THE
DRESSMAKERS
OF
PROSPECT HEIGHTS

ALSO BY KITTY ZELDIS

Not Our Kind

THE
DRESSMAKERS
OF
PROSPECT HEIGHTS

A Novel

KITTY ZELDIS

HARPER

An Imprint of HarperCollinsPublishers

THE DRESSMAKERS OF PROSPECT HEIGHTS. Copyright © 2022 by Kitty Zeldis. All rights reserved. Printed in Canada. No part of this book may be used or reproduced in any manner whatsoever without written permission except in the case of brief quotations embodied in critical articles and reviews. For information, address HarperCollins Publishers, 195 Broadway, New York, NY 10007.

HarperCollins books may be purchased for educational, business, or sales promotional use. For information, please email the Special Markets Department at SPsales@harpercollins.com.

FIRST EDITION

Designed by Kyle O'Brien

Library of Congress Cataloging-in-Publication Data has been applied for.

ISBN 978-0-06-302634-6

22 23 24 25 26   FB   10 9 8 7 6 5 4 3 2 1

For Jennie Fields, a stellar writer and cherished friend
who always knows just what to say, and exactly when to say it.

WINTER

CHAPTER ONE

CATHERINE

Brooklyn, 1924

Catherine Berrill awoke to blood—again. It had happened last month too, but it hadn't trickled down very far, and so left only a light stain on her nightdress, one that she rinsed out immediately before the maid could see it. Nettie knew that Catherine and Stephen were hoping for a child, knew that month after month, their hope was drowned by blood. Sometimes a smear, sometimes a pool. It didn't matter. Blood was blood. Nettie herself had four children, and Catherine didn't want her pity, however well-intentioned.

But today, the blood was far more than a smear. She'd been in a deep sleep, and when she woke, there was a large, crimson stain beneath her, bright and incriminating. Catherine stripped the bed, but she wasn't sure what to do with the sheet—she could hear Nettie bustling around in the kitchen below, so there would be no way to

3

conceal it. And though she could have bundled it up and thrown it away, there would still be its disappearance to account for; Nettie took pride in her meticulous housekeeping. So, leaving the sheet on the floor, she cleaned herself up, secured the necessary flannel pads in her underclothes, and went downstairs.

"There's a soiled sheet in our room," she said. "I left it by the bed."

Nettie looked up; she was pouring Catherine's coffee into a delicate, bone china cup. "Oh, that's too bad, Mrs. Berrill," she said. "Would you like me to bring your coffee upstairs, so you can have it in bed? Since it's your time and all . . . It won't take me a minute to put a fresh sheet on."

Catherine's face burned. Of course Nettie knew why the sheet was soiled. The maid always knew all the secrets of a house.

"No, I'll take the coffee in the back parlor," she said. "Just like always."

"And a cinnamon bun? Fresh baked this morning. Mr. Berrill thought they were perfection—heaven on a plate," he said.

Catherine had to smile—her husband was an optimist, an enthusiast, a man with a perpetually sunny disposition, inclined to see the best in everything and everyone. To Stephen, a freshly baked cinnamon bun was indeed cause for rejoicing. Even so, she was glad he'd already left for work. She didn't think she could stand his unquenchable good cheer this morning.

Nettie brought in the coffee and Catherine sat at the small table and looked out at the backyard. It was winter and nothing was in bloom, but come spring, there would be snowdrops, forsythia, and then lilacs, and in the summer, peonies and miniature roses of the palest pink. The warm weather would bring new growth, new life, but she, Catherine Delman Berrill, would remain barren, her womb wasted and empty. Abruptly, she got up from the table, so that the cup rattled and coffee pooled in the saucer. The cinnamon bun remained untouched.

"I'm not very hungry," she said to Nettie. "I'm going out, and I won't be back for lunch."

"Dinner's baked fish tonight," said Nettie.

"Oh, that's right—it's Friday." Stephen didn't eat meat on Fridays, a habit ingrained from childhood. Although the thought of food sickened Catherine at the moment, she said, "I'm sure it will be delicious, Nettie."

It was a relief to be outside. She could walk along Vanderbilt Avenue, past the big arch at Grand Army Plaza Avenue and into Prospect Park, where she'd follow its winding paths and cross its expansive Long Meadow. If she walked as far as the pond, she'd see the ducks, and maybe even the pair of swans that swam calmly on its surface. She liked tossing them stale bread crusts; unlike the ducks, they didn't lunge and push one another out of the way, but accepted her offering in a regal, dignified manner. But the park was apt to be bleak and deserted on this gray, chilly day, so she headed in the other direction, toward the busier Flatbush Avenue.

She only hoped that she wouldn't run into one of her in-laws, as several of them lived nearby, on Union Street. When she and Stephen first moved into the house on St. Marks Avenue she'd been delighted to have his family so close by. She'd fallen in love with his parents, who'd welcomed her instantly, and his six siblings too—he was the eldest of a big Irish brood.

But Catherine couldn't bear seeing any of them today, especially not Bridget, to whom she was closest, and who knew all about Catherine's yearning to have a child. And Molly, his other sister, was pregnant with her second—no, Catherine really didn't want to see her either. Just as she reached Flatbush, she saw the new little dress shop she'd noticed before but never gone into. Although her closets were full enough, she decided it might provide a sorely needed distraction, and she climbed the stoop leading to the glass-paned double doors. There was a small sign attached to one of them:

DRESSES BY BEATRICE AND ALICE
PLEASE RING FOR ENTRY

A girl of around fifteen or sixteen responded to the chiming sound. Was she Beatrice or Alice? "Good morning," said the girl. "Would you like to look around?" She was pretty, but it was her dress that really stood out. It combined a persimmon-colored gathered skirt with a sage-green bodice and sleeves; the sleeves were adorned with tassels, as was the skirt. Something about it seemed of another time—skirts had not been so full for a while—but the effect was more avant-garde than retrograde. Before Catherine could comment, she was greeted by another woman, who looked to be in her forties. With her olive skin and dark hair that was elegantly twisted and gathered to show off her long neck, she was arresting. Compelling.

Like the girl who'd answered the door, the older woman wore an unusual dress, hers in blue-and-white-striped wool with knitted and fluffy sleeves. "Hello," said the woman. "I'm Miss Bea and this is Alice. Please look around and feel free to ask us any questions." Her voice held the faintest trace of an accent. It sounded European, but Catherine couldn't pin it down any more than that.

"Nice to meet you," Catherine said. Was the woman staring at her or was she imagining it? She began to look at the clothes on display, mostly dresses, no two of them alike. Here was a frock fashioned from a glorious butterfly-print silk with a black satin capelet at the shoulders; there was a simple emerald-green column made from an unfamiliar but appealing material that was both luxurious and soft. Its only adornment was the sash of aubergine velvet that extended from one shoulder to the opposite hip.

There were no labels in any of the dresses, and Catherine couldn't begin to guess where they were from. She only knew she'd never seen anything quite like them before. Despite her gloomy mood, she was intrigued and asked if she could try on the green dress. The material felt so good when she touched it; what would it be like to have it on her body, against her skin?

Alice carried the dress over to a changing area enclosed by an ivory, watered silk curtain. "Won't you step inside?" Her accent was clearly southern—so neither of these women was a New Yorker. Were they related, though? She wasn't sure.

Catherine took the dress and, once inside, began to disrobe. When she had the green dress on, she stepped out again, Alice came over and began to fasten the buttons in the back. The dress felt even better than she imagined. "What's it made of?" she asked.

"Silk knit jersey," said Miss Bea. "It's mostly used for undergarments but we got hold of a bolt and wanted to do something with it."

"So you make the dresses here?"

"Yes. Though mostly Alice remakes them."

"Remakes them? What do you mean?"

"We take existing dresses and combine various parts to come up with something new. Sleeves from one, a skirt from another—like that. Though the one you're wearing is an original. It was my idea actually."

Catherine walked over to the mirror. The woman who looked back at her was unfamiliar. She was glamorous, yes, but even more, she was composed, she was in complete control of her life. Her future. The day's dark mood seemed to lift, banished by this altogether unusual dress. Maybe the dress was a sign of something—something good. Maybe she'd wear it and soon enough, she'd be with child and would need to have it let out.

". . . the sleeves are just the slightest bit too long, but Alice could easily fix them." Miss Bea was looking at Catherine's reflection in the mirror yet it seemed to Catherine that she was not focused on the sleeves at all, but on her face. It was unnerving.

"What?"

"The sleeves—I was saying that—"

"I'll take it," Catherine blurted out.

"It's very becoming," said Miss Bea. "Alice, can you pin the sleeves?"

Alice came over with a pincushion and tape measure. When she was done, Catherine stepped back in the dressing area to change, then handed the dress to Alice, who disappeared behind another, much wider ivory silk curtain in the back.

"That's our work area," Miss Bea explained. "I can have the dress for you tomorrow. Will that be all right?"

"Tomorrow is fine."

"If you give me your name and address, I'll have it sent round when it's done."

"How much do I owe you?" She hadn't even asked what the dress cost.

"Eight dollars."

Catherine would have happily paid more for it. "And the alteration?"

"No charge. Now if I could just get your name." Miss Bea's pen was poised above a small pad.

"Catherine Berrill, 127 St. Marks Avenue."

The pen dropped and ink splattered, black drops sprinkling the pale cream-colored rug and the bit of stocking revealed by the strap of Miss Bea's shoe. "Excuse me," the older woman murmured as she knelt to retrieve it. She didn't seem to care about the ink——or maybe she didn't even notice. When she looked up again, her face had paled, and this time there was no mistaking it—she was staring at Catherine, seemingly transfixed.

"Well, thank you very much." Catherine held out the bills but Miss Bea, still staring, ignored them. "The payment," she prompted. This was all so strange. Strange and uncomfortable.

"You're welcome." Miss Bea took the bills and hastily stuffed them into the pocket of her dress.

Catherine fastened her coat and drew on her gloves. She loved the dress, she truly did, and she was sure that if she continued to look around, she would find others that were equally appealing. These women were clearly gifted. But Miss Bea's manner was so unsettling, so *peculiar,* that Catherine didn't care to shop any further. She hurried out and down the stoop, walking swiftly away, quite certain she would never set foot in that shop again.

CHAPTER TWO

BEA

Bea had seen her. At last, she had seen her in the flesh. Face-to-face. After the searching, the hoping, the waiting, the scheming. The young woman she'd been seeking, Catherine Delman, now Berrill, had walked up those steps and right through the doors. She clearly resembled the photograph the detective had provided, though in the sepia-tinted image, the dazzling blue of Catherine Berrill's eyes were not visible. But today Bea had recognized them—they were unmistakable, even though she had spent years trying to stamp out the memory of their unusual shade, and of the only other person she'd known who possessed them. For years, she'd succeeded. If she didn't allow the memories to bubble to the surface, she could live as if they weren't there. Until she couldn't.

Bea's growing disquiet had begun with something that had nothing to do with her: the Great War that was raging in Europe. President Wilson had kept America out of it for the first three years before deciding to send troops. That was when the department of the Navy had pressured the city to end legalized prostitution. She had been forced to close her business in the notorious New Orleans neighborhood known as the District and say goodbye to her life as a madam, a life that had sustained and occupied her for more than twenty years. She'd been in her forties, still relatively young, and still healthy, her spine straight, her waist narrow. Only a few strands of silver glinted in her dark hair, and her face was mostly unlined. She didn't want to operate her house—one of the finest and most well-known in those circles—undercover, living as an outlaw. So she was faced with the task of figuring out what, exactly, to do with the rest of her life. Unmoored in those first strange days, she took to rising early and embarking on long, solitary walks. Some mornings she headed toward Tchoupitoulas, where a ripe, primal smell wafted up from the nearby river. Other days she'd go deep into the Quarter, peering into courtyards, tossing the occasional coin—without wishing—into a fountain, wending her way down alleys whose bricks were slick with moss. In Jackson Square, she spent too much time watching a disheveled and practically toothless old woman as she scattered birdseed to an adoring flock. Bea had the uneasy feeling that she was seeing her own future.

As she walked, stray memories from childhood flitted through her mind: the slight furrow of her father's brow, even when he napped, the raucous sound of her brothers' laughter as they chased each other through the big stone house. What her room in that house had looked like, the heavy curtains that surrounded the bed and that, when pulled closed, created a cozy alcove for sleep, a meal during which she dripped borscht onto her starched, white pinafore and tried, unsuccessfully, to hide the evidence from her mother. But Mama hadn't been cross, not at all, and it was she, not the maid, who had accompanied Bea upstairs to find a fresh one.

The empty hours allowed Bea to dwell on these memories. Some were sweet. Others were bitter, even gruesome. What had happened to her father, for instance. Yet terrible as that had been, his story had an ending she knew, and there was harsh comfort in that. What about the story whose outcome was unknown to her? It had no conclusion. She had just willed it away from her awareness, buried it deep inside of her. Now it was coming back, asserting itself loudly, stridently. It haunted her, taunted her even. And eventually it drove her to Chartres Street, and the shabby, second-floor office of a detective named Isadore Vernou.

Vernou was a small, pallid man with a center part and a droopy mustache. Sitting across from him, the scuffed and stained oak desk between them, Bea told him who it was she wanted to find. He'd nodded, taken down the information she was able to provide—all of it more than a quarter century old—and said he'd see what he could do.

For a long while, she heard nothing and feared her search would be in vain. It was almost a year later when he contacted her; he'd found a promising lead, but in the end it had led nowhere. Or at least not to the place she was desperate to go. Her house, where she'd allowed the girls to stay until they'd found other lodgings, emptied out. The rooms, which had been filled every day and every night, were now silent. Only Alice and a couple of servants remained.

Then influenza swept the country, and New Orleans became a plague city. People Bea knew, young people, healthy people, died in droves. The newspapers reported on the deaths, the grim numbers mounting; funeral followed funeral. Everyone stayed in, and if they had to go out, they hurried about their business, their faces covered by masks. It was in the middle of this epidemic that Bea heard from Vernou again, and this time, he was certain he had the information she was looking for. So excited was Bea to get this news that she donned a mask and hurried to his office, where he presented her with a name, an address, and miraculously, even a photograph over whose sepia-toned surface she ran her fingertips gently, as if she could absorb the image into her skin. "You're sure?" she had asked.

"Quite sure."

"So what do I do now?"

"That's up to you."

"What if you're wrong?"

"Then I'll refund half your money. I've got to be paid something for my time. But I won't be. You'll see."

"It means I'll have to go to New York. To find her." Bea stared at the photograph, hoping to find an answer, a clue, lodged somewhere in it. "What will I say?" She spoke softly, as if to herself.

"That's up to you," Vernou said again. "I provide my clients with information. I don't tell them what to do with it."

It took Bea some time to act on what she'd learned—she didn't want to travel while the disease still raged, and there was the matter of selling her house and almost everything in it. But finally, the epidemic subsided, the house and its contents were sold, the journey made. Vernou had not disappointed her. Catherine Berrill was the woman she'd been seeking—her eyes alone would have convinced Bea. She had to see those eyes again. To see Catherine again. Having come to the shop once, she might return, though Bea was well aware that she had behaved oddly and might have put her off.

Alice walked back into the front parlor. "There's something on the carpet," she said. "Look, it's on your stocking too."

"It's ink," said Bea. "I dropped a pen."

"I'll get some bleach," Alice said.

The bleach lightened but didn't eliminate the spots on the rug. Bea didn't care, she just moved one of the tufted seats to cover it. The stocking she would keep, a reminder of the day, the precise moment her search had ended.

"Are you all right?" Alice asked. "You seem upset. Did she say something? I thought she seemed pleasant enough."

"Yes, I mean no, no, it wasn't anything she said, it wasn't anything at all. I'm not upset." She looked at Alice, who clearly didn't believe her. "Please don't worry. I'm fine." She hadn't told Alice that she had been looking for Catherine, that this woman had been her whole reason for coming to New York.

They'd arrived a few months earlier, in December. Bea's initial impression of New York was not rosy; in fact, she thought it was an awful city—gray, dreary, filthy. On her very first day in the fabled metropolis, she had been forced to pick her way through the revolting mess left behind by both horses and dogs, piles of mold-spotted potato skins, rotted lettuce leaves, empty liquor bottles, and the bones of God only knew how many chickens, picked clean. The throngs of people who hurried along the wide avenues appeared dour, and in some cases malevolent; the tall, soot-stained buildings seemed to glare down at them. And perhaps worst of all was that New York was so very cold. Bea had spent the first years of her life in Russia, where it certainly had been colder, but the next three decades in New Orleans had blunted both her memories of and tolerance for the chill. The biting wind made her eyes tear, her nose run, and sliced through her new coat—it had seemed so fashionable, so chic, back when she'd bought it on Magazine Street, and it offered no better protection than a dressing gown. How had she not anticipated this?

Alice seemed to share her revulsion, and though she didn't complain, she acted as if she had been bludgeoned into silence. Bea had spent much of their trip north on the *New York & New Orleans Limited* prattling on about landmarks she'd read about but never seen: Central Park, the Plaza Hotel, the New York Public Library, the Metropolitan Opera House. And the train itself bolstered this glamorous if imaginary picture gallery—the observation car with its enlarged windows and sweeping, panoramic views, the cunningly designed compartments, the single red rose placed in the bud vase that sat on each table in the dining car.

But when they found themselves thrust unceremoniously into the pure bedlam of Pennsylvania Station, Bea felt she'd deceived Alice and her own words mocked her. There were so many people, all rushing, shoving, muttering, scowling. Getting out of the terminal was a challenge, and being outside was even worse, what with the teeming sidewalks and streets choked by automobiles, horse-drawn wagons, and bloated, monstrous buses. After twenty fruitless—and freezing—minutes trying to hail a taxi, Bea finally succeeded; she had practically stepped into its path to flag it down. Sitting inside, Alice was clearly terrified. It was the first time she had ridden in a such a vehicle, and she clutched the front seat, alarmed by the speed and the blaring horns of other motorists around them.

When they finally arrived at the hotel on Upper Broadway, they went upstairs, undressed, and went straight to bed. Bea slid down the well of sleep as if drugged. But the next morning, she had to face the city again —pulsating, chaotic, more foreign than she could have imagined. Maybe it had all been a mistake—the visit to the detective, the knowledge he had given her, the plan to come north. Her decision was hardly irreversible, though. She and Alice could just turn around and go back, of course they could—but back to what? Bea knew her life in New Orleans was over. And since she'd adopted Alice in all but a legal way, the girl's life there was over too.

Breakfast the next morning was a subdued meal, with Alice answering only in monosyllables. Bea sipped her coffee, an ersatz, bitter brew, and began to devise something like a plan. The hotel was a temporary oasis. Thanks to Vernou, she had trained her sights on Brooklyn, and a neighborhood called Prospect Heights where he said Catherine Berrill was living. But even though Bea had the address, she couldn't just show up at the house and announce herself; she had to bide her time and find the right moment. Right moment, and the right words too. She rehearsed them endlessly in her head, but everything she came up with sounded false, hollow, and thoroughly wrong.

On the first morning, she had a more immediate concern: how to deal with the cold. She thought of the broad avenues of her home city, its denizens draped in fur and leather—elemental materials with which to face the most brutal elements—and an idea came to her. The hotel concierge seemed a little puzzled by her request, but he consulted a directory and was able to provide the address of a furrier who specialized in secondhand and refurbished garments and whose downtown shop could be reached via the subway at Eighty-Sixth Street. Alice was horrified by the idea of descending underground; she was sure they would be suffocated or crushed. Bea didn't like the idea either. But millions of people in New York City traveled by subway, and if she and Alice were to become New Yorkers, they at least ought to try it. "Everyone else is doing it. They don't seem afraid."

"Maybe they're all insane," Alice said as they stood outside the station. "Or idiots."

Bea took her arm and they went carefully down the stairs, avoiding the other people rushing by them. The subway train hurtled into the station almost as soon as they reached the platform and Alice clapped her hands to her ears. The lurching ride caused her to collide into the woman standing next to her. "So sorry," Bea said to the woman, who glared at Alice with such hostility that Bea put her arm around the girl's shoulders, an instinctive gesture of protection. When the woman exited the train at the next stop, Bea felt something inside her unclench, just a little. She'd get used to it. They both would.

The address she sought was only a couple of short blocks from the subway station. After climbing a narrow and splintered flight of stairs, Bea tapped on the frosted glass door whose block lettering read NED RAPPAPORT, FURRIER. A man she assumed to be Rappaport opened it almost immediately, as if he'd been waiting for them. "Come in, come in," he said genially. His Russian accent was as thick as her own had once been.

Bea looked around the showroom, where animal pelts were tacked to the walls, stuffed onto shelves, and piled on every available surface, including the floor. There were also a pair of sewing machines, a battered mannequin, and a metal rack crammed with coats, mostly made of fur but several of cloth as well.

"You'd like to see a fox, maybe?" Rappaport asked. "Or a sable? It belonged to a fancy lady and she only wore it a few times before she dropped dead, may she rest in peace."

"No fox," Bea said. "No sable. And I want your best price, since I'm going to be buying two furs—one for each of us." She gestured toward Alice, now stroking the arm of a leopard jacket. Then she began to look through his merchandise methodically until she found two suitable coats that she tried to wrestle from the tightly packed rack.

"Let me." Rappaport struggled a moment before he finally freed them both. "Mink. A good choice. Warm, but light. Won't weigh you down. Do you and the young lady want to try them on?"

Alice slipped hers on and stood before the dust-streaked mirror.

The fur was worn away at the cuffs and the pockets. "It's very soft," she said uncertainly. "But it's not in such good condition . . ."

Bea nodded. The one she'd selected for herself was even more flawed—there were several slashes between the pelts, as if someone had gone at them with a knife.

"I'll let you have them cheap," Rappaport said eagerly. "For the price of cloth practically—"

"I'm not done yet." Bea answered him in Yiddish, a language she knew just well enough to construct the simple sentence.

Rappaport looked surprised. So did Alice. "*Du bis ein Yid?*" the furrier asked.

You're a Jew? In Russia, the answer to that question would have been fraught, but in the United States it was less so—a cause for derision at times, but not a blow to the face, a kick in the groin. Bea nodded and returned to the rack, where she pulled out two more coats, one of black wool and the other camel, both quite large. When Bea asked her to take off the fur and try the camel, Alice seemed disappointed. "The fur would be warmer," she said.

"Of course it would. That's why I'm going to ask Mr. Rappaport to use it as a lining." Bea turned to him. "Could you do that?"

"You want to buy fur only to hide it?"

"Not hide it. Use it in a different way." In this new life, she would need practicality, not opulence. She handed him Alice's mink so Alice could try on the black coat. Immediately she was enveloped by the volume of fabric—perfect. "You can do the same with this one—use the other mink to line it, take it in where you need to. The condition of the pelts won't matter, though you'll have to stitch mine back together. And we could use belts . . ." She pulled the coat away from her body so that it formed a tent. "There's enough material here for that, isn't there?"

"Plenty," said Rappaport.

"Excellent. How soon can you do it?"

"Tomorrow maybe. Or the next day for sure."

"What about by tonight?"

"Tonight? I don't know. I'll have to get a helper——"

"You have two machines," Bea pointed out. "And I'll pay you extra."

"All right," Rappaport said. "Come back at eight."

Once they were out of the shop, Alice asked, "What was the language you were speaking back there?"

"That? It was——"

Just then a passing automobile came dangerously close to Alice, and Bea yanked her back from the curb, and then cautioned her about keeping far back from the traffic in the future. The topic of languages slid away.

When they returned to the shop some hours later, Rappaport was ready for them. He was good at what he did; the coats were well tailored, stylish, and best of all, *warm*. And since his helper was still there, Bea bought a moth-eaten mink jacket and had the woman fashion two fur headbands, one for her, one for Alice, that fit snugly around their ears. "What a good idea," Rappaport said. "I'm going to have Minnie make a few more. I'll bet I sell them all by the end of the week."

Bea looked at Rappaport. "You're a good businessman," she said.

"And you, madam—you're an even better businesswoman."

Bea froze. How could he have known just how apt a statement that was? Was he mocking her, insulting her? No, she was overwrought, that was all. Of course Ned Rappaport didn't know who she had been, or what she had done; there was no way he could have. She'd taken the precaution of changing her name yet again. Now she was Beatrice Jones—just to make doubly sure that her past couldn't catch up with her. As she ushered Alice out of the shop and back into the darkened but still busy street, she was even more determined to make sure that it never would.

CHAPTER THREE

BEA

After the encounter with Catherine in the dress shop, Bea felt something akin to a mild intoxication. Her thoughts fizzed as she thought of how Catherine had looked in the dress, the emerald color making her eyes seem more blue than green. Her voice was pleasant, her manners refined—she'd clearly been raised well. She was married. Did she have any children yet? Bea felt eager, almost desperate, to know more.

The next day, Alice was getting ready to deliver the green dress, its sleeves now an inch shorter, but Bea stepped in. "I'll do it," she said.

"Are you sure?"

"Yes, I need to get some air. I'll be right back—it's just up the street." She didn't want to share her real reasons with Alice. Why involve the girl in all that, especially when Bea didn't even know what she was expecting, or why, exactly, she had embarked on this search. She had done it not out of logic, but out of instinct, unmediated and raw. Her feelings frightened her a little, but if she kept them to her-self, she could contain the fear.

Walking quickly, Bea crossed the busy avenue and slowed only when she reached the house. It was a handsome limestone with two leaded oval glass windows punctuating the facade and a pair of urns flanking the front doors, which were painted a glossy black. A mature wisteria vine, twisted and knotty, clung to one side of the building.

The curtains were open and Bea tried, without being too obvious, to get a glimpse into the parlor window. What was visible was fan-ciful and bright—wallpaper in an intricate pattern of golden apples and pale green leaves, the top of a plum-colored armchair with a pat-terned shawl draped casually across it. The woman who lived here had unconventional ideas, at least when it came to decor. Bea could only hope that would extend to other arenas as well.

After ringing the bell, she was greeted by a servant who thanked her and took the parcel. Had she really expected Catherine Berrill to open the door herself? And then invite her in for tea? Irrational as it was, Bea felt deflated and, on the way home, tried to bolster her own sense of purpose. Just finding Catherine was clearing a hurdle and meeting her an even higher one. Who could say what might happen next?

From that day on, Bea continued to hope that Catherine Berrill would return to the shop; if she did, Bea resolved to behave in a calmer, less erratic manner. She rearranged the window, constantly changing the display in the hope that one of these dresses would catch Mrs. Berrill's eye and draw her back in. But although the clien-tele continued to grow—one woman told another, one brought her friend, another her sister, her mother, her daughter—Catherine did not return. Bea felt choked by frustration. To have come this far, and gotten this close, only now to be stymied—it was truly intolerable.

She began to dream in Russian again. Long ago, when she'd first arrived in America, she had dreamed only in her mother tongue. She'd heard her grandmother's voice saying *devushka*—little daughter— as she cupped Bea's face in her hands, her mother saying *bozhe moy!*—my goodness!—when something surprised her. But as the English she heard all around her crowded her head by day, it had begun to dominate her dreams at night too.

Now, the Russian of her girlhood was back. And it wasn't just the words, the sounds, there were images too, no longer just isolated ones, but fully formed scenes, as detailed as if she'd written them long ago and had taken them out now to read again. Bea woke from these dreams unsettled. For so long, she had kept the past locked in a box, rarely taken out, never shared. But she no longer seemed in control of her thoughts. The past would not stay quiet or hidden away. In fact, it seemed as palpable as the present, living and breathing alongside her. It refused to remain on the periphery. No, the past demanded attention, and even more—it demanded a reckoning.

CHAPTER FOUR

BEA

It was Alice who had given her the idea to open a dress shop. The day after their trip to Rappaport's, they had taken the subway to Brooklyn. Alice seemed less alarmed this time, and when they emerged from an underground station at Grand Army Plaza, they were both relieved to see that the streets were far less crowded and hectic than those in Manhattan.

"Is this where we're going to live?" Alice asked.

"We are," said Bea. "Do you like it?"

Alice had looked around at the bare trees, the tidy rows of houses, the gentle incline that led to the top of the hill where they stood. Across the avenue was a low wall that enclosed a large park. She didn't quite smile, but her expression softened. "Yes," she said. "I think I do."

The rental agent led them through the neighborhood, which was filled with narrow structures, each packed tightly against its neighbor. Bea thought the houses looked constricting. Even worse, many were built of a dull, mud-like substance called brownstone. The rental agent extolled its virtues, but Bea thought the material was crude and unappealing. And because windows were only at the fronts and backs of the buildings, she imagined their interiors as dark and gloomy.

There were only two houses available. One of them was made of limestone, and quite ornate. It was directly across from Prospect Park, but the monthly price was more than Bea wanted to spend. The other was rather run-down, and Bea had no desire to live in such a derelict place. "Haven't you anything else?" she asked.

"I've got something on St. Marks Avenue," he said. "But it's very close to Flatbush Avenue, and I thought you might want something a bit quieter."

"You have a house on St. Marks?" Bea was practically vibrating with suppressed excitement. It was the name of the street Vernou had given her, the one where Catherine Berrill lived.

"It so happens I do."

The house in question was made of that deplorable brownstone, but its condition was excellent and, as the agent mentioned, just above Flatbush Avenue, one of the main arteries of the neighborhood. It had three stories, a bay window on the parlor floor, several good-size rooms upstairs, and a kitchen—not that Bea had ever cooked much—that gave onto a south-facing garden. But it was the location that decided her—just minutes away from the house whose address was by now imprinted in her memory.

"We'll take it," said Bea. She and Alice followed the rental agent back to his office on Seventh Avenue to sign the necessary papers and pay the first two months' rent. There Bea learned that the owner was an elderly widower, now traveling abroad. He'd left the house partially furnished, though the parlor floor, with its two large front rooms and smaller back one, was empty. "The most valuable pieces went into storage," the agent explained. Bea didn't mind. She'd use what was there and find a way to fill in the rest. She was good at that sort of thing—she'd had so many years to perfect such skills.

One evening shortly after moving in, Bea and Alice were walking back toward the house when they stopped to admire the display in the hat shop on their corner. Bea was especially taken by a maroon tam made of mohair. Of course Rappaport's fur headpiece was warmer, but it wouldn't be winter forever; she could stop in the next day and try it on. As they continued on, Bea saw that the light in the front parlor of their house had been left on by mistake. There in the window were a few of her extravagant dresses hanging on the metal rack provided by the moving company; she had asked if she might hold on to it for a few days until she could get an armoire.

"Look at all your pretty gowns," Alice had said. "They look like they're in a shop window."

"You're right," said Bea. "They do." The dresses—the Jacques Doucet black silk lace, the ivory satin ball gown from Worth, the peach chiffon bedecked with gold paillette-trimmed lace, a triple-tiered skirt, and ruffled underpinning from Callot Soeurs—had been an integral part of Bea's life in New Orleans. The Doucet she'd worn on New Year's Eve, the chiffon, with a matching mask, on Mardi Gras, the Worth on so many evenings she couldn't even count them all . . . she'd been the most elegant, most tasteful woman in the District. Everyone had said so. So while she couldn't imagine having any occasion to wear these dresses now, she hadn't been able to part with them either, and she'd brought most of her elaborate wardrobe up to New York.

"A shop," she continued. "We could put it on the parlor floor, you know. We're so close to the avenue—there would be lots of foot traffic. And we could put out a sandwich board to let people know we're there." It was also convenient to have the hat shop so close by. Women in the mood to buy a hat might want to buy a dress too. Bea's mind began to hum with possibilities.

"And sell . . . your dresses?" Alice wasn't quite following.

"Not as they are, no," said Bea. Those dresses, though lovely, were out-of-date. Women were wearing very different sorts of garments now—more streamlined, less fussy. The designers she'd learned to revere were being supplanted with a new, young crop of talent like Coco Chanel, Elsa Schiaparelli, and Paul Poiret. Their designs allowed—no, encouraged—women to dispose of their corsets, their bustles, their stiffened petticoats and crinolines. "But maybe they could be refashioned somehow." Wheels started turning in Bea's mind. "I'd need your help."

"My help? Doing what?"

"We'd buy secondhand dresses, good ones of course, and you would redo them. Make them over somehow." With her supervision and Alice's skill, those dresses could be altered in ways that would make them seem more modern. Each one would be a unique creation. One of a kind.

"Like you had Mr. Rappaport do." Alice understood now.

"Yes, exactly." They were at the front door, where Bea fumbled with a key not yet familiar to her. "Do you think you could? That is, would you like to?"

The issue of what Alice was to do was a somewhat delicate one; Bea had hoped she would go to school, but so far, Alice had refused to even consider it. This distressed Bea, for the girl was poorly educated and it put her at such a disadvantage. But Bea was not Alice's mother. Six years ago, Alice had been orphaned while living in Bea's house. The girl had no one to turn to, nowhere to go, and Bea could not in good conscience put her out. And at first, Alice had been grateful, docile, and eager to please; Bea grew fond of her. But more recently,

Alice had changed, becoming moody or silent by turns, and Bea had learned to tread carefully.

"I think I would," said Alice after a moment. And then, with more certainty, "Yes."

They went into the parlor, where wooden crates were still scattered around the bare space. But in Bea's mind's eye, the room was filling up quickly. A chandelier, she thought. Blown glass, from Venice. Pale rugs—sky blue, dove gray, peach, blush pink, champagne. Tufted cushions where customers could sit. A large mirror with a gilt frame over the mantel. Another that was full-length.

The more Bea thought about it, the more invested she became. Not only would it be a way for her to establish herself in the neighborhood, but it would also give her something productive to do. She didn't like being idle. The money she stood to make wasn't essential— years of careful financial management, assiduous saving, and the sale of her house had left her comfortably provided for—but it couldn't hurt either and would provide a nest egg for Alice. Without lessons or schooling, there wouldn't be enough to occupy her, and working in a shop could serve as an alternative. They would become a team— the ideas for the dresses would come mostly from Bea, and the actual work of creating them would fall to Alice.

It didn't take long for the rooms to assume the shape Bea had envisioned. She sought and quickly received the landlord's permission, and she was able to redeploy a few pieces of furniture that were already in the house. The rest she purchased, at reasonable prices, along with several trunks filled with women's clothing that had been left unclaimed at a storage company on the Bowery. Soon everything was in place: chandelier, mirrors, and several brass clothing racks, somewhat more ornate than the one loaned to her by the moving company. The back room, with its window overlooking the garden, was furnished with a sewing machine, a trio of mannequins in different sizes, and an expansive pine table, a work surface for Alice.

Soon Bea was able to put out her shingle, having created what she hoped was an inviting, intriguing shop that had no parallel in the neighborhood or perhaps anywhere else in the city. And the shop had only been open for just a little over a month when Catherine Berrill had walked in—just like that. But now Bea realized this meeting was only the beginning of the journey, the first small steps. She still had so far to go before she could share the well-guarded secret that had been resting like a boulder on her heart for all these years.

CHAPTER FIVE

ALICE

Alice didn't much like living in New York, but then, she hadn't expected to. When Bea had first proposed the idea, she couldn't imagine why she would want to live in such a place; if Bea had been so intent on leaving New Orleans—and Alice *did* understand that—they could have gone to any number of other southern cities, like Atlanta or Montgomery or Charleston. Instead, they had come to this nasty, dirty, and perpetually cold place. Whatever for? She didn't feel she had the right to question Bea's decision. But that didn't mean she would be happy about it.

* * *

The first time Alice had seen the exterior of Bea's house in New Orleans—pale yellow bricks, arched windows, mahogany double doors painted dark green with beveled glass insets—she had stood staring, enraptured by its elegance. She'd never seen such a palace,

30

much less expected to live in one. Helen finally tugged on her hand. "Come on. We can't stand here all day."

Alice followed her inside, to a double parlor all done up with upholstered furniture and rugs in pastel colors—soft pinks, peaches, and greens. The lofty ceilings were covered with plasterwork so fancy that it made Alice think of cake frosting. She was a little nervous at the idea of living in a house like this. Would she know how to behave? What would be expected of her? And she was shy; how would she ever get used to living with so many other people?

She had been only ten, her mother not even two weeks dead. Her big sister Helen had gotten home to Belle Chasse too late; all that was left to do was arrange the pitiful funeral. Then she'd brought Alice back to New Orleans, since no one else wanted her. On the way, Helen talked about her life there. "Miss Bea has one the grandest houses in the city," she said. "Even though it's not the biggest, it's still the best. You can see it from the train when it pulls in—it's right across the street from the station."

"Right out in the open? Everyone knows what it is?" In Alice's experience, what her mother had done, what Helen now did, was something they kept hidden—or tried to.

"Everyone. It's legal in New Orleans, at least in that one neighborhood. They call it the District. The police know all about it, and they don't mind a lick. Police chief's even one of her customers. I've been with him myself once or twice." She looked over at Alice appraisingly. "You know, you could go to work for her too."

"Me?" Alice was horrified. "No. Not yet." *Not ever,* she thought, but did not say. Alice had formed her own opinions about this sort of work. Sometimes it involved drinking. Sometimes there was laughing, other times, shouting. Almost always there was panting, moaning, and grunting—she heard all this from the other side of the bedroom door and she wanted to stay as far away from it as possible.

"You might change your mind when you find out how much money you could make. More money than you could ever imagine." When Alice was quiet, Helen continued. "It's not so bad, really. Sometimes it's even fun."

Fun? Alice didn't think so. Her mother hadn't seemed to be having fun. But Helen was years older than Alice, and had left home some time ago; maybe New Orleans had changed her.

Miss Bea came into the parlor and Alice's fear about being able to fit into such an environment intensified, like a cloud of gnats swarming around her head. The woman was dark-haired and slender, with an angular face and stern expression.

"This is my sister, Alice," Helen said.

Unsure of what to do, Alice attempted a curtsy but stumbled a bit, resulting in more of a clumsy bob.

"Hello, Alice." Miss Bea's voice was low and not unpleasant; she had some of kind of foreign-sounding accent.

"She had nowhere to go and I had to bring her back with me," Helen said. "I hope you don't mind." Miss Bea said nothing, so Helen continued. "I thought maybe she could start working here. You can see how pretty she is. And men would pay a lot for someone so young."

How could Helen *say* this? Alice had already told her—

"They would, but they won't pay it here," Miss Bea said, her tone clipped. "I'm not in the business of selling children. But she can stay, and we'll figure out something else for her to do. She won't start seeing men until she's at least eighteen—old enough to decide for herself."

Alice stared at her. Miss Bea may have looked stern, but she had just rescued her. Eighteen. That was eight years away—a long time. Anything could happen by then. Maybe Helen would meet a rich man who would fall in love with her and take both of them away from this life. It wasn't impossible. And in the meantime, Alice could work at something else. She knew she had to earn her keep and was willing, oh so willing, to try.

First she was sent to help Cook. Within a week, she had managed to break several dishes and two expensive goblets, and let the water boil off from a pot of potatoes, ruining both. Also, being in the presence of so much food was too great of a temptation, and she couldn't help stuffing her apron pockets with biscuits, rolls, and boiled eggs every chance she got. Miss Bea hadn't gotten angry. "Keep her out of the kitchen," was all she said.

Alice felt bad about all the trouble she'd caused and was even more determined to prove herself useful in some way, so she volunteered to clean out a room that one of girls had recently vacated. Turning first to the bed, Alice wrestled the sheets from the mattress and wadded them into a bundle; she had seen the copper washtubs outside the kitchen door and she could bring them down there. Surely that would be helpful. Then her attention was caught by several fans that had been left behind, pinned on the wall—arcs of pleated silk, one prettier than the next. This one showed a branch of pink blossoms, another, a flock of long-legged birds, still another, a little building set among some trees.

"Would you like to keep them?"

Startled, Alice turned around. Miss Bea was in the doorway.

"The fans?"

Bea nodded.

"I couldn't, I mean—"

"Take them. Put them on the walls of your room if you like."

"Really?" Alice took down one of the fans and held it in front of her face. She wouldn't pin them to the walls; she would add them to her treasure chest. Well, it wasn't a chest, just an old wooden box that used to hold seed packets. In it she kept pretty stones, and a long, blue-green feather she had found, as well as a sachet Helen bought her and a lock of her mother's hair.

"Really," said Miss Bea. "Take them with you when you're done." She left the room.

Once she was alone again, Alice began to clean in earnest. She dusted, she swept, she carried a heavy pail of sudsy water up the stairs, sloshing only a little bit onto the carpet, and mopped the floor. She found rags and vinegar to use on the windows and the mirror over the bureau.

Miss Bea returned just as she was finishing. "It's sparkling in here." It was clear from the tone of her voice that she was pleased. "You did a good job."

"Thank you, ma'am."

"Have you been through the dresser drawers?"

"Oh no. I didn't think to, that is, I—"

"That's all right," said Miss Bea. "We'll take a look together." She opened the top drawer of the bureau; it was empty save for a sprinkling of loose face powder. The second drawer was also empty, but the third contained a deck of cards and, folded in a sheet of tissue, an embroidery hoop, a packet of needles, and several loops of thread. Everything looked brand-new.

Alice had no interest in the cards, but the embroidery hoop and the rest of it were things she would have loved to own. There were so many things she could do with the lovely, jewel-bright colors. She'd learned to embroider a few years ago and found the activity immensely soothing—the neat, tiny stitches and orderly designs were a shield against the fractious atmosphere of her home, the yelling, the drinking, the hitting. And here were the tools she needed to take it up again; look, there were even a couple of printed patterns—

"Would you like the embroidery things as well?"

Embarrassed, Alice averted her eyes; had her longing been so obvious? The older woman had already given her the fans. Now she would think Alice was a greedy, grasping girl. But when she looked up again, Miss Bea didn't seem displeased at all. "You might as well take them," she said. "No one else will."

In her spare moments, Alice started to embroider. Her fingers had a memory of their own, and her needle darted in and out with an accomplished certainty. The knotted buttonhole stitch, the rice stitch, the seed stitch, and so many more—she remembered them all, and used them to embellish handkerchiefs, both for herself and the other girls in the house, who, as soon as they saw them, clamored for their own. She started with an initial in the corner, and then added something else, usually a flower but sometimes a bird or a heart. Miss Bea hadn't asked, but Alice made one for her too, the *B* large and fanciful, and below it, a crown.

"It's lovely, Alice," she said. "But why a crown?"

Alice shrugged. "I don't know. It just seemed right."

Miss Bea looked at her. "You're a deep one, aren't you?" she said at last. Alice didn't quite know what she meant by that, but the comment filled her with pride.

She had been in the house for about a month when the storm hit. It was a mighty thing, the wind howling like an animal, the windows rattling in their frames. Miss Bea had everyone gather in her suite; the rooms were the highest in the house and, in case of flooding, the safest. They all huddled together as the rain pelted the roof. Frightened, Alice went to sit beside Helen, who had moved off by herself. But Helen seemed distracted; she wasn't in the least bit comforting.

"Are you feeling all right?" Miss Bea asked her, joining them.

"Yes," Helen said. Her eyes were closed and her arms wrapped around her knees. "I mean, no."

35

"What's wrong?" Miss Bea's voice was gentle. "Is it the storm?"

Helen opened her eyes. "It's not what's out there, Miss Bea. It's what's in here . . ." She put a hand to her belly.

"Pregnant." Miss Bea sighed. "How far long?"

"Three months."

"Have you thought about what you want to do?"

"Yes," Helen said. "I have. Do you know of anyone who can . . . take care of it for me?"

"Know who?" Alice asked. "Take care of what?"

Helen said nothing; it was Miss Bea who laid a hand on Alice's shoulder and said, "Don't worry. Helen is going to be fine. She just needs some medical attention."

"For the . . . baby?" Alice said.

"There won't be a baby," said Helen in a flat voice. "You can count on that."

Just then there was a loud clap of thunder outside, and Alice ran to the window.

"Come away from there," said Miss Bea.

Alice was frightened. "What if it breaks and the room is flooded? We'll all get swept away."

"This house is sturdier than you think. Just like your sister. Now come and sit by me, and we'll ride it out together."

Alice left the window and went to sit with Miss Bea. Cora, one of the girls, started to sing a hymn, and pretty soon they'd all joined in, even Helen. The sound of their voices didn't drown out the sounds of the storm, but it gave them something else to listen to.

Eventually, they began to get tired. One of the maids was sent to find blankets and pillows, and after they'd been handed out, everyone curled up wherever there was a space. Helen went right to sleep, but Alice was far too worried to doze off. What was going to happen to her sister? Who was this person Miss Bea knew and what exactly was he going to do? Alice turned this way and that, unable to get comfortable.

"What's troubling you?" There was Miss Bea, right beside her.

Alice hesitated. She wasn't used to confiding in other people.

"You can tell me." Miss Bea's voice was gentle. "Is it that you're concerned about Helen?" When Alice still didn't reply, Miss Bea said, "Let's go out in the hallway so we don't wake anyone." She got up and Alice followed her. The outside of the window on the landing was coated by a single sheet of water.

"Helen's all the family you have left, isn't she? There isn't anyone else."

"No." Alice could barely get the word out.

"Tell me about your mother," Miss Bea said.

Alice looked at Miss Bea in astonishment. No one had ever asked her such a question. What could she say? What *should* she say? Her mother worked for a man in Belle Chasse. He didn't live with them, but he showed up sometimes and spent the night. Other times he'd send different men. They used to spend the night too. That man, the one her mother worked for, sometimes hit her. She put up with it though. She must have thought she had to. Helen's daddy upped and left when she was less than a year old. That's how Mama got started. Her parents put her out and she didn't have any other way to support her baby. She wasn't even sure who Alice's daddy was. But all Alice said to Miss Bea was, "I miss her."

"Of course you do."

There was more too. Alice's mother used to buy them things— candy, ribbons for their hair. Once she bought them pinwheels— Alice's was blue and Helen's was pink. Even when the man broke her jaw because he was so angry at her for spending the money, she'd said, "I have to give something to my two sunshines." That's what she called them—her sunshines. Alice didn't tell Miss Bea any of this either. But somehow those words—*of course you do*—were enough.

In the morning, Alice borrowed a pair of galoshes from one of the servants and followed Miss Bea outside. Except for two broken windows in the kitchen, the house was mostly untouched. Only the Chinese magnolia had suffered, ripped from the earth and tilted at a sharp angle. But before Miss Bea attended to any of that, she said she was going to take Helen to see a man in the Quarter. Alice pleaded to go along; Miss Bea said no. So Alice had to endure Helen's absence with a mixture of panic and grief, sure that whatever happened to Helen at the hands of that man, she wouldn't survive it. But she did, and Alice had to be held back from flinging her arms around her sister when she returned some hours later. "You'll have to be careful with her for a few days," Miss Bea said. "She's fine though. You can see that for yourself."

And Helen did seem fine, but Alice kept checking on her just the same. "Would you like a drink?" she asked. "I can run down to the kitchen to get it for you."

"There's a pitcher and glass right here, honey," said Helen. "You don't have to fret so."

Soon, Helen was sitting up in bed, asking for her mirror and comb. And within a couple of days, she returned to work. It was understood that Alice was to be elsewhere when her sister was entertaining customers, so she kept away from their room until the evening was over. After waiting for the customer to leave—he was a husky fellow, with a bristling beard and hair covering the backs of his hands—Alice slipped back inside and sat on the foot of Helen's bed while her sister washed up and changed into her nightdress.

"Are you all right?" Alice asked. "That man who was here—he didn't hurt you, tear anything inside . . . ?"

"Oh, sugar, there are plenty of different ways to make a man happy. Not all of them are on your back." Alice had an inkling of what she meant—back in Belle Chasse there had been someone, a man, who made her do things—but no, she wasn't going to think of that now. As long as Helen was unharmed. That was what counted. Alice got ready for bed as well and fell into an easy sleep until she was woken sometime later by the sound of Helen's raspy breathing. She'd kicked all the covers to the floor and was thrashing around in the bed. "I'm so hot," she said. "I'm burning up."

"Here's the water." Alice reached for the pitcher but Helen was quicker; her hand shot out and knocked it away. It fell to the floor; Alice looked down to see a jumble of broken glass and a rapidly spreading puddle.

"Look what you did!" Helen snapped.

"What I did? Helen, you—"

"You stupid cow! Get out of here!"

Horrified, Alice looked at her sister. Her face was flushed and she was breathing hoarsely.

"Why are you still standing there? I told you to get out."

Alice ran up to the fourth floor. Miss Bea's door was closed. She was sleeping. Alice hesitated, but she thought of Helen—feverish, raving. She knocked on the door.

"What is it?" Miss Bea appeared with her hair unbound and loose to her waist. She looked younger, and also kinder.

"It's Helen! She's sick. You have to come!"

Miss Bea reached for a wrapper, which she pulled on as they hurried downstairs. When they entered the room, Helen was babbling. "I told him not to touch me there, but he didn't listen. They never listen! Why don't they listen?" Tears dotted her cheeks and she brushed them away impatiently.

"Who touched you?" Alice asked.

"The devil, of course!" Helen cried. "He's here now. Can't you see him? Smell him? Or has he got you under his spell too?"

Miss Bea told Alice to fetch a cool compress and to press it to Helen's forehead.

When she did, Helen pushed her sister away. "Get out of here!"

"Helen it's me, Alice!"

"You're not Alice," she sneered. "You're an imposter! Get thee behind me, Satan! I told you to get out of here—go!"

Helen's railing woke some of the other girls, who came out into the corridor, but Miss Bea sent them all back to bed, and then had one of the houseboys go in search of McAndrew.

"Who's that?" Alice asked, but Miss Bea didn't answer. She was giving all her attention to Helen, whose face was blotched and eyes glassy. Miss Bea tried to reapply the compress but Helen resisted, so Bea took hold of her wrists.

"Don't hurt her!" Alice said.

Miss Bea looked over at Alice. "You shouldn't be here."

"Please don't make me leave." Whatever happened, she needed to see it.

"All right. You can stay. I'll keep holding her wrists and you apply the compress."

Alice did as Miss Bea told her. Helen's skin was hot and dry but at least she stopped fighting and let Alice apply the cool water to her face and chest. Soon her eyes closed.

"There," said Bea. "She's sleeping now. That's good. Maybe she'll feel better after she's rested."

"Do you think so?" asked Alice.

There was a pause and then Bea said, "We can only hope."

But a short while later, Helen's eyes opened and she began a low, droning monologue. She was cold. Chilled to the bone, could she please have a blanket, a shawl, for the love of God, a fire? Bea brought a blanket, and wrapped it around Helen's shivering form.

An hour passed and then another. The drapes were open and dawn lit the window. Helen was no longer conscious. The red fever spots were gone, leaving her skin blanched and ghostly. Finally, the house-boy returned with the news that McAndrew wasn't there; no one knew where to find him. But it was too late anyway. Alice could see that. Helen took her last breath just a little after noon; Alice was holding her hand. Miss Bea covered Helen's poor, pale face with the sheet and led Alice away.

After her sister's death, Alice was afraid to sleep in the room that they had shared; it felt haunted. Miss Bea offered to set up a cot in her own sitting room, just temporarily, and Alice managed to get some fitful rest there. Helen had been dead for about a week when Alice had a dream about their mother, sitting high up in a tree, calling down to her. Alice heard her voice, but hard as she tried, she couldn't see her; she was hidden behind the dense screen of leaves. Desperate to make contact, Alice tried calling out in response. No sound came from her mouth. Soon Mama's voice faded away and Alice was alone. She woke to a weight of sorrow greater than any she'd known before. The silence of this unfamiliar room was pressing down, crushing her. She had to get out of here, find someone, anyone. Miss Bea was just beyond that door, sleeping. What if Alice were to go into her room, wake her . . . she had done it once before, but she couldn't bring her-self to do it again. Miss Bea might feel annoyed, even angry, at being woken.

Alice stared at the door, willing it to open, but it remained shut. She started to cry. *Stop it,* she told herself. *Stop it right now.* But she only cried harder.

Then to her amazement, there was Miss Bea, hair loose and unbound like that last time. "What is it, Alice?" she asked.

Alice's weeping had taken on a life of its own. She was sobbing so hard she couldn't speak for a moment, and she clasped her arms tightly around herself, as if to keep from falling apart. Miss Bea crossed the room and sat on the bed. She didn't gather Alice into an embrace the way Alice's mother would have; instead, she put her hand against Alice's shoulder. Restrained as it was, the small gesture stopped the tears. "It will be all right," said Miss Bea. "Everything will be all right." And in that moment, Alice believed her. This woman was not warm like her mother sometimes was—no hugs, no caresses. But in her steadiness there was both balm and tonic. Alice wiped her eyes and settled back onto the pillows. "Close your eyes and try to sleep," Miss Bea said. "I'll be here."

Eventually, Alice was given another room, this one near the kitchen. People were passing all day long and much of the evening too. She heard voices, the clanging of pots and pans, water being poured; the activity was reassuring to her. It was clear that she would be allowed to stay on in the Basin Street house, avoiding the gentlemen who came in their evening clothes—Miss Bea was adamant on that—and always remaining behind the scenes, ready with her needle, her thimble, her spools of thread. When Miss Bea bought her a sewing machine, Alice was thrilled. What had taken hours could now be done in minutes, and she continued to make herself useful, even necessary. But they hadn't ever talked about what Alice's future would be, and when Bea—she had eventually, at Bea's suggestion, dropped the *Miss*—made her plans to go to New York, it was just assumed Alice would go along with her.

* * *

Now she was here. Bea was the only person she knew in this city, the only person she could count on. What if something happened to her? It was possible after all. Alice had lost her mother and her sister, after all, and she could lose Bea too. Or Bea could decide that Alice had disappointed her and wasn't turning out the way she'd hoped. This business about going to school for instance. Why did Bea keep harping on that when it was clear Alice had neither inclination nor interest? Just the thought of school made Alice's chest tighten.

But Alice was good with her needle. Bea valued that. Valued her. Alice vowed to work even harder, and take on more. Maybe she could come up with some ideas of her own; surely Bea would like that. The thought calmed her. She had a home with Bea, at least for now. And really, wasn't now the best she could hope for?

CHAPTER SIX

CATHERINE

Although the February day was cold, the light had already started to change. It was almost five o'clock, and the sky still held some vestiges of gold. Catherine was grateful that the dark curtain of night that fell so early in November and December was parting, even just a little. She'd been inside all day and though she'd initially been reluctant when Bridget showed up at the door inviting her for a walk, she was now glad she'd let herself be persuaded to venture out. Her sister-in-law was an ebullient presence and Catherine didn't really have to say anything; nodding and smiling were more than enough fuel to keep Bridget's little motor running. Only now she'd stopped in front of that shop where Catherine had bought the green dress. "Oh, let's go in!" Bridget said. "They always have such pretty things in the window."

"Do we have to?" Catherine wasn't eager to make a second visit; that woman, that Beatrice whatever her last name was, had made her uneasy.

"I'm sure Stephen won't mind if you buy a new dress," Bridget said. "That brother of mine loves nothing better than indulging you."

"That's not it," Catherine said. She saw, with dismay, that this Beatrice had stepped into the window and was hanging a small, beaded bag on the arm of the mannequin. For a brief, charged moment their eyes met. The older woman was staring at her, as if she would never stop. Catherine quickly looked away.

"Then what?" Bridget was clearly still hoping she could change Catherine's mind.

"I want to catch this last little bit of sun," Catherine said. "It feels so nice."

"All right," Bridget said, sounding resigned. "Maybe next time."

"Yes, next time," Catherine lied, and she took her sister-in-law's arm, propelling her past the shop.

When they reached the corner, Bridget said, "Speaking of indulgences, Stephen wants to buy Betsy a horse for her birthday."

Betsy was Molly's daughter, Stephen's only niece and also his goddaughter; he doted on the child.

"A horse! This is the first I'm hearing of it."

"That's because the idea just came to him. He saw her riding and thought she was a natural horsewoman."

"She's only six," Catherine pointed out.

"I know, but he said she was far better than all the little girls in the class, and that she ought to have a horse."

Catherine was quiet. She knew that Betsy had been taking lessons at the elegant Bedford Academy on Ocean Parkway, but hadn't been aware that she showed any particular aptitude. Of course, that's because she hadn't asked. Her own difficulty conceiving had made spending time with little Betsy painful for her, and she avoided the subject. And soon Betsy would be a big sister. Tears formed in

Catherine's eyes and she blinked a few times. "Stephen's the very incarnation of a doting uncle," she said at last. And of a considerate husband—he knew how her childlessness clawed at her spirit, and so he hadn't mentioned that he'd gone to see Betsy riding, or that he wanted to buy her a horse. Of course not.

"Molly thinks he's being extravagant, but as you know, it's hard to resist Stephen's enthusiasm."

Catherine had to agree. Hadn't it been his inextinguishable enthusiasm, his buoyant spirit, that won her heart almost three years ago?

* * *

After the lovely graduation ceremony at Vassar—the Daisy Chain girls in their summer frocks, holding hands in a circle, the pride Catherine had felt when she accepted the tightly rolled diploma—she reluctantly returned to her childhood home in Larchmont, New York. She'd had relative freedom in her days as a student, but now she found herself chafing at the parental scrutiny to which she was once again subjected. It was all benign and loving but still, a girl needed to breathe, didn't she? So when Lydia Nesbit, who had lived on her hall in Main Building, invited her to meet in the city, Catherine agreed at once. She and Lydia had spent many afternoon hours sipping tea in the Rose Parlor and gossiping about boys—from Yale, from Princeton, from West Point—whom they'd met at dances and about the lives that awaited them once they left the ivied walls. Lydia was studying chemistry, and thought she might become a teacher; Catherine was majoring in French and dreamed of going to Paris to look at paintings and old buildings, to walk the fabled streets . . . well, whatever she did in Paris would be wonderful, she was sure of it. But on the morning of their planned meeting, Lydia woke with a headache and had to cancel.

Since the day was mild and beckoning, Catherine decided to go alone, a fact she concealed from her mother. She took the train into Grand Central Terminal. From there, she walked downtown, stopping at Lord & Taylor, where, after sampling several scents, some lush, others delicate, she selected a bottle of Guerlain's Mitsouko. Practically purring her approval, the saleslady said, "It's brand-new. And it's a very provocative choice." Catherine sniffed her wrist again. The saleswoman was right—the mélange of bergamot, rose, clove, and jasmine seemed up-to-the-moment modern and even daring. No one else she knew would be wearing it.

After Lord & Taylor, she continued south to Thirty-Fourth Street, passing the grand edifice of B. Altman. At the Anglophile's Table on East Twenty-Ninth, she stopped for an English-style tea: crustless sandwiches, scones with clotted cream and jam, and doll-size fruit tarts—lemon, strawberry, apple—accompanied by a steaming pot of Darjeeling. Even when she'd finished her meal, she lingered in the garden, reluctant to leave. At first she'd been sorry that Lydia had canceled; now she was glad, savoring the solitude that felt both expansive and a little naughty.

Back on the street, she continued walking until she reached Twenty-Third Street, where a store window filled with stationery—creamy note cards bordered in scarlet, cerise, indigo, and emerald, deckle-edged sheets whose matching envelopes were lined in tissue—caught her eye.

She entered the shop to find a counter just to the left filled with fountain pens—her father's birthday was coming up, and a pen would make a nice gift. And perhaps a box of those note cards for herself, or one of the many journals or diaries. But the store was busy—the saleswoman at the pen counter was occupied with other customers, as was the saleswoman presiding over the blank books, and Catherine wasn't sure she wanted to wait—

"Can I help you?"

Her gaze came level with the middle of a tall young man's very crisp and very white shirt. As she tilted her head back, the rest of him came into view: a face broader at the top and narrowing at the chin, which was covered by a neat, brown beard, hair of a lighter brown, eyes in an intriguing amber color somewhere between that of his beard and hair. Then he smiled. Catherine's response was instantaneous and surprising—an unexpected frisson coursed through her—and she was drawn to him, his warmth, his apparent sincerity. But that was ridiculous. He was a salesman, not a suitor. He was smiling because he wanted her to buy something.

"I was looking for a fountain pen." She tried to sound businesslike.

"Of course. Follow me." He led her to where the pens lay gleaming under the glass countertop. "The Waterman is probably our very best. Made in Paris." That smile again. He opened a small drawer from which he took a bottle of ink and a few small squares of paper. Then he reached below the counter to take out a pen. Its case was a swirling, malachite-like pattern of green and black. He deftly filled it with ink and offered it to her as if it were a freshly cut rose. "Why don't you try it?"

Catherine took the pen and began to write her name; the ink seemed to glide from her fingertips through the pen and onto the paper. What a marvelous implement, her father would love it—

"You have such an elegant hand," he said. "Did you have a strict teacher when you were a girl?"

"Not so much strict as a perfectionist. She insisted that we practice over and over until we did it right. She said it was an art."

"My penmanship was wretched," he said amiably. "It still is. Not all the practicing in the world could help. My teachers were merciless. I can't even remember how many times I had my knuckles rapped. Even now, the sight of a ruler brings it all back."

"You were hit?" Catherine didn't like to think of it—hitting a small boy, and over something as inconsequential as penmanship.

"Every week. Sometimes more." He smiled again, and then looked down at the looping letters she'd penned. "Catherine. A lovely name. Is it yours?"

She nodded. Although her name was not of her choosing, his compliment still pleased her.

"Very nice to meet you, Miss Catherine," he said, extending his hand, which was warm and strong, the nails clean and buffed to a soft sheen. "I'm Stephen Berrill."

"Nice to meet you too." Berrill. That was the name on the shop. "Are you the owner?"

"It's my father's store, but I've been working with him ever since I got back from the front, so I suppose you could say that I'm part owner."

"It's a very nice store." She was flustered by the contact. "That is, you have such a nice selection of things . . ."

"Thank you. Would you like to see another pen? Or is there anything else I can show you?"

In the end, Catherine bought the pen, several boxes of the correspondence cards with different borders—she would give a box to her mother—a notebook bound in dark red leather, and a globe whose golden varnish made it appear to be an antique, though Stephen Berrill explained that it was not. That would be for her father as well.

"It's rather a lot," Stephen noted. "I'll have everything packed and sent to you." He was assuming that she wouldn't want to be seen carrying so many bundles; it wasn't considered proper for young women of her social standing.

"I appreciate it," she said. "Thank you." She wrote her name and address on a slip of paper, aware of his watching her hand form the graceful, even letters.

"Perfect," he said. "It will be taken care of right away."

And she knew that it would. The afternoon was waning, so she made her way uptown at a brisk pace, and caught the 4:47 train back to Larchmont. It was just before the evening's rush, and she got a seat by the window. Outside there was a verdant display of trees and shrubs, but Catherine didn't really see it. Instead, she saw Stephen Berrill's amber eyes and easy smile, felt the warmth of his hand when it covered hers. She said nothing of this to anyone, not to Lydia, who came over the next afternoon when she'd recovered from her headache, not to her father, and most especially not to her mother.

The package from Berrill's Fine Stationery and Papers arrived the next day just after Lydia had gone home. Catherine's mother liked the cards and approved of the gifts Catherine had chosen for her father. But Catherine was still thinking of Stephen, trying to come up with a reason to return to the shop. Two days later, when the mail delivery yielded a note from an unfamiliar and admittedly appalling hand, she realized that he'd been thinking of her too. She was glad she'd intercepted the envelope before her mother had seen it and she brought it upstairs, to read in the privacy of her room.

Dear Miss Delman,

I hope you are pleased with your purchases. I so enjoyed meeting you and was wondering if I might take the liberty of calling on you some afternoon? I would welcome the chance to talk with you again. I'd be happy to take the train to Larchmont and meet your parents before taking you out. Please say yes.

With all best wishes,

Stephen Thomas Berrill

Catherine read the note several times, lingering on the final line. *Please say yes.* He'd chosen a heavy, pearl-gray paper; its matching envelope was lined in a muted silver. He was bold, this Stephen Thomas Berrill. Determined. How many men would offer to come all the way up to Larchmont just to accompany a young lady on a walk? Not many, she was sure of it.

Finally, she slipped the letter into the notebook she'd bought, a notebook that was destined to remain empty because she knew her mother would eventually find—and read—it. She'd been a fool to think otherwise and resolved to give it to Lydia the next time they met. If she wanted to see Stephen again—and oh, how she did!—she was going to have to tell her parents about him.

Meredith Delman's response was predictable. "A shopkeeper?"

"He's not a shopkeeper. He's the son of the owner."

"A shopkeeper's son, then," said her mother.

"And what's wrong with that? You say it as if he's a criminal."

"There's nothing wrong with a shopkeeper's son . . ." Meredith said. "For some other girl—a girl who didn't go to Vassar. We sent you there so you would have . . . other opportunities."

"I thought you sent me there to get an education."

"Of course. But to what end if you're just going to squander it?"

"I don't think an afternoon spent with a perfectly nice, perfectly suitable young man is exactly squandering—"

"I hear squawking in the henhouse." Catherine's father had walked into the room. "What's the fuss?"

When the story was presented to Sebastian Delman, he sided with Catherine. "It's just a stroll on a summer day," he said to his wife. "You're making too much of it."

"Am I?" Meredith turned to Catherine. "What about Bradley?"

"What about him?"

"You two are practically engaged."

"Only in your mind, Mother." Catherine had met Bradley Colman at one of the Vassar-Yale mixers when she was a sophomore and he was a junior. He had already-thinning pale blond hair and though over six feet tall, he was always slouched, as if trying to conceal his height, or perhaps his entire self. Catherine liked him well enough but nothing about him excited her. The few times he'd kissed her—the first and only boy who had—she'd felt as if a damp cloth had been pressed over her lips. She was sure it was possible to experience a kiss differently. She was also sure that if she did, it would not be with him.

"He's offered to come and meet us," said her father. "Now, that's a young man with nice manners."

"He's still a shopkeeper," Meredith said. "You would give up your chance with Bradley Colman to keep company with a man like that? You're being foolish. Bradley won't wait around forever. Some other girl will snatch him up."

"Let her!" Catherine said, raising her voice, even though she knew there would be a price to pay for this display of temper.

"I don't know why she's so stubborn," Meredith said to her husband, as if Catherine weren't there. "You work so hard, give your daughter every possible advantage to make a good match, and she defies you at every turn. I don't understand it."

"Merry." Sebastian put his hand on his wife's forearm. "It's just a walk. She's not throwing Bradley over. Far from it, right?"

He caught Catherine 's eye and signaled that she should back him up. And although inwardly seething—her mother *always* did this, *always* made it seem that anytime Catherine expressed her own wishes, her own desires, she was dealing Meredith a mortal blow—she said, "That's true, Mother. I promised Brad I'd see him when he got back from Connecticut."

Meredith looked at her husband's hand as if she didn't quite know what it was. Then she seemed to relax, and put her own hand over his. "I suppose you're right. And we will have the chance to meet this fellow, this *shopkeeper*, first."

"Of course," Sebastian said.

Catherine didn't have anything to add. Instead, she went straight upstairs and pulled out one of the boxes of note cards, the one with the scarlet border, found a pen, and began to write, her penmanship even more embellished and florid than usual.

Dear Mr. Berrill,

Thank you for your charming note. I'd be very pleased if you were to call on me. How is next Saturday afternoon at two o'clock?

Yours,

Catherine Delman

Early the next morning, she walked down to the post office in town to make sure the note went out first thing. And when Stephen Berrill showed up that Saturday with a small bunch of yellow roses for Catherine and a beribboned box of chocolates for her mother, she was almost giddy. When Catherine returned home from their exceptionally long walk, she must have been glowing, because Meredith said, "I've been thinking about that last name—Berrill. Could that be—Irish?"

"I'm sure I don't know, Mother," said Catherine. "And I certainly don't care."

"You don't care? Well, you ought to care. You ought to care very much!" Meredith said. "The idea that you would ignore the likes of Bradley Colman to chase after an Irish shopkeeper's son—"

"I'm hardly chasing him, Mother." Catherine's mouth curved into a smile, remembering. "I'd say if anything, it's the other way around."

Stephen Berrill telephoned the very next day—Catherine had given him the number—and showed up the following week, this time with a box of cigars for Sebastian and a cluster of magenta peonies for Meredith. Despite the running commentary—and disapproval—from Meredith, they continued to see each other all summer long. It certainly helped that her father was on her side and had taken a shine to Stephen. And that Brad was conveniently out of the city, spending a few weeks with his family at their house in Connecticut. That left long lovely days—and nights—for them to get to know one another. Stephen told her about fighting in the trenches of France, an experience he described as *monstrous.* "I saw things I never could have dreamed of," he told her. "Things I wish I'd never seen, things I don't even want to tell you."

Catherine shuddered, glad to be spared; she had no desire to visualize such atrocities.

"But I will tell you this," he said. "There's nothing noble or glorious or heroic about war. It's pure chaos and horror, from start to finish. Anyone who says otherwise is just a liar." He was actually shaking a little, so Catherine put a hand on his wrist. "I was wounded, so they sent me home. I'm one of the lucky ones," he added. "So many of us were killed. Shot, stabbed by a bayonet, blown to bits . . ." He blinked a few times. "My cousin, my cousin James . . ."

"Your cousin . . . died?" she prompted.

"Yes. Just two days before he was going to be discharged."

"Oh," said Catherine. "Oh, how sad."

"We were born a month apart and we were close, practically brothers. And he, he was an only child." *Like me,* thought Catherine. "My uncle and aunt—they took it very hard."

Catherine said nothing but just let the sadness that washed over him wash over her too.

* * *

One evening they took the subway all the way to Coney Island. Catherine had never been before; her mother thought amusement parks were a lowbrow and vulgar form of entertainment. But Stephen made her see it in a different way. "We came here a lot as a family when I was a kid," he said. "And we all had our favorite things. Bridget liked the roller coaster, and for Molly, it was the carousel."

"What about you?" she asked.

"The Ferris wheel." He gestured to the large glowing circle that was almost straight ahead of them. "Would you like to go for a ride?"

They climbed into the car and buckled the leather belts on either end of the bench. Then the slow ascent began, the car swaying gently, the lights below a glittering blanket, like the stars had dropped from the sky. When they reached the top, the wheel stopped, and the car continued to bob in the night. Catherine couldn't recall ever having been so happy until Stephen turned and brought his face close for the kiss she just realized she had wanted for quite some time. When they finally drew apart, he kept his face near hers inclining his forehead so it touched hers. "Marry me," he said. "Please, Catherine, say that you'll marry me."

"When?" she said, and then he kissed her again.

* * *

As Catherine and Bridget neared the Grand Army Plaza entrance to the park, the wind picked up and the sky was a moody shade of gray, just tinged with blue and the last little bit of gold.

"I think we should be heading back now," said Catherine. "I'm getting chilly, aren't you?"

Bridget agreed. Catherine was glad they were taking a different street on their route home and didn't have to pass the dress shop again. Her mood, lifted temporarily, had plummeted again, and right now, she wanted nothing more than to go home.

CHAPTER SEVEN

CATHERINE

Catherine let herself into the darkened house to find all was quiet. This morning, Nettie had asked if she could leave early, so Catherine would serve Stephen the dinner she had prepared, and they would have a nice evening at home. Stephen would light a fire and turn out the lights; they would sit on the sofa, gazing at the bright, crackling blaze. Knowing they were alone in the house would loosen his inhibitions. Instead of waiting until they went upstairs and got into bed, he would want to kiss her, caress her, take off her clothes right here on the floor by the fire. She was lucky to have such an ardent, adoring husband. Even though her mother had not approved, Catherine had known that Stephen was the man she wanted, and she had not let herself be dissuaded.

* * *

"He's Irish," Meredith had said. "And Catholic." It was not clear which of those things she found more objectionable.

"I'm aware of that." Catherine was trying to restrain her temper. "Well aware."

"Really? Then why don't you understand the problem this poses—"

"Problem? What problem?"

Meredith frowned. "All I've ever wanted for you is a chance to come up in the world. And what do you do? You drag us right back down again."

"Merry, you're being dramatic," said Sebastian. "Stephen Berrill seems like a fine young man, even if he is Irish and—"

"Well, of course you wouldn't care about that—your family tree has plenty of bad apples!"

"What do you mean, bad apples?" Catherine asked.

Sebastian looked sternly at his wife. "This isn't the time." Then he turned to Catherine. "She's made her choice. It wouldn't be your choice, I know that. But he's a good man, from a good family—"

"Good *Irish Catholic* family!" Meredith interjected.

"A good and prosperous family. Catherine will be well provided for. You said he lives in Brooklyn somewhere?"

"Prospect Heights," Catherine told him. "He says it's a very nice area. His parents have a house and they want to buy him one nearby. It will be their wedding present to us."

"That means you'll be living in Brooklyn." Meredith moaned. "Instead of a town house in Manhattan or a lovely house here in Larchmont."

Catherine didn't answer but turned to her father. "I love him, Daddy," she said. "I love him so very much."

"And there's nothing more important than that," said her father. "Isn't that right, Merry?" He took his wife's hand and kissed it.

"To think she could have had a Colman . . ." But Meredith must have realized she had been overruled because she had now taken to lamenting instead of fighting.

Catherine looked at her father and mouthed the words *thank you*.

"You'll see," Sebastian said to Meredith. "Everything will be all right."

"No, everything will be wonderful," said Catherine.

"I suppose there's one small consolation," said Meredith.

"What's that?" Catherine asked.

"At least he's not an Italian. Or, God forbid, a Jew."

"That's not too likely," said her father dryly.

"You can't be too sure," Meredith said. "Once you open that door, you can't predict what—or who—will come charging in."

Although Catherine had been charmed by St. Augustine's on Sixth Avenue, a block-long structure where Stephen's sister had married, she mollified her mother by agreeing to be wed at the Episcopalian church in Larchmont where they had always gone for services. "What about your parents?" she'd asked Stephen. "Will they mind? Will you?"

"I just want us to be married," he said. "I don't care where it happens. And if I explain that to my parents, they won't press."

Catherine was relieved. Once the venue was confirmed, she let her mother choose everything else too. She found she didn't care about the trappings. She just wanted to embark on her life with Stephen, a life, she was sure, in which her cup would runneth over with happiness.

After the wedding and a honeymoon in Newport, Rhode Island, Stephen and Catherine settled into a house on St. Marks Avenue, and the extended Berrills were quickly and seamlessly woven into their lives. There were dinners, lunches, spontaneous visits in the late morning or early evening, walks in the park, rendezvous on the main avenues, holidays spent together.

Catherine loved every bit of it. For the first time, she was part of something large and vital, a welcome change from her own childhood, in which she was the sole focus not only of her parents' doting but also of her mother's ever-present surveillance and worry. Whereas with seven children, Jack and Veronica Berrill had learned to loosen the reins, and to Catherine, their lives seemed relaxed and joyful, their house a warm, inviting place. She wanted that for her own house, a place that Stephen gave her carte blanche to decorate.

"You take care of all that," he said. "I'm sure you'll do a better job than I would."

At first, Catherine consulted with Mr. Willis, an interior decorator whom Meredith had hired for her. "Everyone in Larchmont considers him the very best," she had said. "At least, everyone with taste." Privately, Catherine found his ideas predictable, his palette wan. She didn't want to replicate her childhood home or the homes of the ladies her mother knew. She wanted to create something different and new, and she didn't need an interior designer to do it. Instead, she found a pair of brothers with roots in Italy to paint the heavy, dreary dark woodwork white, and to hang wallpaper. But not the prim and dull wallpaper suggested by Mr. Willis.

Catherine searched and searched until she found a small company in Woodstock, New York, that offered the sort of designs she had imagined: exuberant florals, paisleys, and for the front hallway, peacocks preening in a walled garden. Then she covered the herringbone floors with thick rugs in glowing colors, and filled the rooms with generously proportioned sofas and armchairs that encouraged curling up, lounging, and napping. To these she added gaggles of pillows—embroidered, patterned, tasseled—and cozy throws of cashmere and mohair. She collected vases in jewel-toned glass—cobalt, ruby, amethyst, emerald—and ceramic vases with lush, drippy glazes, filled them with flowers, and set them everywhere, and sought out eclectic artwork—a vista of mountains rendered in blurred pastels, a Japanese woodblock print of kimono-clad women holding parasols, a tiny oil canvas that depicted a squirrel risen on his hind legs, his front paws clasped beseechingly together, his black eyes fixed on the viewer.

Catherine dreaded inviting her mother to see the newly decorated house, knowing that Meredith would find fault with her unconventional choices, and when she finally had her over, her fears were borne out.

"I can't imagine what people will say when they see it," Meredith began. She was sitting on a love seat and eyeing the crewelwork pillow cover that came from Greece with frank suspicion. "They might not want to come again, you know."

"If people find my taste so deplorable that it would keep them from my home, then I don't want them here anyway," replied Catherine.

"And your husband—he allowed this?"

"His name is Stephen, Mother." Meredith seemed never to utter his name if she could help it. "And not only did he 'allow' it, he fully approved."

"He's a tolerant man," Meredith said. "Very tolerant."

"Isn't Daddy?" asked Catherine. "It seems to me that he lets you have your way in, oh, just about everything."

"Don't you be fresh, Catherine. It's not for you to judge your parents' marriage."

But it's perfectly fine for you to judge mine, she thought. She was rescued by the chiming of the doorbell. In walked Bridget with one of the younger Berrill siblings, Kevin, whose black hair, blue eyes, and winsome nature diverted her mother's attention for the rest of the afternoon. When they left, and Catherine and Meredith were alone again, Meredith said, "They do have adorable children"—by *they,* Catherine knew she meant the Irish. "Let's hope yours will be as engaging."

"Yes, Mother," she responded, striving for patience. "Let's hope."

Catherine continued her unconventional decorating schemes on the house's upper floors as well. The bedroom she and Stephen shared had paper splotched with enormous cabbage roses, a low bench covered in rose velvet, and gossamer-thin gauze drapes that were shot through with threads of scarlet and gold. One of the two guest rooms was covered in paper patterned with floating umbrellas—some tightly closed, others open and bobbing like parachutes—and the ceiling was the color of an April sky.

But the rooms on the fourth floor were intentionally left empty. Catherine was waiting to fill them because these were the rooms their children would occupy. *Their children.* She couldn't wait for those words to become a reality, and she knew Stephen felt the same way—they both envisioned a big, happy family, much like the one he'd been lucky enough to come from. After their lovemaking, which was ardent and frequent, she would lie awake next to him, imagining those children, their faces and even their names. Violet, Miranda, Charlotte, Delphine, Daniel, William, Arthur—a private litany with a music all its own.

But even though she and Stephen were ready to become parents, Catherine didn't conceive right away. She began to consult books on the subject, traveling to bookstores and the New York Public Library in Manhattan because she didn't want her troubles to be known in the neighborhood. The advice she found was wildly divergent— have marital relations first thing in the morning, counseled one doctor; have marital relations only in the evening, advised another. Or have relations every day during certain times of the month and not at all during others.

At first, Stephen found these directives amusing and even stimulating; he was happy to comply. But as Catherine's urgency turned to desperation, lovemaking became less of delight and more of a chore. Soon she couldn't bear to discuss it and instead left an unspoken sign, like one of her undergarments tucked under his pillow, that indicated her intent. He always accommodated her, but without the ardor of their earliest days. He was trying though, trying so hard. His effort moved her.

Catherine became a woman possessed. It had to happen. No, she would make it happen. This was the month she would find herself with child. In the family way. Quickening, an archaic term she especially liked. Pregnant—the most clinical of all. But whatever it was called, the much-desired state eluded her. Month after month, hope swelled, crested, and collapsed in the same crushing disappointment.

Maybe the problem was a medical one, she wondered aloud to Stephen, who immediately suggested that they consult a specialist. He found someone in the city and accompanied her to the office, which was on Twelfth Street, just off University Place. After the examination, he took her hand as the doctor delivered his diagnosis.

"You're fine," he had said. "No abnormalities, nothing of the sort. You're just nervous, that's all. You need a rest."

A rest? she thought. A rest from what? Her life was easy and good. Stephen could support them comfortably, and she had some money of her own too—her grandmother had left her a nice sum in her will. Nettie did all the cooking; she and another maid did the housework. Catherine was a lady of leisure, maybe too much leisure. She longed for the days to be filled by a baby, its demands and its needs, for the rooms upstairs to be filled with the children who would give her life richness and purpose and meaning.

She was quiet and withdrawn on the trip back to Brooklyn. Not Stephen. He was his cheerful self and even hummed a bit. It just wasn't in his nature to worry. But he took the doctor at his word and surprised Catherine with tickets to Niagara, where they stood in awe before the falls, watching as the water rushed and thundered down. Catherine enjoyed their time there, but she did not get pregnant. Other trips followed—Chicago, then Quebec, where they walked on cobblestone streets and stayed in the most charming of inns. Their room had a canopy bed, and in the morning, they ate croissants with apricot jam and Catherine had a chance to practice her French. And still—nothing.

* * *

The next morning, Catherine slipped out of bed while Stephen still slept. Her plan had worked even better than she'd anticipated; they had made love on the sofa, the floor, and then, after they'd gone upstairs and fallen asleep entwined, once again when they awoke. It was good to be reminded of this connection between them, the mutual desire, the bond. For too many months, she had allowed the failure—and it was *her* failure—to consume her. It had gotten so that she couldn't bear to see women with babies. Or the swollen bellies that would soon result in babies. She didn't know what she would *do* if she and Stephen couldn't have a child. It seemed so unfair, so cruel even, she wouldn't be able to endure it, she really wouldn't—her thoughts went round and round, chasing each other like a pair of angry dogs, nipping and snarling.

But she was going to try to put that behind her and cultivate a new attitude, all the while knowing that an attitude alone couldn't make a difference. Or could it? That month, her time was late, then later still. Then there was the morning she was dizzy, and the smell of bacon frying—usually an enticement to get up and go to the breakfast table—made her ill. She realized, with dawning and tremulous euphoria, that the sickness she felt was not sickness at all, but a sign, the one she had been hoping and praying for—her dreams were coming true, and at long last, she was going to have a child.

SPRING

CHAPTER EIGHT

ALICE

———
———

Brooklyn, 1924

Those first days in Brooklyn, Alice felt like she and Bea were a pair of marbles in a hatbox, rattling around aimlessly. Of course, this was the first time they had lived alone together, just the two of them. On Basin Street, there had always been other people around—the fifteen or so girls in Bea's employ, along with maids, cooks, laundry women, houseboys, a groom, stable hands, and of course the men who came and went every evening, all evening long.

But as time passed, they began to develop something like a routine. Mornings they spent in the workroom together, bolts of fabric draped out across the table, along with jars of buttons and beads, spools of ribbon, lace, and trim. Dresses in various states of completion hung from racks or were displayed on one of the mannequins Bea had ordered. This was Alice's favorite part of the day—working companionably with Bea, the possibilities unfurling like the cloth, experimenting with color, with pattern, with texture, with shape, and with line.

In the afternoons, Bea went into the shop, helping the customers who had begun to frequent it, while Alice stayed in the workroom, sewing. She liked to listen to Bea as she sewed—she was gracious with the women, and knew how to draw them out in a way that had nothing to do with dresses or suits or coats, and they almost always went away with at least one if not several new garments.

On Sundays the shop was closed, and they used the day to search for more clothing and fabric for raw material. A couple of times they took a ferry over to New Jersey, where they walked around an open-air flea market, hot potatoes in the pockets of their Rappaport's coats to keep their hands warm. On the ride back, Bea struck up a conversation with a woman who told her about a neighborhood in the city where they could continue the hunt, and not just on Sundays. "If you like a bargain, that's the place for you," she said.

So the following week they took the subway to the Grand Street station, emerging from the station into a knot of narrow and crowded streets. Here, the merchandise was piled in heaps on top of pushcarts and the vendors expected and even encouraged haggling. To Alice, it felt like the Quarter back in New Orleans. But instead of French or Spanish, the conversations that buzzed around her were in languages that were totally unfamiliar. Bea explained that she was hearing Russian, Polish, Lithuanian, and German—but mostly Yiddish.

"Yiddish?" Alice had asked. Bea's explanation didn't seem all that much clearer—a mixture of German and Hebrew? She had never heard of Hebrew. And how could a language be a mixture?

Around noon, they stopped for lunch and, seated on round stools at a counter, were served bowls of steaming, magenta-colored soup and plates of some kind of dumplings, rolled like little logs, accompanied by sour cream and applesauce.

"Borscht!" Bea said. "I haven't eaten borscht in years. And look, blintzes too."

"What kind of soup is this?" Alice took a taste. It had a slight tang—maybe vinegar?—and a rich, flavorful broth.

"It's made from beets," said Bea. "And the blintzes are filled with white cheese."

"So you've had it before?" Alice asked, then took another eager slurp. Everything was delicious, much more so than the bland pap Bea's Brooklyn cook spooned onto their plates nightly.

"Not for a long time," said Bea. "Not since I was a child."

"Where did you grow up?" Alice had never asked this before, never thought to ask. Bea as a child was something she couldn't even imagine.

Bea hesitated before she said, "Russia."

Alice had only a vague notion of that faraway country. Big. Cold. They had a king . . . no, a czar. And a czarina. But not anymore—there had been an uprising. A revolution. She remembered hearing about that. "Did you like it?"

"Like it?" Bea seemed amused by the question. "It was—home." Bea took her arm after paying the bill. "Come along. We've got work to do."

Back out on the street, Alice took greater notice of the food that was for sale here—pickles pulled and still dripping from brine-filled barrels, bagels and bialys, which Bea said were best with sweet butter or cream cheese, smoked salmon, corned beef, pastrami, herring and slivers of onion in a milky sauce, pouches of fried dough filled with mashed potatoes with the funny name of knishes, a cinnamon-swirled loaf cake with the even funnier name of bobka. Bea seemed delighted by the discovery and, in addition to all the fabric and clothing they had found, filled three bags with groceries, so many that they had to take a taxi back to Brooklyn.

* * *

But ever since that woman had shown up and bought the green dress, Alice felt that this fragile sense of order had been upended. Bea seemed different. Less composed, not herself. She was distracted, beginning tasks but not completing them, forgetting others entirely. Alice had the sense that Bea was looking for that customer when they were out walking in the neighborhood or from the parlor window. Early one morning, Alice found her still in her dressing gown, with the door wide open, staring at the street and shivering. She led her back into the house and upstairs, and even helped her pick out her clothes for the day.

That evening at dinner, Alice confronted her. "You're not yourself," she said. Since the shop and workroom took up the parlor floor, they had taken to eating downstairs, in the room off the kitchen. Although it lacked the high ceilings and elongated windows of the rooms on the higher floors, it was made welcoming by a black-and-gray-veined marble mantel, wooden shutters, and oak floors in a checkerboard pattern.

"I'll be all right," Bea said. "It's just the strain of moving and setting up the shop."

"No," said Alice. "It isn't." She took a bite of poached chicken and chewed it without enthusiasm. "Does it have anything to do with that woman who came in a few weeks ago? The one who bought the green dress?"

Bea looked uncomfortable. "Why would you say that?"

"I don't know. But she upset you, I could tell. You had such a strange look on your face . . ."

"What look?"

"Like you'd seen a ghost."

Bea smiled. It was not a convincing smile but it was a smile all the same. That was Bea—she held herself together no matter what. Alice had never seen her lose her composure. "Your concern is very touching," she said. "Really it is. But I don't want you to worry about me. There's no cause."

"And what about her? That woman—Mrs. Berrill?"

"What about her?"

"She must have said something, done something . . ."

"I think you're imagining all this, Alice. Maybe you're a bit too cut off—spending your days here with me and no one else."

Alice didn't say anything, but Bea was right. Not that she wasn't grateful—Bea had taken her in when she'd had no other place to go, and she'd been so generous too, buying her clothes and whatever else she needed. Still, she *was* lonely here, cut off from the people she'd known and without a way to make new connections, new friends. The glamor of the city seemed elusive; instead, she spent her days sewing. Not that she minded the work. The quiet room, the bolts of fabric, yards of ribbon and trim, the garments turned inside out, exposed and beckoning. She liked following Bea's directions as well as pursuing ideas of her own. What if she put new sleeves on that jacket, or added a pinafore to that dress? Necklines lowered or raised, buttons switched, silhouettes reinvented. Or starting from scratch, like that green dress. Bea had had the original idea but it was Alice who'd figured out how to execute it.

Dressmaking gave her a chance to be good at something, to put her skills to use. But it couldn't give her everything. Back in New Orleans, the house had been filled with girls, well, women, but they acted like girls—gossiping, laughing, brushing each other's hair, rimming each other's eyes with kohl. Oh, there had been plenty of quarrels large and small, tempers flaring, harsh words. Yet beneath all that, there was a sense of kinship, of, well, family.

". . . you could still go to school, you know. Or if not school, we could hire a tutor for you. You don't have to spend all your time in the shop—"

Alice looked down at her plate. Next to the poached chicken was a lump of creamed spinach and another of mashed potatoes. Food for an invalid. Or a baby. She couldn't eat another bite. "I'm sorry, Miss Bea," she said. "I tried it before and I just didn't like it . . ."

"You know you don't have to call me Miss Bea. We talked about that, remember?"

"I remember."

"Well, we don't have to decide anything now," Bea said.

Alice was relieved. "I think I'll go upstairs now," she said. "If that's all right."

"Of course it's all right."

Alice closed the door to her room and sat on the bed. The curtains were still open, and she could see the dark rectangle of night framed by the window. Like the workroom, her bedroom overlooked the garden. Bea thought Alice would like that, especially since they found out there was a Chinese magnolia growing near the back wall. It wasn't nearly so large or lush as the one in Bea's New Orleans garden, but its mere presence, so far north, was a pleasant surprise. Still, it did nothing to make Alice feel less alone, less strange and displaced.

She didn't know why Bea had been so intent on New York. Of course no one had compelled Alice to follow her; she could have stayed in New Orleans. Or gone back to Belle Chasse. But in New Orleans, she would have become a whore—like her mother, like her sister. And Belle Chasse? No, she'd never go back there, not for all the money in the world.

* * *

Peeking over the banister, Alice could see that the double doors to the parlor in the Belle Chasse house were closed. Good—a sign that she was safe and could continue down the stairs. The carpet on this last flight showed a pretty pattern of roses; that was because the boarders who lived on the second floor paid more for their rooms and were more highly regarded by Mrs. Keefe, their landlady. Alice knew that she, Helen, and her mother were not so highly regarded by Mrs. Keefe; the torn and worn-out carpeting—dull brown, no flowers—that covered the stairs to the third floor was good enough for the likes of them.

Even though the doors were closed, Alice scuttled past them in a hurry. They might open suddenly, revealing the parlor that Mrs. Keefe was so particular about keeping clean. But it wasn't Mrs. Keefe, with her broom or her mop, her dust cloth or scrub brush, that worried Alice. It was her husband, a big, hulking man who was as idle as his wife was industrious, and who spent much of the day sitting in the parlor's brocade armchair or playing cards in the kitchen with a few other men.

It was still early—Helen had only just gone off to school—but the day was already hot and promised to be hotter. Squinting in the glare, Alice crossed the dusty road and entered the grocery store on the corner opposite the house. She held a small basket in one hand and a few coins tightly clutched in the other.

"Morning, baby," Mrs. Langley greeted her. "You're here for your mama?"

"Yes, ma'am," Alice said, giving her the coins. "She needs four eggs."

Mrs. Langley counted out the eggs and placed them in the basket, adding a bit of loose straw for protection. "Now you be careful going home," she said. "You don't want those to break now, do you?"

"No, ma'am." Alice looked down at the eggs, whose smooth brown shells she could see beneath the straw. Her stomach rumbled. It had been a good morning. Mama hadn't woken up sick or with that sour breath that she got when she had been drinking. Instead, she'd stretched her arms and called for Alice to come cuddle with her. Even though the room was warm, Alice had slipped under the sheet and let herself be enveloped by her mother's arms. "Go and get some eggs," she'd said. "I've got half a loaf of stale bread. I can cut it and fry up the slices." The bread, soaked in a milk-and-egg mixture, and fried in butter, would be delicious, especially when Mama sprinkled cinnamon sugar on the top. Alice wished she could have a piece of the fried bread right now. Dinner had been some leftover beans and rice, and not all that much besides.

As she stepped inside the house, the parlor doors opened and there was Mr. Keefe. Like he was listening for her. Waiting for her.

"Hello," he said. "You went shopping for your mama?"

Alice nodded, too scared to speak.

"You're a good girl. And good girls deserve a treat, that's what I think."

"No, thank you," Alice managed to say. "I don't want anything."

"Of course you do," he said, stepping out of the doorway and a little closer to where she stood, hand clutching the basket tightly.

Alice wanted to bolt but was too frightened to move. Besides, he was their landlady's husband. Mama had drilled it into her that Mr. and Mrs. Keefe were doing them a big favor in letting them have those rooms upstairs; other landlords might not be so . . . understanding.

"Come on now," he coaxed. "I have something special for you. Very special."

"Well, I . . ."

He took her free hand and led her into the parlor. She could hear the sounds of Mrs. Keefe moving around, and that calmed her slightly; they wouldn't be alone.

"Is that you, Gus? Who's with you?" called Mrs. Keefe. She came into the parlor. "Oh, it's Alice."

"I want to show her the rabbits," he said.

"Rabbits?" Her ears perked up. Alice did love rabbits.

"A whole bunch of them. A mama and her babies," Mr. Keefe said. "Right out back in the backyard."

"Really?"

"Yes, really. Come with me and I'll show them to you. You can leave your basket here."

"Gus, I need you to help me roll up that carpet," Mrs. Keefe said.

"We'll only be a few minutes." Still holding her hand, he knelt down so his face was close to hers. His nostrils seemed very wide, and his stubble-covered cheeks were coated with a sheen of sweat. Reluctantly, Alice set down the basket and followed him through the parlor and the dining room, and out the kitchen door.

"They're right back there." He gestured to the far end of the yard, where a small wooden shed stood by the fence. "When they get a little bigger, you can pick out one for your own. Make it a pet and all."

"Oh!" Alice let herself picture it—a baby rabbit, maybe gray, maybe brown. The image crowded out images of the other times Mr. Keefe had managed to get her alone, the hands that roamed up and down her body, the fingers that slipped under her dress and into her drawers—no, she shouldn't think about that, she should think about the rabbit. Her bunny rabbit. But would Mama let her keep it? She had to, she just had to. Following Mr. Keefe across the grass, she tried to come up with reasons that would persuade her mother to agree.

"Look." He pointed to a crevice between the shed and the ground below. "That's where they go in and out. Do you want to see?"

"Yes, yes, please." Alice got closer to the shed. The crevice was dark; none of the animals were visible. "I can't—"

Before she could finish, Mr. Keefe yanked her quickly around the corner and behind shed, out of view of the house.

"Shh," he said. "Don't say a thing." He knelt and began touching her then, just like before, but this time, his fat, sausage fingers poked their way into her body. She was alarmed—he had not done that before. "Ow," she whimpered. "You're hurting me."

"I told you to be quiet." His fingers continued their awful probing.

Alice was terrified but unable to move. She closed her eyes so she wouldn't have to see his face, which had grown sweatier, practically glistening. So she first felt, not saw, the firm rod of flesh he'd thrust into her hand. Her eyes popped open.

He stood, towering above her, pants unbuttoned. "Move your hand up and down." When she didn't do it, he closed his hand over hers to demonstrate. He sucked in his breath as her hand started moving. "Yes, like that." His hand was still controlling hers. "Harder. And faster." Alice's hand hurt from the pressure. That thing of his was getting fuller, more swollen. Would it burst? Break? Would she get into trouble? Faster and faster, their hands worked together until he emitted a loud groan and finally released her. Her hand, now freed, was covered in something sticky and wet. She wiped it vigorously on her dress.

Breathing hard, he buttoned himself back into his pants. "Now you don't say a word about this to anyone, you understand?"

"Yes, sir." Alice's voice was a whisper.

"Good. Because if you do, I'll kick you and your slut of a mother out onto the street. How would you like that, missy? No place for a rabbit if you're living in the street, is there?"

"No, sir."

"Now get out of here," he said. "And remember what I said."

Alice walked quickly across the yard until she reached the back door. He wasn't following. She stepped into the kitchen, where Mrs.

Keefe was in the kitchen, frying onions. The smell made Alice feel nauseated.

"Did you see the baby bunny rabbits?" asked Mrs. Keefe. "They're sweet little critters, even if they eat every fool thing I try to grow back there."

"Not today," Alice croaked.

"Oh." The landlady pushed the onions around with a wooden spoon. "Maybe next time."

"Maybe." Now the smell was making Alice gag, and she feared she was going to throw up right here, on Mrs. Keefe's freshly waxed kitchen floor. "I'll just be going upstairs now," she said. "My mama's waiting for me."

"All right." Then Mrs. Keefe looked up. "Where's Gus? He was supposed to help me with that rug."

"He's in the yard." She took her basket on the way out and hurried up the stairs. In her haste, she tripped on a bit of frayed carpet sticking up from the top step and the eggs, all four of them, jumped out and landed on the floor.

The door opened. "There you are," Mama said. "I was wondering where you'd got to." She'd slipped on her shiny black wrapper, one with the embroidered birds on the back. Then she noticed the puddle of broken eggs. "What happened?"

"Oh, Mama!" Alice rushed over and threw her arms around her mother's waist.

"Why, you're shaking like a leaf," her mother said, stroking her hair. "Come inside and tell me what all this is about. We'll clean up later."

Still trembling, Alice followed her mother inside and sought refuge in her lap while she told the story—Mr. Keefe, the promise of the bunnies, the thing that he made her touch behind the shed. She took a deep breath, inhaling the fragrance of Mama's lilac-scented talc. Now it would be all right. Mama would make it all right. But instead she felt a sharp slap and her hand flew up to her wounded cheek.

"Don't ever say that about him," Mama hissed. "Not to me, not to anyone. If you do, they'll turn us out and then what? Where will we go? What will happen to us?"

Alice stood up. "That's just what Mr. Keefe said."

"Oh, baby." Mama's eyes filled with tears and she reached over to touch the spot, still red, still stinging. "I'm sorry. I'm so sorry." But Alice moved away and went into the room she shared with Helen. She curled up in a little ball on the bed and stuck her thumb in her mouth, waiting for Mama to chide her, tell her she was a big girl, too big to be doing that anymore. But Mama went out into the hallway, probably to clean up the eggs. When she came back inside, Alice was still on the bed.

"I can heat up the bread and make us cinnamon toast," Mama said. "We don't even need the eggs."

"That's all right," Alice said. "I'm not hungry anymore anyway." And though she could sense her mother staring at her, hoping she would forgive her, Alice refused to meet her gaze.

A week or so later there was another morning when Mama wasn't feeling well, and she asked Alice to run over to the pharmacy for a bottle of Dr. Franck's Grains of Health. The clerk behind the counter had to go in back to find one, and for a moment, Alice was left alone. Her eyes roamed the shop: shelves crammed with tinctures and remedies; a basket of soaps, tins of powder, bottles of scent, nail varnish, cough lozenges, one flavored with honey. Alice liked the taste of honey and was curious about the nail varnish. But something directed her to a packet of Kennedy corn plasters—she didn't even know what, exactly, they were—and she pocketed them. At just that moment, the clerk returned with the pills and Alice made the purchase. There was a covered glass jar with sticks of rock candy at one end of the counter and the clerk took off the lid and handed one to Alice.

"I don't have an extra penny," she said. It was true; she'd spent all the coins her mother had given her.

"That's all right. It's on me."

Alice thanked him and felt ashamed of having stolen the corn plasters, which she didn't even want. She walked home slowly but scuttled quickly past the double doors to the parlor on up the steps; she wasn't going to let herself be caught by Mr. Keefe again. Her face burned when she thought of him, the way he'd tricked her. Though Mrs. Keefe had said there were bunnies, and Alice had looked many times, she had never even seen a bunny back there. Not once.

"That you, Alice?" Mama called out.

"Yes, Mama. I have your pills."

She brought her mother a glass of water, the corn plasters still in her pocket. Several days later, Mama sent her down to Mrs. Keefe with the rent money. She'd seen Mr. Keefe leaving the house a few minutes before, so she didn't have to worry about bumping into him.

"Your mama sick again?" Mrs. Keefe asked as she took the worn bills and smoothed them out between her fingers.

"Yes, ma'am."

"She might have fewer headaches if she didn't drink so much," Mrs. Keefe said. "Liquor is the devil's nourishment."

Alice had nothing to say to that; in fact, she agreed with the landlady.

"Well, thank her for managing to pay on time—even with a headache."

"I will."

A snapping sound from the kitchen caused Mrs. Keefe head to turn in that direction. "Must be the mousetrap," she said and hurried off, leaving Alice alone in the parlor. Across the room was an armchair and next to that, a side table on which sat a wooden matchbox. That was where Mr. Keefe sat and smoked. She saw his face, felt his hand on hers—Alice snatched the box from the table, left the parlor, and went upstairs, the small object practically throbbing in her hand.

* * *

Remembering it now, Alice had an urge to look at those small trophies again. Making sure the door was closed, she reached under her bed for the box that had held her childhood treasures. Here was the matchbox with its picture of a smiling lady holding up a foam-topped glass. And the package of corn plasters, which looked as new as the day she had taken it. The long-ago thrill of these thefts kindled something, a long-dormant but unmistakable heat. She was older now, and she knew better than to steal. She could get caught, get in trouble. But she understood that the urge wasn't something she could control; it controlled her. All she could do was wait to see if it would come again.

CHAPTER NINE

CATHERINE

Now that she was with child, Catherine's days were golden, her nights sparkling. Blessed. Winter gave way to spring, and as Brooklyn throbbed to life around her, she pulsated in glorious rhythm along with it. After the first months, when she felt either nauseated, fatigued, or both, she entered a halcyon period of enormous energy and appetite. Gone were the times when she could barely keep anything down, nibbling salted crackers and sipping ginger ale to calm her queasy stomach. Now she woke hungry and stayed hungry. Nettie outdid herself in feeding her mistress. Mornings Catherine came downstairs to find oatmeal simmering on the stove, and Nettie would serve her a big bowl, adding generous portions of raisins, brown sugar, and cream. Another day there would be waffles, butter pooling in their crisp, still-warm squares, maple syrup—which Nettie had heated—forming a golden circle around them, or scrambled eggs whipped frothy and flavored with dill and bits of smoked salmon. Catherine ate it all and asked for seconds. Food had never tasted so

good, and with every bite, she felt she was feeding the new life growing inside her.

She reveled in her body's physical changes too—the thickening at
her waist that made it look like she'd stashed a pumpkin under her
dress, the taut, full weight of her breasts with their newly darkened
nipples. Catherine knew from her sister-in-law Molly that some husbands were repelled by these developments, but Stephen wasn't one
of them. He told her she was "a goddess" and found her new shape
wildly exciting; they made love with even greater abandon than ever
before. Gone were the tense, workmanlike encounters and in their
place, a rekindled passion. On weekday mornings, he was reluctant
to leave her, and on Sunday, when he didn't have to work, they stayed
in bed until noon. Nettie was off, so Stephen would go downstairs
and assemble a tray that he'd carry back up filled with grapes, slices
of apple dipped in honey, triangles of jam-smeared toast. They'd
make a holy mess of the sheets, but Catherine didn't even care what
Nettie would think.

If the weather was fine, she and Stephen would go walking. Their
favorite route was along the broad thoroughfare of Eastern Parkway
that brought them to the Brooklyn Botanic Garden. "This wasn't
here when I was a boy," Stephen said on one of these days as he
gestured to the manicured beds, the tidy walkways. "None of it.
And now look." They strolled past the Rock Garden and the lovely
Japanese Hill-and-Pond Garden with its bridges and templelike
wooden structures. "We'll take our baby here," he said. "Our babies." He squeezed her hand, and she leaned into him. By the time
they were ready to head back, Catherine was hungry—again—and
they stopped at Grogan's, Stephen's favorite neighborhood pub. Will
Grogan was an old friend of Jack Berrill's, and so Stephen and Catherine were treated like family. She slathered butter on slices of Irish
soda bread while waiting for the beef stew to appear, the fragrant

hunks of carrot, potato, and onion a perfect complement to meat so tender it didn't need a knife.

On the days when Stephen was at work, Catherine walked and walked, sometimes with Bridget or Molly, but often alone. She went back to the Botanic Garden, or Prospect Park, or in the other direction, all the way to Brooklyn Heights. She loved the names of the streets in that area—Orange, Pineapple, Joralemon, Grace Court—and the stately homes that lined them. She'd stop for a cup of tea—coffee gave her heartburn now—and a pastry somewhere along the way and still have an appetite for whatever Nettie prepared for dinner.

It was an especially fine spring, with a spate of fresh, sun-filled days. The visual signs, crocus and snowdrop, soon followed by the glorious yellow forsythia, the riotous colors of the tulips, the red flash of a cardinal, seemed even brighter this year. And was the season always so noisy? Catherine was aware of dripping, melting, the crackling of branches, as if waking up from a long sleep. There was the hysterical chatter of sparrows, the raucous song of blue jays, the cooing of the doves that landed on the garden-facing windowsills. All this was music to accompany the smell—the sharp scent of hydrangeas, the sweeter fragrance of lilacs, and sweetest of all, beach roses, rambling, motley, and intoxicating. After such days, she slept deeply, remembering none of her dreams in the morning.

But in all her many walks near and far, the one place she somehow found herself avoiding was the dress shop farther down on St. Marks Avenue. There was no specific reason for this. The owner and that young girl who worked for her had been pleasant enough. The green silk knit was beautiful. Exceptional. And yet something about her experience there—perhaps it was Miss Beatrice's slightly odd manner, the way she'd stared at Catherine through the window later—discouraged her from returning.

Even as Catherine grew larger, she still felt energetic, almost feverishly so, and looked for projects she could take on—embroidering bibs and learning to knit. But she didn't do either very well, so she turned her attention to decorating the nursery.

"What kind of wallpaper do you want?" Stephen asked. "Maybe a circus scene? Or maybe a garden?"

"There isn't going to be any wallpaper," said Catherine.

"No?" Stephen seemed surprised. "I thought you loved wallpaper."

"I do. But I have something else in mind," she said. "You'll see." Catherine had ordered glazed tiles depicting scenes from nursery rhymes from an English company; she planned to have the walls painted a rich cream color, and then have the tiles installed in a waist-high frieze around the room. She imagined taking a small hand and saying, *Look at Humpty-Dumpty. Isn't he funny?* or *Do you see the old woman and all her little children crammed into the shoe? That's so silly,* as she led little Vi or Danny around the room, reciting the rhymes and pointing out what was in the pictures. She'd also ordered a wicker bassinet, a dresser, a crib, and a rocking chair all in a white enamel finish, and an oval braided rug, as well as a small wooden hobbyhorse with black glass eyes, red saddle, and a real horsehair tail. Once the room was in order, she went up to visit it every night.

Just a week before the baby was due, Molly and Bridget organized a tea at her in-laws' house. They invited all the female cousins and several of Catherine's school friends for a buffet of assorted sandwiches and strawberry shortcake. She sat within the circle of women, exclaiming over the gifts they had brought: a white cashmere blanket trimmed with white satin binding, knitted sweaters and caps, several pairs of booties, a Royal Doulton mug, bowl, and plate decorated with frolicking lambs, and a stack of flannel burping clothes. Then Bridget left the room and returned wheeling in a handsome black pram trimmed in gold and outfitted with several white, lace-bordered cushions. "It's a Hitchings," Bridget said. "That's what Queen Victoria ordered for three of her babies."

"See, it's fit for a prince," said Veronica.

"Or a princess," added Molly, whose own baby girl, Maud, had woken from her nap and was now sitting in her mother's lap.

"Your baby nurse will be so proud to push it round," added Bridget.

"Baby nurse?" Catherine said. "Oh, I won't be having one. I want to take care of my baby myself." She saw Bridget and Molly exchange looks, as if to say, *She says that now but just you wait* . . . Hoisting herself up, Catherine lumbered over to the pram and grasped the Ivorene handlebar. She'd waited long enough for this baby and there was no way she was giving over its care to anyone else. Maybe she'd consider a baby nurse for the second child. Or the third.

After the guests left, Bridget and Veronica helped to gather up all the gifts.

"We can put things in the pram and wheel it over," Bridget said.

"Oh no," replied Catherine. "We can't use that until the baby gets here. It's bad luck."

"Cathy, you're not superstitious, are you?"

"Well no, but . . ."

"We don't need to use the pram," Veronica said. "Jack and the children will carry everything over and we'll keep the pram here for you. Just go home and get some rest."

"Thank you," said Catherine, embracing first her mother-in-law and then her sister-in-law. For the hundredth, no thousandth time, she thanked God, Fate, or whatever for bringing her into this family. She was really one of them now, and her baby would only strengthen that bond. Bridget wanted to walk her home but Stephen showed up and told Bridget not to trouble herself. Then she took Stephen's arm as they walked slowly to their house.

"Tired?" he said.

"A bit." She rested her head against his chest for a moment.

"Happy?"

"So happy!" she told him. "Happier than I've ever been."

He smiled. "Happier than on our wedding day?"

"Yes, because this is the culmination of that day—*Be fruitful and multiply,* isn't that what the Bible says? Well, we're doing it."

"Yes, Mrs. Berrill, we are."

They went up the stoop and after she'd undressed and bathed, Catherine put on a soft, white lawn nightdress that covered but did not fully hide the ripe mound of her belly. She saw Stephen respond to the shadowy form of her body beneath the sheer cloth, but now she really was tired. So tired that she even skipped her nightly trip upstairs; she would visit the nursery in the morning.

"I think I'm going to fall asleep as soon as my head touches the pillow," she said. "Maybe even before."

And she did. But it was some hours later—she didn't know how many—that she awoke in the dark. It was nothing external—no noise, no light, no disturbance of any kind. No, it was something within, something that had infiltrated the fortress of her body. "The baby," she said.

"What?" Stephen was not fully awake.

"The baby, the baby. Something's wrong."

Now he was sitting up and turned on a lamp. "What is it?"

Catherine squinted against the brightness. "I don't quite know," she said. "But for weeks, I've been feeling the baby in there, moving, kicking. Now it's suddenly gone still."

"Maybe it's sleeping," Stephen said.

"No," she said firmly. "Even when the baby sleeps, I can still feel it. Bobbing almost. Like a ball on the water. But now it feels like something inert inside me. Something—dead."

"Don't panic." Stephen swung his long legs out of bed and began grabbing at his clothes. "But let's get you to the hospital."

"I don't think I can walk."

"You don't have to. I'll call an ambulance."

Catherine was still in her nightdress when she was wheeled into the delivery room. The examining physician, Dr. Cunningham, was going to induce labor.

"You're almost thirty-nine weeks," he said. "We can do it now. It's safe."

"But is the baby all right?" Catherine heard that her voice was choked with panic.

"Let's just get you onto the table, Mrs. Berrill." He patted her hand and Catherine had to resist the impulse to swat it away. He was talking down to her, as if she couldn't be trusted to absorb the truth. But then the fight just went right out of her. Or rather, she saw the necessity of redirecting it. What difference did it make what the doctor said? She had a job to do—she was going to give birth.

Whatever they injected her with made the contractions come one after another, like waves crashing down on the shore, and Catherine forgot about the baby, forgot about her fear, forgot everything but the excruciating pain that simply would not stop, no matter how she howled, shrieked, or writhed. Finally, just when she thought the next wave would rip her body in half, something gave and she felt the huge release of fluid and of something solid and weighty—the baby! "Let me see." Her voice, raw from screaming, was only a whisper. "Oh, please, let me see!" But the thing she had borne was whisked away and now the pain began again, only of a different kind. There was more to emerge, her body would not stop, it was gushing, pouring—

"We're going to give you something to help you sleep now," Dr. Cunningham was saying.

Sleep! Catherine didn't want to sleep! She wanted her baby, to see it, hold it, let it suckle. But there was all this other . . . liquid . . . streaming out of her, it was green and foul on the sheets—a jab, more writhing, and then the blackness, like a blanket pulled gently up and over her head.

When she finally awoke, she didn't know if it had been hours or days. She was clean now, clean, dry, and the pain had been muted, located only between her legs, where there was a terrible soreness, and her belly, which felt raw and sore too.

Stephen was seated beside her bed, his face grave and white beneath the beard. This did not bode well.

"The baby?" she asked. "Where is the baby?"

Stephen said nothing, but his lips twitched slightly. Then he began to speak in a low, monotone voice. The baby—a girl—had been born dead. A bacterial infection had caused the death, and had threatened Catherine's own life. Her cervix hadn't sealed properly, which was how the contagion had entered her body and done its nefarious work. Ovaries, fallopian tubes, uterus all hideously infected, and now—all gone. She had been scraped clean. Gutted. Hollow.

"But you're alive," Stephen said. "They saved you."

Alive? She wasn't alive. Catherine closed her eyes and turned her face to the starched and stiff pillow slip. Her heart and soul had been scraped out along with her womb. Stephen was still babbling but she was no longer listening. She was a dead woman; she couldn't hear a thing.

SUMMER

CHAPTER TEN

CATHERINE

Brooklyn, 1924

That June was one of the hottest anyone could remember, but Catherine didn't care. She was in hell after all, and everyone knew hell was hot. In addition to the heat outside, there was the heat within—hot flashes, caused by the sudden change of life she was experiencing, plagued her day and night. Often she soaked through her nightgown, and tore it off impatiently, leaving a wet heap on the floor beside the bed.

Stephen begged her, repeatedly, to go away with him. "My father will give me the month of August off. July too if I want it. It was his idea. He said we needed to get away."

"Did he?" Even those two words required so much effort. It was hardly worth it. She wished that Stephen wouldn't talk so much. Or at all.

"It will do you good. You'll see."

Would she? Catherine closed her eyes and burrowed down into the sofa, hoping Stephen would take the hint and leave her be. Oh, he was trying, they were all trying, the tightly knit clan of Berrills that descended, en masse, when one of their own was wounded or hurting. Molly ordered the tiny white casket lined in white satin. Bridget provided a white christening dress and bonnet for the burial. They rest of them tried to console or distract her. Without her knowledge, they disposed of the gifts and dismantled the nursery, which was gone virtually without a trace. The only thing Catherine could hear was the dull thudding and cracking that came from the men upstairs prying the tiles, the precious-English-tiles-that-she-wanted-to-show-Danny-Vi-or-Lottie, from the walls, and she fled the house so she wouldn't have to listen. The Berrills loved her, she knew they did. They meant well. But they didn't, couldn't, understand. They thought her grief was a load she wanted to set down. It was instead fused to her, a new appendage she would never willingly part with. Grief was the only connection she had to the dead baby, a girl, and she would never surrender it.

"We'll adopt," Stephen said. "Somewhere out there is a baby who needs us, Catherine. We just have to find her. Or him. It's not that hard."

Catherine looked at his earnest face, suffused with love, with worry, with his seemingly inextinguishable optimism, and for the first time, she hated the man she had married. Hating Stephen felt like such a shock that it almost made her want to rouse herself, do something, anything, to get away from this hideous feeling. But the impulse subsided almost as quickly as it had flared.

"I think I'll go upstairs," she said. "I want to take a nap."

"You slept until almost noon," Stephen pointed out. "Let's get out for a bit. We'll have a walk. The gardens will be beautiful today."

"It's too hot for a walk." She looked longingly at the staircase; it was beckoning to her.

"That's why I think we should get away. A little place near the water on Long Island or upstate, by a lake."

"Maybe," she said. Better to placate him so he'd leave her alone. "We'll see." She knew she was hurting him. She was a terrible person to knowingly hurt the man who loved her. But she wanted only to crawl into the embrace of her grief and her mourning. That was the only place where she felt whole.

Catherine slept all afternoon and dragged herself down for dinner, which Nettie served in the garden. A few fireflies looped and circled; Catherine picked at her meal, which tasted like dust, and slapped at a mosquito. If she ate, or pretended to, this would be over, and she could go back to bed.

The next day, Nettie came to rouse her from the welcome escape of sleep. "Your parents want to see you," she said.

"My parents?" Catherine lifted her head from the pillow reluctantly. "What are you talking about?"

"They're downstairs. Your mother said she's not going to leave."

Her parents were in Brooklyn, and in her parlor? A low but malevolent hammering began in Catherine's head. "Tell them I can't see them now. That I'll telephone them when I can but to please, please go away."

"Yes, Mrs. Berrill. But I have to say that your mother, well, she looks very . . . determined."

Determined was one way to put it. Also *stubborn, intrusive,* and *intractable.*

"All right." Catherine knew she was defeated. "I'll get up now. You can tell her I'll be down shortly."

Nettie nodded and left the room.

Catherine's parents had been to the funeral, of course. And they had continued to telephone her regularly, but for the past week or so, she had not taken the calls. It was all too much. Her mother seemed so brittle, as if Catherine's grief were hers and might shatter her to bits. And her father, her darling, beloved father, had the air of a kicked dog, subdued, broken even, but unswerving in his loyalty.

She went to her armoire, pawing at the garments hanging there in an effort to find something cool to put on. Wasn't there a lightweight linen in here somewhere? Her hands stopped their hurried motion as she touched the green dress she'd bought at that shop down the street, never worn, and tucked away until now. Somehow, she never had offered it to Bridget.

As she pulled it out, the sight of its fluid green silhouette enraged her. She didn't want to give it away, she wanted to destroy it. Where could she find a knife, a pair of shears? Her gaze darted around the room and settled on the porcelain hatpin holder that sat on her bureau. The several long pins she saw wouldn't do the job, not entirely. But they would inflict some damage, and that was what she sought. She'd just reached for the longest of them, topped with a smooth, carnelian tip, when a knock at the door stopped her.

"Catherine? Catherine, you open this door at once."

Catherine froze. She could have been twelve and pouting in her childhood bedroom with her mother outside, demanding entry. There was no point in putting off the inevitable confrontation, not when her parents had come all the way from Larchmont. She let her mother in.

Instantly, Meredith's indignation melted and she gathered her daughter in her arms. "You poor girl," she murmured. "You poor, dear girl."

Catherine stood stiffly in her mother's embrace. She knew Meredith was trying to comfort her, and she appreciated the intent. But

since the loss of the baby, she'd become sensitive to touch, even repelled by it.

Finally Meredith released her. "We've been worried about you."

Catherine looked over at her father, who stood awkwardly clasping
his hands together. The expression on his face was exactly as she'd
imagined it, and she had to look away.

"I can see that you're not dressed, dear, but that doesn't matter.
We don't need to stand on ceremony, not now."

"I'd rather get dressed if you don't mind," Catherine said. "Wait
for me downstairs? I promise I won't be long."

Her parents exchanged glances and then filed meekly out of the
room, giving her a temporary reprieve. She found the linen dress,
quickly coiled her hair on top of her head, securing the untidy bun
with a few hairpins. A quick stop in the lavatory to splash water on
her face and clean her teeth. There. It was far from her usual stan-
dard. But it would suffice.

Catherine went out to the garden, where Meredith and Sebastian had
been seated in the shade of the neighbor's mulberry tree and were
sipping what looked like Nettie's limeade. There was a glass for
Catherine as well. "I'm sorry I haven't been taking your calls," she
began.

"That's all right. We wanted to see you. To talk in person." Meredith glanced at her husband. Did that look mean anything special or
was Catherine just imagining it? "We know what this loss meant to
you. Believe me when we tell you we understand."

"I know you want to," Catherine said. "But I'm not sure that you
do. You had a child. Only one, it's true. But one can be enough. One
can be the whole world, in fact. But none . . ." She shook her head.
"None is an empty shell."

"Catherine, this is hard to say . . . but we feel you need medical attention."

Catherine looked at her blankly. "What for? There's nothing wrong with me. All those diseased organs were removed, remember? Cut out of me."

"It's not your body we're worried about." Meredith's voice was gentle. "It's your mind."

"I don't understand."

Her father cleared his throat. "Your mother thinks you should see a . . . psychiatrist."

"Is that what you think? And Stephen too? Have you been discussing it with him? All three of you deciding that I'm not right in the head, that I'm crazy?" she asked, seething.

Catherine knew about the field of psychiatry; she'd even taken a course at Vassar in which she'd read the writings of that esteemed Viennese doctor, Sigmund Freud. Freud had written about many sorts of neuroses, psychoses, and hysterics. But none of those conditions described her state of mind—she wasn't mentally or emotionally unbalanced, not at all. She was *grieving*.

"No one thinks you're crazy, least of all Stephen. But he's worried, he wants to help—"

"If he wants to help, he can leave me alone. You all can. I'm not seeing a psychiatrist."

"Why not?" her mother asked.

Why not? Because I'm not crazy, I'm grieving, don't you see? I had a baby and she was taken from me. Snatched. Now you all want me to replace her like she was a kitten. A pair of gloves.

But she didn't say any of that. All she said was, "I know you meant well by coming here. And that you love me. But I can't talk about it anymore. You'll just have to excuse me." And then she fled, leaving them where they sat.

* * *

The next day, Catherine forced herself to get up along with her husband.

"Good morning," said Stephen tenderly. "Are you joining me for breakfast?"

"I thought I would," she said.

"Good." He smiled as he moved about the room, fastening the buttons on his collar and adjusting the garters of his socks. He was fastidious in his dress, even on the hottest of days.

"But there's something I wanted to talk to you about. Alone."

"And what would that be?" He stopped what he was doing and sat down on the bed.

"My parents were here yesterday."

"Yes, Nettie told me. They've been worried about you."

"You're all worried about me." Now why had she said that? She needed to start again. "And I understand. I do. But they said something that upset me."

"And what was that?"

"That they think I should see a psychiatrist."

"I know," he said. "It was my idea, actually."

"Your idea!"

"Yes." He scanned her face intently. "Please don't be angry with me. I only suggested it because I was so concerned about you. You can't seem to put the . . . baby behind you, to move ahead with your life."

"What if I don't want to move ahead, as you so quaintly put it? What if I want to stay right where I am?"

"Why would you want to stay in such a dark place?" he asked. "If you could let go of the past, you might see your way to a different future."

"You still think we should adopt a baby," she said flatly.

"I do," he said. "There's no reason we shouldn't. Or couldn't. Molly's husband's a lawyer. He could help us." He reached for her hand and she pulled back, as if singed. "Think of it, Catherine. We'd have a baby. You'd be so happy, you could hang wallpaper in that room, or tile it again or have a mural painted in there if that's what you wanted—"

"You think that's what this is about?" Her even tone belied her fury; she was so filled with rage she thought she might burst into flames. "Wallpaper? Tiles? I don't think you understand me." She looked at him as if through a new and disorienting lens. "Maybe you never did. Because if you think I can simply replace the daughter I lost with some other baby, any baby, you don't know the first thing about me."

An hour or so after making an attempt to eat a breakfast of dry toast, Catherine was walking toward Prospect Park. Rage fueled her steps, explosive sparks that threatened to combust on whatever they landed. Her parents, for their inability to understand. Stephen, for the same reason, and for wanting her to put *all that* behind her. But when she got to the park, her anger dissipated slightly. Here, the green canopy cooled the air appreciably and the branches of the trees were alive with birdsong. She had a moment of wishing she could disappear into those trees, become elusive and feral.

She began to walk, avoiding the main paths—filled, it seemed, with mothers and children, governesses and nursemaids with children, pregnant women soon to bear children—and instead penetrating the park's less-frequented interior, picking her way carefully through twigs and rocks. There, right in front of her, was a butterfly, orange and black wings spread to their fullest extent.

It was a monarch, not so unusual but lovely still, and she stood looking at it, feeling privileged because it submitted to her gaze without fluttering away. It took a moment for her to realize it was dead. Gingerly, she picked it up and turned it over. Its body was spotted too—white on black—and its slender legs were covered in tiny fibers and ended in delicate, pronged feet. What had killed it? There was no clue; the creature was intact.

Somehow it seemed wrong to just place it back on the path, where it was so exposed, so vulnerable. Looking around, Catherine saw a cluster of toadstools, a bulbous and almost comical eruption. One of them was quite large, and she set the butterfly down under its expansive cap. Then she picked up a smooth, green leaf and covered it. She exhaled deeply and continued on her way.

The path twisted, turned, and soon she began to climb—it wasn't too steep but even in the relative cool, she began to feel winded and stopped to rest. It would be nice to have had something to drink but the thought was not enough to get her to leave the park. She didn't feel at peace here; she didn't believe she would ever feel at peace again. But she felt slightly less wretched, and that was enough. She could see, though, that the afternoon was waning, and Nettie would be wondering where she was. Wondering—and reporting to Stephen. Reluctantly, Catherine turned and began to go back in the direction from which she had come.

The chipmunk off to the side of the path—how had she not seen it before?—was curled on its back, paws stiff, eyes closed. When she picked it up, the small body left a smear of blood in her hand. She remembered the blood that had stalked her, haunted her, the serial disappointments now almost a sweet memory. Back then, the blood meant there was still a chance, still a hope she'd have a child. Now there was none. Sinking down in the dirt, Catherine began to sob, pressing the dead creature to her chest. Oh, she'd be a fright when she got home. What would Nettie say—or tell Stephen? She willed herself to stop crying and focus instead on clawing the ground with her bare hands until she'd made a depression deep enough to bury the chipmunk. She covered it with dirt, and then found a small gray stone and two acorns to set on the spot.

Nettie was predictably horrified by Catherine's appearance when she returned home. "Mrs. Berrill, you're bleeding!"

"No, actually I'm not."

"But the blood . . . are you all right?"

"I'm fine. Truly I am. Would you be so kind as to draw me a bath?"

"Yes, of course, right away, right away. I can help you get out of those things—"

"No, that's not necessary, Nettie. Just prepare the bath. Please."

Catherine watched as the blood—there wasn't much—dissolved into the hot water, first in little swirls and then disappearing altogether. Nettie had brought in a cake of gardenia-scented soap and a washcloth, both of which Catherine used. She'd broken several nails with her frantic digging but at least her hands were now clean. And during dinner—again served in the backyard —she made a particular effort to seem like her old self. She knew Nettie would have told Stephen everything, and she didn't want him to start asking questions, or worse, getting someone to spy on her.

"You know, I was thinking that you're right—we should go away somewhere." Catherine took a bite of her salad, a dish she could actually tolerate, though not enjoy.

"Really, darling? You'd do that? I'm so glad!" Stephen 's eyes were especially bright—tears?

Once again, Catherine felt ashamed of herself. Shame seemed like her constant companion these days. She knew he loved—no, adored—her, and felt the loss of their child almost as keenly as she did. But his hovering irritated her and she had to resist the urge to twitch off his solicitous touch, the light kiss on the cheek, the arm that would try to encircle her waist. As for the passionate nights and mornings they'd spent together, the very thought repulsed her.

Fortunately, she was not forced to reject him, not yet. Her body still hadn't healed fully, and he understood, and didn't press her, that wasn't his nature. But one day she'd be mended, or her physical self would, and he'd want to resume their marital relations. She didn't know what she would do when that time came because she felt like she never wanted him to touch her in that way again.

Her little ploy worked. She ate enough of the salad, pushed the other food around on the plate until it seemed like she'd eaten it, and got down a few spoonfuls of Nettie's dessert, something cloyingly sweet and smothered in cream.

Stephen seemed mollified by her performance. He didn't question her about her day, and in return, she feigned interest in the travel plans he presented to her, pretending to consider the relative merits of the seaside or a lake.

The next day was Sunday, and so she couldn't escape but had to accompany him to mass at St. Augustine's. His family was there, most of them: Veronica and Jack, the younger boys, Kevin and Michael, Bridget, but mercifully not Molly or her children. After the service, there was the obligatory lunch at which the Berrills tried their best to cocoon her with love. Had they always been this inclined to touch, pet, embrace her? She'd thought it was just Stephen, but no, it was all of them, stroking her as if she were a lapdog. Vaguely she remembered how she'd loved that about them at first. Now it made her want to scream. The afternoon ended, and pleading a headache, Catherine retired early. Tomorrow was Monday; Monday Stephen would go off to work and she, well, she could go to the park.

It became her habit, then, to walk those hidden paths and search for creatures—sparrows, chipmunks, pigeons, once, a blue jay, its feathers so brilliant, so gaudy that they seemed like a refutation of death, and another time a small brown rabbit, black eyes still open, merest bit of a tail. It wasn't even a search, really. It was as if these animals called to her in some silent language. And she listened. She heard. There were days when she found nothing for an hour, two, or even more. And then, on her way back, she'd find three bodies within forty-five minutes.

And now she came prepared. She'd bought a trowel and a pair of sturdy gardening gloves at Garber's Hardware on Seventh Avenue. "Going to plant some marigolds, Mrs. Berrill?" Mr. Garber asked genially. "Or do you prefer petunias?"

"Marigolds, yes." Catherine carried her equipment in a straw basket along with a canteen she'd found among Stephen's things, now filled with water. She didn't care about eating, and as a result, her dresses seemed to collapse on her, but she did get thirsty.

Now it was easy to dig small holes and cover them with dirt and leaves. Then came the sweetest part, the search for things to mark the spots. Catherine had decided it couldn't be anything she brought from home or a store; she could use only what she found, a rule she and her friends devised when, as little girls, they made fairy houses in their backyards. Stones of different shapes and sizes were good, as well as interesting leaves or petals. Sometimes she used acorns, or small, soggy pinecones, remnants from another season. Once she found a carved ivory button, and another time, a battered cigar clip that might even have been gold. Rusty nails, a cloisonné com-

pact with a broken mirror, whatever was cast off, lost, discarded—
she was drawn to these objects too, and she gathered and left them
as markers of lives lived. She never visited Greenwood Cemetery,
where her baby was buried. She didn't think she ever would. But
this improvised cemetery soothed her a little. She was grateful she'd
stumbled on something, anything, that did.

Stephen had rented a house in Greenport, Long Island, where they
would spend a week. Catherine would miss her solitary rambles
in the park but thought that the shoreline might provide different
opportunities for her creations. She imagined dead crabs, jellyfish,
sandpipers, or even a gull. She could bury them in the wet sand. To
mark the graves, she'd choose from a glittering wealth of shells, bits
of sea glass, and who knew what else? The only problem would be
getting away from Stephen. She would not try to explain her ritual to
him. He'd never understand.

The day of her last trip to the park before they left for the seashore
was the hottest day yet. Even amid the trees, the air felt heavy, crushing. She didn't stay long and found only a single bird—a robin, its
beak pointing like a miniature dagger at the sky. Why was it called
red breast? The front of the bird was a rich, burnished brown, not red
at all. She buried it neatly and, since she could find nothing of interest
to use as a marker, settled for some twigs, which she laid in a cross-
hatched pattern over the mound of dirt. That was enough.

She drained the canteen and started home, the sun still high and
fierce in the sky. Outside the park was a long row of benches that
faced out toward Prospect Park West. It was on one of these that
she sank down, setting her basket between her feet and tilting her
head back. She could feel perspiration under her linen dress, and under the crown the of her straw hat, moisture, like a diadem, circling

her head. Even though her house was only a short distance away, she couldn't walk another step; she had to stop and close her eyes. She might even have dozed for a moment, slipped into that sweet envelope of sleep, before she became aware of the fact that someone had joined her on the bench.

Opening her eyes took a great effort, but she did it. There was the woman from the dress shop, the older of the two. And just like that time in the shop, Bea, that was how she'd introduced herself, was staring right at her. But Catherine was too tired to feel any sense of outrage or alarm and when she spoke, her voice was calm, not indignant.

"You again," she said. "You were staring at me that day in the shop. You're staring at me now. Why?"

"I'm sorry I was—am—staring. It's just that I've wanted to meet you, find you, for such a long time. So when we actually met, I almost didn't believe it was you."

"You wanted to find me? Whatever for?"

Bea twisted her hands together for a moment. Her fingers were long and fine, her skin slightly olive in tone. And she wore a ring set with an arresting, blue-green stone, iridescent and glittering. An opal, that's what it was.

"It's a simple reason," said Bea after a moment. "The simplest of all maybe." She twisted the ring around and around on her finger, the stone disappearing for a second, then shimmering anew as the light found it, the color an enchantment. "I wanted to find you because you're my daughter."

CHAPTER ELEVEN

BEA

Catherine Berrill had never returned to the dress shop and Bea had come to accept that she never would. The one and only time the younger woman had wandered in, Bea had lost her composure, dropping things, almost gawking. It was foolish of her, indulgent even. She'd come so far and waited so long, only to have squandered her chance.

She consoled herself by thinking it had been a chance, but not her only chance. Catherine still lived nearby. Bea watched her walking up and down the street, and even though she was always on the opposite side, Bea was able to become familiar with her habits and routines. That was how she learned that Catherine was pregnant—she saw her swelling. Burgeoning. And though the road separated them, Bea thought Catherine looked happy.

And then all at once, her form, full to bursting, deflated. No more swollen belly. Now she was as flat as before. She must have given birth by now, but where was the baby? Catherine continued to walk up and down the street but was accompanied by no pram, no nursemaid.

It was odd; most women would want to spend at least a little time with an infant, even if they assigned the bulk of its care to someone else. But as the weeks went by, Bea deduced that something had gone terribly wrong in Catherine's life. She grew thinner, noticeably so, and was never with either of the women she had often been with— a freckled blonde and a plump brunette with children of her own. A few times Bea had even followed her at a discreet distance. Catherine carried a basket and went deep into the park, which was where Bea always lost her trail.

Then came a bit of luck. The blond woman came into the shop, and she was one of those chatty customers who wanted to talk as much as browse. "I love this one," she said, holding up a striped linen to which Alice had added flowered sleeves and rows of lace on the cuffs and hem. "But I love this one too." The second dress had an empire waist from which rows of tiny pleats descended. It was a shimmering bronze organdy and embellished with jet-colored buttons.

"Why not try them both on?" Bea brought the dresses to the changing area.

"Thank you, I think I will."

During the appraisal of the dresses, Bea learned that the woman's name was Bridget Berrill, so it was easy enough to ask, "Are you by any chance a relation to a Catherine Berrill? She stopped into the shop some months ago and bought a lovely green dress—one of Alice's originals."

"Catherine's my sister-in-law." Bridget had come out from behind the screen and was smoothing the dress down over her hips. "Do you think it's a little tight?"

"We can probably open the seams—Alice, can you come out here for a moment?"

"It's nice that you two live so close." Bea chose her words with care. "It must be very comforting to have family nearby."

"Isn't that the truth?" said Bridget. "And it was never more true than this year. Oh, she went through a terrible time, Cathy did." Bridget went on to say Catherine had been expecting a baby but that she lost it just before it was due to arrive. "She was devastated," she continued. "Poor lamb. Having children was what she wanted most in the world. And now she can never have them."

"She could adopt," Bea found herself saying.

"That's what we all keep telling her, my brother Stephen most of all. But she won't hear of it." Bridget went back behind the curtain and emerged wearing the other dress. "Oh, I think I'll just have to take both of them. Can you have the alteration done on the first one and when it's finished, have them both sent over to me? I'm on Sterling Place."

Bea sat there after she left, staring out the window. So Catherine had lost her baby, the baby she'd wanted so desperately; decades ago, the baby that Bea didn't want was born into the world and thrived. What a strange and twisted symmetry.

"Bridget Berrill." Alice had come over to where Bea was sitting, dress still in her hands. "She's related to Catherine Berrill, isn't she?"

Bea nodded. She couldn't even speak, not just yet.

"Well, I'll fix the dress and deliver it tomorrow."

"Thank you, Alice," said Bea.

"You're welcome." She ducked back behind the curtain and a moment later, the sewing machine began to hum.

As the weather grew warmer, Bea continued to look out for Catherine and, occasionally, to follow her to the edge of the park. On one of those days, she waited for a while, hoping, even sensing, that if she stayed nearby, she might see her again. And she was right. Only a short time after Catherine had gone into the park, she came out again, looking damp and flushed. She sat on a bench right at the top of Carroll Street, and it was there that Bea joined her and said the words she hadn't believed she'd ever get to say, not until the minute they had left her mouth and hovered in that fragile space between them: *You're my daughter.*

Catherine had looked at her as if she'd just announced she planned to fly to the moon. This was not the reaction Bea expected, and it unnerved her. "I'm the woman who gave you up when you were born. You were—are—my daughter."

"I knew you were strange when we first met," said Catherine. "But now I see you're not strange. You're absolutely mad. I wasn't adopted—I don't know where you got such an idea."

Bea was not surprised. "So they didn't tell you. Well, I can understand that. But I can tell you that your adoptive father is Sebastian Delgado. Or it was then. I found out he'd later changed it to Delman. I never met his wife but I know her name was Meredith."

Now Catherine was staring at her in a different way, a way that suggested Bea had hit the mark. "How do you know all this?"

"Because it's what happened to me. To you. Sebastian took you away, up north and back to his wife, to raise you. He promised he'd be good to you, and it seems like he was. He was, wasn't he? And Meredith too?"

"You may have found out the names of my parents but that still doesn't mean—"

"There was a ring," Bea said. "A cameo set in platinum with a circle of tiny diamonds around it, ten in all. I counted them. When Sebastian came for you, I gave it to him. And I asked him to give it to you. Judging from your face right now, I'd say he did."

"I've got to go," Catherine said. She stood abruptly and swayed on her feet; Bea reached out a hand to steady her. "Don't, please don't touch me." But then she sank back down to the bench and looked at Bea. "What do you want?"

"Want?" said Bea. "To get to know you. I missed so many years of your life. I don't want to miss any more." When Catherine didn't answer, Bea continued. "I'm sure this comes as a great shock and I'm sorry for that. But I had to tell you."

"I don't think I can talk to you now. I have to think, I have to . . ." Catherine pressed her hands to her face.

"I understand," Bea said. "Ask your parents. They'll confirm what I've told you. Or at least your father will, I feel sure. And then if you want to talk some more, come to see me. I'll be in the shop. You know where it is." She stood and walked away, and it took every bit of self-control she had to refrain from looking back. But now that she had uttered those life-changing words, she had to retreat, and let Catherine come to her.

CHAPTER TWELVE

CATHERINE

Bea knew about the cameo. Despite the heat, despite her fatigue, Catherine sped home and up the stairs. Bea may have been able to find out the names of her parents; doing so wouldn't have been all that hard. But the ring? That detail was too precise, too specific to have been guessed at or uncovered in any way other than the one the woman had described.

Once in her room, Catherine went straight to her leather jewelry case. The little cameo was right where she had left it, in a compartment of its own. Her father had given it to her on her sixteenth birthday. "It belonged to my grandmother," he said. "I know she would have wanted you to have it." Catherine had believed him; why wouldn't she? It was a lovely thing, delicate and precious. But Stephen had given her an engagement ring, and another, with a cluster of pearls, as a birthday gift, and she'd been wearing those instead. Then when her fingers had grown swollen during the pregnancy, she'd taken off all her rings save her wedding band and hadn't put them back on.

The cameo slid easily onto her finger, and the diamonds—and yes, she counted ten of them—formed a delicate outline for the carved profile. Meredith hadn't been too impressed. "It's pretty enough," she'd said. "But what a shame to waste platinum on a mere cameo. Now if that had been a diamond . . ."

Her parents. She had to talk to them. Immediately. So even though she still wore both her hat and shoes, which were uncomfortably constricting, she went downstairs to place the call. Waiting for someone to answer, she envisioned the phone on the stand just off the kitchen. Her father would be in his study or perhaps on the veranda, but the back windows would be open and he'd hear the ring. Or her mother would be the one to answer and—Catherine put down the receiver. She realized she didn't want to tell them about her encounter with Bea. Not just yet.

She needed to live with it for a time on her own, to make what sense of it she could. What if her parents corroborated Bea's story? That would mean that Bea, not Meredith, was her mother. *Her mother.* Those words were like a rock hurled into the formerly placid surface of her life, shattering it beyond repair.

She was still standing there with the phone in her hand when she was startled by Nettie, who had come up quietly behind her. "I just wanted to be sure you were all right, Mrs. Berrill."

"I'm fine, absolutely fine." It wasn't true: Catherine didn't think she would ever be fine. But no one wanted to hear that.

The cottage Stephen rented was charming, she had to admit, and she accompanied him on walks along the beach in the mornings or late afternoons. The lifeless fish and crabs littering the shore didn't really tempt her; that particular urge to gather and bury the dead had subsided. All she thought about was Bea. So many questions she hadn't asked, though she knew she would have the opportunity to ask them—if she chose. But her questions might yield answers she wouldn't like. What could have compelled her to give up her baby? Catherine couldn't imagine it. Even if she were destitute, without family or friends, she'd find a way, she knew she would. This line of thinking was a form of self-torture though. She'd never have to make such a choice because she'd never have a baby. She had been walking alongside Stephen, allowing him to take her arm, but she suddenly speeded up, as if she could outpace the thoughts that continued to torment her.

Stephen hurried behind her. "Where are you rushing off to?" he called.

She didn't turn around. "I just wanted to get moving. The air is— bracing."

"I told you the seaside would be a tonic for what ails you." He had sprinted to catch up and took her elbow again.

"Mmm." Catherine neither agreed nor disagreed, and only looked down. They were both barefoot, she with her skirt pulled up to one side, Stephen with his cuffs rolled above his ankles as the foam-tipped waves eddied around them. "Let's go swimming," she said.

"Now? It's almost time for dinner."

"Dinner can wait."

"All right." Clearly, he wasn't going to give her an argument, not about this, not about anything.

They returned to the cottage, changed into their bathing costumes, and went back down to the beach. The sun was just beginning to dip, and its orange light glazed the surface of the water like syrup.

Stephen waded in as far as his knees and stopped. "It's cold."

"It's glorious!" She plunged right in. The waves lifted the skirt of her bathing costume so that it floated around her, a sodden parachute. She was waist deep, then shoulder, and then she immersed herself completely. When she emerged, she shook her head, sending droplets of water flying.

"You're all wet!" Stephen said.

"Of course I'm wet! I'm in the water." Catherine began a brisk crawl along the shoreline. Stephen tried to keep up, but she soon left him behind. The waves were gentle and only tugged at her; she was a strong enough swimmer to withstand them. It had been so long since she'd gone swimming. Too long. Her parents had sent her to a summer camp for girls in Connecticut because her mother had heard that the place was filled with "the right sort of people." It was there that she'd learned to swim, first in a lake and then in Long Island Sound, from the fearless Miss Foley, who maintained that it was an "essential life skill, young ladies! An essential life skill!" So Catherine knew enough not to venture out too deep and instead to swim parallel to the shoreline.

The sky was an extravagant canvas of pinks, violet, and molten orange; a wave, larger than the rest, rose up and over her and she emerged sputtering. She supposed she ought to get out now; Stephen was a tiny figure in the distance, doggedly making his way toward her. But what if she didn't get out, what if she swam out farther, much farther than was wise or safe? He wouldn't be able to get to her, not in time. And the beach was deserted. By the time he'd gone for help, it would be too late. The idea, forbidden and dangerous, awakened something in her, a longing to surrender herself to the great and boundless ocean. She'd read that you struggled only for a little while and then it was easy, so easy to give in.

Once the struggle was over, she'd be at peace. She wouldn't wake every morning feeling as if she had swallowed ground glass. Her lifeless body would float in the water, yielding to the current until she eventually washed up on the shore, like one of the creatures she'd collected in her ramblings. Poor Stephen, he'd be filled with self-recrimination—the seaside had been his idea, he'd been the one to press her. And in that moment, she felt sorry for him, sorry for the grief she'd already inflicted, and that greater grief that was in store. But Stephen had a heart that was fundamentally glad. He'd mourn, but he'd recover, and when he did, he'd find someone else to love, to marry, to give him the children she could not.

Catherine continued to swim, her mind not even aware of the swift, sure strokes of her arms, the controlled and forceful kicks of her legs. She began to veer away from the shoreline, as if pulled toward the horizon. Stephen was still far away. Good. The sun sat on the water now, a glowing disc of fire that beckoned to her. She'd swim toward it and when the water took her, she would relinquish her hold on life with its brilliant glow stamped on her mind. Farther and farther she swam, instinctively moving in and out of the waves, which was not helping her to realize her intent. So she stopped swimming and waited.

The next wave was bigger, fuller than the last few and rose up before her with an impressive and indifferent majesty. She had only to let it crash and bring her down, down, down. Then the end would begin. It was cresting, it was ready to break—

The wave slammed her, wrenching her body with unexpected force. She went under, eyes open, lungs assaulted, twisting and writhing. This was not the gentle end she imagined; her body's struggle took over, and she kicked and thrashed until she finally broke the surface again, coughing and heaving as she expelled the water that she realized would not be her grave.

When she calmed down sufficiently, she began to swim again, this time in a diagonal toward the shore until she finally reached a place where she could stand. Stephen was running frantically toward her, a comical figure in his striped swimsuit. When he was close enough, he splashed in to grab her, lifting her right out of the water and into his arms. "Oh my God," he said. "I couldn't see you, I thought you'd gone under, oh sweet Jesus, you're alive, you're alive."

Catherine allowed him to carry her all the way up the beach and to the sandy, pebble-strewn road that led back toward the rented cottage. His bare feet must have hurt but he didn't complain. Nor did he ask what had happened; maybe he sensed that the answer was one he wouldn't want to hear. She didn't tell him either. Her grand plan had failed—miserably, foolishly. Now she would be the object of greater worry, and scrutiny, her actions noted, her freedoms questioned if not curtailed. But there was little to be done. She'd tried, but hadn't succeeded. Life, with its random and nonchalant cruelties, its abrasive edges and precipitous drops, was too powerful a force, and in the end, it was life, and not death, that had claimed her.

The day after she returned from Long Island, Catherine found herself seated in Bea's back garden, a glass of sherry in her hand. Now that she knew who Bea was, the lure was too great to resist. So many questions to ask, so many things to say. She still hadn't told her parents—her adoptive parents, actually—about their meeting. Nor had she told Stephen. She would, of course, but in her own time. If Bea had been surprised to see her appear in the shop, she didn't reveal it. "Today is the cook's day off, but we can sit out back. Would you care for a sherry?" she'd asked. "I know it's illegal, but I've always kept a bottle or two in my cupboard."

Catherine finally spoke after she had taken her first sip. "So you've never met Meredith?"

"No. I dealt only with your father. He came by himself."

"My mother doesn't care for New Orleans," said Catherine. "I think she thought it was . . ."

"Beneath her?" supplied Bea.

Catherine was surprised. "How did you know? Yes. Beneath some idea she had about herself. Who she wanted to be. Who she wanted me to be."

"Mothers can be like that," Bea said.

"Was your mother that way too?"

"Oh. No, no, she wasn't. She had other concerns."

"Such as?"

Bea looked at her sadly. "Best not to start there," she said. "What else do you want to know?"

"Everything. Anything. You have an accent—where are you from?"

"Are you certain you're ready to hear it?" Bea asked.

"Of course I am." Catherine was impatient. "Why else would I have come back here? You have to tell me. Tell me everything."

CHAPTER THIRTEEN

ZHENECHKA

Ekaterinaslav, 1878–1896

My father was a gentle man. He never raised his voice, let alone his hand, to any of us, and was even mild and soft-spoken with the servants. Perhaps this was because he was so pious—prayer shawl, beard, faithfully devoted to the rituals of Jewish observance. My mother—who was beautiful and always mindful of her beauty—did not fully share his conviction, and I knew that she chafed at some of the rules he held so dear. But they managed to find a balance that suited them; discord in our home was rare, and, when it occurred, it was never too loud or alarming. Did Sebastian and Meredith quarrel when you were a child? I'd like to think not.

We lived in Ekaterinaslav, a good-size city on the Dnieper River. We were prosperous, a fact notable because we were Jews. The source of the prosperity was a tannery on the outskirts of the city, owned and operated by my father. He had built his business up hide by hide, barrel by stinking barrel. It was a profession allowed to our kind chiefly because it was so odious few Gentiles wanted to engage in it. The tannery was a place I seldom visited. The stench of the urine used in the tanning process coupled with the sight of the splayed animal skins on the walls drove me gagging from there in minutes. But he turned a good profit, my father did, and our lives reflected that.

The house where I was born and raised stood firmly at the end of a quiet street, nestled between a pair of maple trees whose leaves turned a brilliant scarlet every fall. It was made of pale gray stone and had a solidity, a permanence to it that I never questioned. It seemed to me as if it had grown up right from the ground. The house had always been there. It always would. And more importantly, it would always be our home.

Behind the house were gardens, one for flowers, and another for vegetables. A handful of chickens pecked earnestly in the dirt, and a dappled cow, kept for milking, lived in a small, tidy shed. My father wouldn't allow animals in the house—he founds cats untrustworthy, dogs obsequious, and the canary I petitioned for a noisy nuisance. But one of his clients had given him a tortoise, a large, imperturbable creature, which he allowed to live outside, where it would make its ponderous way about our property. I followed the tortoise slavishly, wanting to elicit from him some shred of affection, or barring that, acknowledgment. There was none, and after I eventually gave up, the bruise of rejection eventually turned to dislike.

The inside of the house was as grand as the exterior: a spacious double parlor lit by crystal chandeliers, parquet floors, and velvet drapes that pooled beneath the windows. There was also a handsome black piano, at which I took lessons, and I attended weekly dance classes at the shabby home of a former ballerina who taught the minuet, the waltz, and the five positions as well as a few exercises done at a barre.

My older brothers, Max and Sasha, were sent to a military academy when I was quite small and spent their holidays in Yalta, with my parents, who traveled there to meet them. I was deemed too young to accompany them and remained behind with my wet nurse, Ludmila, in whose soft arms and lap I'd always found comfort. Back then I wasn't Beatrice or Bea; I was Yvegenia, *though Ludmila called me Zhenechka, and so everyone else did too. Mine was a largely solitary childhood, though not an unhappy one. You didn't have any sisters or brothers, did you? The man who helped me find you didn't mention any.*

When I was about seven years old, my father announced that he was engaging a tutor for me; Mr. Bixby, from Cambridge, would be coming several times a week.

"Is it really necessary?" Mama had asked. "I'd rather she worked on her embroidery and her music."

"She can do all that and have lessons too," Papa said. "The world is too big and changing too quickly to keep her sequestered. She needs to be educated in a more modern way."

"For what? To be a wife and mother?"

"Why shouldn't wives and mothers be educated?" he countered.

"I wasn't," Mama said, her tone a little huffy.

"And you are without peer, my darling," Papa said. "But these are different times, and we have to adapt." And that was that.

I was grateful Papa had prevailed and eager to meet my new tutor. I hated embroidery, and my starched bit of cambric in its tight, wooden hoop was always speckled with blood. Music was more tolerable, though I had no real ear for it and found practicing tedious. But what Mr. Bixby had to offer was of interest. He taught me arithmetic, at which I was quite good, and languages—English, French—at which I was even better. And then there was the geography lesson, during which I was enraptured by the spinning of the globe, tilted on its axis, and the colorful maps he pinned to the nursery walls. How vast the world was, how varied and how wide. The names I learned—the Congo, Madagascar, Arabia, Siam—formed a poem that reverberated in my soul. Finger tracing the mountain range in southwestern France or the winding path of the Nile, I promised myself that one day I would visit all of these places, that I would live in them the way their exotic names lived in me.

Soon I asked if Mr. Bixby could come five days a week instead of three. I knew that Ludmila felt hurt, but I was no longer satisfied by the decorous walks we took or the childish diversions she could devise, like cutting out paper dolls or spinning a hoop on the paving stones alongside the house. When Mr. Bixby and I went walking, he pointed out birds, trees, plants, and even insects, offering the gift of their Latin names too. Latin was something else he promised to teach me one day, if Papa allowed it.

One year, my parents decided not to go to Yalta and instead Max and Sasha came home during a school holiday. I had not seen them in quite some time, and they seemed like strangers. Even when I was upstairs with Mr. Bixby, I was distracted by the noise they made—running, stomping, clattering through the house. Their raucous laughter rang down the hallways, up the staircase, and out the windows. When they finally stopped to take notice of me, it was to treat me like a small pet or doll—scooping me up and tossing me in the air, exclaiming over my ringlets, fashioning a swan from the dinner napkin or shadow puppets on the wall. They were astonished by my rattling off the multiplication tables and asking, in English, if they would like butter and jam with their bread.

"She's the smartest little girl in all of Russia," said Sasha.

"Why just Russia?" Max asked. "Why not all of Europe?"

I grew less fearful of them and began to enjoy the way they made the house hum with their boyish energy, their high spirits. Yes, they were big and they were loud, but they were kind and loving too. Mama smiled in their presence, and Papa's eyes gleamed with pride as he looked up at them, his two fine sons in their crisp school uniforms, brass buttons bright against the blue serge, collars stiff and brushed.

I had gleaned from talk at the dinner table that it was not usual for Jewish boys to attend military schools; dispensation had been given in large part because of Papa's success. Neither Sasha nor Max wore a prayer shawl as he did, and neither had a beard. "Better for you boys to blend in," Papa said, even though he chose to display his own religious faith.

The year I turned thirteen, my brothers graduated from the military academy. This time, I accompanied Papa and Mama, the three of us tucked in the carriage, a wool blanket covering our legs as the air had not yet yielded the chill of winter. The glossy brown mare trotted briskly along, and we passed fields and forests where the remnants of the winter's snow still clung to a few of the branches. We stayed overnight at an inn whose proprietor was cordial until he noticed the fringes of the prayer shawl that hung down below Papa's waistcoat. I could see the man's expression change so completely that I thought he might hand back our money and put us out. Instead, he turned away and spat loudly into a polished brass spittoon. Mama's face reddened at the unmistakable insult, but Papa seemed unruffled as he gestured for us to follow the man up the stairs to the room.

We arrived at the academy the next day and sat together in a crowded auditorium as Sasha, Max, and two dozen or so other cadets marched one by one across a platform to receive a certificate and a handshake from a uniformed man in an elaborately plumed hat. Later, there were outdoor exercises with glinting swords and still later, shooting demonstrations. With each new burst of fire, I jumped back a little.

Then the guests went back indoors, where we were served little frosted cakes on silver platters and pink, sparkling punch on whose effervescent surface darker pink berries floated. It was only after I had consumed two cups that I learned a liberal amount of vodka had been added to it. I had to go outside, behind some trees, where Mama held my head as I vomited.

Sasha and Max were different after their graduation, calmer and less rambunctious. They were tender with Papa and especially with Mama, rushing to hold the door or pull out a chair for her. Sasha left home first, promising our weeping mother that he'd return home safely. He was off to Peking, where the czar's troops were intent on vanquishing the Chinese rebels who'd been burning *churches and killing Christians. The rebels were called Boxers, which I found confusing, as the name conjured images of shirtless men in a ring, swiping at each other with large, comical-looking gloves. Mr. Bixby explained that they were actually proponents of martial arts and that they were in the midst of a violent rebellion against the foreigners they believed had taken over their country.*

I went up to the third-floor schoolroom in search of the globe and found the large pale green expanse that was China. Although I was not in the habit of praying, I prayed every night for Sasha's safe return. After a few weeks, Max, who seemed adrift without Sasha, was called up too. Now I said fervent prayers for both of them.

I couldn't know if they prayed too, but they did write, and in the letters they would each add lines meant just for me. I'm going to bring you back a jade pendant—or would you rather a brooch? Sasha asked. Max wrote that he missed me and urged me to continue my studies with Mr. Bixby. I've told everyone here about you. Write me back in English or French so I can boast some more.

The next letter was about Max, not from him—killed in an explosion, his body torn to bits—and when Mama read it, she dropped to the floor like she was something inanimate, a load of bricks or logs. Papa had to drag her to a chair, and Katya, who had replaced Ludmila in our household, rushed to pour her a glass of brandy. It was only days later that we got another letter. Sasha wasn't dead, thank God, but badly wounded; he'd been shot in the leg and sent to an infirmary to recover. After an anxious week, we finally received a letter from him. *The doctor here is an overworked, harried man who, when finding out I was a Jew, made it clear that I could not expect much attention from him. So, Mama, please send what you can in the way of food and supplies—clean bandages, food, whiskey, tea, anything really.* Mama put down the letter. "What are we waiting for?" she said. "You heard what he said—we have to start making a package right now!"

Concern for Sasha's welfare eclipsed Mama's grief for Max. Setting aside her embroidery, she began a frenzy of knitting—socks, a muffler, a vest—her needles clicking furiously into the night. She dispatched Katya to buy tins of tea and biscuits, and even several links of sausage, carefully hiding the *traife* from Papa. Bottles of vodka were packed in sawdust and newspaper.

Once the package was assembled and mailed, Mama began a daily vigil of waiting for the postman. When a letter from Sasha did arrive, she ripped it open, trying to find in it something to contradict what was clearly worsening news. *My leg is no better, and the infection seems to be spreading. It's making me weak and I'm unable to walk without a cane.*

"At least he's still walking!" Mama said. "That's a good sign!" I turned to Papa, who quickly looked away. That didn't sound like a good sign to me. Not at all.

Subsequent letters told of gangrene, of fevers, of plans to amputate the leg. And then the final letter, not from Sasha but with an official seal, red and shiny, that Mama wouldn't open, but thrust into Papa's hands. "Esteemed Sir and Madame, we are very sorry to inform . . ."

After this, Mama's mane of black hair turned white, and though she wouldn't speak of my brothers, I could see that their deaths had broken her. She became clinging and fretful, wanting me always nearby. During my lessons with Mr. Bixby, she sat in a chair at the door, her once perpetually busy hands now still and tightly clasped. And I was aware of her coming into my room late at night, sometimes rousing me from sleep.

Mama's grief seemed to have taken over mine, so I had to blunt it, bury it, lock it away. Only once I remember seeking out Papa for something and finding him alone in his study, his face in his hands, weeping quietly. I didn't need to ask why, I only knelt and put my arms around his legs, wetting the wool of his trousers with hot, salty tears of my own.

Spring came fitfully that year, and when it arrived, Mama finally seemed a little better. Papa told me that he had thought of a way to pull her out of her despair. He had to go to Moscow for three weeks on business, and when he returned, he would take us both to Paris.

To my enormous relief, this seemed to work: my mother roused herself and began preparing for the trip. She selected bolts of fabric to give to the seamstress to sew our traveling costumes and made an appointment with the local milliner, where she ordered new straw hats—hers with a cluster of red silk poppies on one side and mine with a sky-blue grosgrain band around the crown. The three weeks passed quickly enough. But Papa still hadn't come home.

"There's nothing to worry about," I told her. I was sixteen by then and beginning to assume a more adult role in the household. "Business is probably good. When he comes back, his pockets will be stuffed with rubles."

"Maybe," Mama said. "Maybe not. Anyway, I don't care about the rubles. I just want him to come back."

Two more days passed with no word. I had begun to worry too, though I didn't tell my mother. Mama had been through so much already; it was essential to buoy her hopes, not crush them. She had resumed her vigil for the postman, who came every afternoon just after lunch. "Here's a letter for you, Mrs. Kharshova," he said one day. She practically snatched the envelope from his hand, but when she saw it wasn't from Papa, she left it on the hall table without opening it.

The next morning, just before dawn, I was awakened by a heavy thud that seemed to come from downstairs. No one else was up, so I put on my dressing gown and went down to investigate. The parlor and dining room were quiet and there was no noise from the kitchen either. Perhaps the sound had come from outside? I went to the heavy oak front door, but when I tried to open it, it wouldn't budge, like something was obstructing it. All my pushing and straining were to no avail, and finally, I gave up and let myself out through the kitchen door and walked around to the front of the house. Dew soaked the hem of my nightdress and through the thin soles of my slippers I felt every stone on the path. The sky had lightened enough so that I could see the large canvas sack, the kind used for mail, that had been blocking the door. What in the name of God could it be?

The sack was gray with grime, and stained with dark splotches. I loosened the cord that drew the fabric together at the top, but when I had opened it to a diameter of about five inches, I stopped. There, in the opening, I could just see the top of Papa's head—I recognized his silvery curls, now matted with dirt, and with what appeared to be blood.

Inside, I felt a percussive clash in my head, my chest. I knelt beside the sack. My father was inside. No, not my father. His corpse. How, when, and where he died were unknown. There were only these sad remains, dumped under the cover of night in front of the house.

I looked up to see my mother and Katya standing over me. They too must have been wakened by the noise. "It's Papa," I sobbed while my mother clawed at the sack's opening and tried to pull the body from it. It was only then that I saw his battered face, dark bruises clouding his forehead. One eye was reduced to a swollen slit.

"Madame, no, that's enough. Come inside now." Katya vainly tried to pull her away, but Mama fended her off and managed to get my father's head, shoulders, and entire torso free before she threw herself on the body, crying his name over and over as she pressed her cheek to his, her tears mingling with the crusted blood.

"Mama, you have to be quiet," I said sternly, worried that one of the neighbors would hear. None of them were Jews, and it had always been our habit to keep our distance and not call undue attention to ourselves. She understood and stopped crying, silently watching as

Katya and I moved the sack enough so that we could open the front door and then drag it into the house. I locked the door firmly and Katya took my mother away to wash up.

The house where I'd lived my entire life suddenly felt strange, and no longer safe. I wandered around for a few minutes, trying to regain my bearings. I finally sat down in the parlor and stared at the intricate arabesques of the rug—deep blue, scarlet, plum, and bottle green. It was fully day now, the soft gray light visible through the gap in the drapes. I finally lifted my gaze from the rug. There was blood on my slippers and on my hands too. I understood that I would have to take care of things; my mother was in no condition to do what needed doing. Which was . . . exactly what? I thought of that gruesome package just inside the front door. The body. My father's body. It would need to be buried.

Grateful to have an immediate task to which I could apply myself, I washed my hands, dressed quickly, and went to call on the rabbi, who lived in a small house near the synagogue. He had me wait in his book-lined study while he sent for the good men of the chevra kadisha, who would wash the body and prepare it for burial later that day.

After Papa had been returned to the earth, the rabbi took me aside and gave me the prayer shawl that had been slashed and burned, and was now filthy too. I cleaned and mended it as best I could, and then tucked it into the trunk where I kept the garments I'd begun assembling for my trousseau. Those conversations—about the possible matches I might make, their relative strengths and drawbacks—felt like they had occurred long ago, in another life.

My mother was unaware of the prayer shawl's existence or anything else that went on in the house. She took to her bed, where she remained for several days, drapes closed to keep out the light. She refused any food, even broth proffered by a concerned Katya.

"See if you can have a word with her," Katya said. Mama smiled weakly when I came into her room, and drank some tea to please me but still wouldn't eat. "She'll waste away," Katya fretted.

But when my father's right-hand man from the tannery showed up, she agreed to see him. Along with several of the more senior workers, Vova had come to the funeral the day we buried my father. He'd grasped my shoulders and kissed me on the brow. "Your papa was a good man," he'd said. "I know he's in heaven now, looking down at you." Today, Vova seemed very agitated. He refused a glass of tea and roughly kneaded his hat in his dye-stained hands as he waited for my mother to come down.

Finally my mother appeared, dressed entirely in black. Vova got right to the point. "There's been a fire, Mrs. Kharshova. No one was hurt, but there's been a lot of damage. Equipment, supplies, skins— all gone." The hat was now a mangled wad of dark cloth.

"A fire? How did it start?"

"We don't know. I'm always so careful and the other workers, you know they're a good lot and devoted to your late husband, may he rest in peace, just like I was."

"My husband had insurance—there's a policy somewhere. Perhaps in his office or the safe upstairs . . ."

Vova shifted uneasily. "I know about that policy, madame. But the brewery nearby was damaged too. And since they're claiming the fire was our fault, they want damages. I'm worried they'll take most of the insurance money. Or all of it."

There was a long silence. When Mama spoke again, it seemed she was choosing her words very carefully. "Vova Andreyovitch, are you suggesting that the fire could have been . . . arson?"

"I couldn't say for sure, but yes, it could have been . . ."

"So then we must go to the police," she said. "Right away. "I'll have Adik harness the horses and——"

"Madame, do you know who the chief of police is?"

"Of course I know who the chief of police is. I'll see if I can get an appointment with him today, and if I can't, I'll wait in his office until he'll see me."

Vova looked at her with pity. "Do you also know his brother-in-law?"

"His brother-in-law? No, but what does that have to do——"

"He's the owner of the brewery."

"Oh," said Mama. "I see."

The tannery, which we visited later that day, was a blackened, ash-covered shell. My mother wept inconsolably the entire ride back to the house. But I didn't cry; all my tears seemed to have dried up. All I could think was how fortunate it was that no one had been hurt or killed in the fire, because if they had, we would have been blamed for that too. And money wouldn't have solved that problem. Only blood, our blood, would have made it right.

Mama's torpor was over. As Vova had guessed, every last ruble paid by the insurance company went to the brewery; there was nothing left with which to rebuild and start again. Not that she would have wanted to. She decided that we would leave Russia, and make the great journey across the ocean, to America. She had a distant cousin who'd gone there and written to her about his new life. He lived in New Orleans. It had been hard at first, he told her. But there were no pogroms, no one who vanished and turned up as a corpse. And it was warm, he wrote. So warm. I was afraid of making such a long journey. "We can sell the house and go to Moscow," I said. "Or St. Petersburg. I could get a job."

"What sort of a job?" Mama asked.

"As a governess. Or a lady's companion."

"And what good would that be?" Her expression was grim. "It will only happen again. Oh, we'll the sell the house all right—the house and everything in it. And then we'll leave this country. Can't you see, they don't want us here? Open your eyes, daughter."

She was right. The seemingly secure and protected life of my childhood was a built on a fault line, and that line had just cracked wide open, leaving us at the edge of an abyss. I had never seen such hatred up close before; the pogroms my parents had sometimes spoken of in low, fearful voices had happened long ago, before I was born and then once when I was a small child. And of that night, I remembered not the terror, only the kindness of the local priest who hid us in the church, his unkempt beard reaching almost to his waist, and the wooden crucifix that he wore. That priest, where was he now? But it made no difference. He couldn't save us this time. No one could.

My mother was forced to sell our house for far less than it was worth. The buyer, a shrewd businessman from a neighboring town, didn't bother to hide his smugness. The same thing had happened when she went out daily to sell its contents, bit by bit. It was as if everyone smelled our desperation. My father's murder and the loss of the factory had turned my mother from a respectable matron to a vulnerable widow. She came away with enough money to give something to each of the servants, our train fare to the port city of Riga, and our passage across the Atlantic by steamship. There was a scant amount left over. "It's not much," my mother said. "But it will have to do."

"I can go to work when we get there," I told her. "As a governess. Or nursemaid."

"You should be thinking about a husband, not a domestic position," she told me. "We'll find a matchmaker as soon as we're settled. And I'll look for work—embroidering or even, if it comes to it, taking in laundry." I didn't want to contradict her, but this seemed unlikely. My mother had grown even more frail in these last months. Her ribs were visible when she asked me to help her undo the corset she really didn't even need to wear, and her wristbones looked like two knobs protruding from the sleeves of her dress. And then, just two short weeks before we were to leave, her heart gave out. I was the one who found her, cold and still, hands still clutching the counterpane. For the second time that year, the members of the chevra kadisha came to wash the body of someone I loved and prepare it for burial.

The death of one's mother is an enormous loss, perhaps the greatest one I had experienced, and I grieved for her. But somewhere inside I knew that although she wanted to leave the Russia that had scorned and spit on her, she didn't want to leave the place where her husband and sons were buried. And so in the end she didn't. I had her laid to rest near my father and could only hope that she was at peace.

CHAPTER FOURTEEN

BEA

New Orleans, 1898

With nothing left for me at home, I went to Riga on my own, the train rushing through forests of birch and pine, over rivers, and through tunnels, towns, and cities. I'd sold my mother's train ticket at home, and once in Riga, I found another buyer for the ship's ticket. I'd have enough money to get me started in America, but I knew it wouldn't last long. I'd also had a few pieces of her jewelry sewn into the hem of my coat, but they were stolen my first night on the ship as I slept—I was too gullible to know that was the first place that thieves looked.

My mother had written her cousin in New Orleans to say we were coming and received a prompt reply. The ship arrived in September; I was not prepared for the heat of the place. In Russia, that month already had a crisp, autumnal feel. But in New Orleans, the air was moist and thick enough to slice. It sapped my energy and made me sleepy. What little clothing I had was unsuited for the climate, and I felt like I marinated in sweat all day long. When I found my way to the address on the back of our cousin's letter, his landlord told me that he had recently died—the same week as my mother—and that he'd left no money at all. He'd actually owed money; I left quickly, lest the landlord try to collect the debt from me.

I found a cheap and respectable place that let rooms, and then an agency where I could apply for a job. Thanks to Mr. Bixby, I spoke decent though accented English, and I knew I was attractive enough. I used a little of the money I had to buy a dress of moss-green linen. It was a cheap thing but it fit well, and I knew it played to my strengths both in terms of cut and color. In Russia I'd owned many beautiful dresses; my mother had employed a dressmaker who came to the house twice a year. But most of them had been sold and the few I had kept were too heavy for the climate.

I filled out the application carefully. On the boat, I'd met a young woman named Ludmila Petranova who told me she was going to be-come Lucille Peters when we reached America. I could see the wis-dom of her decision, though I had no idea about how to choose a name. It seemed bizarre to abandon one of the most essential links to who I had been in favor of something I just made up. So I hadn't done it and now here I was, with that blank space waiting. I glanced down at the newspaper I'd been carrying in the crook of my arm. Here was an advertisement for Beatrice face powder, illustrated by an attractive woman with her face turned in profile. I wrote *Beatrice* in the empty space. What next caught my eye was an ad for Carr's Garden and Lawn Ornaments, with a lovely image of a statue of a nymph amid a grove of trees. The sound of "Carr" was not so far from Kharshova. My hand hovered over the space for just an instant before I filled in that blank too.

I learned that there was a position open with the Phillips family, who needed someone to tend to their youngest son, Teddy, who was about a year old; the older boys, George and Matthew, were in the care of a governess who also gave them lessons. The lady at the agency felt certain Mr. and Mrs. Phillips would approve of me despite my accent. "The important thing is that you're neat, clean, and respectable." She handed me a slip of paper with the address. "It's in the Garden District."

"Garden District," I repeated, liking the sound of it. "Can I walk there?"

She sighed. "I suppose so. Let me draw you a map. You can go over now. Mrs. Phillips receives visitors in the afternoons."

The Phillips house was like nothing I'd ever seen—white, with four columns in front that supported a curved balcony above. Two stained-glass panels shone on what I guessed were the landings of the stairwell; the windows were very tall and were lined with white lace panels. I went up the three shallow steps and lifted a brass knocker shaped like a pineapple.

A dark-skinned maid let me in. In Russia, I'd never seen such people before but here in New Orleans, they abounded. I found them interesting and often beautiful, their skin tones ranging from lightest cocoa to deep, almost bluish, black. The variety of the faces I saw gave me the hope that maybe I'd come to a place of greater acceptance or even tolerance than the one I'd left. But soon I came to understand that New Orleans was a rigidly stratified society, with the whites at the top, everyone else beneath them. Just like Russia, only there it had been the Christians. What stratum did the Jews occupy here in New Orleans? I didn't yet know.

I followed the maid to the back porch, where I sat on a wicker settee; two matching wicker chairs faced me, and in the corner of the room was a brass stand with a cage. In it, a pair of finches with startling red beaks darted around nervously.

"Beatrice Carr?"

The name still didn't seem like mine, but I turned to see a small woman in a white eyelet dress. This was Clara Phillips. Her light brown hair was done in braids that had been pinned to the top of her head and pearls dangled from her earlobes.

"Pleased to meet you." I remembered conversations with Mr. Bixby. We would have tea parties at which such phrases would be uttered but I had never imagined I would actually have to use them in any way that was not academic.

Mrs. Phillips asked for references but beyond the woman at the agency, I had none. This gave her pause but she was eager to hire someone—"I have three boys, and I can tell you three are a handful"—and she did not press. I think too she liked my modest attire and clearly wellborn ways. Then she took me upstairs to see the baby, who was asleep in his crib. He was a fair-haired child, and he lay on his back, arms and legs splayed in innocent abandon. "He's like a cherub," I told her, and it was clearly the right response because Mrs. Phillips hired me on the spot.

I was given a small room on the third floor and told I could move in immediately. I was so grateful I could have grasped her hand and covered it with kisses but I restrained myself. I instead walked back to the agency to tell them I'd been hired and then I took the street-car to my rooming house, where I collected my valise and settled my bill.

I worked six days a week for the Phillipses, but on Sundays they all went to church and then to visit family, and I was given the day off. I spent my free day exploring the city, eager to learn its broader con-tours and its finer nuances. Mostly I walked, literally wearing holes in the leather of my shoes, but a few times I indulged and took the streetcar, a fabulous red contraption that went from uptown, along St. Charles Avenue, all the way downtown, almost to the Quarter. The car was a deep, shiny red and ran on an electrified rail. Stepping into it, I felt as if I'd stepped into the future, and I felt hopeful as I gazed out the windows at the grand houses we passed. Fluted columns, wide porches that went all the way around, and stained-glass windows all caught my eye. This too was the Garden District, and at first, I remained safe within in it.

But in time, I grew curious about other parts of the city, and I began venturing farther downtown, where it was immediately apparent the atmosphere was different. The streets were more densely packed here, with people walking, smoking, talking, hurrying. Girls strolling arm in arm, their laughter like a melody, a maid emptying a chamber pot from a window up above, splashing the hem of my dress with its foul contents. I thought of Yekaterinoslav Avenue in my home city, with its orderly rows of shops, hotel, and post office—how sedate and tame it seemed in comparison.

At the corner of Canal and Basin Streets I came across Krauss Department Store, a respectable emporium that sold elegant wares. But just a little farther on was a café and chophouse that took up half the block and advertised providing food and drink at all hours of the day. Music blared out into the street, and through the doors that frequently opened and closed I caught glimpses of several enormous arched mirrors behind the bar, and an ornate ceiling that blazed with what seemed like a hundred lightbulbs. This was Anderson's, and the other servants at the Phillipses' told me it was the gateway to the more licentious parts of the city.

I soon found that they were right: just beyond Anderson's were the ornate mansions where all manner of carnal pleasures were bought and sold, in the infamous area known as the District. In this part of the city, prostitution was legal and the brothels were allowed to operate out in the open. I had heard of such places but in my sheltered girlhood had never seen them for myself, nor ever imagined I would. One of these buildings was more splendid than the next, and even though I didn't dare to enter any of them, I could guess at the opulence within.

If I turned and went down some of the side streets, things changed yet again. The farther I went from Basin Street, the greater the squalor and desperation. Some of these streets were devoted completely to single rooms with private entrances. Since the occupants often stood in the open doorways, I could see that a room consisted of a bed, a washstand, and little else. The women who presided over them were blatant in their attempts to lure customers, hiking up their skirts to show their garters—and more—or pulling at the necklines of their gauzy dresses to reveal shoulders, cleavage, and in one memorable instance, breasts.

I was both scandalized and fascinated by this glimpse into a world that was so different from any I'd known, and these walks reminded me that a combination of circumstances had severed me from my past. I was alone, accountable to no one other than myself, and although I often felt loneliness sharp as a blade to my heart, at other times I felt a great sense of freedom. I remembered those long-ago days when I would spin the globe and when it stopped, point my finger at some random spot about which Mr. Bixby would elaborate. I couldn't have put my finger on New Orleans even if I'd wanted to, but as I made my way through it, both the sordid and the beautiful, the birds, trees, and flowers all still so unfamiliar, it seemed as strange and wondrous as any of those places I'd imagined.

Beyond the wickedness of the District lay the Quarter, which was also tawdry but in a different and more appealing way. The clusters of low-slung buildings in creamy colors—salmon, buttercup, the blue of a robin's egg—were charming, as was their ornamental ironwork. And I especially loved the sheer abundance of the outdoor stalls: blossoms, from palest white to deep aubergine and crimson, willow baskets piled high with fruit and vegetables, tables on which were strewn bolts of fabric and spools of thread and ribbon, jars of buttons, burlap sacks spilling their dark, glossy beans, tin buckets where live fish swam round and round, and gutted fish carcasses splayed over mounds of shaved ice, scales glittering in the sun. Sometimes I indulged and bought myself a paper cone filled with strawberries, small and misshapen but uncommonly sweet, or a glazed confection that resembled the ear of an elephant and whose delicate pastry shattered in my mouth when I took a bite.

It was on one of these Sundays, when I was still so new to America and wandering around the streets of New Orleans like a dazed calf, that I met him—Richard Clayton Robichaud. I had been walking in the Quarter, wilting from the heat, which I had not yet grown accustomed to. I longed for the cold back home: ice-blue mornings, winter sunsets that glowed like embers lining the horizon. And the different kinds of snow: fine as sand, stinging my cheeks, cotton-like white balls that piled thick and fast, and big, wet flakes that looked like flowers raining down from the sky. But there was to be no snow here, not ever, and I would have to find some other form of relief—perhaps a glass of cool, sweet tea? I deliberated about spending any of the precious coins in my purse—the tea cost two cents. But if I walked back to the Phillipses' house, I could have a free glass. Mrs. Phillips kept an etched glass pitcher full of cold tea on the sideboard in the dining room and I was permitted to help myself at any time. The house would be empty, and I could sit in their garden for a little while undisturbed. Just as I was deciding to return to the house, I looked up, and there he was.

Of course I didn't know who he was then, or anything about him. I only knew that he was the most beautiful man I had ever seen and I had to stand there and look at him. He was perhaps a shade under six feet tall, with lustrous light brown hair combed away from his forehead. His eyes were a clear, light blue, the color of a tropical sea, a rarely seen fish or bird, an opal. He was clean-shaven, with two deep dimples when he smiled—which he did as soon as he noticed my graceless stare. His teeth were white, even, and straight, with only the smallest gap between the two front ones, one I wanted to touch my tongue to. The thought—so unprecedented, so shocking—made me look away, down at my worn and rather scuffed shoes.

"How do you do?" he said.

"Charmed, I'm sure." If only Mr. Bixby could have heard me.

"You're not from here," he said.

"No." Even after all my practice, my accent was still very pronounced. "I'm not."

"Where, then?"

"Russia," I told him.

"St. Petersburg? Moscow?" He looked intrigued—those were marvelous cities, famous the world over.

I shook my head. "Nowhere so big, or so grand."

"You're far from home," he said.

"Very." I didn't add that there was no more home. All that I'd known as home was gone forever.

"I've never met a young lady from Russia before." He bowed slightly at the waist. "I'm Clay Robichaud."

"Beatrice Carr." I gave him the name that still didn't feel like my own.

He looked surprised. "That doesn't sound like a Russian name," he said.

"It's not. But I'm not in Russia anymore."

He laughed, the sound so silvery, so appealing to me. "No, I suppose you're not." Then he asked, "Are you on your way to an appointment, Miss Carr? Or just out for a stroll?"

"Just a stroll," I said.

"Would you allow me to accompany you?"

In Ekaterinaslav, I wouldn't have spoken to a strange young man I met in the street, let alone allowed him to walk with me. But I wasn't in Ekaterinaslav any longer and the old rules did not apply.

Clay was still waiting, and as he waited, he extended his elbow just the merest bit. I had never walked arm in arm with a young man before, yet I was drawn by the singular pull he exerted. I placed my hand on his arm, and as we began to walk down Chartres Street together I felt as if I were floating above the pavement. I was not yet eighteen, still deep in mourning for my family, my country, the life I had left behind, and a handsome young man had stopped in the street to smile at me. Smile and offer his arm. And that, it seemed, was all it took. I understand if you disapprove of my conduct. You weren't raised that way, and neither was I. But remember that I no longer had parents to guide and direct me; I was in this, as in everything, quite alone.

CHAPTER FIFTEEN

BEA

After that Sunday, Clay and I met regularly every week. Being courted was a novel experience; my family tragedies had prevented that next phase of my life from unfolding. He took me rowing in City Park and for rides on the carousel. One Sunday he rented bicycles, and when I told him I couldn't ride, he spent the afternoon teaching me. There were walks, talks, and visits to ice cream parlors and cafés. During the time we spent together, I told him all about my life in Russia. He seemed fascinated by—and sympathetic to—the hardships I'd endured; by his own admission, he'd never met anyone like me, a young woman who once had a position in the world and then lost it.

"Yet you're not bitter," he said.

I considered this. "No, I'm not. I miss my family terribly. But I managed to escape. I'm here, aren't I?"

"Yes." He took my hand. "You are."

Clay also asked me to speak Russian, which delighted him, though he understood not a word. He also admired my penchant for memorizing poetry, a habit instilled by Mr. Bixby and which I had continued to cultivate on my own. I knew that when I recited Shakespeare's sonnets—Mr. Bixby had me start with those—my pronunciation was deplorable. But Clay seemed enchanted just the same. And he was perhaps most intrigued by the fact that I was a Jew—that too was new for him.

"There must be other Jews in New Orleans," I said, though I hadn't yet encountered any.

"I'm sure there are, but our paths haven't crossed. My mother is a good woman but she cares about things like that."

"Like what?"

"Like associating with people who attend the same church, and have the same values."

"Your mother—she wouldn't like my being Jewish. She wouldn't like me."

"But I like you." He put a hand to my cheek. "You're unique. Soulful."

These were pretty words, but I discerned their real meaning. You're different. Strange. Not one of us. Yet I said nothing. That Jews were hated was a given in my experience; better that Clay should view me as some exotic creature to be prized than one to be reviled. But the exchange underscored how divergent our lives were. Apart from the charmed hours we enjoyed on Sundays, I had no idea about how he passed his time when we were not together. "What is it that you do?" I asked him once.

"Do?" He seemed perplexed by the question.

"Yes. Do." I was accustomed to a world in which men did something.

"I'm not sure I know what you're asking."

"Your profession. Your work."

"Oh, that." He dismissed the idea with a shrug. "My father has an importing business, if that's what you mean."

"So you work with him?"

"Not really. I'll take it over one day, I suppose. But it doesn't much interest me."

"Then what does?"

"My horses. I breed them, you know."

He had mentioned going to the stables. But could this be considered work? "To race? To sell?"

"Both." He seemed eager to leave the topic.

"What else?"

He took my hand and smiled. "You."

At the end of each afternoon we spent together, Clay brought me back to the Phillipses' house. On one such day, I thought I saw a curtain shift at the window. Was I being watched? I hoped not but decided that in the future, I would have Clay walk me only as far as the corner.

The following Sunday, Clay asked for more details about my position in the Phillips household. "The children—I'm fond of them," I told him. "And Mrs. Phillips is very kind. This dress I'm wearing? She gave it to me. The shoes too. If Teddy is napping, she lets me sit in the room where George and Matthew have their lessons, which is helping my English so much. And she lets me borrow whatever I like from their library." I enjoyed reading but had brought no books with me from Russia; they were far too heavy.

"And what about Mr. Phillips?"

"What about him?"

"I don't know . . . a pretty girl like you, alone in the world. Some employers might try to take advantage . . . does he?"

"No," I said. I didn't like Mr. Phillips and I didn't want to talk about him. Although he was not a heavy man, his face was doughy. His gold-rimmed glasses had thick lenses that made it hard to see the expression in his eyes, and an enormous mustache covered his upper lip entirely, as if he wished to hide it. He was prematurely bald, so perhaps he grew the mustache in compensation. He was condescending to his wife and harsh with his children. He spanked George and Matthew regularly and on one awful occasion, he caned George for some infraction. The cries that child made were so pitiful that I didn't know how Mrs. Phillips could stand it. But why was I thinking about Mr. Phillips when I was with Clay? I quickly banished him from my mind.

That was the first day that Clay kissed me. We were in City Park again, but in a more secluded part, and he'd brought a blanket so that we might sit upon the grass. We kissed for a long while and when his hands strayed to my breasts, I felt an exhilaration and a desire I hadn't ever experienced. I knew that I should not allow this intimacy. But my newfound freedom—the obverse of my exile—gave me permission. Who would know? Who would judge? I hope, Catherine, that you won't. Finally, we moved apart.

"When I kissed you, you didn't say stop or pull away. You don't seem worried about whether I'll think you're a nice girl." Clay stroked my hair as he spoke.

"I am a nice girl," I said.

"The nicest," he said gently.

"And why would I pretend I don't want you to kiss me when I do want it—I want it very much."

"Oh, Bea . . ." He took me in his arms and kissed me again.

The next time we met, Clay asked if I'd like to go somewhere new with him. It was a secret, he said. I followed him through the Quarter until we came to a small brick building set back behind an enormous willow tree. By now I was familiar with the kind of fil-igreed metalwork that wrapped around the upper story. The front door was painted a glossy black and a large ceramic pot of geraniums stood right beside it.

"What is this place?" I asked.

"My father owns it," he said. "And I have the key. Would you like to come inside? It's very pretty and I think you'll like it."

I knew full well that accompanying a young man into an un-occupied house was not a prudent thing to do. But this wasn't just any young man—this was Clay, with whom I was in love. I had ex-perienced so much grief in my young life; I was not going to turn down the possibility of happiness when it was handed to me.

I followed him past the foyer and into a sitting room, where I perched on a small settee. Clay sat down on an armchair but quickly got up to join me. When he began to kiss me, I wasn't surprised, and my body responded instinctively. But when he started to undo the buttons of my dress, I pulled back.

"We shouldn't."

"Do you want to?"

"I . . . I don't know. I suppose I do but . . ."

"But it's not right, well-bred young ladies don't allow such liber-ties."

"Exactly," I said, relieved that he understood. I remained within the circle of his arm, and when he began to kiss me again, it was with greater delicacy and restraint. This in turn inflamed my own desire and I almost wished that he would start unbuttoning my dress again.

But he didn't, and soon the afternoon had wound down and it was time to return to the Phillipses'.

The next Sunday we went back to that house, as I'd known we would. "Why does your father have this place?" I asked this time. "He doesn't live here, does he?"

"Oh no," Clay said. "But sometimes he likes to . . . entertain here."

"You mean, a woman?"

"Well, yes."

"I see." This was the house where his father brought his mistresses. I knew about such things; I had overheard conversations my mother had with her friends about husbands who strayed. "Doesn't that bother you?"

"We've never discussed it, actually."

"Yet you have the key." And then I understood. His father had given him the key in case he too wanted to entertain someone in this house. Someone like me.

"Would you rather not be here? We can leave if you like. I wouldn't want you to do anything you don't want to do." He stroked my face and neck; I remembered his caresses from last week and was stirred all over again.

"No, I want to stay," I said. "At least I think I do." He began kissing the places he had been stroking.

"If you want me to stop, all you have to do is say so," he said. "I would never force you."

But I didn't want him to stop, and this time when he began to undo the buttons, I let him, and I let him slide his hands into the chemise's opening. From there it seemed so easy to let him lead me up the stairs to a bedroom. Inside, the wallpaper depicted cavorting cherubs, the white curtains were edged in white fringe, and a brass chandelier hung directly over a sleigh bed piled high with pillows and covered by a white matelassé spread.

Clay gently pulled me down and I let him strip off my chemise, unfasten my corset, and take off my petticoat. I was quiet while he hastily removed his own clothing, not quite believing what I was about to do. I had been brought up to wait for marriage, but that was in another world, another life. Mere months ago, I had left Russia a nearly destitute orphan. And now there was Clay. It was enough. Even the small, sharp pain I felt when he entered me didn't trouble me—the first time was supposed to hurt. "It will be better," he promised.

Can you understand all this? Any of it? I know you might think less of me for giving myself to a man before I was married. But you asked me to tell you everything, and so that's what I'm doing. I'm trying to explain how and why that came to be. I'll keep trying.

Clay and I made regular visits to that house. He—or someone else—must have gone there in our absence because the bedroom, the only room we frequented, was always clean and sweet-smelling, the linens fresh and pressed. Sometimes I'd find a spray of flowers on the bureau, or a package of sweets tied with a pastel ribbon.

I lived for our time together but was still mindful of my role with the Phillips family. Mrs. Phillips seemed cordial enough, and I knew the boys—not just Teddy, who had become my own precious darling, but also George and Matthew—were fond of me too. But the more I came to know Mr. Phillips, the less I liked him. When Matthew started wetting the bed, Mr. Phillips insisted that he be made to wash out the soiled sheets himself. The sight of the poor child kneeling over the copper washtub, his small arms in the hot water, filled me with pity.

So I began to get up a little earlier than usual to check Matthew's sheets. If they were wet, I changed them myself and bundled them in with the rest of the laundry. I never knew whether Bitsy, the maid, suspected; she never said anything to me. Matthew seemed to know though. He sometimes came to my room in the afternoons, and once he rested his head on my knee when we were in the study. I made sure no one else saw the signs of our growing attachment, for although it was not forbidden, it was clear to me I was supposed to concern myself with the baby only.

At first Mr. Phillips largely ignored me, but as the time went by, he seemed to take a greater interest in what I wore, and would occasionally compliment me on a dress or hat, even if they had first belonged to his wife.

And then there was the night that I put Teddy to sleep in his room on the second floor and climbed the back stairs to my room on the third. It didn't have the romance or flair of the cherub-strewn bower I visited with Clay, but I had come to appreciate its more modest charms—the hooked rug, narrow bed covered in a faded patchwork quilt, pine armoire, marble-topped bureau. Over the bureau there was a mirror, and above the headboard was a picture of the Virgin Mary holding the Infant Jesus. I suppose it never occurred to the Phillipses that I might not be Christian—they hadn't asked, and I hadn't said. At first the picture unsettled me, but after a while I decided the baby looked like Teddy and so I ceased minding it.

I'd started undressing when I noticed a large, tissue-wrapped parcel on the bed. A bright band of ribbon wound around it and curls of ribbon sprang from the lavish bow at the center. A present, obviously. But not from Clay; he would never leave anything for me here. I undid the ribbons and pulled the tissue away to find an exquisite chemise and matching petticoat, both of the finest batiste; the petticoat was bedecked with yards of lace, three rows deep. I lifted the chemise up and held it to the light. I somehow knew that Mr. Phillips had left it here, a thought which both sickened and frightened me.

I remembered the questions Clay had asked me about him. At the time, I was able to say no, Mr. Phillips had never behaved in a way that was forward or rude. But that was no longer true. I hastily stuffed the chemise back into the tissue and put the entire parcel under the bed.

The next night, I found another wrapped package, this time an even more expensive-looking peignoir set of pale peach satin. I lay awake a long time, pondering what to do. There was no one in the house I could consult, no one to whom I could turn for advice.

The following night there was nothing new in my room, and nothing the night after. I was relieved. Perhaps Mr. Phillips had been satisfied by simply leaving the underthings in my room. I certainly hoped so.

But about a week later Mrs. Phillips went to Baton Rouge to visit her sister. I watched from my window as her husband put her into the carriage that would take her to the railway station. That evening, Miss Molyneux, the governess, was nursing a toothache, so after I'd settled Teddy in for the night, I put the older boys to bed. George and Matthew were rowdy, jumping on the beds and swatting each other with pillows. I was worried their father would hear, so I promised them a story if they would settle down. Miss Molyneux didn't believe in bedtime stories, rather a quick kneel for prayers, then lights out and no talking.

The boys were very intrigued by the idea and listened raptly, George stopping me with a question now and then, Matthew snuggling against my collarbone. He smelled warm and fresh—like a just-baked biscuit. "I like you so much better than Miss Molyneux," he whispered.

"I like you too."

When they were asleep, I went to my room, but before I could undress, I heard a knock. It was Mr. Phillips. "May I come in?" It wasn't a question.

"Yes, sir." I stood aside and let him pass.

I saw him looking around the room, as if in search of something. Finally he asked, "Did you get my gifts?"

"Your gifts?" Of course I knew what he meant. And I had a vague, unsettling idea of what might be coming next.

"Yes. The petticoat, the peignoir . . . where are they? I'd like to see them."

I could feel the flush starting to prickle somewhere on my neck and rise up to my cheeks. I knelt to retrieve the delicate garments from under the bed and laid them out on top of it. "Everything is very pretty, sir. Very pretty and very fine. But they're too expensive. I can't accept them. Let me give them back—"

"Have you tried them on?" He ignored me. "They might not fit. If they don't, I can exchange them for ones that do."

"I've already said that I don't want—"

"This has nothing to do with what you want. It's about what I want. Do you understand?" I said nothing and he continued. "Try them on."

"Excuse me?"

"You heard what I said. Try the things on. The batiste first."

"But, sir . . ."

"You can just pretend I'm not here. I won't touch you. I only want to watch."

I couldn't believe what he was proposing. Did he really think I would agree? I'd have sooner taken all the finery and hurled it out the window. "I'm sorry, sir, but I can't do that—"

"You can and you will. Otherwise I'll tell my wife about the trips you and Mr. Robichaud make to that house in the Quarter. Do you really think she'll keep you on once she hears how you spend your free time?"

How did he find out? I was too shocked to ask.

"Don't look so surprised," he said. "I have a lot of friends in this city. And I make it my business to know something about the people in my employ." When I still didn't move, he added, "Go on. What are you waiting for?"

I began to undo my dress and to loosen my underthings. My fingers shook a little and I knew my face was a bright, mortified shade of pink.

"That's right." His breathing was heavier. "Take everything off. Then put on the white things, and look at yourself in the mirror. Like you would do if you were alone."

I obeyed his directions, turning away as I stripped and stepped into the new underthings he'd bought. The batiste was soft and very fine; nothing of such quality had touched my skin in a long time. I moved to the mirror and I could see him behind me now. He was rubbing himself urgently, and as I adjusted the fabric over my breasts, I saw that he'd unbuttoned his trousers. I tried to keep my eyes away from the white, pulsating bit of flesh and soon I heard his sharp intake of breath, followed by a loud groan. I didn't move.

"Now give me the chemise."

"Excuse me?"

"You heard me. Take off the chemise and give it to me."

I was puzzled. He had given it to me; now he wanted it back? But I did as I was told. He used it to wipe himself off, and then tossed it on the floor, near my feet, before leaving.

I was deeply shaken by this incident and couldn't wait to confide in Clay. It seemed he had known such a thing might happen; he'd even hinted at it. But during the intervening days, I changed my mind. Telling Clay could color his feelings, and despite himself, he might think less of me. I didn't think less of myself though. I simply understood that Mr. Phillips was going to be part of the price of my survival here in New Orleans. I'd already survived so much. I would survive this too.

CHAPTER SIXTEEN

BEA

This is an especially unsavory part of the story and I hope you don't judge me too harshly, Catherine. I was taken advantage of by someone who ought to have protected me, or at the very least not preyed upon me. He knew I couldn't tell and he took advantage of that.

Mr. Phillips became a frequent visitor to my room. He would ask me to wear the underthings he'd left for me, or to put on the new slips, chemises, corsets, and petticoats he continued to bring. Sometimes these garments were demure and virginal, but some seemed quite scandalous, like the ensemble made of red satin and trimmed lavishly in black lace. It made little difference though—I found them all equally abhorrent. Then he would step back and we would begin our little charade—he'd pretend to be invisible as I moved around my room.

I soon learned to manipulate the situation to my own advantage. Certain gestures or actions—putting a finger in my mouth and then touching that same finger to my nipple, delicately sniffing under my arm before I washed—sped up the whole process. Once he'd gone, I stripped off the garments and stuffed them into my valise—I didn't want any of the other servants to see them. Later I would wash them, and hang them in my room to dry, making sure the housemaid didn't come in to clean until they had been put away.

I continued to keep these interludes a secret from Clay. The secret weighed on me at first, but I began to see that secrets might need to exist, even between two people who were in love, just as differences could exist between them too. I had already accepted that Clay was not the sort of man my father had been—he lacked the drive and the ambition. And the fact that he'd always been comfortable and protected left him incurious about the fates of those who were not.

"How come all the colored people in New Orleans are servants?" I asked.

"Not all," he said.

"Well, then most."

"They're not well educated," he said. "Being servants is the only thing they're suited for."

"Why aren't they educated?"

"Why?" The question surprised him. "I don't know. It's just not done."

"Just because something's not done doesn't mean it shouldn't be. In Russia, women aren't given an education, but my father insisted that I have one."

"I never thought about it that way."

"If they had educations, they could be much more than servants—they could become lawyers or bankers or teachers—"

"Bea." Clay smiled and took my hand in both of his, a gentle cage. "You're such an idealist. Maybe even a reformer. I'll bet that years ago, you would have been an abolitionist."

"Abolitionist?"

"Those firebrands who opposed slavery."

"Of course I would have," I said. "Wouldn't you?"

Winter came to New Orleans, though it was so mild I could scarcely recognize it as such. But I wondered if my body was registering the changes in temperature anyway, because in December I became sick, gripped by brief but powerful spasms of nausea in the mornings, and the occasional bout of dizziness during the day. I tried to hide my symptoms, even as I worried I might transmit them to Teddy or the older boys. It was Bitsy, after having caught me retching into an enamelware basin, who enlightened me. "Honey, you're going to have a baby," she said. "Didn't you know?"

Didn't I know? No, I did not. All those months I had been meeting with Clay I was aware of the possibility of such a thing, but he'd shown me how to take precautions—a cake of coarse brown soap to wash with—and I trusted him. "It will keep you from getting in the family way," he had said. I used the soap faithfully after every time we'd been together, and so when my monthly time was late, I hadn't been especially worried.

Bitsy brewed me a cup of chamomile tea and while I sipped it, I quickly mapped out a plan. Today was Wednesday. I would see Clay on Sunday—that was when I would tell him. He would be surprised—as I'd been—but it would be a happy surprise. Or so I hoped. He loved me—of this I was certain. And I loved him.

When Sunday came, I was up early and stepped into a rose-sprigged dress that had once belonged to Mrs. Phillips. It was a little tight but not noticeably so, and I thought it was becoming. I arrived at the house in the Quarter and went around the back to let myself in. Clay hadn't arrived, so there was time for me to pinch my cheeks and bite my lips for color; I'd been looking peaked and wan lately. I heard the key turning in the lock and then Clay appeared with a tiny bunch of violets. He pressed them into my hands and drew me close for a kiss. When he released me, he took my arm and propelled me toward the stairs.

"I want to talk," I said.

"We'll talk all you want." He'd already taken off my hat and had begun unpinning my hair. "Later."

"No, it has to be now."

So we sat downstairs and I could see him fidgeting. I had to get right to it.

"I'm going to have a child." There, the words were out.

"A child! Are you sure?" I nodded. "I thought the soap . . . It wasn't supposed to happen."

"No," I said. "But it has."

He stood up and went to the window so I was unable to see his face. I felt plunged into darkness. Would he be angry? Recoil?

"My darling girl!" He'd turned around and crossed the room to kneel before me. "I'm surprised, of course I'm surprised. It's not what we intended. But it will be all right. No, it will be wonderful." He took my hands and kissed them.

"Are you saying that—"

"Marry me, Bea. Marry me and we'll be a family. You, me"—he touched the front of my dress where the buttons were starting to strain—"and the baby. Our baby."

I closed my eyes and let happiness and relief flood through me. He wouldn't cast me aside; we'd be married and we'd be together— forever.

"Bea, you haven't said anything."

"Yes." I opened my eyes. "I'm saying yes."

"We should do it as soon as possible. Maybe even elope, and then tell my parents later."

His parents. Why hadn't I thought of them? He'd never brought me to meet them, never even suggested it. And I hadn't asked either. "What do you think they'll say?"

He stood again and began to walk around the room. "They might not be so happy. Not at first, anyway. My mother has it in her head that I should marry the daughter of one of my father's business associates."

"But you don't want to?"

"No, I don't and I won't. I've told Mother this over and over, but she won't listen."

"What if she's angry with you? And your father too?"

"That's why we should elope. Once it's done, they won't have anything to say about it."

Was Clay right in thinking his parents would come to accept me? He hadn't even mentioned the fact that I was Jewish, another—significant—reason for Mrs. Robichaud to object. And if they didn't accept me, would they show their displeasure by withholding their money? I had no knowledge of Clay's financial situation because it hadn't mattered to me. But if we were to support a child, it mattered now.

"You're so quiet. And you look sad. You should be happy. I'm happy!" He leaned over to kiss me and the kiss grew more insistent. "There's still time for us to go upstairs."

"What if your parents cut you off? What will happen to us then?"

"Is that what you're worried about?" he asked. "You needn't be. I've had an income of my own since I was twenty-one. It's not lavish, but we'd manage. And think of the baby, Bea. No one can resist a baby. Certainly not my mother." He stood and tugged on my hand. "Now please don't fret anymore."

* * *

Later I walked back to the Phillipses' house, thinking about Clay's response. He'd said and done everything I'd hoped and prayed he would—asked me to marry him, reassured me about his family and how he would support us. Yet still I felt uneasy. I looked at my left hand and touched the place where the ring would be. I needed no diamonds, no jewels, just a simple band of gold that would protect me, and my unborn child.

For the next few days, I did my best to keep up with my work, but I was often distracted. I had little appetite but I forced myself to eat so I wouldn't feel weak. I slept deeply at night, and when I woke, I could barely summon the will to leave my bed. I'd lie there and hear Teddy, who had just started calling out my name in the mornings—BeaBeaBeaBea—and I'd think of the child I was carrying. Boy or girl, fair or dark? What did it matter, as long as he or she had a father and a name?

I stumbled to Teddy's room and lifted him from the crib, his little arms reaching up to meet mine. One morning I felt so ill that I brought him back to my room and into my bed. I let him babble next to me as I dozed, his little body tucked into the curve of my own. Bitsy found us and shook me awake. "The missus, she's asking for you," she said. "You better come down now." I knew Mrs. Phillips had been observing me. How much did she know? I couldn't be sure. But I did know my position was becoming less secure every day.

The next time I heard a knock at my door, it was she, not Mr. Phillips, on the threshold. "I think you know why I've come," she began. I said nothing. Why should I make it easy for her? "It pains me to have to do this. The boys are very fond of you. And Teddy especially will miss you when you go." I would miss him too, but I wasn't going to tell her that. "But I can't have a woman in your . . . condition . . . in my household and around my children. People will talk." I had yet to say a word and I could see this flustered her. I imagined she expected me to plead and beg for my job. When I didn't, she was at a disadvantage. This was a revelation and I drew strength from her discomfort. "I'll give you two weeks' wages if you're out before the boys are up tomorrow."

"Yes, ma'am," I said, finally breaking my silence.

She put her hand on the doorknob but then turned back to me. "There's something else." Again, I waited. "You have some . . . undergarments . . . that I'd like you to give to me." Two red spots appeared in her cheeks. "I think you know what they are."

So she had known. All this time he had been coming up here and she had known. My revulsion for her husband was dwarfed by my towering disgust for her. How could she have let this happen? I looked at her steadily as I said, "Are you sure you want them? They're not very . . . clean."

Mrs. Phillips looked as if she'd been slapped. But she said nothing more, only turned and hurried down the stairs. I waited until she had gone before I went in search of Bitsy so I could say goodbye.

"Let me know where you'll be staying," said Bitsy.

"I will."

"At least you'll never have to see him again. That much is a blessing."

"Who?" She didn't mean Clay, did she?

"Mister Phillips. I know he came to your room. And I know what he did there."

"You do?" I was mortified.

"You're not the first," she said gently. "And you won't be the last either."

After Mrs. Phillips let me go from her employ, I went to the house in the Quarter; I had told Clay what had happened and he said I could remain there while he planned our elopement. He had a cousin who was a priest up in Alexandria; he would marry us. I was uneasy about this—I was Jewish and surely that would matter. But that worry was crowded out by others; Clay still needed to find a way for us to get there and a place where we could stay. In the meantime, he cautioned me to remain indoors and out of sight.

That first week Clay came to see me several times. He brought some pralines in the hope of whetting my appetite, but they were so sickeningly sweet they made me gag. He also brought several books and a couple of large, loose dresses, as my own clothes barely fit me. The next week he came again, this time with a small cameo ring. The delicate profile was set in an oval of platinum that was studded with several tiny diamonds. "It's not a proper engagement ring, but it's been in my family for some time and I thought you could wear it until we can pick one out together." He slipped it on my finger—a perfect fit.

"It's lovely," I said. "Was it your mother's?"

"My grandmother gave it to my sister, but she never wears it. By the time she misses it, we'll be married."

His words reassured me, and after he'd gone, I'd look at the ring—a stand-in for a wedding band—and feel confident in our future together.

But the following week he didn't come at all. As the days passed, I grew more and more worried. Had he changed his mind? Decided to abandon me? Or had something happened to him? I tried to distract myself by reading the books he had brought me—the volume of poetry, the novels by Miss Jane Austen.

But it was useless. My worry had turned to panic, and so on Sunday, I set out for the Phillipses'. I concealed myself some distance from the house, and when I saw them leave for church, I went around to the kitchen and knocked. Luck was with me because Bitsy came to the door. Without uttering a word, she stepped outside, shut the door, and ushered me around the side of the house to the shed where the gardening tools were kept. We went inside; a rake, a broom, and a wheelbarrow were the sole witnesses to our conversation.

"Are you all right?" she asked.

"All right as I can be." I told her where I was staying and how Clay's visits had ended so abruptly and without explanation. "Maybe you can help me," I said. "If you know someone in that house, you can find out what's going on. Perhaps he's gone away. Or he's taken sick."

"Robichaud." Bitsy seemed to be rolling the syllables around in her mouth. "I heard that name before. His daddy is rich." She looked at my belly. "Mr. Clay, he knows about this?"

"Yes. He wants to marry me. Or that's what he said." I no longer had faith that this was true.

"You go back now," Bitsy said. "And stay there. I think I know someone who can tell me. And when I find out what happened to your boy, I'll come to the Quarter and let you know."

"Oh, would you?" I felt hot tears stinging my eyes and I grasped her hand to kiss it. "Thank you, Bitsy. Thank you and God bless you. And I'll pay you for your trouble—"

"Worry about that later," she said. "Now go."

I waited nervously for the rest of the day, and the day after that. Bitsy came knocking the following morning, rousing me from my light sleep.

"Have you seen him? Is he all right?" I asked.

"No, I haven't seen him. But I heard about him. And he's not all right. He's dead."

"Dead!" I sat down heavily on a striped chair near the door. "How is that possible?"

"Yellow fever," she said. "It took him fast. Julie told me—she works for the family. She said it started with chills and aches. He went to bed, but he didn't feel better. He turned yellow and started to vomit. Came up black as pitch."

The word made my stomach, still easily roiled, convulse, and I hurried to find a basin. I came back, still wiping my mouth with a damp cloth. "Are you sure? Maybe it was someone else." She must have made a mistake. Clay couldn't be dead.

"No, it was him. Made sure before I told you."

I closed my eyes against the next wave of nausea. I'd heard people talking about yellow fever. Years ago there had been an epidemic that killed thousands. But I could not reconcile my image of Clay—beautiful, immaculate in his dress and habits—with the horror of the disease.

"Funeral is tomorrow morning."

"Where?" I opened my eyes. "That big church in Jackson Square?" I had seen the grand white edifice of the St. Louis Cathedral, though I had never been inside it.

She shook her head. "Our Lady of Guadalupe," she said. "Over on Conti Street."

I must have looked surprised that Clay's family would choose that church over the far more ostentatious St. Louis. "That's where they bring fever victims," she added. "Then they can take them to the cemetery next door. No one wants to be dragging that corpse—I mean, his body—all over town, spreading the disease."

Corpse. The person who had been Clay was now a corpse. Again, my stomach churned and a sour taste arose in my throat but the impulse subsided. "I want to go," I said.

"Not a good idea."

"You don't understand. I have to go."

She sighed. "I suppose it'll be all right. Just be sure to cover yourself up. You don't want any trouble."

No, I didn't. Before Bitsy left, I tried to give her some money, but she wouldn't take it. "You'll be needing it now," she said. "And maybe one day, you can do a favor for me."

"Anything," I said and hugged her tightly.

I didn't go to bed that night. Instead, I sat in the striped chair, not moving. I had seen death up close before—my father and my mother. And yet Clay's death felt incomprehensible. This was the New World, not the old one. And I imagined that in it, someone like Clay was protected, untouchable. As the night wore on, I began to wonder whether I too might catch the fever; we had been together only days before he became sick. And for a little while I almost welcomed the possibility.

When I saw the sky growing lighter at the window, I washed my face, cleaned my teeth, and wrapped myself in the most generous shawl I had. Then I walked to the church on Conti Street. Red tile roof, stucco and brick, it had a decidedly Spanish look—by then I knew that the Spanish had been here too and they'd left their mark.

I waited at a discreet distance as the black-clad mourners began to arrive. There were so many of them. As they filed into the church, I kept back. I'd seen funeral processions in New Orleans before— musicians playing their instruments as they followed the casket through the streets, people joining in until the procession became a parade, noisy and even exuberant. There was no such exuberance here though. Everyone was somber and quiet.

I saw an elegantly attired couple, he in a tall black hat and she with her face and head swathed entirely in black netting. I moved a little closer, for a better look, sure that these were Clay's parents. Walking right behind were a girl—the sister he'd mentioned—and a young man I guessed was his brother. Just as the last mourners entered the church, a pair of horses came clomping down the street, pulling a covered black hearse, and stopped in front of the church's doors. A group of young men carefully took the coffin from the back and, with solemn steps, carried it inside. I felt faint when it passed me but forced myself to remain standing; I didn't want to attract any attention. I waited a little while and when I heard music, I crossed the street and slipped inside, staying close to the door so I could escape easily if the need arose.

Once when I was a child my mother and I had been walking by a church just as the service was letting out. Through the open doors, I could glimpse some of the brilliantly colored figures painted in panels on the walls. That man with the shield and the lance—who was he? And what about the woman with the sword? The gaunt, mournful figure nailed to the cross that was at the very front of the church was familiar, though—that was Jesus. I felt a rush of pity; compelled by his suffering, I wanted to go inside, touch the image, as if that would somehow alleviate his agony. Before I could, a man in a fur hat and fur-trimmed overcoat—I recognized him from our street— muttered *zhid* and someone else said, more loudly, "Go home, Christ killer." My mother grabbed me roughly. "Hurry up," she said, her grip so tight that my hand ached through my glove.

But no one here seemed to notice me, and my fear subsided. I didn't pay much attention to the service, keeping my eyes on the coffin. It seemed to dominate the space, and the rest of the church's interior was only a backdrop for it.

The priest who'd been officiating stepped aside and a few of Clay's relatives and friends spoke. I continued to stare at the coffin, still not quite able to believe that he was inside. And yet he was. That was why we were all here. When the service came to an end, a very large, white-haired man sat down at the organ and began to play as the pallbearers picked up the coffin once again. The net-swathed woman was attempting to rise from her pew, as if she meant to impede their progress down the aisle, but the man seated beside her wouldn't allow it. Finally, the woman ceased her struggle and the coffin proceeded. What would Clay's mother, or any of them, have said if they'd known that a piece of Clay was going to live on in the child I carried? It seemed essential to tell them.

So I waited until the funeral had concluded and then I discreetly followed them, at a safe distance, to the cemetery next door where Clay's coffin was placed in an aboveground marble vault—the earth did not receive all the dead in New Orleans. And then I continued to follow them, all the way to what I gathered was their home on St. Charles Avenue. With its curving double-gallery bay windows, and pillars that framed an elaborate stained-glass sunburst over the front door, this house made the Phillipses' house seem quite modest. When the family had all gone inside, I went up to the massive front door and rang the bell.

A colored maid in a black uniform and white apron answered. "Servants and trade round the back," she said, ready to shut the door in my face.

"I'm not a servant or a tradesperson," I said.

"Then who are you?"

"Family." It was audacious, but it was not entirely untrue.

She studied me for a moment before saying, "You don't look like family."

"Please," I said. "I need to speak to Mr. or Mrs. Robichaud. It's urgent."

"Wait here," she said and then closed the door.

When she opened it, she was standing with the woman I'd seen at the funeral. Genevieve Robichaud. She had taken off her veil, and her unadorned face was marked by her grief. But she had the same blue eyes as Clay had, and it was into those eyes that I looked as I began my appeal.

"My name is Beatrice Carr. I knew your son," I began. "He gave me this ring." I was still standing on the porch; neither she nor the maid had invited me in.

Mrs. Robichaud looked down with an expression of distaste but then her eyes widened—she had seen the ring. "Where did you get this? Are you a thief?"

"No. I told you—Clay gave it to me."

"How do you know his name? Who are you?" Her voice had scaled up, and she was joined at the door by the man I assumed to be Clay's father.

"What's all the commotion?" he asked.

"It's this young woman. She says she knew Clay. And she has Christina's ring—look!" She grabbed my hand roughly and held it out for him to see.

He peered at down at the ring and then up at me. "I don't understand," he said.

"Neither do I," said Mrs. Robichaud.

"Miss," Mr. Robichaud said, "won't you come in?"

Finally, what I'd been hoping for. He led me to a small but opulent room with green lacquered walls, a leather sofa, and a half dozen or so fringed paisley pillows.

When I sat down and began to speak, I was so nervous that I stuttered at first. My thickly accented English sounded appalling to my own ears but I had no other voice, no other words. "I knew your son quite well," I said. "I loved him and he loved me. He asked me to marry him—that's why he gave me this ring."

"Marry him!" Mrs. Robichaud exclaimed. "That's impossible."

"No, it's not."

"Why would he do that?" her husband asked.

"I told you: we were in love."

"And this so-called love—was it . . . intimate . . . in nature?"

I nodded. "Yes. And I'm going to have a child. His child."

"Ah," Mr. Robichaud said, sitting back against the cushions. "Now I understand."

Mrs. Robichaud turned to face him. "You do?"

"Of course. Young lady—"

"She says her name is Carr. Beatrice Carr."

"Miss Carr, may I ask where you met my son? Was it in . . . the District?"

"No, of course not!" I was insulted but not surprised.

"I mean, young men will be young men, and even Clay might have been curious and wanted to see what you ladies had to offer." He shook his head. "But curious or not, my son was not going to marry a girl like you."

"He loved me." *Luffed me*, it came out.

"You may have thought so. He may have thought so. But marriage . . ."

Abruptly, I stood up, wanting to leave before the tears that had formed splashed down my cheeks. This had been a fool's errand—I should have known that. "I didn't expect you to approve. But this baby I'm carrying—this is your grandchild."

"Don't even say such a thing!" Mrs. Robichaud cried.

"Really, Miss Carr, there's no way you can prove it's Clay's."

"No. But you can't prove that it isn't, can you?"

"Henry, it's true, it's true, how can we ever be sure—"

"Stop." Mr. Robichaud held up his hand. "We'll have none of this nonsense. Not another word. Miss Carr, I'll do you the courtesy of letting you keep the ring—"

"But it belongs to Tina! Don't give it to her, the little harlot—"

"Keep the ring and not report you to the police for theft."

I began walking out of the room and toward the front door, and Clay's father followed me, his hand to his pocket, pulling out his billfold. "Here's a little something to help you out . . . If you are, as you say, in trouble, I'm sure you can use it." He handed me two five-dollar bills. I wished I'd had the strength to crumple and toss them to the floor. But I took them without another word. Then I left. That was the last I saw of your paternal grandparents, Catherine. They might well be alive, along with his sister and brother. But I don't imagine you'd want to seek them out—they didn't want to know my story, and I doubt they would be sympathetic to yours.

I had nowhere to go, no one to turn to. That afternoon, I wandered around until I ended up in one of the poorer parts of the city, where I knocked on doors, offering to do any sort of work—cleaning, laundry, chores of any kind. Finally, someone took me in. She let me stay, and when I had you, she introduced me to your father. I didn't want to let you go, but it seemed the only way, the best way. And looking at you now, seeing what a wonderful young woman you've become, I can see that I was right.

CHAPTER SEVENTEEN

CATHERINE, BEA

Brooklyn, 1924

She'd been born to an unwed mother. Catherine could not contain her shock, and after listening to Bea's lengthy confession, had left the backyard again abruptly, barely saying goodbye. For days after, Catherine went over the story in her mind. Her father must have known some of Bea's background, but how much? Her mother? Most likely not. She would ask them, of course—when she was ready. For now, she would tell no one. Bea was *her* discovery, *her* secret, and she held pieces to a puzzle Catherine hadn't even known existed. A puzzle Catherine now had to solve. The only way to do it, though, was to speak to Bea again.

She showed up unannounced again at the house late one afternoon. Bea invited Catherine to join her out in the backyard. The maid served cold tea and biscuits before withdrawing. Catherine saw a movement at the window upstairs and spotted that girl, Alice, looking down at them. When she saw Catherine looking at her, she stepped away.

"You said the name you chose for yourself was Carr . . . but you call yourself Jones now. Why?"

Bea looked a bit flustered. "I changed it again when we came to New York. I wanted a fresh start. A clean slate."

Catherine thought her response was a bit odd, but she didn't dwell on it.

"My mother didn't care for New Orleans," mused Catherine. "She never went with him when he visited for work or to see his family and she wouldn't let me go either."

"Yes, you told me that."

Catherine was quiet for a moment and then she said, "It must have been hard for you to give me away."

"It was the hardest thing I ever did," Bea said. "So hard, I had to hide it from myself. I couldn't admit it or look at it for years."

"And then what changed? Why did you come looking for me after all this time?"

"The feelings I thought I'd put behind me came clamoring back. And there was so much suffering—from war, from the influenza epidemic. It made me rethink my past, my life. I couldn't stop thinking about you, and about what I'd done. I'm not even sure what I imagined or hoped would come of this. I only knew that I had to find you."

"Well, you've found me, and it seems like you went to considerable trouble to do it. Was it worth it?"

"I can't say yet. You and I—we're intimately connected, yet we're strangers. We don't know each other at all. We can take things slowly and see what happens. That is, if you want to."

"I might as well." She was here, wasn't she? Something had drawn her in. "What have I got to lose?" Catherine reached for her glass and saw the tiny diamonds on the ring sparkling in late afternoon light. "The ring," she added. "If you hadn't kept it, hadn't given it to my father for me . . ."

"I wanted you to have something of mine—I thought the ring would connect us somehow."

"You were right about that," said Catherine. "It was the ring that made me believe you."

The tidy deck of cards that had been Catherine's life was now up-ended, tossed into the air and left scattered. Unlike her parents, her husband, and his family, Bea had nothing invested in whether Catherine picked the cards up and reassembled them in their previous order. She didn't judge, and best of all, she didn't advise. Catherine soon became a regular visitor at Bea's house, spending as much time there as she could. With Stephen she was vague about where she passed her afternoons, and he knew better than to press her. They almost always sat in the small yard out back; the maid would bring them a pitcher of cold tea and a plate of biscuits. Once the maid had left, Bea would produce the bottle of sherry she said she'd had since before Prohibition, and they'd sip it from tiny, ornate glasses. She found she was most comfortable at Bea's, most at ease with herself.

After the day on the bench when she'd first told Catherine her story, Bea listened more than she spoke, and when she did speak, she was measured and calm. Catherine came to appreciate the vestigial traces of her accent, the way she inclined her head when she was considering something Catherine had said, the deliberate way she moved and walked. She couldn't have said whether she liked Bea, or wanted anything more from her than this: the garden, the conversation, the sherry, for Bea always served her a glass. But for the time being, it was enough.

* * *

Bea was surprised at how many of her conversations with Catherine seemed to center on some aspect of being Jewish. At first, Bea was hesitant to discuss the matter. Back in Russia, it had been dangerous to live openly as a Jew. Even the memory of her father's desecrated prayer shawl could bring it all back. Still, in America—and especially in New York—being a Jew seemed less perilous. Yet that fear, which had seeped into her at a formative time, was still there, sediment that remained. She would overcome it for Catherine though; for Catherine, she would overcome a lot.

"I've barely even met a Jew before," Catherine said. "And now I find out that my own mother is one."

"And, according to Jewish law, you're a Jew as well."

"So I am," said Catherine. "Imagine that." Then she added, "Meredith didn't know. I'm sure of it. Maybe my father did, but she didn't. She had a hard enough time with Catholics. Jews were even more . . ."

"Unacceptable? Intolerable?" Bea asked.

Catherine nodded. "She said bad things about them. That they were greedy. Coarse. Not to be trusted."

Now it was Bea's turn to nod. "I've heard it all before. Also—we killed Christ."

"I've heard that too," said Catherine. "But it doesn't make any sense. If God wanted Jesus to sacrifice himself for us, then his dying was part of that plan. Why be so angry over what was preordained?"

"People have been less . . . philosophical about the subject. But Jesus wasn't crucified by Jews—that was a Roman idea. A Roman punishment."

"Maybe it's all for the good," Catherine said.

"What do you mean?"

"Well, why does everyone have to be the same? What's the matter with being different?"

Bea laced her long, elegant fingers; the opal sparkled and blazed. "Why indeed?" she said with a rueful smile. "Here's something else that tends to be overlooked. Jesus himself was a Jew. So were his parents."

"I suppose that's true but I never thought much about it."

"Most people don't."

Catherine prodded her for details that Bea had to reach far back into her memory to supply. Hers had not been the most observant of families, but there had been a festive meal the evening before Rosh Hashanah, when the family cook killed three large capons to serve all the guests who gathered round their table. There had been a dish with raisins and carrots, challah breads baked into round loaves, a honey cake that left a sticky, delicious residue on the plate that Bea would scrape up with her fork when no one was looking. At Pesach, they went to visit her mother's sister, where she sat at the damask-swathed table, fidgeting during the interminable seder, until they were finally, *finally* allowed to eat, the glazed duck, the color of mahogany, resplendent on its blue-and-gold-bordered platter. When they were done, there was the mad rush, all the cousins running through the house in search of the afikomen. She was one of the youngest and never found it, but when her older cousin Mikhail did, he gave it to her so she could claim the prize—a silver coin and a bar of chocolate wrapped in red-and-gold paper that had come all the way from St. Petersburg.

"That must have been fun," Catherine said. "Like hunting for Easter eggs."

"I loved visiting my cousins. We were a gaggle. A tribe almost."

"I missed that," Catherine said. "Just like I missed having sisters and brothers. That's why I wanted to have lots of children. Of course, I'm not going to have any now."

"You lost your baby." Bea knew the story, but it would be different if Catherine told it.

"I did. And I haven't put it behind me." Her expression was fierce. Defiant. "They all tell me that's what I have to do. Look ahead, not back. But I can't. I don't even want to."

"They?" Bea asked.

"My parents. Stephen."

"Your husband?"

"My husband." There was a weighted pause.

"Are you happy with him?"

"I was. But I don't know anymore."

"Why not?"

Catherine looked away. "I don't want to talk about him. I want to talk about you—and what it was like growing up Jewish. What else do you remember?"

Bea would have liked to know more about Catherine's husband, and even to meet him. But it was too soon to raise the idea. So, reaching down into memory's jar again, she tried to come up with the stories Catherine was eager to hear. "My mother lit candles on Friday nights. She was less religious than my father, and sometimes they argued about that. So lighting the candles was a concession to him. I think she liked it though. She had a beautiful silver candelabra that she kept on the center of our dining table. She'd put a lace shawl over her head and raised her hands to say the blessing. I liked to watch her."

"Do you remember the prayer?"

Bea shook her head. "It was so long ago . . ."

"That's too bad," Catherine said. "I'd like to hear it. Learn it even."

Bea said nothing. Losing her baby notwithstanding, life had been kind to Catherine Berrill. She retained an innocence so far from Bea's own experience that she seemed like a creature of a different species. At her age, Bea had lived through—and lost—so much, and by contrast, Catherine still seemed like a girl, intrigued by the novelty of Bea's background. She thought being a Jew was nothing more than an amalgam of quaint or colorful customs, rituals, and holidays, and naively imagined she could assume that identity—or at least the parts of it she liked—with no more consequence than donning an elaborate gown for a costume ball. "Perhaps you will," she said, and leaned over to refill Catherine's empty glass.

"Could you find a way to teach it to me? Look it up in some book or other?"

"Why?"

"I don't know. I'm—curious. About you, your background."

Bea knew she should find Catherine's interest touching. But she didn't. If Catherine probed too hard, dug too deeply, she might uncover bits of Bea's story that had to remain secret, otherwise this fragile thing they were constructing, word by word, sip by sip, would instantly collapse. Still, she didn't want to appear unyielding, to alienate the girl she'd been seeking for so long. "I'll see what I can find," she said, and hoped she could leave it at that.

CHAPTER EIGHTEEN

ALICE

Manhattan, 1924

Alice meandered along Allen Street. She knew she was headed away and not toward the house in Brooklyn, but it was a lovely Sunday afternoon, and the shop was closed, so she didn't need to rush back. Anyway, she knew Bea would be talking to that woman, Catherine Berrill; it seemed like that was all she ever seemed to do these days. Catherine showed up almost every afternoon or early evening, and once she did, Bea was interested in nothing besides her. Alice was annoyed by Catherine's presence and, if she were being completely honest with herself, jealous. Catherine had been to college. She spoke French like they did in Paris, not the smattering of it Alice had picked up in New Orleans. And Bea herself was different in Catherine's presence. She seemed more animated somehow. She almost glowed. No, Alice was in no hurry to get back.

Her morning had been spent on the Lower East Side; by now she was comfortable enough with the city to venture there on her own. Today she had found an unusually rich trove of clothes and fabric: a velvet evening cape trimmed in feathers, a two-piece raspberry brocade with crystal buttons down the back, two lengths of fabric—one a riotous jumble of roses, the other a fine merino wool in a rich shade of goldenrod. She'd also picked up several yards of black braided trim and, best of all, a crumpled fur stole with a cigarette hole on the front.

It was the fur that she was thinking about as she walked. It could be steamed, which would release the wrinkles, and she could add some decorative element to cover the hole. Or she could do something entirely different—a vest maybe? Add it to the bodice of a dress? She would have to get a different set of needles though; she didn't have any that would pierce the thick pelts. Maybe she should head back to Orchard Street . . . But where was she now? She'd veered west and found herself in an entirely different sort of neighborhood.

The buildings were similar to those she'd just left—three- and four-story brick, fire escapes girding their facades—but the shops that filled them were different. Some sold cheese in great, pale gold wheels, and others mostly meat—she saw hams hanging from hooks in the ceiling. There were ones that sold spaghetti, and bakeries whose windows were filled with triple-tiered cakes topped by sugar flowers and sugar birds, most of which were closed. But what were open were cafés, three of them on a single block. Alice was drawn in by the green-and-white-striped awning, the metal tables and chairs—all occupied—on the sidewalk and most of all, by the strong smell of coffee. Oh, how she missed the taste of really good, strong coffee.

Inside the café she chose, the aroma was even stronger and she sat down at the single vacant table. It took a while before a waiter appeared, but that was all right. She needed time to decipher the menu, handwritten on a chalkboard, since nothing looked familiar. Finally, she decided on a caffe latte, which she thought might be like a café au lait, and two long, dry cookies studded with nuts from a pile that sat under a glass dome on the marble counter. The waiter returned swiftly, and the coffee was as delicious as she would have hoped. Finally, someone who knew what it was supposed to taste like. She dipped the cookie into the hot brew to soften it and took a bite. If she ordered yet another one, maybe she wouldn't be hungry for dinner, which suited her just fine; she didn't need to sit through another meal with Bea, listening to her talk about Catherine the whole time.

She began to look around. Two old men played chess at one table; three old women gossiped at another. The group closest to her was the largest, and several tables had been pushed together to accommodate them. Everyone at that big table, boys and girls together, was young, not all that much older than she was, and they looked as if they were having such a good time, talking, laughing, taking forkfuls of pastry from each other's plates with an easy familiarity. She must have been staring, because the boy nearest to her leaned over and said, "Would you like to join us? I'm sure we could get another chair in."

"Oh, I don't know, I mean, I wouldn't want to disturb you or—"

"You're not disturbing us at all. We're a pretty friendly bunch."

"Well, if you're sure that—"

The boy stood, took the empty chair across from her, and squeezed it in next to his. Then he slid her bag, which was on the floor, over to her new seat. "Come on. You can bring your coffee and biscotti." He smiled. "I'm Sheldon, by the way."

"Alice." She sat down next to him.

"Hey, everyone," Sheldon addressed the group. "This is Alice. Say hello."

"Hello, Alice!" chorused a few voices. One of the boys waved at her.

"That's Arthur," Sheldon said. "But you can call him Artie. We all do."

Artie had black hair, and eyes so dark they seemed black too. Alice found him quite handsome, which flustered her, so she turned back to Sheldon. She had only recently started to notice boys with any interest. In the past, boys—well, men really, but she didn't distinguish—had made her uncomfortable and she had kept her distance. "Do you work together?" she asked.

"No. School. We're at NYU."

Alice didn't know what that was, so she just nodded.

"And where are you in school?" asked Sheldon.

"Oh, I don't go to school. I have a job."

"And what would that job be, Miss Alice?"

"I'm a dressmaker."

"Ah, so your bag is filled with your . . . raw materials." He reached down and rubbed a bit of the merino wool between his fingers. "So where do you ply your trade?"

Was he making fun of her? She couldn't tell.

"At a shop in Brooklyn."

"But you're not from Brooklyn," he said. "That accent is a dead giveaway."

"I'm from New Orleans." No point in mentioning Belle Chasse; they were not likely to have heard of it.

"New Orleans! Now isn't that something! I've always wanted to go to New Orleans. Carnival, Mardi Gras . . . people in New Orleans know how to have a good time."

She decided he wasn't making fun of her, just being friendly. Though he wasn't handsome, like Artie, she did want to keep talking to him, and when he invited her to accompany him to a party in the neighborhood, she hesitated for only a moment; some of the girls who had been seated at the table were following along, so it wasn't as if she was going off alone with him.

* * *

"It's just a few blocks away," he said, hoisting her bag onto his shoulder. Artie fell into step with them and Alice tried not to look too pleased. Maybe at the party she'd have a chance to talk to him.

"So you're joining us?" Sheldon asked.

"I thought I would," said Artie. "Maybe Vincent will be there."

"Dream on," said Sheldon, and Artie laughed.

Of course, Alice didn't know who Vincent was or why Sheldon seemed to think he was unlikely to attend, but she kept quiet. They came to an apartment building, where Sheldon stopped and rang the buzzer. "Here we are." Almost at once, a girl popped her head out of an upstairs window and looked down. "Sheldon! You did come!"

"Of course I did!"

"Catch!" The girl tossed something out the window. Alice saw a bit of red streak by and then heard something metallic hit the pavement. Sheldon knelt to pick it up——a key, tied to a red ribbon.

He let them in, and she and Artie followed him up several flights of stairs——was it four or five? she'd lost count——to a hallway where a door was wide open. The girl from the window looked at Sheldon, squealed "I've missed you!" and threw her arms around him.

"Missed you too, Posy," said Sheldon, handing her the key. "You remember Artie? And this is Alice. She's from New Or-leeeans." He stretched out the second syllable.

"Yes, of course. Nice to see you, Artie." Then she looked at Alice. "New Orleans! How glamorous! How divine!"

A brothel, even on Basin Street, was hardly divine, but Alice just smiled. Sometimes it was better to say nothing and let other people do the talking.

Sheldon said, "We'll put your bag in the bedroom and then you won't have to worry about it." She waited until he reappeared. Then he walked her around the apartment, which was filled with chatter, with smoke, with music. Most of the girls had cut their hair to chin length, and some had bangs. One wore a turban and puffed on a cigarette in a long, black enamel holder. When Artie wandered off to talk to Posy, Alice's gaze followed him. Other than hello, he'd said nothing to her. The song playing on the phonograph was "I'm Always Chasing Rainbows," and a couple was dancing, or more accurately swaying around the floor in each other's arms. Even though the whole country had been dry since 1920, it was clear that those two were drunk.

"They've had too many." Sheldon was at her side. "But one's not too many. Can I get you a drink?"

"It's against the law," said Alice.

"Is that what's stopping you? Don't worry. We're all friends here."

"No, that's not it." She'd seen up close what drinking did to people—it made them angry, like the man her mother worked for, or weepy, like her mother. Then there had been the occasional drunk at Bea's—loud, sloppy, or both. Bea had always had them put out.

"Oh, so you're a teetotaler. A regular Carrie Nation."

"It just doesn't agree with me."

"Then I've got just the thing." He led her over to a large, cut-glass bowl surrounded by an array of cups. The bowl was filled with something white and foamy; bits of pineapple floated on the surface. "Here, try this." He filled a cup and handed it to her.

She took the cup. "Is it made with milk?"

"Cream of coconut," he said.

"I love coconut." Alice took a sip. It was sweet. But she detected something else too. "Is there liquor in it?"

"Just a little. Otherwise, it would be too sweet. Liquor gives it a little kick."

"I thought liquor was hard to get around here."

"Not if you know where to go," Sheldon said. "And Posy always does."

Alice sipped again, the coconut almost-but-not-quite masking the harsher taste of the alcohol. The party grew more crowded. Girls danced with boys or other girls, some very well and others quite badly. Someone was singing, loudly and off-key, over the music coming from the phonograph.

Posy had wandered away from Artie and began to talk to Sheldon and Alice again.

"So Vincent's not coming?" he asked.

"Of course she's not, you idiot! She's won a Pulitzer Prize—she has better places to be!"

"But when I invited her after she spoke to my poetry class, she said she'd try."

"She?" Alice was confused. "Vincent is a girl?"

"Edna St. Vincent Millay," Sheldon said. "You've heard of her, right?"

Alice shook her head.

"She's a poet." The disdain in Posy's tone was clear. "A brilliant poet. A *famous* poet."

Alice's face must have revealed her ignorance, because Sheldon said, "Maybe they don't go in for poetry down south. Anyway, it's too bad about Vincent. She's such a dazzling personality. I heard her recite once—it was like a performance. The entire room was filled, not a seat left. I had to stand in the back, but it was worth it."

"Why don't we do a reading?" Posy asked. "Right here. I'm sure I have at least one of her books." She wriggled through the dancing bodies to a shelf on the far side of the room and pulled out a dark red volume. "Found it!" she called loudly. Then she went over to the phonograph and plucked the needle from the record, and some of dancers began to protest. Posy cut them off. "New activity," she announced. "Since Vincent can't be here tonight, we're going to invoke her spirit by taking turns reading from her latest book." She began positioning the people closest to her. "Come on, gather round." Posy continued directing until most of the guests had formed a large, loose-knit circle. "I'll start."

She opened the book and began reading, but Alice couldn't follow. She didn't have an ear for poetry, and when she'd been forced to recite it while at school in Belle Chasse she'd found the experience mortifying. She didn't understand so many of the words, and even those that she did, she couldn't pronounce. Her classmates tittered openly, and even the teacher couldn't hide her exasperation. Alice was mercifully allowed to sit down, though the teasing went on for days afterward.

Everyone clapped when Posy finished; she took a dramatic bow before passing the book on to the next person. More poems, more clapping. They might as well have been reading words written in another language. And soon it would be Alice's turn. She'd have to read in front of all these strangers, college students no less. They would laugh at her, look down on her; it was clear Posy already did.

Extricating herself from the circle, Alice slipped into the bathroom and shut the door. She would wait until the reading had finished before venturing back in there again. In the meantime, she splashed water on her face and smoothed her hair. There was a knock.

"Just a minute," she said nervously. "I'll be right out."

"Alice, it's Artie. I was worried about you."

He was? She'd been wanting to talk to him since she'd gotten here. She opened the door. He stepped inside and shut it again.

"What happened?" he asked.

"I didn't want to have to read a poem," she said.

"Oh, Posy and her parlor games. Don't pay her any mind. We can sit on the fire escape until they're done."

"We can?"

"Why not?"

She followed him out of the bathroom and toward a window that gave onto the fire escape. On the way, he picked up two cups of the punch and set them on the sill until they'd both climbed outside. The day was still cloudless and mild and when he handed her a cup of punch, she didn't say no.

"So you're from New Orleans," he said.

She tensed for a moment, expecting more teasing. But there was none. He was nice, nicer than Sheldon, and unsettlingly handsome. She found herself wanting to touch his face, his hair. These were new feelings; she'd certainly never thought about touching a boy before. If anything, she'd wanted to avoid being touched by one of them for as long as she could. By the time she and Artie went back inside, the poetry reading was over and the phonograph started up again, this time playing "Rock-a-Bye Your Baby with a Dixie Melody."

"This one's for you, New Orleans girl," Artie said. "Come on, let's dance."

Alice stepped into his arms. He felt so solid. So strong.

"You're very pretty, you know," he said softly into her ear. "You have that southern belle charm."

And what, exactly, was that? Had her sister had it? The girls who worked for Bea? But Alice didn't want to think about that. She was feeling happy and a little dizzy too. The room was warm. So warm. She gave herself over to the dance and when it was through, accepted another cup of punch, which she drank very quickly this time. It didn't cool her off though.

"It's so hot in here," she said. "Can we go back out on the fire escape?" That had been nice, the city streets below them, the blue sky above.

"There's someone else out there now," Artie said. "But we can go into the bedroom."

Bedroom. There was something about that word. It was a warning. An alert. But she was being silly—Artie was a gentleman. And besides, there were other people around. There was no danger here.

The bedroom was empty, and so much cooler than the front room.

"Now, that's better, isn't it?" He stepped closer.

"Yes, it is."

His arms moved around her and he leaned down for a kiss. She was startled. She'd never been kissed by a boy before. But he was gentle, not pushy at all.

"There," he said when he lifted his face. "Did you like that?"

"I did," she said shyly.

"Come on then." He took her hand and pulled her down to the bed. Then he began kissing her again and this time, she was kissing him back. She heard a noise at the door. Someone else had entered the room. It was Sheldon. What was he doing here? She expected Artie to stop kissing her but he didn't. Only now she didn't like it because Sheldon was watching—that spoiled everything. She wanted to say so but her tongue wouldn't cooperate. Why was she feeling like this, so muddled, so confused? Could it be the punch? How many cups had she had? She remembered the sweetness, the creamy texture, the bite that followed. She was drunk, that was it. Very drunk.

Another noise. It was a click of some kind, like a bolt sliding into place. That wasn't good. And now she was feeling sick, really sick. Extricating herself from Artie's embrace, she leaned back on the bed slowly until her head found the pillow. The window was open and she could see a rectangle of pale sky, its color just starting to fade. She needed to rest, just for a minute, one little minute . . .

"Are you all right?" Artie asked. His voice seemed to come from a distance.

"Yes, fine . . . I need to rest for a bit. Then I should go home."

"Of course. Put your feet up. I'll unbuckle your shoes so you can get comfortable."

Thank you. Did she say that or just think it? It was hard to tell. She heard murmuring. Artie was still here. Sheldon was right beside him. They were above her, and both smiling, and before closing her eyes, she smiled back.

It was some time later when she awoke and sat up on the bed. She was alone. Looking at the window, she could tell that the sun had gone down. What time was it? Her eyes scanned the room but there was no clock. She had an impulse to lie down again because her head felt so heavy, her temples throbbing. But she wouldn't let herself and instead rose and walked over to the mirror that hung on the wall near the door. What she saw shocked her. Her hair was a mess. She had no idea where her shoes were, but they were not on her feet, and her stockings were down around her ankles. Her blouse was buttoned wrong and her skirt wasn't buttoned at all. Worst of all, she felt sore and bruised, but not anywhere on the surface of her body—the dull pain emanated from somewhere deep within.

Now she really did have to sit back down. What had happened to her? It didn't matter, she just had to get out of there, to get home. Quickly, she buttoned and straightened her clothes, refastened her stockings, and found her shoes, which were way under the bed and furred with dust. There was a brush on the bureau and she used it to tidy her hair. There, in a corner, was her bag of fabric and trimmings. It seemed so long ago that she'd bought those things, like a different day entirely.

Tentatively, she opened the door. The party was still going on, though many of the guests had left. Alice looked for Sheldon and Artie but didn't see them. No one took any notice of Alice.

She descended the stairs and managed to find a subway that would take her back to Brooklyn. The train emerged from its tunnel to cross the river; the water was gray, almost metallic. She'd been gone longer than usual. Much longer. Bea would be worried; what would she tell her? About the party? The punch? Or what Sheldon and Artie may or may not have done while she was passed out on the bed? By the time Alice got to Brooklyn, she had worked herself into a lather. She hurried up the stoop and unlocked the door.

"Bea?" she called out. "Bea, it's Alice. I'm back."

No answer on the parlor floor and no answer upstairs either. Alice turned and headed down to the kitchen. Empty. But the door was open, and there was Bea, sitting in the garden, with a lantern on the table to dispel the dark. She was talking to someone whose back was turned. Alice didn't need to see the woman's face to know it was Catherine Berrill—again.

Standing in the doorway, Alice waited for Bea to break off her conversation. It seemed a long while before she did. "Are you just getting back? Would you like to join us?" she said. "There's some sliced fruit and a bit of cheese left too—"

"No, that's all right. I'm not hungry." Alice was feeling too wretched to be hungry. Oh, why didn't Catherine leave already? Didn't she have a home of her own? All Alice wanted to do was sit with Bea and put into words what had just happened to her—if she could even find such words, because she wasn't entirely sure what had.

Now Catherine turned around as well. "Hello, Alice."

"Hello." Alice knew she sounded sullen, but it was clear she wasn't going to get to speak to Bea alone tonight. "I hope you'll excuse me. I'm tired and I want to go to bed."

Although she went upstairs, Alice didn't go to bed. Instead, she went to the workroom, where she could look down on the two women from the window. They seemed so at ease, so comfortable with each other. It had taken Alice quite a while to feel so natural around Bea; for the longest time, she feared Bea would put her out, and so she had to try extra hard, be extra good, to make sure that didn't happen.

Alice felt the weight of the day, with all its budding hopes, confusions, its strange and unsettling end, weighing down on her. She really did need to sleep. She went to her room and got undressed in the dark, afraid to look at her body, because of what it might reveal. In her mind's eye she could still see the two women seated at the table; it seemed that they would be there always, and that while they were together, there would be no place for her.

Now the fatigue was gone and she felt fully awake. Awake and oh, so very sore, even—no, *especially*—in places that she wasn't accustomed to feeling soreness. Maybe she could take a warm bath. Yes, a bath might be just the thing—

"Alice?" Bea was outside her door, tapping on it gently. "Alice, are you still up?"

"Come in." Alice pulled the chain on the lamp. Catherine must have left. Jesus be praised.

Bea crossed the room and sat down. "I just wanted to see if you were feeling all right," she said. "I thought that earlier you seemed . . . troubled."

"I'm fine," lied Alice.

Bea waited before replying. "Is there something about Catherine Berrill that bothers you? It seems you don't like her."

Everything about her bothers me. And no, I don't like her. But these words remained in Alice's mind. She didn't say them. She didn't dare. "I don't dislike Catherine," said Alice carefully. *I hate her.*

"I'm glad because as I'm sure you've noticed, she's been spending a lot of time here."

"Yes, I've noticed." How could she not have?

"But I'm sure you're not aware of why she's here so often. Of why I want her to be here so often." Alice said nothing, so Bea went on. "Even though we met only months ago, Catherine and I have a strong connection. Very strong."

"Is she part of your past?"

"She may be the biggest part." Bea looked down at her knotted fingers and Alice was aware of how uncomfortable she looked. This alone was concerning; Bea had such self-control. "You see, she's my daughter."

"Your daughter." Alice said the words quietly but inside her head, they were exploding, sending off flares and sparks. "I didn't know you had a daughter."

"Because I wanted it that way. I had her when I was very young. I was alone, and had no way to support her or raise her and I gave her up for adoption. I never talked about her after that."

"How did you find her?"

"I hired a detective. It took a while but eventually he was able to locate her. She was living in Prospect Heights."

"So that's why we came to New York," Alice said, even more deflated. "It was about her." Everything had been about her.

"Yes," said Bea. "It was."

"I see," Alice said. And she did. Catherine was the one who mattered to Bea, the one she cared about, the true daughter. Alice had been a stand-in, only tolerated until the real thing came along. She was not prepared for how disposable this made her feel. How unloved.

". . . this doesn't change anything between us," Bea was saying. "You'll have a place with me for as long as you want one. The shop is doing well, you're doing well in it. You have a future as a dressmaker, if that's what you want."

Is that all Bea could say after such a revelation? Alice didn't know what she wanted, except for this horrible conversation to be over. "I'm glad you told me." That was a flat-out lie.

"I am too," Bea said. "Keeping it from you felt wrong. And I hope you and Catherine get to know each other. Care for each other, even. You might find you have things in common. Things you can share."

Alice didn't reply and Bea stood up. "I'll let you get some sleep now. You said you were tired." And she laid her hand on Alice's arm before she left.

When she was alone, Alice curled up tightly under the light blanket, trying to make herself as small as possible. Trying to disappear. It was a warm night but she was shivering as if she had a fever. Maybe she did. Maybe she had a raging fever and this whole ghastly day—the party, the drinking, the boys, and what went on in that room and now Bea's startling disclosure—was all a dream. But she knew it was nothing of the kind. The party seemed to have happened days or even weeks ago; she couldn't connect with it now. One thing was clear though—she would not tell Bea about it. No, that was the last thing she would ever consider doing.

CHAPTER NINETEEN

CATHERINE

Brooklyn, 1924

Catherine felt Stephen's hand first on her waist, and then, a moment later, move under her white lawn nightdress until it reached the base of her spine, the place she had always loved him to stroke before she turned over and lay on her back. But now his touch was unwelcome, and she remained rigid, hoping he'd think she was asleep. After a brief time, he withdrew his hand, expelling a sigh so loud she was sure she was intended to hear it.

After the baby was born, she had felt sorry that she was rejecting him. But in the months that passed, the feeling had hardened into something like a shell or armor—protection. She lay very still, willing herself to fall asleep, and after a while she did.

In the morning, she heard him first in their shared bathroom, noisily washing up and making exaggerated sounds while brushing his teeth. Then she heard him moving around the room—bureau drawers being closed with a smart smack, armoire doors pushed so hard they creaked on their hinges. He was intentionally trying to rouse her, but once again she feigned sleep. There was silence, and after a while she heard the bedroom door open and then close. She sat up, thinking she'd succeeded. But there he stood, arms folded across his chest, a frown settled on his face. "You were pretending," he said. "Just like last night."

"So what if I was?"

"You keep pushing me away. Why?"

"You know why."

"No, I really don't." The frown dissolved into a beseeching look. "Is it because there's . . . someone else?"

"Someone else?" she spat. "Yes, there's someone else."

He looked alarmed. "Who is it? You have to tell me."

"You know who she is. We buried her in Greenwood Cemetery."

"Catherine . . ." He crossed the room, sat on the bed, and tried to take her hands. She resisted at first but then let him. It made no difference. She still wouldn't forgive him. "You've gone away from me, in spirit and in body. You're out so much of the day, I know because Nettie tells me. And then in the evenings too. I have no idea where you go or what you do. I wander around this house that you created looking for you, missing you."

"I visit Beatrice Jones." Catherine had so scrupulously guarded her secret; why? Now she wanted to tell Stephen everything. To tell them all.

"Who's that?"

"My mother."

"What?"

"My real mother. I was adopted."

"You're not making any sense. Are you sure you're all right?"

"Stop implying that I'm crazy, because I'm not. And I didn't believe her at first either. But she knew about the ring." The little cameo was on Catherine's finger now and she extended it toward him.

Stephen took her hand and began to rub her palm. "I'm not sure what this has to do with anything."

The gentle contact affected her; she hadn't let him touch her in so long. And she needed to slow down. After all, she'd had weeks to absorb this new information, information that had changed her relationship to just about everything and everyone in her life, including him. So she told him the story, trying to include every detail. "And you know what else? She's a Jew. And that means I'm a Jew as well."

"That seems almost beside the point, doesn't it?"

"I don't know. I don't know anything anymore. Except that my parents shouldn't have kept it from me."

"Why?" As far as they were concerned, that woman—Bea, that's her name, right?—was the past. They were giving you a new future."

"She gave birth to me."

"That doesn't make her your mother."

"Then what does it make her? They should have told me just so I didn't have to find out about it in this way—"

"Catherine, you're angry. But maybe not with them. Or not just with them. I know you've been angry with . . . me."

"I was! I am!" she said. "So angry!"

He was still rubbing her palm, gently, insistently. "Why, darling? Can you say?"

"You didn't fight hard enough! You let them eviscerate me without question, without a struggle. And you don't even care that the baby died. You've just gone on with your life, whistling and humming like you haven't a care in the world. I'm not just angry, I'm enraged—"

"You're wrong," he said. "Completely and entirely wrong. I begged that doctor not to do it, pleaded with him to find another way. There wasn't one. Or not one that would have kept you alive. I'd already lost a child. I couldn't lose you too." And then he began to cry, great heaving sobs.

Catherine was shocked. She had never seen Stephen cry. Never. She didn't quite believe that he could. "Don't," she said. "Please don't." She used her free hand to touch his face and he suddenly leaned over and pressed himself tightly to her breasts. He needed *her* to comfort *him*. This was new; he had always been her support, her ballast.

Stroking his hair, she let him sob. But she didn't cry with him. She was tired of crying, tired of being so sad, tired, even of being angry at Stephen—tired of everything and yet, as that day at the shore had shown her, not tired enough to relinquish her hold on life. Since then, she'd been living on two parallel tracks—one that she shared with Bea, which now seemed more real than anything—and one that she shared with everyone else. Today, though, by telling Stephen, she had done something that forced the two tracks to intersect.

His sobs quieted. "I'm sorry you felt I've failed you."

"Maybe I've failed you. Maybe we failed each other. We were both hurt but we couldn't give each other any solace." In truth, she hadn't even tried; it hadn't occurred to her that he'd needed it too, needed it badly.

"I tried," he said. "I tried as hard as I knew how."

"I know," she said. "And I know it's your way to look for a silver lining, to find hope wherever you can."

"It is," he said. "That's what I wanted, more than anything. I knew how sad you were, and that day on the beach, oh God, I'll never forget it—"

"You knew what I was thinking? What I wanted to do?"

"Of course."

"But you never said anything."

"Did you want me to?"

She thought for a moment. "No."

"I was walking a tightrope with you, trying to find the way to lead you out of the darkness but also trying to respect your need to stay in it."

They sat close, his head still resting on her chest. "I want you to meet her," she said finally.

"Meet who?"

"Beatrice Jones, of course."

He lifted his face, still tear-streaked, to look at her. "Meet her . . . Are you sure?"

"Very sure. I want to have a dinner for her, here. My parents too."

"What about my family?"

"Yes, though maybe not all of them at once—I don't want to overwhelm her. But your parents, certainly. What do you think?"

"It will be strange, most likely. More for your parents than mine, but probably them too."

"So you think I shouldn't do it?"

"I didn't say that. No, I think you should."

"You do?" She felt closer to him in this moment than she had in months.

"Yes. In fact, *we* should invite her. The invitation should come from both of us. She's part of you, just like I'm part of you. Our families, well, they'll have to accept it. And I think they will. It will take time. But they will."

"That's the optimist in you talking," she said softly. His head was pressing on her breasts, his mouth near her nipple, separated only by the merest bit of fabric. Her desire for him, a dead thing for so long, was beginning to stir and rustle. The gentle prickle of his beard against her skin, his citrus-infused cologne reminded her of what she used to feel for him—that swooning, that wonderful, glorious letting go—and what she wanted to feel for him again. Yes. She did want that.

He must have sensed the shift because he lifted his face to kiss her. She kissed him back, ardently, and when they moved apart, she pulled her nightdress over her head, a single, bold movement, and then tossed it behind her. She had never been so frank with him before, never communicated her feelings so openly. A man was supposed to initiate, she had been told. But now, as she sat there shivering in the cool morning—it was still August, but the air had the feel of the coming season—she didn't care. "Come," she said softly. "Come warm me up."

Stephen didn't go into work at all that day. After their frenzied, passionate reunion, they slept, woke, and then made love again, this time more slowly. Nettie finally knocked early in the afternoon. "Everyone all right in there?" she called.

"We're fine, Nettie. Just fine." Stephen looked at Catherine and then they both started giggling. "We'll be coming down for lunch in just a bit."

"Very good, Mr. Berrill."

"Are you hungry?" he asked Catherine.

"So hungry!" And she beamed at him, the first smile she'd sent his way in a very long while.

Catherine waited until lunch at her parents' home was finished, and they were all sitting out back on wrought-iron chairs that had been placed in the shade of a massive oak tree. She knew that before she threw herself into planning any dinner, she had to tell her parents that she'd connected with Bea. Instinct told her that this conversation should take place at their house, where they would feel more comfortable, more secure, so she telephoned to let them know that she and Stephen would be coming up on the train for the day.

A pitcher of lemonade sweated on the table, and Meredith was passing around a plate of shortbread. "You seem to be doing . . . better," she ventured. "Your father and I are so pleased." Meredith shot Sebastian a nervous glance.

Catherine felt sorry for her; she couldn't imagine how what she was about to say was going to affect her mother. She'd talked it over with Stephen, trying out many different ways of putting it, but none of them felt right.

"Just wait until we're there," he'd advised. "You'll know what to say then."

She looked at him now and he seemed to be nodding, imperceptibly. The day was hot, but the leafy branches offered ample protection from the sun. Somewhere a bird called and a pair of squirrels chased each other around the trunk of a nearby oak.

"I am feeling better," Catherine said. "So much better that I'm planning a little dinner party."

"A party!" Meredith clapped her hands together like a girl. "What a marvelous idea. You can show off your house. It's so . . . original."

Catherine knew how much Meredith was trying, given her feelings about her daughter's decor.

"Yes, that will be nice but it's really to honor a special person. Someone I want you both to meet," Catherine said. "Well, actually, Father's met her already." She saw Sebastian's smile fade a little and a slightly confused look take its place. "Her name is Beatrice Jones and she's from New Orleans."

"Who is she? Why do you want me—us—to meet her?"

Catherine ignored Meredith's questions; she was looking at her father.

"I never knew her last name," Sebastian said carefully. "Only her first—she was called Bea, though. I do remember that."

"What are you talking about?" Meredith also looked at Sebastian. "None of this is making any sense."

"Beatrice Jones, the woman who gave birth to me. My mother."

Like a pair of startled doves, Meredith's hands flew to her mouth. She turned to her husband. "We agreed we weren't going to tell her. You *promised* me."

"I didn't tell her," Sebastian said.

"That's right. He didn't. Bea hired a detective to track me down and she found me. She rented a house up the street, just so she could be close. We've been spending time together—"

"You what? Catherine, how could you! Keeping such a secret from us—"

"And what about the secret you kept from me?"

"There was no reason to tell you," said Meredith. "None. It was all in the past. We wanted you, we took you, we raised you. We loved you." Her voice quavered.

"And I love you both. Very much. But this isn't about that. It's about my knowing, truly and completely, who I am, where I came from. Instead, you let me live a lie."

"We just didn't want to hurt you," Sebastian said.

"You had family in New Orleans. Business too." Catherine was now remembering. "You used to go there. Mother and I never went with you. Why not?"

"Well, you were in school, and we didn't want to pull you away. And the summers, they were so hot, not a good time for—"

"You didn't want to go," Catherine said, looking at her mother. "And you didn't want me to go, did you?"

"I suppose not." Meredith looked down at her lap.

"They were Catholics in Daddy's family, isn't that right?"

"My father was Catholic," Sebastian said. "His name was Orlando Delgado. He died when I was baby. Later, my mother got married again—to a Protestant. But she loved my father and wanted me to keep his name, so I did—"

"Until Mother persuaded you to change it."

"Delman was just easier to say, to spell. What harm was there in changing it? I felt more comfortable with that name, just like I felt more comfortable with people of my own faith and——"

"And then I went and married a Catholic. No wonder you were so horrified."

"You're getting all excited," Meredith said. "It's not good for you."

No, Meredith was wrong. This *was* good for her. Knowing the truth about herself, her family—how could that be bad? Finding out she'd been adopted explained so many things, like why her mother was so worried about her all the time. Why she didn't favor either of them; they were both fair, and she was dark and had those unusual blue eyes. Blue eyes that came from Clay Robichaud, the man Bea said was her father. "That's why you kept harping on adoption," Catherine said. "Because you'd done it."

"You're right," said her father. "We did. And look how well it turned out—for all of us. It saved our lives, your mother's and mine. So we thought it would be the same for you."

"It's bad enough that all this is being dredged up. Why do I also have to meet this woman?" Meredith asked. "I don't think I want to. No, I'm sure I don't want to."

"I do," said Sebastian. "I remember the first time I met her like it was yesterday. She'd clearly been through a hard time, poor girl. But she was brave and she held her own, yes, she did. I remember that too. I'd like to see her again."

"So see her on your own! Leave me out of it!"

"Don't you understand?" Sebastian gestured toward Catherine. "She's come back to us, Merry. Catherine's come back. You said you would do anything to help her. Well, now's your chance to prove it."

Stephen had been silent this whole time, but now he said, "I know what a shock this must be. But it's so important to Catherine. Can you do it—for her?"

Meredith looked at her daughter, then her son-in-law, and back again. "I don't know if I can," she said. "Maybe one day in the future, but for now? The answer is no."

CHAPTER TWENTY

ALICE

Sitting at the worktable, Alice looked out of the back window and seethed. She was supposed to be sewing—Bea had given her instructions for two new dresses, and there were always alterations—but she was distracted. Down below, Bea and Catherine Berrill were huddled again, the two of them talking, talking, talking. Bea's explanation about why they were always together hadn't made Alice feel better; it had only made her feel worse. The memory—hazy, and all the more frightening for that—of that day in the Village had burrowed somewhere deep inside her. She would tell no one, and she would work to forget that it ever happened.

Alice couldn't actually hear what they were saying, but the murmur of their voices was enough to rile her. As ever, she was excluded from their tight circle; the few times she'd crossed paths with Catherine, she could barely bring herself to be civil. Imagine Bea saying that she hoped they'd become close, that they had things in common.

A burst of laughter from below hit her like a slap, prompting her to look up from the dress whose waist she should have been letting out. What could they be laughing at? Alice knew Bea served her guest— her *daughter*—sherry during these visits. She didn't seem to care that she was breaking the law. Maybe it was the sherry that made even the most humdrum conversation entertaining.

Alice closed the window, not caring that the room would be stuffy. It was better than being reminded of her exclusion. Bea never had time for her anymore. Those long mornings spent together in the workroom had been replaced by notes Bea left for her: *try using that pale green satin with purple trim* or *think about ways to use the dark gray raw silk because we have a lot of it.* The shopping trips they'd made to New Jersey and Orchard Street had petered out too. "You can go on your own now," Bea had said. "You don't need me." But Bea was wrong. Alice did need her, and now more than ever.

It didn't help to brood, so she decided to concentrate on her work. But she put aside the dress she'd been working on and moved on to a new project, one that was all her own. She'd found the fabric—a navy bengaline moiré—on one of her shopping trips and used it to create a long jacket that she'd lined with red silk. The contrast between the two colors was bold and unexpected, even if the lining would only be seen in glimpses. But instead of pairing the jacket with a skirt, Alice decided to make a pair of wide-legged trousers. It was kind of a daring thing to do; women didn't wear trousers, of course, and there weren't any for sale in the shop. All the more reason for her to experiment.

Without a proper pattern, Alice was left on her own, but she had a pair of men's pajama bottoms she'd purchased to use as a guide. By turning them inside out, she was able to see how they had been stitched together. It really wasn't all that difficult, and soon she was ready to cut the fabric. Then she had another idea. What if she used the red silk to line the trousers as well? And extended the lining beyond the hem, adding a touch of brilliance against the subdued navy? Alice became so immersed in the project that when Bea appeared in the workshop, she was surprised.

"I was wondering what had happened to you," Bea said. "You didn't come down for dinner."

"I'm sorry, I just lost track of time."

Bea smiled. "So you finished the dresses?"

"No, not the dresses." Still annoyed, but eager to show Bea what she had been doing, she laid the jacket on the worktable. "This. And this too." She put the trousers alongside it. They were not quite done.

Bea picked up the jacket. "It's very nice, and very well done, but Catherine was just saying that she thought navy was dark for summer."

Catherine was saying! Since when had Catherine's opinion counted for anything having to do with the shop?

". . . especially with that lining, it's going to be heavy . . . And trousers?" Bea was still talking. "I don't know, Alice. They're certainly original. But I don't think our customers are going to like them. We're in Brooklyn, you know. Not Paris."

Alice was crushed. She hadn't realized just how much she'd wanted Bea to exclaim, to praise, to fuss. Until she hadn't. But she certainly fussed enough over Catherine.

". . . and I do wish you had made sure to finish the other two dresses first, especially since I've been asking you to do them."

"Yes, of course." Unable to meet Bea's gaze, Alice looked down at the brilliant bit of red edging the trousers. What a waste.

"Don't you want to eat something? You must be hungry."

"I'm not actually." Alice began folding up the jacket.

"Well, I'm sure you're tired. You can start on the dresses first thing tomorrow."

"I'll do that," said Alice. "First thing."

The next day, Alice woke early and got right to work. She skipped breakfast and had only an apple for lunch, but she finished the two dresses so that Bea would have no cause to complain. Only Bea wasn't here now. Alice was alone. When the shop was busy, she didn't mind because she liked dealing with the ladies who came in. They were generally pleasant and always complimented her on what she was wearing. But when the shop was empty—and as they had moved into the heat of August, this was more often the case— being by herself made her feel isolated. Lonely. She hung the two dresses on a rack in the shop so Bea would see them as soon as she got home.

The doorbell rang, and grateful for the distraction, Alice hurried to answer it. To her surprise, there was a man standing on the stoop.

"May I help you?" she asked. Sometimes a man did come in, looking to buy his wife or sweetheart a present.

The man—young and clean-shaven, wearing a straw boater— pulled a card from the pocket of his checkered coat. "Robert Mueller," he said. "*Brooklyn Daily Eagle*."

Alice looked down at the card he'd handed her and then back up at him. "That's a newspaper, isn't it?" She thought she might have seen it at the newsstand on Seventh Avenue. Or was it something Bea occasionally had at the house?

"Yes, it's a newspaper, one of the city's best, if you don't mind my saying so."

Why would she mind? And what did he want from her?

"I'm looking for Beatrice . . ." He consulted a small pad that he'd also pulled from his pocket. "Beatrice Jones. Would that be you?"

"No. I'm Alice. But Beatrice—Bea—is out. Do you want to wait?"

"Thank you," said Mueller. "I'll do that if you don't mind."

As soon as Bea came in, Alice handed her the card. "There's someone here to see you," she said. "A man from a newspaper."

"Newspaper?" Bea looked at the card. "Did he say what his business was?"

"No. Just that he wanted to talk to you."

Mr. Mueller stepped forward. "Miss Jones?" he said, extending his hand. "I'm from the *Eagle* and I want to do a story on the shop."

"You do? Whatever for?" Bea asked.

"Well, you've developed a little following. Lots of admirers singing your praises. And yours too," he said hastily, looking over at Alice.

"That's very nice, but I'm not sure it warrants a story—" said Bea.

"Oh, but it does. It does. I promise I won't take up much of your time—I just need to gather a little background information and then perhaps you can walk me around the shop and show me some of your most special creations."

Bea relented and, with Alice by her side, recounted how they had come to open the shop. When she got to the part about Rappaport, she asked Alice to fetch the coats. "These were our inspiration," she said. "It really started there." She walked him around the shop, explaining what had been done to various garments, and acknowledging Alice's role in the process. But somehow, she made Alice sound like a servant. Or was Alice just imagining this? Mueller nodded and was jotting down notes on his pad. Bea then sent Alice to the kitchen to fetch some drinks and when she returned, they were both sitting down.

". . . so you got your start in New Orleans," Mueller was saying.

"Yes, I'd come there as a young woman and had some other jobs before I turned to dresses. I had a position in a dress shop for a while."

"Jobs such as . . . ?"

"I had worked as nursemaid, and did some domestic work as well. But I always had an eye for fashion. And Alice—that's Alice Wilkerson—is uncommonly gifted. She can take my visions and turn them into reality."

"I see, I see." He was busy scribbling.

Alice wondered if he would make an effort to find out if what Bea said was true. Wasn't that what newspaper people were supposed to do? Check facts and so forth?

Mr. Mueller closed his notebook. "Thank you so much for your time, Miss Jones." He turned to Alice. "And yours too, Miss Wilkerson. I'll let you both know when the article will run."

There was an especially busy day in September when Bea asked Alice to bring three dresses to a customer who lived in Greenwich Village. Earlier that month, the *Brooklyn Daily Eagle* had published the article and the response had been immediate. Regular customers reappeared after the summer lull, and they were joined by so many new ones. There were even some from Sutton Place, like the pair of fancy ladies who arrived in a big, shiny automobile that sat idling out front while they browsed. Bea was spending more time in the shop now, which Alice appreciated, but Catherine still stopped by on many evenings.

The article had generated so much new business that they would soon need to hire another person to help with the deliveries, but for now, Alice was still doing it. it. The address, on Washington Square, brought Alice to a street she thought she recognized. After she dropped off the dresses, she wandered around until she found the building in which the party had been held.

She stood looking up at the window out of which Posy had stuck her head. Alice was not stupid enough to imagine that she could summon Posy—or Sheldon, Artie, or any of the others she'd met that day—simply by standing there, and yet she didn't move. She tried, vainly, to summon the elusive memories of that afternoon. If she only knew what had happened, maybe she could make some peace with it.

Finally, she started walking again but not toward the subway. Instead, she let instinct lead her back to the street with the cafés, and yes, there was the place she'd joined that table of students, the green-and-white awning looking jaunty in the September sunshine.

The café was filled with customers again, but today the other shops were open too, and she saw women with string bags bulging with onions, carrots, tomatoes, and loaves of bread. Boys played at something with a stick and a ball in an empty lot; she heard their gleeful shouts when one of them got a hit. Another knot of boys was hunched over a game of marbles; a trio of girls took turns jumping rope, chanting in unison.

Mother, mother, I am sick
Send for the doctor quick, quick, quick.
Doctor, doctor, shall I die?
Yes, my darling, by and by.

What a gloomy rhyme, she thought, hurrying away and then stopping in front of a bakery window. She was hungry and everything tempted her, including the aroma of freshly baked bread, but before she could go in, she heard a crash and turned around.

There on the sidewalk was a woman, old, who had evidently been trying to water a window box filled with geraniums. The watering can must have slipped from her grasp, because it was now on the sidewalk, water spreading everywhere, including under Alice's feet. "Are you all right?" she asked.

"Yes, yes," the woman said, a thick accent coloring her words. "But what about you? Did your shoes get wet? Be careful."

Stepping over the puddle, Alice righted the now empty can and handed it back to the older woman.

"I shouldn't have filled it so full," she said, shaking her head. "I was trying to save a trip up and down the stairs. And now look. I've just made myself more work."

"Let me help you," Alice said and followed the woman up to a second-floor apartment, refilled the watering can, and then went down to water the geraniums.

"Thank you," the woman said when Alice returned with the can. "You're a good girl. A very good girl. Let me give you something for your trouble."

"No," Alice said. "Please no. I was glad to do it."

"Are you sure?"

"I'm sure."

"All right, then. I'm lucky you came along. You live around here?"

Alice shook her head. "I live in Brooklyn."

"I don't know Brooklyn," the woman said. "I've been in this neighborhood for thirty years and I hardly leave it. This is my shop."

Alice only just noticed that the geraniums sat below an oversize window onto which the words SCORCIO'S TAILORING AND MENDING were painted in curling black script.

"Are you . . . ?"

"Giovanna Scorcio. Tomasso—that's my husband—is the tailor. I do the mending."

Alice looked into the shop, where a shiny black Singer sat on a table surrounded by tools of the trade—pincushions, tape measure, shears. Spools of colored thread stood neatly on a shelf behind it.

"Nice to meet you, Mrs. Scorcio. I'm Alice Wilkerson."

"Well, if you come back this way again, you stop by and see me," Mrs. Scorcio said. "Let me at least get you a pastry. Napoleon, éclair, cannoli—they're all good."

"Next time," Alice said. She'd been gone long enough; she had work to do.

"All right. Next time," said Mrs. Scorcio.

As soon as Alice returned to the shop, Bea went out. Taking her seat at the sewing machine, she reached down into the alterations basket; it was always full these days. The unfinished navy trousers were stashed in her room. She wasn't going to finish them anytime soon. Or maybe ever. There was so much else to be done—too much really—and she felt overwhelmed. When the telephone rang, she expected it to be one of the customers asking when her dress was being delivered. Instead it was Mr. Mueller from the *Brooklyn Daily Eagle.*

"Hello, Miss Wilkerson," he said.

"Hello, Mr. Mueller. Let me get Miss Jones for you. It will only take a minute."

"I didn't call to speak to her. I called to speak to you."

"Me?"

"Yes. The article got such a nice response that my editor wanted me to do a follow-up piece about you. You'd be a nice human interest story. Young dressmaker-as-apprentice, learning her craft from an expert—"

"Bea's not an expert." The words just seemed to have popped out, unintended. She had not meant to sound so . . . resentful.

"No?" His tone registered surprise. "She certainly seemed to know a lot about fashion, and she said she had experience in New Orleans."

Bea knew a lot about fashion? Apparently not enough to appreciate Alice's very forward-thinking trouser suit. One day women, fashionable women, would wear such garments. Alice was certain of it. Bea was just wrong. "Oh, she had a lot of experience in New Orleans."

There was a pause. "She said she'd worked in a dress shop. Where was it?"

"Basin Street." Again, the words seemed to leap out of her mouth, unbidden; what was wrong with her?

"Basin Street," he repeated thoughtfully.

Alice regretted her reply immediately. Basin Street was known well beyond New Orleans, and he might know what for.

"And you two met exactly how? She said your mother was her friend . . . ?"

"Well, yes, but . . ." Alice stumbled her way through the rest of the conversation, one lie tripping over another. Finally, she told him she heard the doorbell—yet another lie—and hung up the phone. She had no idea what he would make of what she'd said.

She tried to return to work but was too unsettled to concentrate. Finally, her guilt got the better of her and she picked up the telephone, asking the operator to dial Mr. Mueller's number.

She would take it back, every last bit of it, and tell him that she didn't want to be featured after all. But the reporter was not at his desk; an impatient-sounding man asked if she wanted to leave a message.

Alice didn't know what to say to that. She wanted to speak to Mr. Mueller, she truly did. But if he called back, there was a good chance Bea would answer, and how would Alice explain why she'd called him in the first place?

"No message," she said at last. "I'll just try him again."

"Suit yourself, girlie." And then he hung up without saying goodbye.

CHAPTER TWENTY-ONE

ALICE, CATHERINE

Abraham & Straus had to be the most elegant store in all of Brooklyn, if not of New York. White-gloved attendants ran the bronze elevators. An interior courtyard lofted up to a series of skylights above, and the elaborate system of pulleys hanging from the intricately carved ceilings whisked shoppers' money into the store's silver vault. The store was so glamorous that it even had live mannequins, beautiful girls modeling the latest fashions, in its front windows.

Alice loved coming here; it transported her to some other realm, far from the prickly reality of her own circumstances. Dazzled by the spectacle, she moved around the ground floor. She knew that upstairs there was a fur salon that must be a far cry from Rappaport's showroom, and an art gallery, but for now this was enough. She wandered over to a counter featuring costume jewelry—glittering, frivolous things studded with beads and fake jewels. Sidling her way into the knot of women, she waited until the young and harried salesgirl noticed her. "Is there something you'd like to see?" she asked.

"The pins, please," Alice said.

"Which ones?"

Alice didn't actually care—one was as good as another—but she pretended to consider the options. "The parrot, the heart, the pig, the flower, and the circle. And oh, that bracelet there, yes, the enamel one."

"You certainly like pins," the salesgirl said. She brought out the items. Alice picked up the parrot. Hideous, but what did it matter? She wanted it, she wanted it desperately. The salesgirl was watching her closely.

"Excuse me." A woman to her left accidentally bumped her, and Alice stepped aside. "That's a darling little pin," the woman said. "If you're not taking it, may I have a look?"

"Of course," Alice said.

The salesgirl turned to get the mirror that was on the far end of the counter, and Alice knocked the remaining pins and the bracelet to the floor. In the confusion that ensued, she was able to take the heart and slip it into her shoe, where it was uncomfortable, but not uncomfortable enough for her to remove it. Then she quickly walked away. The salesgirl might not remember the number of pins she'd brought out. And she might think one of them had skittered off somewhere. In any case, Alice would be long gone by the time she figured it out.

Flushed with her success, she moved on to a counter that sold hair ornaments. There were no customers here, but the two saleswomen were deeply engaged in a conversation. Shouldn't one of them have gone over to help out with the jewelry? Alice felt a pull toward a black velvet bow attached to a band. It was too big for her pocket, but she deftly took it and put it in the bag she carried, making sure to push it as far down as she could, and then covering it with her scarf to conceal it from view.

Next, she took a curved marble staircase down to the food hall, where she was overwhelmed by the choices—nuts, confections, tins of cookies and chocolate, delicacies of every kind. Her gaze settled on a round box of violet-flavored candies. Without stopping to think, she took them, as well as a square box that contained six chocolate creams, and best of all, a tin of caviar that cost five dollars. She'd tried caviar in New Orleans, where Bea had sometimes served it on New Year's Eve, and found the slimy, salty taste disgusting. But the tin itself was a gorgeous thing, red with a silver fish leaping from whitecapped blue waves.

Someone was offering petits fours samples from a tray, and although they were too sweet and the icing stuck to her teeth, Alice ate two of them, her heart slamming with excitement, with shame, with the terror that she could be caught. She should go now, this minute. Instead, she found herself taking two small wheels of Camembert, each in a round, twine-tied wooden box, and adding them to her bag. There. Something that had been coiled tightly inside her had loosened.

She went back up the curved staircase, and toward the exit. But just as she got there, she felt a hand on her arm, and looked up to see a nicely dressed woman wearing a wide-brimmed felt hat and carrying a large parcel. She looked like just another shopper, but Alice had the feeling she was not. She stepped back, quickly calculating how she could elude the woman by retreating into the store and making a dash for a different exit. But they were quickly joined by a man in a blue jacket with a white carnation in his buttonhole who clearly worked for the store too. "I'll need you to come with me," he said quietly.

Realizing she was trapped, Alice meekly accompanied him. The woman in the hat followed just behind. Alice's panic began to rise like an incoming tide. Would they call the police and cart her off to jail? Her mother had been taken to jail several times. Usually it was when she was drunk, and she didn't go easily; once, she'd cursed and yelled so much that the policeman snapped handcuffs on her wrists.

It didn't seem to bother her; it was Alice who had gone scarlet with mortification.

The man with the carnation touched her elbow, indicating that she should turn left. They had reached the bank of elevators, and as doors slid open and closed, a fluctuating cluster of people stepped in and out of the cars. Spying an exit that led to one of the side streets, Alice took a chance and darted away from the man and his companion, who had to dodge several shoppers in order to chase her. Then she dropped her bag containing some of the stolen goods on the floor, causing the man to stumble over it. The woman helped right him and that brief delay gave Alice the advantage she needed. She sidestepped a pair of dapper gentlemen and shoved a large woman out of her way. "How rude!" She heard the woman's indignant voice behind her but Alice was going, going, streaking toward the doors that were a beacon to safety. To freedom. But before she could escape, another man wearing a carnation blocked her path, giving her two original pursuers a chance to catch up.

"You're coming with us." The first man gripped one of her arms tightly enough to make it hurt, and the woman with the hat gripped the other.

Alice saw that with the two of them holding her, she wasn't going to get away. And as she rode beside them in the elevator, she saw that the woman had recovered the bag with all the things Alice had tried to steal. They got off on the top floor, where the ceilings were lower and the entire ambience far less posh than below. The man with the carnation sat at a desk, across from Alice; the woman in the hat sat beside her. Between them was the bag of goods.

"Young lady, we've been watching you for a while today. It seems like you were on a bit of a spree, and now you're in trouble. Big trouble. What do you have to say for yourself?"

What could she say? Alice looked down at the bag. There was nothing in there she actually even wanted; why had she gotten herself into such a horrible predicament?

"Cat got your tongue?" he said. "All right. Let's try this a different way. What's your name?"

Alice remained silent.

"You'd better tell me," he growled.

The woman gave him a reproving look. "Why don't you tell us your name, dear? It will go better for you if you do."

She sounded nicer than the man; maybe she would understand. But how could Alice hope to explain behavior to them that she couldn't explain to herself?

"Come on now," the woman coaxed. "You must have a name and I'll warrant it's a pretty one."

"Alice," she choked out. "Alice Wilkerson."

"There, that's a start." The woman looked at the man as if to say I-told-you-so. "Now can you tell us the names of your parents?"

"My parents are dead." That much was true.

"Oh, I'm sorry," said the woman. "So the name of your guardians, then. You look too young to be on your own."

"I'm older than I look and yes, I am on my own, all on my own—"

"Where?" The man threw that word at her as if it were a stone. "Where do you live?"

Alice fell silent again. If she told them her address, they would call Bea and she couldn't bear that. As awful as this exchange was, Bea finding out about it would be even worse.

"If you refuse to cooperate, I can call the police. Maybe a night in a jail cell will change your mind."

"He's right, you know," said the woman. "Store policy about shoplifters is very strict and so—"

"Her name is Beatrice Jones. My guardian." Alice didn't say *mother* because Bea had never been that to her. Bea was generous, Bea was fair. But she held back; it was like she kept her heart on a leash. Alice's own mother might have yelled, might even have struck her. But she had been free with her caresses; Alice remembered her mother plaiting her hair, fixing the Cream of Wheat just the way she liked it, with sugar and a drizzle of cream, gathering her in for a hug or pulling Alice onto her lap. "We live on St. Marks Avenue."

The woman and man exchanged looks and Alice saw the woman nod ever so slightly. So she hadn't been nice, not at all. She was just pretending.

Waiting for Bea's arrival was excruciating. Would she berate Alice in front of her interrogators? Tell her she had to leave the house? But when she got there, Bea didn't raise her voice or show any anger at all. If anything, she was apologetic and conciliatory, offering to pay for the stolen items. Since they had not actually left the store, the man and woman told her it wasn't necessary. Her manner disarmed them both, and they were willing to let Alice go without pressing charges. "But she's not welcome here ever again," said the man. He turned to Alice with a hard stare. "Do you understand? Never."

"I understand." Alice's voice was barely more than a whisper.

The trip home, in a taxicab Bea had hailed for them, was silent. Once at the house, Alice wanted nothing more than to slink upstairs to her room and remain there for the rest of the day. Bea, however, broke the silence and asked Alice to please join her in the workroom, where the maid brought up a tray with two cups and a pot of tea. Bea poured a cup for Alice, clearly not remembering that Alice didn't drink tea, never had. Somehow this minor lapse felt unbearably wounding.

"Why?" was all Bea said. And when Alice said nothing, she continued, "Why did you need to steal, Alice? Don't I give you everything
you need? And an allowance besides?"

It was true. Alice never went without anymore, not like when she
was a little girl. Bea had even urged her to open a bank account,
though she hadn't done it; having money of her own was still such a
novelty that she preferred keeping it close at hand, where she could
count it whenever she wanted.

"Can you explain it to me? Because I don't understand."

Alice just looked down at the tea, which she hadn't touched. "I
don't drink tea!" she blurted out. "I hate tea!"

"Alice, what does tea have to do with anything? What's the matter
with you?"

Alice was trembling now. "I'd like to be excused."

"But we haven't finished talking. We've barely started."

"I have nothing to say." Alice had never spoken like this to Bea;
she had never spoken like this to anyone. "Are you going to ask me to
leave? Put me out?"

"Why no," Bea said, and seemed surprised. "I'm not going to do
anything of the sort. But I would like to know why—"

"If you're not going to kick me out, I'm going to go upstairs. Please.
Just let me go upstairs." And then she left the room without another
word.

After that, she and Bea were painfully cordial with one another. Alice
sensed that Bea was mystified by her, even a little bit afraid of her.
And she found she liked the feeling. But despite the mortification of
having been caught shoplifting, she felt compelled to rifle through
Bea's things when she was alone in the house. Bea! It was despicable,
but Alice's hands had a will of their own, and sought a coin here and

there. A single glove—who stole just one glove? Then it was a dollar bill from the top dresser drawer where Bea kept her money. While rooting through the drawer, Alice found a showy pair of faux-pearl earrings and a matching choker wrapped in tissue. She recognized them as leftovers from Bea's Basin Street days; Bea never wore them anymore. Alice felt she had to have them, and when she left the room, she did.

* * *

Now Catherine could throw herself fully into her plans, even if Meredith wasn't going to be joining them. She consulted with Nettie on the menu, changing her mind several times, placed orders with the florist, also subject to several changes, and asked her mother-in-law for advice about the menu. Then there was the issue of Alice. She supposed she had to extend the invitation to her as well; not to do so would make a statement. The wrong sort of statement, as if she had taken a position against a child. Alice was, after all, just a girl. But she was so unpleasant, even sullen, and had made no effort at all. Catherine would invite her, though. For Bea's sake.

The day before Catherine's dinner was to take place, Bridget paid her a call. She'd already told her sister-in-law about the discovery of this family member and her plans for dinner, explaining that although this wasn't the ideal moment for her to be introduced to Bea, she hoped there would be other occasions.

"Lovely to see you as ever." Catherine kissed Bridget on the cheek, as was their custom. "But I don't have all that much time. I need to discuss the desserts with Nettie. I know she'll be offended if I order it, but there's a new bakery on Union Street and they have something called a praline cake—pralines are a New Orleans specialty, you know?—and I thought it would be a nice nod to Bea's life there."

"I don't think you want to make any references to Bea's life in New Orleans." Bridget looked uncommonly serious, her freckles quite pronounced against her pallor.

"No? Why not?"

"Then you haven't seen it."

"Seen what? Bridget, are you unwell? You look—ghostly."

"Here," said Bridget, handing her a rolled-up copy of the *Brooklyn Daily Eagle*.

"Oh, the article about the dress shop. Yes, I thought it was very nice too. Bea says it's brought her a lot of business."

"Not this article."

"Whatever are you talking about?"

"Look. It's on the front page."

Catherine did as Bridget asked, puzzled until she saw the headline. PROSPECT HEIGHTS DRESSMAKER REVEALED TO HAVE SCANDALOUS PAST. As she quickly scanned it, certain words came hurtling off the page as if they were buckshot. *Prostitute* was one of those words. It was repeated numerous times. Also *madam* and *brothel*.

"This can't be true." She thrust the paper back at Bridget. "These are lies, everyone single one of them. Nothing but filthy, disgraceful lies. She can sue for libel. She *should* sue. Has anyone spoken to Gregory? I'm going to get in touch with him immediately . . ." Gregory Murphy was Molly's husband; he had a small law practice on Montague Street near the courthouse.

"Catherine," Bridget put a hand on her arm. "I'm afraid all these things are . . . well, they're true."

"How would you know? You've never even laid eyes on her! If you had, you'd never believe this smut-sheet, this *rag*. Not for one minute."

"I've spoken to Gregory. He knows a couple of people at the paper, and he called to check. The information came from a reliable source."

"What reliable source?" Catherine asked.

"That girl she lives with. I believe her name is Alice."

Alice—the girl Bea rescued, the girl Catherine had never liked. Could she have made all this up? If so, why? None of it made any sense. "They based this whole libelous article on the word of a young girl?"

"Of course not. Gregory said that the reporter did his job and made multiple calls to substantiate the claims. He talked to a lot of people. He even found photographs—he went down to New Orleans to research the story."

Catherine was still holding the paper, but now she dropped it to the floor. She'd throw it out immediately, but it didn't matter whether she threw it away or burned it so that nothing remained but ash. She'd never be able to forget—or forgive—the horrible, disgraceful things she'd learned about the woman who had given birth to her. Not ever.

CHAPTER TWENTY-TWO

BEA

Bea was surprised not only by all the new business the newspaper story had generated, but also equally by her own reaction to her success. The shop had never been a goal in itself; it had been a decoy, designed to lure in Catherine Berrill, and to a lesser extent, a way to give Alice's days some structure and purpose. But now it had become a prize all its own, and she took immense pleasure in designing new garments and gathering the materials that served as both source and inspiration. She'd made several more trips to the Lower East Side, as well as to flea markets around the city, persistent in her search for things she found interesting, offbeat, and unexpected. A fabulous magenta-and-teal panel that had no doubt been a drape or curtain in some elegantly appointed home, a banquet-size tablecloth of impeccably tatted lace, a woven serape, a heavily embroidered caftan that would have been at home in the souks of Marrakesh—these were the treasures that fired her creative spirit.

The shop was now so busy that she was actively looking to hire another seamstress as well as a delivery person. There was too much work for Alice alone, and Bea didn't want her to be unduly burdened. Also, she'd started to feel uncomfortable around Alice, even more so after the day she'd picked her up from the department store, so she wanted to have someone else in the house to dispel the tense atmosphere. Their relationship had changed, that was certain, but into what was still unclear. Alice was growing up, and growing away, and Bea was surprised by the sadness this caused her. It would have been easy to paint Alice as ungrateful and disloyal. But maybe, just maybe, Bea had played a part in the rift. She knew herself to be reserved and distant; reserve and distance had been her armor for so long. Alice could have misread her behavior, especially since they'd come to Brooklyn. On Basin Street, they had not been alone together, so reliant on one another's company.

Maybe it was not too late to change things, though. Bea went out of her way to seek out Alice's company even when they weren't working. She made sure Alice knew she wanted her to attend the dinner Catherine was planning. But Alice remained stubbornly aloof. She wouldn't go to the dinner. Pressed for a reason, she offered none. Of course it had to do with what had happened at Abraham & Straus; Bea knew Alice must still be mortified, and needed to keep her distance to salvage what shreds of pride she could. But Bea had been shaken by the incident as well. How had she not seen that there was so much churning below Alice's meek exterior? What else had she missed? She was almost relieved when Alice continued to rebuff her overtures; she really didn't know how to deal with this new side of her.

It was October, and just a day before the dinner was to take place, when Bea went downstairs into the shop to find things a bit out of order. Nothing alarming—just a few dresses that had been left on cushions, and one that had slid to the floor. Some of those on hangers were pulled at odd angles while others had been crammed together. Alice generally tidied both the shop and the racks before she went upstairs for the evening, but clearly she hadn't done so last night. And come to think of it, she was nowhere to be seen this morning.

Bea went over to open the shutters at the front windows and when she did, she saw a sizable group of women outside. Customers? So early . . . and so many? That was highly unusual. Unprecedented, actually. She looked more carefully. Several were carrying signs. SHOP OF SHAME. SOUTHERN FILTH. When they noticed the shutters opening, they started to yell and even through the closed windows she could hear the cries of *slut, whore,* and the calls for her to be evicted, banished, tarred and feathered. And then there was the word that Bea knew always hovered at the periphery—*kike.* Quickly, she closed the shutters again and tried to calm the exploding rhythm of her heart.

What was happening? Where was Alice? Was she safe? Carefully, Bea crept toward the window again. Some of the women—the crowd consisted mostly of women—were trying to come up the stoop to the front door but were stopped by a pair of police officers. Police! Why had they been summoned? Were things that out of control?

Moving away from the window, Bea sat down and tried to focus. This was not the first time she had been under siege. Far from it. She had to be calm, so she could think. Clearly, these were references to her past in New Orleans. But how had the information been transmitted to these women? That was the missing link. And Alice. Where in the world was Alice?

Sitting there was doing no good. Bea went back upstairs and began to pack. She didn't know where she would go, but her instinct for flight was well honed. As she was gathering her things, the doorbell rang; in her present frame of mind, it made her jump. At first she wasn't going to answer but the bell kept ringing, the sound seeming ever more insistent. She went downstairs and cautiously peeked through the lace curtains that covered the glass panels.

The first thing she saw was Officer Duggan. He was a regular presence in the neighborhood and she'd gotten to know him. When he learned that she and Alice were on their own, he'd developed a protective, almost avuncular attitude toward them. Why was he here now? To arrest her? She stood there frozen until she heard a voice outside. "Miss Jones? Are you all right in there? It's Mr. Bonville, the rental agent. I'm here with Officer Duggan. When I saw the crowd, I went over to the station house and asked him to escort me here. I need to talk to you."

"I'm afraid to open the door," she said. "There are so many of them out there."

"Miss Jones, I won't let anyone in," said Officer Duggan. His Irish brogue was as thick as ever, and somehow reassuring. "And I've got backup in the street. This group may be noisy, but they aren't dangerous."

Cautiously, Bea unlocked the door. Immediately the swell of angry voices rose up. *There she is, there she is! The dirty kike whore! Throw her out! Evict her!* Mr. Bonville slipped in and Bea locked the door again. "Let's get away from here," she said and brought him downstairs to sit in the kitchen, which was empty. So the cook was gone too. Something had happened and both the cook and Alice knew what it was. Only Bea remained in the dark.

Seated across the table from him, Bea knotted her fingers tightly. "What in the name of God is going on? It seems that nothing less than my head on a pike will satisfy them."

"Oh, Miss Jones, I'm sorry, I'm so sorry. Nothing like this has ever happened before and I really didn't know what to do. But after that article—"

"What article?"

"You mean you didn't know?"

"Know what?"

"Oh my, oh my." He reached into his briefcase and handed her a newspaper. It was the *Brooklyn Daily Eagle*. "Read it," he said. "I'll wait."

Bea said not one word, not a single word, while she read. It was all there: her early life in Russia, her illegitimate child, how she came to find herself in the District, the years on Basin Street. Thank God they didn't mention Catherine by name—at least there was that. When she was finished, she pushed the paper back toward Mr. Bonville.

"It came out yesterday, and the daughter of the owner of this house, she lives over on Plaza Street, read it. Then she cabled her father in Europe. The long and the short of it, Miss Jones, is that they want to break the lease and for you to vacate the premises as soon as possible."

"Can they do that? Legally, I mean?"

"Yes, they can. There's a morals clause, and something like this"— he touched the newspaper—"is grounds for termination. He wants you, and the dress shop, out, effective immediately."

"Out," Bea repeated. "Immediately."

"It's for your own safety, Miss Jones. Surely you can see that."

"Oh, I can see that all right. I can see a lot of things." She stood. The sooner she dismissed this odious little worm, the better.

"I'm glad you understand," Mr. Bonville said nervously. "And if you need help with finding a place to stay—"

"I won't be needing any help from you," she said. "I can manage quite well on my own. I'll be out today, but I will need to come back to get my things. I'm not giving up my keys until I do." Though there wasn't much—it was only the dresses she wanted. The dresses she and Alice had collaborated on, created together. Alice. Where was she now? And what was her connection to the commotion, this up-roar? Somehow, Bea was starting to get a sense of what that might be.

"Oh yes, of course, of course." He was clearly relieved she wasn't putting up more of a fuss. But why would she want to stay here now, anyway? Her mother had known when it was time to leave; even now, all these years later, her behavior had set an example Bea was smart enough to follow.

Mr. Bonville emerged from the house where Officer Duggan awaited him. Police backup had arrived and the crowd had been dis-persed though some of the signs had been left behind; Bea looked out the window to see the words DIRTY JEW staring up at her from the gutter.

She finished her packing and then sat down to write a quick note, which she placed in an envelope, and then exited through the kitchen door into the backyard, note tucked safely in the single bag she car-ried. There was no access to the street this way, but she hoisted the bag over the back wall and then managed to get over it herself too, coming down hard on her ankle. She'd noticed that the owners of a house that abutted hers had a basement door that was often left open, perhaps to air out a musty space. She had a hunch it wouldn't be locked now, and she was right. Bea walked in, went through the basement, up the stairs, and waited for a time on the landing until she had determined all was quiet. Then she darted the short way from the ground floor hallway to the door and outside again, leaving the door unlocked behind her.

She found herself on Prospect Place, where there were no signs of the crowd, but still she felt anxious, as if she were being hunted. She'd taken the precaution of donning a wide-brimmed hat with a heavy veil, hoping it would conceal her identity, at least until she reached Catherine's house, which was only a short distance away. Once there, she walked up the steps and slipped the letter under the door. If Catherine hadn't seen that article yet, it was only a matter of time before she did. Bea had no way of gauging what her reaction would be, or how she would respond to the request in the letter.

She continued walking, out of Prospect Heights and into neighboring Park Slope, which felt safer in this moment. Her progress was slowed by her ankle, which had started to throb, and she hoped it wouldn't swell. Finally, she reached the Third Street entrance to Prospect Park, where a pair of full-size bronze panthers stood sentinel. Although they appeared identical, upon closer inspection, the two were distinguishable from each other—their stances differed, as did the inclination of their ears. Yet both were self-possessed and proud. Bea sat down on a bench below them, relieved to give her ankle a rest. Looking up at their powerful, muscular bodies, their implacable gazes, she tried to draw strength from their presence as she sat waiting—and hoping—that her daughter would arrive soon.

FALL

CHAPTER TWENTY-THREE

ALICE

Little Italy, 1924

By now, it was easy for Alice to find her way back to the street with all the cafés, but she walked right past them and straight into Scorcio's Tailoring and Mending. An old man was bent over the shiny black Singer; he glanced up when he heard her come in.

"How can I help you?" He had a full head of steel-gray hair and steel-rimmed glasses.

"I'm trying to find Mrs. Scorcio," she said.

The man looked her up and down. "Can I tell her who's asking for her?"

"Alice," she said. "Alice Wilkerson."

He nodded, as if this meant something to him, and then rose, with some difficulty, to shuffle off behind a faded curtain. She heard him calling his wife's name up the stairs. He came back out. "She'll be down. You want to sit?"

She did. Mr. Scorcio went back to his sewing while she looked around. She could see the geraniums beyond the window and inside, on the sill, an orderly arrangement of small plants. Alice didn't know their names, but she could see they were well tended. The opposite wall was dominated by a large crucifix, which was surrounded by several illustrations of the Virgin Mary and other saints whose names she didn't know.

Finally Mrs. Scorcio appeared, smiling. "It's you!" she said. "You came back. I hoped you would." The warmth of her greeting made Alice want to weep. "You want that pastry now? Tomasso can mind the store while we go next door to Paulo's. He's my cousin, and we always eat and drink for free."

"Thank you, but I'm not here for a pastry," she said.

"No? What then? A sandwich? He makes panini too—cheese, salami, prosciutto—what do you like?"

"A job." Alice had to make an effort to keep her voice level. "I need a job."

At this, Mr. Scorcio looked up from his work.

"A job," said Mrs. Scorcio. "Doing what?"

"Sewing." She realized she'd never mentioned the work she had been doing for Bea. "I'm a very good seamstress. That's what I was doing in Brooklyn—I worked in a dress shop."

"But not now," Mrs. Scorcio said.

"Not now."

"How long ago did you leave your job?" asked Mrs. Scorcio.

"Just today."

Mrs. Scorcio seemed surprised but didn't ask any more about it. She instead had questions about what Alice had done, what she could do if she came to work for them. Alice felt on firmer ground here. Mrs. Scorcio turned to her husband and began to speak as if Alice weren't there. "You've been saying that you could use a helper," she said. "And your eyes—well, they're not what they used to be. What do you say we try her out for a bit?"

"You want to hire her right off the street?"

"I know her. She's the one I told you about. She helped me with the geraniums that day."

"Well . . . I've got several jobs piled up. We could bring down the other machine—"

"You have another sewing machine?" Alice asked.

"We do," said Mrs. Scorcio.

"Set it up here, so I could keep an eye on her."

"Yes, that would be good," Mrs. Scorcio said, nodding. "You'd look over what she's doing, train her even . . . When could you start?" she said to Alice.

"Today," Alice said. "Right now, if you like."

"We haven't even discussed what we could pay," the older woman said.

"Oh, I'm sure whatever it is, it'll be all right." She had no idea of what to expect. Bea had been paying her, but Bea also bought the food and took care of Alice's other expenses. And gave her a place to live too. All that, and look what Alice had gone and done—no, she couldn't think about that now.

". . . you said you lived in Brooklyn," Mrs. Scorcio was saying. "You came by subway? How long does it take?"

"Oh, I'm not living there anymore," said Alice.

"So where do you live?" Mr. Scorcio asked.

"At the moment, nowhere." When she saw that this admission surprised them, she hurried to say, "That is, I'm trying to find a place. Maybe you know of someone in the neighborhood who could rent me a room, even a shared room . . ."

Alice saw the Scorcios exchange looks again; it was Mrs. Scorcio who spoke first. "There's a little room in the back," she said. "There's not much to it—just a bed and a bureau. Sink and toilet are out in the hall. No bath—that would be upstairs on the second floor."

"That's fine, that's perfectly fine," Alice said eagerly.

"Wouldn't you at least like to see it first?"

"No, I know it will be—" She stopped, knowing that she seemed desperate. Well, she was desperate. Early this morning she'd gone into the shop to tidy up, which she hadn't gotten to do the night before, and saw the angry mob clustered out front. The signs they carried. The words they chanted. She understood—too late—that she was the cause of all this. That conversation with Mr. Mueller had given him reason to pursue the story further. He'd done some digging and he'd struck gold.

Alice had immediately felt sick with remorse. She'd done this to Bea—Bea, who had taken her in, and kept her from a life of selling her body before she even knew what that meant—and she couldn't face her. Or herself. So she ran back upstairs and hastily packed her things as well as the money she'd been saving, glad she hadn't opened a bank account. She hastily crammed what she could carry into a bag, and in her frantic packing, came upon the tissue packet containing the choker and earrings. Should she leave them behind? No. She grabbed them and stuck them in too.

Now she really did have to hurry. Bea was still not awake, but Alice knew she would be soon. The crowd outside was growing; still she had to risk it. She opened the door a crack and then a little wider. She stepped outside. *That's her, that's her! No, it's not—can't you see? That's a girl. Beatrice Jones is a grown woman. Older. Old. A hag! A witch!*

Alice wanted to rush down the stairs and sprint away, but she had to lock the door behind her. Otherwise, these enraged women might storm the house and hurt Bea. Her hands were shaking as she fumbled with the key and then slid it back under the door; she could hear the crowd behind her and some of them were starting to come up the stoop—

"Step back, step back all of you!"

Alice looked round to see a policeman gesturing to the women to keep away. It was Officer Duggan—thank God!

"It's a free country!" someone shouted. "We have the right to assemble."

"On the street, you do," said Officer Duggan. "This here's private property and I'll thank you to get off it unless you want to see the inside of the paddy wagon."

The two women, one tall and gaunt, the other round as a grouse, stopped where they were. Officer Duggan kept them from getting any closer. "Miss Alice, you seem like you could use some help," he said.

"I just want to get to the subway station, that's all."

"All right then. Stay with me and I'll get someone to walk you over."

And now, here she was, with the chance of a new start in front of her.

Alice quickly adapted to her life at the back of the Scorcios' shop. She woke early, dressed, washed her hands, face, and neck at the sink, and went out front. There, she'd attend to whatever small jobs had not been done the night before, and do the pressing for the garments that were going to be picked up. By then, Mr. Scorcio had come into the shop and Alice went upstairs to their apartment, where Mrs. Scorcio made her a *macchiato*—it meant *stained,* she told her—and gave her fresh bread with butter and fig jam that she made herself.

"Eat," she said, trying to get Alice to have another slice. "You're nothing but bones!"

Throughout the rest of the morning, she helped Mr. Scorcio with the tailoring. Most of these clothes belonged to men, and Alice hadn't worked on men's clothing before. But she grew to appreciate the fabrics—the gabardines, the tweeds, the herringbones—and the nuances involved in altering the cut of a jacket, the fit of a pair of trousers. This was the first time she had the benefit of working alongside someone who was as experienced as Mr. Scorcio; her previous training had been a smattering of this and that. Much of what she'd learned she'd picked up on her own. It wasn't as much fun as the work she'd done at Bea's, but she felt she was learning something important, a foundation for some as yet unrevealed goal.

As for Bea, she tried without success to put her from her mind. She thought about her all the time and felt constant remorse about the torrent of hate she'd unleashed on her. What if she'd been hurt? Alice checked the newspaper the Scorcios brought in—of course they didn't read the *Brooklyn Daily Eagle*—to see if there were any stories about the incident, but found none. No, there was nothing to be done about it. Had she wanted to banish Catherine from Bea's life? Well, she'd probably done that, but she'd ended up banishing herself too.

She put all her effort into making this new life work. Whenever there was a woman who came in, she always hovered around eagerly to see if she could offer any novel suggestions for altering or embellishing a garment. But none of these women were interested in the flights of fancy that Bea had admired and encouraged in her. They wanted only the tamest of changes—tucking here, letting out there, shortening, lengthening. It was, in truth, boring.

So she put her excess energy into other things—sorting the buttons that the Scorcios kept in a big glass jar, for instance. Papering the shop with the pages from the stack of *Vogue* magazines she'd found when she brought the trash pail to the curb. Luscious silks from American looms, hats from Paris, a change in the length of skirts—in Alice's view, these illustrations added to the atmosphere of the shop. Mrs. Scorcio thought so too and rearranged the pictures of the saints to give them more room. "They give the place some class," she said. Alice used more of the magazine pages to decorate her little room too, and scrubbed the grimy window until it looked perfectly clear. There was nothing much to look at out back though—just other tiny, concrete-paved yards filled with clotheslines whose flapping garments were bright against the sliver of sky.

Alice adopted the habit of scattering bits of stale bread to the sparrows, and pretty soon, they came looking for her in the mornings, twittering madly as they flitted about. Sometimes a pair of shy blue-gray doves alighted as well; Alice kept very quiet so as not to disturb them. She even began feeding a stray dog who wandered back there from time to time. He was so thin every rib was visible, and he cringed when anyone came near. "Starved and beaten," was Mrs. Scorcio's verdict and she started setting aside bits of meat that she had Alice give him. Pretty soon, he too became a regular at the back door.

Mr. Scorcio was teaching her about tailoring; Mrs. Scorcio, about food—at least Italian food. "These long, tube-shaped ones, they're called ziti," Mrs. Scorcio said. "The ones that look like bow ties? Farfalla. The skinny ones? Pasta per capelli d'angelo—angel hair. There's a name for every kind, and a sauce to go with it."

Alice's favorite was tortellini—different, she learned, from tortelloni—which Mrs. Scorcio served with a sauce made of butter, cream, and Parmesan cheese to which she'd add peas and bits of prosciutto. Sometimes she made her own pasta, and Alice liked to watch her deft hands roll, flip, and flatten the dough. Other days, she sent

Alice to Raffetto's, on Grand Street, and to the cheese shop, where she'd pick up fresh ricotta and a quivering ball of warm mozzarella wrapped in cheesecloth.

While Mrs. Scorcio plied her with food, Alice tried to deflect her many questions. When the older woman asked how old she was, she padded her real age and said eighteen; Mrs. Scorcio looked doubtful but didn't contradict her. "And what about your people?" she asked. "Your mama and papa—don't they want to hear from you? Are they worried about you being all on your own?"

"My parents died years ago," Alice said. At least that was the truth.

Mrs. Scorcio made the sign of the cross. "May they rest in peace," she said. "So you're an orphan. One of God's own." And over Alice's protests, she refilled her bowl with another helping of rigatoni Bolognese.

In the evenings, she joined the Scorcios in their apartment, a compact space into which so many things—figurines of girls and boys, goblets of etched glass, painted pitchers and bowls—had been crammed. The overall effect was cozy, not cluttered, though. Mr. Scorcio sat with the newspaper while Mrs. Scorcio knit, the clicking of her needles punctuating her running commentary. Seeing Alice's interest, she began to teach her. Mrs. Scorcio examined her neat rows of stitches, impressed by how quickly she'd caught on. "Golden needles, that's what I'm going to call you."

On one of these evenings, Alice showed Mrs. Scorcio the jacket and trousers she'd made. "You designed this?" Mrs. Scorcio exclaimed. "All by yourself? Tomasso, come have a look." And she turned the garments inside out so he could see how they had been constructed.

"This is good," he said. "Very good."

"It's more than good," Mrs. Scorcio said. "This girl has real talent."

The next day, she hung the outfit in the window of the shop. Alice found herself wishing Bea could see it there.

As the days grew shorter and chillier, Alice felt her energy lagging. She had to drag herself from the narrow bed in the mornings, and longed for a nap after every meal. Other than that, she felt fine—no headache, sore throat, cough or cold. And she looked like she was blooming—Mrs. Scorcio told her so. When she regarded herself in the shop's mirror, reflected back at her was a softly rounded face, rosy cheeks, and bright eyes. Had her face ever been so full? In fact, she couldn't remember the rest of her as being this full or rounded either; she was straining at the fronts of her dresses and having trouble buttoning her skirts.

"I can see my cooking is having a good effect on you," Mrs. Scorcio said. "You've got some meat on your bones now. And that dress— it looks tight."

"It is a bit snug," Alice said.

"Why don't we make you a new one?" Mrs. Scorcio said.

"A new dress? Really?"

"Yes, of course. I have lots of fabric tucked away. Maybe a flannel or a wool, now that we're getting into the colder weather." She reached for a box on a shelf and brought it down.

"See, this one's nice." Mrs. Scorcio's hands swiftly sorted through the neatly bundled lengths of cloth. "Or what about—no, I have a better idea. Let's remake one of my old dresses. I have one I think will be perfect. Come."

It was almost lunchtime, so they left Mr. Scorcio in the shop and went up to the apartment, where Mrs. Scorcio opened her pine chifforobe. "Here it is." She pulled out a dress made of two kinds of fabric—a navy-and-bottle-green plaid that had been paired with navy-and-bottle-green dots. It seemed rather daring for Mrs. Scorcio, whose wardrobe was limited to dresses or skirts of black, gray, or dark blue; on Sundays, she wore a white blouse she boiled on the stove with bleach and over it, a black crocheted shawl. Alice liked the patterned dress and imagined that changing the buttons or adding a new collar would give it even more flair.

"It still looks a bit big, but I can pin it for you and then you can do the altering when you have the time."

"Thank you, Mrs. Scorcio," Alice said. "Thank you so much." She began to unbutton the dress she was wearing, and after stepping out of it, she laid it on a chair. When she turned around again, she saw Mrs. Scorcio staring.

"What is it?" Alice's camisole and slip were also tight, she'd recently noticed. "Is something wrong?"

"Don't you know?" Mrs. Scorcio said.

"Know what?"

"It's not just my cooking. You've got a baby in there."

"A baby!" Alice sat down on the chair, right on top of her dress. How was that possible? But she knew. Of course she knew.

"You must have had some idea," Mrs. Scorcio said, looking embarrassed. "You and your fellow . . ."

"I don't have a fellow." Alice got up, and grabbing her dress, hurried to put it back on.

"We can still make over the other one for you," said Mrs. Scorcio. "You're going to need it."

Alice nodded miserably and stepped into the plaid-and-dotted dress. As Mrs. Scorcio pinned and tucked, she thought of the first day she had come to this neighborhood. The awning. The café. The party at which she went into the bedroom with Artie and Sheldon. She had tried to dismiss that possibility from her mind, tried to believe that they hadn't actually done that to her. Maybe one or both had unloosened her clothes, kissed her, touched her . . . but *that*?

She'd been drunk, passed out. Would they really have taken such advantage?

"I'm going to leave some room." Mrs. Scorcio was kneeling beside her, extracting pins from the pincushion she always wore on her wrist. "No point in making it too tight."

Alice said nothing.

"Do you know how this happened to you?"

"No."

"Really? You have no idea?"

Alice shook her head; she couldn't even look at her.

"Come on now. You're a bright girl. You must know—"

"I don't know anything! And please, *please* don't keep asking!"

There was a silence and then Mrs. Scorcio said, "All right. But if you change your mind, you can tell me later."

Alice kept her gaze averted. She wouldn't change her mind and tell Mrs. Scorcio later. She wouldn't tell her—or anyone else— *ever.*

That evening, when Mr. Scorcio was settled in with his newspaper, Mrs. Scorcio brought Alice down to the shop on some pretext.

"I know you don't want to tell me what happened," she said. "But is there anyone else you can tell?"

Alice thought of Bea. "No," she said. "No one."

Mrs. Scorcio put an arm around Alice's shoulders. "I was young once too. I know what can happen to a girl, especially when she doesn't have anyone looking out for her. And I can help."

"You can?" Alice couldn't see how.

"You remember the church we go to? The Immaculate Heart of Mary?"

"I do." Alice had been to Mass with them a couple of times.

"I know the priest there very well. He'll take the baby."

"Take the baby?"

"Yes. You can't raise it on your own—you're just a baby yourself."

"I'm not a baby, I'm—"

"Sixteen, if you're a day. I knew you weren't eighteen. So how are you going to manage? No, you give the baby to the priest. He won't breathe a word to anyone. Anyone except . . ."

"Except who?"

"He always knows of a couple who wants a baby but can't have one. They come to him, unburden themselves. And if it happens that there's a baby who needs a home, he makes sure the couple finds out about it."

"You mean I should give my baby away?"

"It would be for the best. For you—and for the baby."

Like Bea had done with Catherine. The thought flashed, lightning quick, across Alice's mind. Someone had told her the same thing. And had it been for the best? It hadn't.

"No," she said. "I won't."

"Think it over," Mrs. Scorcio said. "You don't have to decide this minute."

That night, when the Scorcios went up to bed, Alice went into the shop, took off her clothes, and stared at her naked self in the mirror. Yes, she looked fuller, plumper, but a baby? How could Mrs. Scorcio be so sure? She put her hand on her newly swollen belly and to her amazement, she felt a fluttering inside. Something was moving! She put her nightdress back on and went into her little room. The pretty, fashionable ladies from the pages of *Vogue* seemed to mock her. What would they do if they found themselves in her situation?

The next day, she resumed her place next to Mr. Scorcio in the shop. He had been showing her how to do a rather complicated tailoring job on a man's tuxedo jacket. She'd been eager to master these skills, but today she couldn't concentrate on the rich, black fabric under her fingers. He must have seen the trouble she was having since he suggested that they stop for lunch earlier than usual. Alice was just grateful he didn't say anything more.

Tired as she was, sleep eluded her at night. She was in no position to be a mother. But she couldn't stop thinking about Bea. Hadn't her life been ruined by giving up her baby, not the other way around? She'd have been better off if she'd kept Catherine, found some way to care for her. She wouldn't have found her way to the District, to a brothel, to Basin Street. Maybe the obvious answer wasn't really the answer at all. If only she could have talked to Bea. If only. Now it was too late. Unless it wasn't.

A few days later, she said goodbye to the Scorcios, thanking them effusively them for all their kindness, and promising to stay in touch. "You know where to find us," Mrs. Scorcio said. "We'll be here until they carry us out, feetfirst." And they each kissed her goodbye, Mr. Scorcio on the forehead, and Mrs. Scorcio on both cheeks.

Wearing the newly altered wool dress Mrs. Scorcio had given her and carrying her valises, Alice returned to Brooklyn. The need to see Bea had grown stronger and stronger. She had no idea of whether Bea would speak to her, much less take her back. But she had to try. Bea had been in this same position—pregnant and alone, with no one to turn to. Maybe she would feel sorry for Alice. Maybe.

But when she reached 77 St. Marks Avenue, she found it shuttered and dark. The sign for the dress shop was gone and in its place was a discreet sign that said TO LET. She rang the bell anyway. Nothing. She rang again, and then a third time.

Alice walked back down the stoop. Of course Bea was not inside, that was clear. Where had she gone? Alice didn't know, though she had an idea of who might. Catherine Berrill was the last person Alice wanted to see or talk to—ever. But it looked like she was going to have to do it anyway.

CHAPTER TWENTY-FOUR

CATHERINE

===

Brooklyn, 1924

From across the street, Catherine could see Bea seated on the bench, waiting. Her perfectly erect posture made her seem imposing and in command rather than shamed or cowed. Well, why not? She'd been revealed as brazen and shameless; why would she look otherwise? But her costume was straitlaced and sober: a high-necked, dark dress, large black hat with a black net veil covering her face. It was the costume of a widow, not a whore. Oh, but Bea was good at dissembling. Very good.

"You came," she said when Catherine drew closer. "I wasn't sure you'd want to see me."

"I didn't. I don't. But this will be the last time. You can count on it."

Bea nodded but said nothing and when the silence stretched on too long, Catherine burst out, "Do you blame me? You lied to me. Lies, lies, and more lies."

Bea seemed unruffled. "Of course I lied."

"Aren't you ashamed of yourself?"

"For lying? No. If I hadn't, you would never have spoken one word to me. As it was, I had a chance to get to know you. And you—you came to know me."

"How? You didn't tell me the truth."

"I told you the truth about what mattered. About what was essential."

"And what was that?"

"I was driven from my home, traveled thousands of miles by myself. I fell in love, found myself pregnant, alone, without family or friends. I told you that someone took me in—well, someone did. I just didn't tell you that she was a madam. And at first, all I did was clean and scrub. Then you were born and I thought I was giving you up as a way to save you. And myself. But I was wrong, at least about that part of it."

Catherine looked unconvinced. "Were you?"

"Afterward, I felt more bereft, more despairing than I'd ever felt before. I think I knew nothing would ever be quite right with me again, but it was too late. It was so easy to slip into that foul stream. I was already in it, it was all around me. I didn't care what happened to me."

"That much is evident."

"And then I began to see that the way to move out was to move up. To become a madam myself. Then I could assume control of my life."

"And what control that was—bringing other girls to their ruin."

"Whatever had happened to them to make them choose that life, it happened long before they met me."

"I can't believe how you're trying to justify yourself!"

"Not justify. Explain. There's always a reason, if you can stop judging long enough to see it."

"You deserve to be judged."

"Not for that."

Catherine was quiet for a moment. "I don't know why I came," she said. "I wish I'd never met you. You've brought only shame and disgrace to me, to my family—"

"You're forgetting that I'm your family. And the disgrace you feel—well, you've chosen to feel it."

"No!" Catherine stood. "You're not my family and if anyone ever says you are, I'll deny it. I can lie too, you know."

"Not to yourself. Never to yourself. I know that much about you."

"You're wrong. You don't know me. And after today, I won't know you. Goodbye, Bea." Catherine turned and walked away. She'd have to forgo seeing Bea's reaction, but nothing would make her turn around to look.

Walking home, she was too filled with indignation and disgust to be aware of putting one foot in front of the other. To think that she had discovered her *real* mother, her *true* mother, and only to learn that she was a vile woman, without morals or scruples. Catherine felt something sizzling inside, hot and ugly, and she knew what it was— hatred. Yes, she hated Bea. And nothing would ever change that.

She returned home to find Stephen waiting anxiously at the window. By the time she'd climbed the stoop, he was at the door to meet her.

"Are you all right?" he asked.

"I will be," she said.

"Did you talk to her? What did she say?"

"She hasn't an ounce of shame in her. Not a drop. She's led the most deplorable, wicked life and she feels no remorse. I can't understand such a person and I don't even want to try."

Stephen gathered her in his arms. "I'm sorry she turned out to be such a disappointment to you. To all of us."

Catherine pressed her face against the starched freshness of his shirt. "So am I," she murmured. "So am I."

Catherine knew Stephen was worried she would slip back into that dark place she'd fallen into after the death of the baby. They all were, the Berrills and the Delmans, and she could feel them watching her closely, waiting for a sign. There was none. Yes, she'd been disappointed by Bea, bitterly and irrevocably, but the experience hadn't broken her. There was still something in her that wanted to live, and to be happy. But how? That was what she'd have to discover. She thought of those months during the summer when she'd gathered the dead creatures and laid them to rest. She'd been building something then, creating something, and it had brought her a measure of peace. What if there was a way to find that peace again? The answer seemed close by, but she hadn't found it yet. Soon, she told herself. It was autumn now, with winter close at hand. Maybe in the spring . . .

There was a day she was walking along Eighth Avenue when the street seemed suddenly full of people—she realized it was Saturday, and they were all coming from the big temple on the corner of Garfield Place. She'd seen the building dozens of times and knew it was where Jewish people worshipped, but she felt no connection to it. Only now she felt herself pulled into their wake, suddenly curious to know what the inside of the building looked like. Why did she even care?

But still, Catherine found herself there the next Saturday too. She had noticed that the women were dressed up, so she'd worn her walking suit with the Chesterfield coat, passementerie trim, and frog closures so that she would fit right in. The service had ended and people were heading for the wide double doors. She moved easily among them, nodding and smiling. Some people even smiled back, which emboldened her further, and after a moment, she very casually slipped inside. There were still a few stragglers, adjusting a coat or hat, or chatting to a companion. No one noticed her.

The interior was round, with the pews arranged in a semicircle, like an amphitheater. Stained-glass windows. Red carpeting. These facts told her nothing. There was something more she wanted, a yearning that had started when she'd first learned that Bea, and by extension she, was Jewish. The knowledge had been working on her, boring into her consciousness, forcing her to reconsider what little she knew about Jews and how they fit—or failed to fit—into the larger world. The death, no, murder of Bea's father was horrifying and contained details Bea disclosed only after repeated questioning, and even then with great reluctance. And yet it had taken Catherine all this time to make the stunningly obvious connection: Bea's father was her own *grandfather*. Her *grandfather* had been murdered, her *grandfather's* body stuffed into that filthy mail sack and sent back home. She was not off to one side of the story, she was squarely in it; this was part of her heritage, her legacy. Had she been raised by Bea, she would have had to face the contempt and hatred that Bea had experienced. That would have been part of her legacy as well.

The temple was empty now, and the lights went on and off a couple of times. They were closing up; Catherine realized that if she didn't leave now, she could be locked in here for hours. Hastily, she retreated down the central aisle and into the street again.

All week long she told herself that she would not return to temple, that it was a waste of her time and energy—and yet, the following Saturday, there she was again. It was a chilly fall day, with a brisk wind shaking the leaves in the trees. Hands deep in pockets,

Catherine let herself blend into the crowd, waiting for the chance to enter the building a second time. Maybe she could go upstairs. Or down. There might have been something she'd missed, some clue or hint about how to make sense of this new information about herself.

She was just about to enter the temple when she noticed a girl walking ahead of her. The girl was carrying two valises and a hatbox, so it was obvious she wasn't coming from services. Catherine was torn. She wanted to go inside again, but the girl distracted her. There was something about her. Catherine's curiosity had to be satisfied. She wasn't abandoning her plan, only postponing it. The temple would be there. The girl would not.

Back outside, Catherine scanned the sidewalk, searching for her. But she was not to be found. Annoyed with herself, Catherine decided to go home, no longer in the mood to go into the temple. She walked quickly back toward her house. To her surprise, she saw the girl standing on the front stoop, valises and hatbox beside her, her back to the street. When Catherine reached the stoop, she called out, "Can I help you?" The girl turned. It was Alice.

"What are you doing here?" Catherine hadn't given much—well, any— thought to what had happened to her.

"I'm looking for Bea. I thought you might know where she went. The house—it's empty."

"I don't know and I certainly don't care." Catherine had reached the top step and now stood face-to-face with Alice.

"All right then." Head bowed and shoulders slumped, Alice picked up her valises. "I'll keep looking. I'm sorry I troubled you."

Her coat, which was unbuttoned, opened and revealed the startling truth. "You're pregnant!"

"I am." Alice sounded miserable and immediately Catherine began filling in the story's blank spaces. Bea would have cast her out—of course. Alice was the one who'd set that newspaper reporter on his sordid task. So where had she been? What had happened to her? And more to the point—where would she go now?

"Do you want to come in?" Catherine was surprised by her own words. Alice said nothing. "You might as well. It's going to be cold tonight, and you don't want to be outside—not in your condition." They were into November already, and the temperature had dropped.

Alice followed her into the house, where Catherine took one of the bags and led her upstairs to the fourth floor, to the room-that-was-to-have-been-the-nursery-but-now-never-would. There was no wallpaper, of course, but there was a bed and some other furnishings, all of it taken care of by Bridget and Molly. Since the room's promise had so cruelly betrayed her, Catherine didn't consider it a true part of the house anymore and avoided it whenever possible.

Alice set down her bag and hatbox as she looked around. "You're very kind," she said softly. "Thank you."

The compliment made her feel twitchy and Catherine felt the urge to shake it off. But she just said, "You can stay tonight if you want. We have dinner at six on Saturdays because the maid leaves early."

"I appreciate that." Alice's voice was low. "Dinner and the offer to stay."

"What plans have you made? Surely you didn't think Bea was still going to be here, did you? And even if she were, it's not likely she'd take you back." Hadn't Alice just told her she was kind? Well, she wasn't. In fact, she was being quite unkind, but really, was this girl so naive?

"I don't really know what I thought. I didn't have anywhere else to go. I thought Bea would understand . . ."

"Maybe so. But what were you thinking when you went tattling to that reporter? She may have been a . . . woman of no virtue, but she was good to you."

"I know." Alice sounded like she was about to cry.

"Then why . . . ?"

"It was because of you, really."

"Me! What did I have to do with it?"

"Bea and I—we had each other. We weren't close, but we were together. And then she found you, and there wasn't room for me anymore . . ."

"She didn't mean to shut you out." Catherine realized she was in the odd position of defending Bea. "And she did try to include you. She was going to bring you to dinner to meet my husband and my father."

"She told me." She was studying Catherine's face. "I didn't tell that reporter about her past, you know. I just said something that made him want to dig deeper and find out for himself. But really, all I wanted was for things to be like they'd been before—before she found you."

"I don't see how you thought that was going to be possible." How could she not have understood the nature of her disclosure or have foreseen the damage it would do? "And in any case, I don't know where she is."

"Do you know how I can find her?"

Catherine tried to contain her exasperation. "No. I don't."

"I see." She looked downcast and said, "If it's all right with you, I'd like to lie down for a bit now. I'm tired."

"Of course." Catherine went downstairs to ask Nettie to set another place. And she was waiting in the front room when Stephen got home; she wanted to fill him in before dinner.

"And who is this girl again?" he asked gently.

"She was some kind of ward of Bea's. She never adopted her formally but she'd been living with her and supporting her. The girl's an orphan—she doesn't have any family."

"So where will she go after tonight?"

"I haven't the faintest idea."

Dinner was less awkward than Catherine expected, largely because of Stephen. He kept the conversation light and easy, telling her stories from his Brooklyn boyhood and about the slapstick antics of Charlie Chaplin and Buster Keaton.

"The Flatbush Pavilion is just a short walk from here. Catherine and I go over there about once a week, don't we?"

Catherine nodded. Why was he so intent on trying to entertain her?

"What if we take you sometime?"

"That would be nice. I've only been to a picture show once."

Catherine was ready to fling her dinner roll at her husband.

After dinner, Stephen made a fire in the parlor and brought out a box of checkers. While the logs snapped and popped, he played two games with Alice. She won both times, and Catherine suspected he let her. While they were setting up the board for a third game, Catherine went to make sure there was an extra blanket and fresh towels in the room upstairs. She looked at the two valises and the hatbox, now stowed neatly by the door. Nettie had probably hung up some of Alice's things, because she saw a nightdress that had been folded and placed by the pillow.

When she went back downstairs, she found Stephen and Alice in the kitchen, where he was attempting to make hot cocoa for all of them, though it seemed as if all he was making was a mess. Catherine had never known Stephen to go into the kitchen other than to help himself to something Nettie had just taken out of the oven. She sent them back to the parlor and took over, preparing a tray with cups, saucers, a pot of cocoa, and a plate of Nettie's gingersnaps. Alice and Stephen had moved on from checkers to cribbage, which Stephen was trying to teach the girl.

"Maybe that's enough for tonight," Catherine said. And after they finished the cocoa and cookies, they all went up to bed.

When they were alone, Catherine asked, "Why are you being so nice to her?"

Stephen had curled up beside her. "She's a guest in our house. Isn't that reason enough?"

"I never liked her."

"Oh, that's apparent."

"Is it?" Catherine felt a moment of regret over this and then decided, why? Alice had made her own antipathy known right from the start.

"I feel sorry for her."

"That's so like you." For a moment, her anger spiked. But then she reminded herself that his empathy was one of the things she loved about him. She was fortunate to have such a kind, generous man as her husband. She moved closer to him.

"I'm just trying to imagine what will happen to her after tonight."

"I'm sure I don't know."

"So we're just going to turn her out? Where will she go?"

Catherine was silent for a while. "Are you suggesting we let her stay here?"

"We have the room."

"That's hardly a reason."

"True. But if she stays, it wouldn't inconvenience us in any way."

"I don't care," said Catherine. "It's not about convenience. I just don't want her here, that's all." Why was she even having this conversation?

"All right," Stephen said. "But we can tell her in the morning, can't we? No point in waking her up now."

Was there just a hint of reproach in his tone? Well, so what if there was? The idea that Alice had, and didn't want, what Catherine could never have, and so desperately wanted, was beyond galling. She closed her eyes, but sleep wouldn't come. She got up, intending to go downstairs and fetch the new issue of *House & Garden* to distract herself, but as she approached the staircase she glanced up. There was light coming from the floor above. So Alice was awake too. Catherine waited for the glinting satisfaction of spite but instead she thought of a girl, very much alone and frightened, taking temporary respite in a strange room and wondering what in the world would become of her.

Realizing the magazine wouldn't help, she went back to her bedroom. Stephen had turned on the lamp and was sitting up in bed.

"What's wrong?" But she knew. Of course she knew.

"It's Alice," he said. "I don't want to press you. Still, I wish you would reconsider, Cathy."

Cathy. He had been the first one to call her that and hearing it made her thaw, just a perceptible bit. She allowed herself to imagine Alice growing larger every day. Alice giving birth. Alice with an infant. Catherine would have to witness all of it.

"We won't do it if you're dead set against it, or if it will . . . upset you in any way. But putting her out seems so heartless."

He knew how she felt about pregnant women, women with babies. But Alice wasn't a woman. She was a girl. It was different somehow. "What if we said she could stay for a little while . . . maybe a week? That way we could see how it goes . . ." Catherine said.

"A trial period." He was nodding. "See how we all feel about it."

"You're assuming she's going to say yes."

"It's not as if she has a lot of choices. In fact, I'd say she has none."

Stephen turned out the light and Catherine lay down next to him. An enormous exhaustion overtook her. Was she really going to allow this? What if she couldn't bear it? Stephen had pulled her into his embrace. He believed in her—her capacity to be forgiving, generous, kind—more than she believed in herself. But that was a good thing, wasn't it? She would try hard to be the person he thought she was. Or could be. And having come to that decision, she was finally able to give herself over to sleep.

The next morning over breakfast, Catherine told Alice that she and Stephen were willing—she couldn't quite bring herself to say happy—to let her stay with them until the baby was born.

"You'd do that for me? After what I did?"

"What you did was wrong," Catherine said. "But you're young and I'm willing to believe you didn't understand the repercussions."

"No," said Alice. "I didn't." She didn't sound young in that moment, not at all. "But I'm grateful that you'll let me stay. I'll try not to be a bother to you. Maybe I can even help you out."

"Help me out?" Catherine couldn't hide her incredulity. "Doing what?"

Alice smiled shyly. "Sewing, of course."

At first, Alice stayed in her room, where she busied herself with mending and minor alterations, which was indeed a help, as neither Nettie nor Catherine cared for doing them. Catherine saw Alice only at meals, during which she ate heartily but said almost nothing. Then Stephen's mother came over with a sewing machine that had been sitting unused in a closet and offered it to the girl. Catherine saw the flicker of interest in Alice's expression, and the next day, she left the house after breakfast and returned late in the afternoon carrying two large bags of fabric.

"Do you have a table I might use?" she asked. "I need space to lay out the material before I cut it."

"Of course," said Catherine. And even though they didn't actually own a suitable table, she sent Stephen out to buy a collapsible one and set it up in Alice's room. Soon Catherine could hear the steady whirr—a pleasant, and even cheerful sound—most of the day and often in the evening too. The door was often closed, but when it was open, Catherine would find a reason to pass by the room and often stood in the doorway, chatting. Once, after she'd been standing there for about fifteen minutes, Alice invited her to come in and sit down. This too became a pattern—Catherine keeping Alice company as she sewed. They talked about what Alice was making or the merits of one kind of fabric over another, but avoided the big, hard subjects, like Bea, or what Alice planned to do when the baby came, or how she'd gotten herself with child in the first place.

As Catherine watched Alice work, her respect for the younger woman grew. She didn't need patterns but could improvise easily, using dresses she owned as templates for new ones that would fit her expanding body. Catherine couldn't help but note the changes; she remembered the various stages she'd gone through, the initial thickening that became an entity unto itself—a taut, round ball that preceded her wherever she went. There was regret in watching what she would never experience again, but Alice's extreme youth and fear prevented the envy from overwhelming her. Whatever was happening to Alice's outward appearance was no indication of her inner state. Her body was growing a baby; were her heart and mind preparing to be its mother?

After she'd made a few dresses, Alice turned to making baby clothes, and had soon produced a layette of tiny, beautifully sewn garments. Catherine showed a few to Molly, who asked if Alice might consider sewing some things for her girls. Alice complied by making a pair of smocked dresses with pinafores whose hems she embroidered, rompers that buttoned at the shoulder, and nightdresses with ruffles and matching robes. Molly's friends admired the clothes and asked where they could get them; before long, Molly was hosting afternoon gatherings where Alice's creations were sold.

When Molly gave Alice the money from her sales, Catherine wanted her to set it aside for the baby, but Alice said no, she wanted to contribute to her room and board, and insisted on splitting the revenue with Catherine and Stephen. Not only did Catherine admire Alice's talents, but she also respected her desire to pay her own way in the world, and not rely on charity. Still, it seemed wrong to take money from the girl, so Catherine put it safely away and planned to give it to Alice later. Surely she would need it. Her insistence suggested she was more mature than Catherine had previously thought. And maybe there were other ways in which she hadn't given Alice sufficient credit, and she began to regard her with a degree of respect. Which made the question of the baby's father all the more compelling. During all this time, Alice had not said one word, not made one reference, to him; if Catherine wanted to know, she would have to ask.

She waited until they were alone to pose the question.

Alice was silent. "I'd rather not talk about it," she finally said.

"You don't have to," Catherine said. "But whatever it is, I promise I won't judge you harshly."

"It's just that I haven't talked about it before," she said.

"All the more reason for you to talk now," said Catherine. "It might even do you some good to unburden yourself."

Alice seemed to consider this and then began to speak. "I met some boys—their names were Sheldon and Artie—at a café in Greenwich Village and they invited me to a party," she began. Her head was bent over her sewing, though the machine was still. "I wanted to go. It was lonely living with just Bea—no one my own age to talk to. I thought a party would be fun. And at first, it was."

"Was there alcohol? Did you have anything to drink?" Catherine said gently.

"I didn't want to. I know what liquor does to people and I detest it. But Sheldon kept giving me punch, coconut punch. I knew there was liquor in it—I could taste it. He said there was only a little in there to keep it from being too sweet."

"I see." Catherine could see very well.

"Anyway, I got drunk. I didn't mean to but I did. And then the room was so hot, and Artie took me into a bedroom and . . ."

"And what?"

"And he kissed me."

"Did you want him to kiss you?"

"Yes, yes, I did. I liked him. But then the other boy, Sheldon, came into the room and I didn't like that but I was feeling too woozy to tell them. And then I fell asleep."

"Could they have put something else into the drink? Something even stronger than alcohol?"

"I don't know . . . maybe. What I do know is that when I woke up, my clothes were all undone and I was sore . . . I managed to get home and since I didn't remember what had happened, I tried to tell myself nothing had."

Catherine absorbed all this in shocked silence. The vulnerability of girls was such a fearful thing. It occurred to her that Bea had been such a girl once too, but she quickly banished the thought.

"You never saw those boys again? Had no way to find them?"

Alice shook her head. "I didn't even get their last names or where they lived. All I knew was that they talked about a school called NYU."

"New York University. The students must have been there."

"I suppose so."

"What did Bea say about all this?" asked Catherine.

"I never had a chance to tell her."

"Why not?"

"Because . . . she was always with you. I didn't think she cared about me anymore."

A surge of something—pity? compassion?—welled up in Catherine. How petty she'd been to harbor any grudge against this girl at all. She was a child. A child to whom terrible things had been done. There'd been no one to speak for her, no one to protect her. Even Bea, who rescued her once, hadn't managed to prevent this awful thing from happening. Well, things would be different now. She'd make sure of it.

The next day, Bridget showed up with knitting needles and yarn. "I was cleaning out my drawers and found all this," she said. "I started something—I'm not sure if it was a shawl, a scarf, or a blanket—but I'm never going to finish it. Maybe Alice could do something with it. She's so handy."

By this point, Alice's swollen belly was making it hard for her to sit hunched over the machine, so she took the yarn and needles and switched to knitting. Now Molly could sell her winsome creations—fringed and tasseled scarves, mittens patterned to look like puppies' faces or ladybugs, hats that tied under the chin or caps festooned with pom-poms—to the same ladies who had bought the baby clothes. And even though Alice spent much of the day knitting, she could hardly keep up with the demand.

"You're so creative," Catherine said as she watched the needles fly. "I envy you."

"Whatever for?" Alice asked. "You're very creative too."

"Me? I don't sew, knit, embroider, or crochet. And I can't sing, dance, draw, or paint. I don't do anything creative."

"But look at your house. You put it all together yourself and it looks wonderful. Just wonderful. I've never seen such a house."

Catherine was flattered. "You like it then?"

"I love it! Don't you see—that's your skill. Your gift. You could do for other people what you've done here. You'd be very successful."

Catherine was less sure—her own taste was idiosyncratic in the extreme. But she had derived enormous satisfaction from assembling and arranging her home. And even those graves she'd created over the summer, the ones that brought her a sense of peace at the worst time she'd ever known—weren't these homes, too, final ones, that she had been driven to create? Maybe Alice was on to something, and Catherine could find a way to develop and hone what seemed to be her natural skills.

She made some telephone calls and then took a trip into Manhattan to pay a visit to the Metropolitan Academy of Interior Design Arts, a school located on lower Broadway, above a barbershop and next door to a wholesale producer of silk flowers. She studied the brochure all the way back to Brooklyn and learned that students could take classes in drawing, measuring, creating scale models, the magic of mirrors, lighting, bringing the outdoors in, pattern and color, the use of faux finishes. Then she presented it to Stephen at dinner that night. "I want to enroll," she said.

Alice leaned over. "Can I see it?"

"There's a nine-month program with a certificate at the end."

"And that's what you want to do?"

"Yes," she said.

"Well, I think it's a fine idea. When could you start?"

Catherine returned to the school to ask more questions and to fill out the application. New classes began in January; that wasn't so far off.

At Thanksgiving, Catherine's parents took the train from Larchmont to join the lavish celebration at Stephen's parents' house. Veronica's table was set with her best Limoges, and she filled their plates with roast turkey, two kinds of stuffing, cranberry relish, a sweet potato soufflé, and more. The Berrills had already accepted Alice into their midst. But Catherine's mother, who'd been informed of the arrangement and told they were *performing an act of Christian charity* by taking the girl in, still had reservations.

"It may seem all right now," she said to Catherine. "But, darling, what are you going to do when that baby is born? Why, it won't even have a father. Whatever will she put on the birth certificate?"

"I'd say she has more important concerns, wouldn't you?"

"That's what comes of allowing someone like this, this Beatrice, into our lives," Meredith went on. "Naturally she would associate with a lower class of people."

"This Beatrice, as you call her, does happen to be the woman who gave birth to me." Catherine was surprised by her own sense of resistance. Hadn't she been the one to sever all connection with Bea?

"Well, yes, but we agreed you're not going to speak of that again."

"I know. But this is just between us. We don't have to pretend."

Though it seemed they did. Some weeks earlier, Catherine had been visiting her parents and tried to talk to her father alone, asking him if what Bea had said was true. He was clearly uncomfortable and got up from the room on some pretext or another. When he came back, Catherine's mother was with him. Intentional? Hard to say.

But later, when Meredith was showing Stephen something in her garden, Catherine tried again. "Please don't put me off this time," she said.

He studied her. "You really want to know, don't you?"

"I *need* to know."

He sighed deeply, as if the breath were being pulled from his core. "All right then. I'll tell you if you promise to keep it between us. Your mother knows most of the story. But not all of it." He glanced out the window to the garden, reassured that Meredith was deeply engrossed in the botanical conversation. "Eloise, the woman who ran the house where Beatrice lived when she gave birth to you, was someone I'd known for years, long before I met and married your mother. You could say we grew up together. She'd just come from England—Liverpool. She was very lively . . ." He stopped, clearly remembering. "When her life took a turn for the worse, I didn't abandon her. She was an old friend. An old and dear friend. And look at what she did for us—she brought us together. Sometimes the ends do justify the means."

So Bea's story *was* true.

"You've never told Mother all this?"

"I haven't."

"And you never will?"

"I don't think it would benefit her to know. Do you?"

"No."

Catherine thought about the life her father had had on his own, apart from his life with her mother and with her. Had that woman, that madam, Eloise, been his—well, his lover? She wouldn't ask, though she wished he would tell her. Her reticence came from some newfound regard for him as a separate person, not just her father or her mother's husband, but also a man with a past that didn't include either of them. Still, there was one last thing she did have to ask.

"When you first met her, Bea that is, were you aware that she was a . . . prostitute?"

"I'm not sure that she was. Eloise said she'd shown up pregnant and begging for work. She took her on to do the cleaning."

"So her becoming a prostitute, that came after? That's what she told me. But I didn't believe her."

"I do. But does it really matter?"

"I thought it did," she said. "Now I'm not so sure."

"I would have wanted you anyway. Where you came from was of no concern to me. I took one look at you and knew you belonged with us. And I was right, wasn't I, Catherine? You've been our girl all these years—our girl, your mother's and mine."

"Thank you." Catherine's eyes were brimming. "For everything." She leaned over to embrace her father.

"Bea's great misfortune was our great blessing," he said. "It doesn't seem fair, does it? It doesn't seem fair at all. But that's the way it was."

CHAPTER TWENTY-FIVE

BEA

═══

Manhattan, 1924

Bea walked up the steps to the Madison Park Foundling Hospital and Home and opened one of its heavy oak doors. It was cold, which meant she wouldn't be able to bring any of the babies outside today. That was too bad—she so enjoyed taking them to sit amid the quartet of trees in the courtyard, or for excursions around the neighborhood.

"Good morning, Miss Bea," said Dora, the third-floor nurse. "Nice to see you again."

"Good morning." Bea removed her coat—Rappaport's creation was now in its second season—hung it on the rack, and then followed Dora upstairs.

"Will you be on the third floor today?" the nurse asked.

"Yes, and if there's time, I'll stop by on the second too."

"Well, you know you're welcome wherever you go, Miss Bea. You're a saint, that's what you are. A regular saint."

Bea hardly thought of herself as a saint. Dora didn't, couldn't, know that the babies in this hospital—all of them orphaned, and none of them older than two—gave her as much as she gave them. No, they gave her more.

The third floor, like the two below, was shaped like an extended H, with two long corridors joined by a shorter, horizontal one. The shorter corridor had two sinks, two changing tables, and four chairs. In the longer corridors were the two lines of cribs, each about six feet apart. It was at the far end of a long corridor that Bea began her rounds today.

"Hello, Ginny. How are you?" Reading from the handwritten tag attached to the crib, Bea leaned over and picked up the baby, whose wispy, dark hair stood in wayward tufts on her head. "Let's give you a little coif today." She took the baby to the changing table and pulled out the little comb she kept with her for this purpose. After her hair was smoothed, Bea checked her diaper—clean and dry—and then hoisted her up onto one hip so that they could take a stroll down the corridor. "Look at the clouds." Bea pointed upward through one of the windows. "And see? There's a bird." Ginny pressed her tiny palm to the glass. "That's right—clouds. Sky. Bird." She continued, commenting on whatever she saw down below—a man walked a waddling dachshund on a leash, a flower seller tried to interest passersby in his wares. After a few minutes, she returned Ginny to her crib and picked up the next baby.

For the last few months, ever since she had stumbled upon the hospital, this had been her routine—several mornings a week spent talking to the babies, playing with the babies, coddling and even singing to them, as long as no other adults were in earshot. It started as a diversion but soon became something essential, and Bea planned her days around this activity.

After she'd been hounded out of the house on St. Marks, she had found a hotel where she could stay temporarily and signed in there under the surname White. It was clear she'd have to reinvent herself yet again. Brooklyn was tainted—and possibly dangerous—so she crossed the river to Manhattan, where she was able to rent two small furnished rooms and a bath in a four-story house near Madison Park. There was a larger suite of rooms available on the parlor floor, with high ceilings and ample windows. But the windows faced the street, which made her feel vulnerable, and she worried it might be noisy. The fourth floor was more secluded and therefore safer, she felt. She soon discovered an iron ladder that led to the roof, climbed up, and saw the city spread out before her. The streets were full of people, all busy, all heading to or from somewhere, to someone. When she'd lived in Brooklyn, she'd never even considered going up on the roof; there had been so much to tether her to the world below. But now she felt cut off, and adrift, reason enough to come up here to look at the expanse of the sky, which was blue and cloudless and cold.

She had the feeling in her early days there that she no longer mattered to anyone. Was not even *seen* by anyone. How strange to find herself so unmoored. So alone. She'd been alone after the deaths of her brothers and parents, alone when Clay died and the Robichauds rejected her, alone when she'd given her baby to Sebastian Delgado, and now she was alone once more. Maybe it was her natural state, and perhaps it would be easier to stop trying.

But Bea couldn't shake her worry about Alice, now adrift in the city, and she considered going to the police or even another detective. When Alice had left her, the act had wounded her more than she would have expected. She'd never felt like the girl's mother, so why did her absence tear at her at night as she tried to sleep, and in the morning when she woke to a steady drumbeat of dread? In those moments, she'd resolve to search for her more actively. But then she'd consider: What if she found Alice only to be rejected? And then there was Catherine, whom she'd moved heaven and earth to find. Bea should have been honest with her from the start, taken the risk of revealing her true self, but it was too late for that now.

Such thoughts could drive a woman crazy, and Bea did feel that her isolation might bring on a kind of madness. So even on the chilliest days, she forced herself to go out, usually with a destination in mind—the Metropolitan Museum of Art, the main branch of the New York Public Library. Other days she just walked, and the city that was revealed to her was almost always brand-new, and almost always surprising. New York was so much bigger than New Orleans; Bea sensed that it would take weeks, if not months, to get the full sense of its size and scope.

One morning she headed west on Twenty-Third all the way to the Hudson River, and then back the same thoroughfare, to the East River. On the way she passed Berrill's Fine Stationery and Papers and felt the heat rise in her face, the instantly accelerated thrumming of her heart. Catherine had mentioned Stephen's family's store to her many times. Bea stood in front of the window, thinking she might go in and ask for news of her, give him some message—but that was ridiculous. Catherine wanted nothing to do with her. Best to just walk on by. Yet she couldn't do it. She stood there for several minutes before finally walking in and glancing around, just as if she were any other customer.

"Can I help you?"

Bea found herself looking up at a tall, bearded man with an affable expression. This was Catherine's husband, Stephen, she was sure of it. She could have said she was simply browsing and let him walk away. But she wanted to prolong the contact for a little longer, so she asked for help with a fountain pen. Stephen had sold one to Catherine the first time she had gone into the store; she remembered the story well. Bea feigned interest in the different pens he showed her, though they each seemed as good as the other. If she hoped he would say something personal, she was disappointed. He remained unwaveringly professional and unfailing polite. After paying for the pen she finally selected, Bea left the store, stuffing the package into the recesses of her bag. She would not go into the shop again.

She discovered the foundling home by chance on one of her walks when it had suddenly started to rain and she'd found herself without an umbrella. After ducking inside the front door, she was greeted by a baby's cry. Looking around, she saw a woman seated at a desk who asked, "May I help you?"

"I'm not sure. What is this place?" Bea shook off her coat and stamped her feet; rainwater puddled around her shoes.

"The Madison Square Foundling Hospital and Home."

"Hospital?"

"Well, that's only part of our mission. Not all of the babies are sick. In fact, most of them are quite healthy, really."

"Then what are they doing here?" Bea was distracted. The wails of that baby, wherever it was, had intensified. Wasn't anybody going to do anything about it?

"Waiting to be adopted, of course. Is that why you're here? To adopt?"

"Me? No. I just stepped in to get out of the rain."

"And good you did," said the woman, whose name tag read MRS. WARREN. "No sense catching your death out there. Would you like a cup of tea? We serve tea and sandwiches in the lounge every day from eleven to one. It's just down that hallway."

"Thank you, maybe I will," said Bea. The screaming of the baby was still disconcerting to her. Why didn't someone see to it? "I'm curious about the babies. What do they do all day?"

"We have people coming through regularly," Mrs. Warren explained. "Would-be parents that are looking to adopt. And there are the nurses, of course. But they're so busy, so the babies are mostly in their beds. No one has time to play with them, if that's what you mean."

"Or pick them up when they're screaming?"

"Oh, yes, of course." Mrs. Warren turned her head in the direction of the sound. "Someone will go see what that's about."

"When?" Bea was aware she had no leverage here. After all, what was she prepared to do about it? And then it came to her, the most natural and obvious thing in the world. "Maybe I could go and see what's ailing that baby. And perhaps hold or walk with it?"

Mrs. Warren looked at her with frank surprise. "You want to pick up a crying baby?"

"Don't you think someone should?"

Although Mrs. Warren was clearly puzzled by Bea's request, she nonetheless led her upstairs, toward the sound of the wailing, to meet the floor nurse, who seemed quite harried. She plucked the shrieking infant from her crib and unceremoniously handed her to Bea. "Her name's Pauline. Or I think it is," she said. "That may be an older tag that wasn't replaced."

Bea looked at the baby who may or may not have been Pauline. Her face was flushed and there was hair plastered to her head with what must have been a combination of sweat and tears. Bea used her handkerchief to pat the little cheeks dry. "Let's have a stroll, shall we?" Rocking the baby gently as she went, Bea walked the length of corridor and back again. The baby's sobs lessened, and with a final hiccup, she was—at last—quiet. "She's wet, and should be changed," Bea said to the floor nurse.

"They were all changed not an hour ago," the nurse said, sounding defensive.

"Still, she's wet—check for yourself."

The nurse reached over and patted the baby's bottom. "Why, so she is." She shook her head. "There are so many of them—there's no keeping up."

"I can change her." Bea took the baby to a table that was covered by an oilcloth pad stacked high with folded diapers, next to a glass jar filled with diaper pins and a tin of Brownie Skin Ointment. The smell from the covered diaper pail next to the table was over-powering. Although it had been many years, Bea remembered her time with the Phillipses and knew what to do. After depositing the sodden diaper in the pail, then cleaning and coating the baby's skin—which was covered in an angry rash—with ointment, she pinned on a fresh cloth and then handed her back to the nurse. "I think she'll be all right for now."

Bea watched as the floor nurse set the baby down in her crib. Two other nurses hurried by; they didn't even look at the baby, or at any of the other babies they passed. Bea understood why. These women looked like they were busy from morning until night. They didn't have time to hold a baby just for the sake of holding one. Or play peekaboo, patty-cake, or anything else. But Bea did.

The hospital had no formally designed program for what she pro-posed, but no one raised any objections either. On the contrary, the director, a woman of perhaps sixty with a bun that looked painfully tight, was delighted by Bea's offer to volunteer. "Why, you'd be a pair of hands from heaven," Mrs. Baumgarten said. "And we could certainly use them."

Once she settled into this new routine, it occurred to Bea that she had been unconsciously readying herself for it. Shortly after decamp-ing for Manhattan, she'd made a final evening trip to the house on St. Marks, face well hidden by the black-veiled hat, and had the cab wait while she collected her own clothing as well as all the inventory left in the shop. Most everything was sent into storage, as the fanciful, elaborate garments seemed wrong for her present circumstances, and she filled only a suitcase with simpler clothes. Even then she sensed she needed new garments for a life that would be more active and less ornamental than the one she'd known.

She went uptown to Macy's in Herald Square, where she was drawn to the kind of modern, two-piece outfits women had started wearing during the war—a belted, hip-length jacket and matching skirt in navy blue, an unstructured periwinkle silk jacket and pleated skirt from the English company John Redfern. She also bought one of Redfern's versatile silk jersey traveling dresses; it put her in mind of the green jersey dress Alice had made, and Catherine had bought. The memory of Alice and Catherine stung. Abandoned—and possibly betrayed—by the first, excoriated and banished by the second. But she wouldn't allow herself to dwell on either of them.

Since her new clothes didn't require the elaborate armature of the past, Bea also shopped for streamlined brassieres, simple chemises, and comfortable knickers. What a liberation. She remembered the punishing undergarments of her youth, and the time it had taken every day to put them on and take them off. And when a baby at the foundling hospital wound his little hand through a tendril of Bea's hair and yanked it hard enough to bring tears to her eyes, she decided that her long tresses were a liability. She found a hairdresser on East Nineteenth Street and asked for a short, stylish bob. As the barber worked, her shorn locks, the dark intertwined with the gray, fell to the floor around her. There was a moment when she wanted to say *wait, let me gather them,* but the barber's boy came along with his broom and with a few deft movements, swept them away.

That night, as she stood in front of the mirror in her room, Bea looked at her hair, and then at the spare wardrobe that barely filled the armoire's rack. She had not been this unencumbered since she left Russia. Back then she'd mourned the loss of every gold chain and bracelet, every crystal goblet and perfume flacon, her sealskin coat with its matching hat and muff. Now there was no mourning, only the sense that she was moving into new territory, a place unfamiliar and undefined; she needed to shed as much baggage as she could for the journey ahead.

Bea purchased two more items she felt would be useful—one was a white wicker buggy and the other, a cart with four wheels, an enclosed seat, handlebars, and a long pole with which to control it. The smaller babies were content in the buggy, but the slightly older ones liked pushing the cart along with their pudgy legs.

The little girl she'd met that first day was one of them. Her name was not in fact Pauline but Raisa, a name that aroused Bea's curiosity. When she asked the director about the baby's background, she learned that Raisa was indeed Jewish, as she'd suspected, and that her parents had come from Russia. "Tragic story," Mrs. Baumgarten said. Raisa's mother had died of the Spanish flu, and her grieving father had then jumped from the roof of their five-story apartment building. "The rest of the family was back in Russia," said Mrs. Baumgarten. "There was no one to take her." Bea felt a special kinship with this child, and though she loved spending time with all the babies, Raisa quickly became her favorite. She would buy her things—a new dress, a hat, a rattle—and no matter which floor she visited, she always stopped by to see Raisa. And it seemed the baby girl was growing attached to her too, waving her hands excitedly in the air when she saw Bea approach, face breaking into a smile when Bea picked her up and held her close.

Her time with Raisa and the others scratched at long-dormant emotions, ones she'd last experienced when she had lived with the Phillipses. She'd never felt this tenderness, even intoxication, with her own child; the circumstances of her birth were too devastating and chaotic to have allowed for that. But now, freed from responsibility, and able to willingly, easily give, her affection for these babies could rise up and bubble over.

While Mrs. Baumgarten and Mrs. Warren both expressed their gratitude to Bea, the actual nursing staff mostly ignored her, and in one case, seemed to resent her. When she suggested that they form a little group for some of the older children, Nurse Morgan—the woman who'd insisted that Raisa was not wet—snapped, "What would be the good of that?"

"They would benefit from playing with one another," said Bea. "It would give them a different kind of stimulation."

"Well, who would organize such a thing? It's not like we have so much time on our hands, you know."

"I could do it. We could set up an enclosed outdoor area in the courtyard." The idea was taking more concrete shape in Bea's mind. "Buy some inexpensive fencing, perhaps wood. That ought to be sufficient to offer them liberty but keep them safe."

"It seems like a lot of trouble," Nurse Morgan said skeptically.

"These babies are alone in the world. Don't they deserve a little extra effort?"

Nurse Morgan said nothing. But a week or so later, Bea was surprised to learn that her plan had been implemented—and that the head nurse took the credit for it. At first she was annoyed but then decided it was the babies that counted, not her pride.

Once the fencing had been erected, she took it upon herself to bring out small groups of children for twenty minutes at a time. The ones who could toddle were delighted by their freedom, and the ones still in a pram seemed to respond just to the fresh air and change of scenery. This success made Bea think there might be other possible enhancements to the space. She visited the New York Public Library, where she read about young children and their social development.

She was especially excited by the idea of a sand table—a zinc-lined enclosure filled with grains of sand. When dry, the children could pour the sand using tin vessels. When damp, they could mold and build with it. Bea could just picture it: a group of children sitting contentedly in the enclosure, building hills, castles, mountains . . . entire villages and cities made of sand!

Nurse Morgan did not share Bea's vision. "What a ridiculous idea! There will be sand in their eyes, their noses, their ears . . . They'll eat it. Or throw it at each other—"

"We would do it in small groups," Bea said. "They would be supervised."

"Every cat in creation will find it. The thing will be teeming with germs and bacteria in no time—"

"Not if we cover it at night. A heavy tarp would do it."

"What about the sand that would be tracked into the building, and into their cribs? I hate to think of the mess it would make."

"As I said, the groups would be small, so we could supervise. The children would be brushed off, their clothing and shoes shaken out before going back inside—"

"There will be no sand." Nurse Morgan's voice was firm, her tone final. "Now is there anything else you'd like to discuss?"

This time, Bea was more than annoyed, she was angry, but knew she had to tamp down the feeling. Challenging Nurse Morgan would not get her what she wanted. But perhaps a discussion with Mrs. Baumgarten might. Unlike the nurse, Mrs. Baumgarten loved the idea and almost immediately authorized its construction, which Bea had volunteered to pay for. She watched the workmen hauling the heavy bags; the sight of the golden sand pouring into the enclosure filled her with satisfaction, which only deepened when she was able to bring the children in to play. She quickly developed a routine—four or five children at a time, twenty minutes per group. Sometimes she would climb in and play with them; it had been so long since she'd used her hands for any such purpose.

But though Bea had emerged victorious, Nurse Morgan was not one to back off easily. Although she was around Bea's age, she had the energy of a very young woman. No matter what time Bea arrived, Nurse Morgan seemed to be there already, and she was still there when Bea left; did the woman never go home to eat and sleep, or just march down the hallways at a brisk pace, dispensing medication and directions with equal aplomb, twenty-four hours a day? The other nurses didn't necessarily like her, but they all respected her, and when they had a question or needed guidance, it was Nurse Morgan whose help they sought.

Nurse Morgan continued to grumble about sand in the building, though Bea never saw any and was scrupulous in cleaning off the children after their play, and insisted that sand had gotten into the drain and would clog the pipes. Bea didn't believe her as the water in the sinks she used seemed to go down easily enough. And she often took Bea to task for other infractions, such as keeping the children outdoors a little longer than planned or spending more time with Raisa than the others.

"Favoritism is frowned on," said Nurse Morgan. "And if you don't adhere to the schedule, the whole day will be thrown off-kilter."

Bea could have pointed out that surely an extra few minutes out in the sunshine was worth a slight disruption in the schedule, or that her attachment to Raisa in no way harmed another child, but she didn't because she sensed the other woman was being deliberately antagonistic. Better to avoid an open confrontation if she could manage it.

Despite Bea's efforts to steer clear of her, Nurse Morgan nevertheless managed to corner Bea in the small room where the nurses went for a break; she had chosen a time when the two of them were alone.

"I've been looking for you," the nurse began. "We need to talk."

"What about?" Bea asked. It was still early, and on the way she had stopped in a bakery to purchase several small Linzer tortes. She had just taken one out of the bag and been about to bite into it when Nurse Morgan interrupted her. Bea put down the torte, thinking of its raspberry filling; her stomach growled.

"It's your attitude," Nurse Morgan said. "Superior. Haughty. You think you know better than the rest of us, but really, who are you? Where did you come from? You just wandered in off the street, and you come in giving orders—"

"Not orders, suggestions—"

"And you went right over my head about this sand table or whatever it is. Such a nuisance."

"The children love it," Bea said quietly.

"Would you let them gorge themselves on sweets all day or toddle right off the roof because they loved it? Children don't know what's best for them."

"Maybe not, but I fail to see how playing with sand is a hazard—"

"I've decided to talk to Mrs. Baumgarten," said Nurse Morgan. "You might as well know it now."

"Know what?" But Bea saw where this was leading.

"I'm going to ask her to forbid you to come here anymore."

"Why?" Bea saw a chasm open up in front of her, precipitous and vast. Her time at the foundling hospital had saved her; she knew that now. Just the thought of being barred made her feel inconsolable. But she was not going to let herself be cowed so easily.

"I just don't want the order I've established upset by a newcomer. It's not right. It's not fair. And I won't put up with it."

"So this isn't about the babies at all. It's about you. And me." Bea suddenly understood; it was so obvious that she wondered why she hadn't seen it before. "You think I'm trying to show you up, make all your hard work seem inconsequential."

"That's ridiculous," said Nurse Morgan, but she looked decidedly uncomfortable.

"Is it? I don't think so."

"Mrs. Baumgarten knows me, she trusts me implicitly." There was something almost pleading in Nurse Morgan's tone.

"I'm sure she does, but she also appreciates and respects me. And the hospital's board members were very pleased by the sand table. Mrs. Baumgarten made a point of telling me so."

"Well, maybe I was too hasty in my judgment about that," Nurse Morgan said stiffly.

"Maybe?" Bea saw her advantage and pressed it. "I'd say definitely."

"I've given years—decades actually—of my life to this place, so naturally I wasn't too receptive when you—"

"It wasn't just a matter of being unreceptive," Bea said. "You rejected my first idea and then claimed it as your own. You couldn't do that with the sand table, so instead you want to discredit me, or even banish me. But don't you see—if you try to improve your standing with Mrs. Baumgarten by undercutting mine, it won't work. In fact, she might end up thinking less, not more, of you."

Something flitted across Nurse Morgan's face. It was fear. Bea knew it well because she'd experienced it in the past and it had left a mark. Hadn't fear kept her from throwing Mr. Phillips out of her room? Or tearing up the money the Robichauds had given her and throwing it at their feet? Nurse Morgan was afraid of her, worried that Mrs. Baumgarten's good opinion of Bea might somehow tarnish her view of the nurse. Bea softened. Nurse Morgan was an experienced and dedicated professional. She'd been doing her job, and doing it well, for years. Maybe she and Bea didn't need to be adversaries. Maybe they could be allies instead. She picked up her Linzer torte again and then offered the bag to the nurse. "Please," she said. "Won't you have one?"

Nurse Morgan hesitated. "It's not that I couldn't see the value in what you were proposing," she said. "But these projects—they require so much more work, and I—well, all of us really—are already worked to the bone. It's enough to make sure that our charges are fed, changed, and kept healthy. Or given treatment if they need it. Adding on things like outdoor playtime and sand tables . . . well, it all felt like too much." She took a tart, though, and when she bit into it, the powdered sugar that clung to the corners of her mouth made her look less adversarial. "I'm sorry," she said. "I hope you can accept my apology." It was clear these words were difficult for her to say.

"Apology accepted." Looking at the nurse's pained expression, Bea could clearly see how much these words had cost her.

They were both quiet for a moment while Nurse Morgan finished the cookie and then wiped her mouth. "That was very good," she said. "Did you bake it?"

"Me? Oh no. I don't know my way around a kitchen at all."

"But you do know your way around a nursery."

"Thank you." She could have told the nurse about caring for Teddy Phillips, but any personal disclosures seemed unwise. And at that moment, a couple of other nurses entered the room for their breaks, so Bea could occupy herself by passing around the rest of the Linzer tortes.

After that conversation, Nurse Morgan gave her no further trouble and even began to solicit her opinion on a couple of occasions. Bea was grateful for the truce, especially when the nurse started making a point of finding Bea in the break room and offering her sweets that she had made—almond crescents, marguerites, divinity candy, candied grapefruit rind. But she never sat down and joined her; she simply left the treats and went about her busy day. Bea was actually disappointed by this; now she was curious about Nurse Morgan and wanted to get to know her better. She considered writing a note suggesting that they go out to dinner sometime, though it was not the sort of risk she was unaccustomed to taking. What if Nurse Morgan thought her unprofessional or strange and said no? Even if she said yes, such a meeting was still potentially awkward. They might find that outside the confines of the hospital they had nothing to say to each other. Yet Bea yearned for the company. Her evenings were long and lonely. While she was pondering whether to chance it, Nurse Morgan extended an invitation of her own.

"I live just off Madison Park, on Twenty-Fifth Street," she said. "It's a short walk from here, and I was hoping you might want to come over for dinner one evening."

"Dinner? At your home?" Bea was flabbergasted.

"My apartment, yes. And I promise there will be a proper meal, not just sweets."

Bea arrived at the apartment on the dot of seven, unprepared for how anxious she felt. She realized how reclusive and unsocial she had become in recent months. And for years, her social interactions had been predicated on business—she'd overseen the selling of women's bodies in New Orleans, and women's dresses in Brooklyn. When Tess Morgan—her given name was Teresa and she'd asked Bea to use Tess outside the hospital—opened the door, Bea almost didn't recognize her. She'd never seen the other woman in anything other than a uniform, starched cap always pinned securely in place. To- night she wore a two-piece gray dress with a dropped waistline, and a silver link chain from which an oddly shaped silver pendant hung. Her hair, brown mixed with gray, was pulled back in a low bun at her neck, and silver hoops glinted at her ears. Her appearance was altogether more chic than Bea would have imagined, and the apart- ment, with its streamlined furniture and forward-looking art—one painting that consisted of blurry, concentric circles, another that was composed entirely of small, brightly colored squares—was equally tasteful in a restrained way. Tess was clearly a woman of discernment and style; Bea never would have guessed it.

"Thank you for inviting me." Bea had brought flowers but instead of offering them to her hostess, she kept the bouquet clutched to her chest until she realized it and handed them over. Tess arranged the flowers and then invited Bea to sit at the rectangular table, where two candles burned in a pair of heavy, crystal holders. They ate the sole meunière and green beans Tess had prepared, as well as the dessert of baked Alaska.

"I had no idea you were such an accomplished cook."

"Skills honed in another life," Tess said as she cleared the table. "I rarely cook for myself these days."

When they moved to the sitting area, she on the sofa, Bea on the chair, she took a cigarette from an enamel box and lit it. "Do you mind?" she asked.

"Not at all." Bea was feeling less nervous now. The conversation had unfolded easily enough—the hospital, the babies. Nothing too personal or intimate. So she was surprised when Tess said, "You do have a real affinity for the children. A gift, even. Surely you've had at least one of your own."

Bea went very still. Where to begin, how to explain? *I had a daughter but I gave her away. Then I found her and lost her again. And I had another daughter but she ran away. I haven't seen or heard from her in months.* Had Alice been her daughter? She hadn't behaved like a mother to her, not really. She had no right to claim her.

". . . I'm sorry," Tess was saying. "I didn't mean to pry. I should know that the answer to that question can be . . . fraught. It certainly is for me."

"I'm not sure I understand."

"I had a child," Tess said. "A daughter."

She'd said *had*.

"Isabel. She was such a bright, lovely little thing. A sprite. A fairy."

"Then what . . . ?"

"She was five—almost six, just a month shy of her birthday. One Monday, she was her usual enchanting self, getting into everything, begging to use my best pearls and fox throw to play dress up . . . Tuesday she was droopy, Thursday she was battling a raging fever, and by Friday, she was gone. The infection had raced to her brain and it killed her." Tess exhaled and a large plume of smoke dispersed about her head.

"I'm sorry," Bea said. "So sorry."

"The light went out of my life. There was no consolation, no peace. My husband found consolation, though it wasn't with me. He left the marriage and started over with someone else."

"But you couldn't."

Tess looked at her steadily. "That's right. I couldn't. I could change my life, though. I enrolled in a nursing program and gave myself over to my studies. I had the best marks in the class, the best marks in the history of the school in fact. When I graduated, I came to work at the foundling home."

"That was very brave," said Bea.

"Brave?" Tess took a deep drag of the cigarette, as if she were drawing sustenance from it. "No. Desperate. I turned my back on my former friends, and my frivolous existence. I gave up the apartment I'd shared with my husband so I could be close to the hospital. I wanted to lead a life of service—it helped me to believe Isabel's death hadn't been entirely in vain."

"And you have." Bea was incredibly moved by not only Tess's story but also the honesty and dignity with which she told it. Could she have done the same? She wasn't certain.

"What about you, Bea? I've always sensed that you had some sorrow you were carrying. Maybe we recognize that in each other."

"Maybe we do."

Tess nodded as she extinguished her cigarette, and reached for another. "I have plenty of time," she said. "That is, if you're inclined to tell."

Here was her chance. "May I have a cigarette?" she asked. Bea had smoked only on rare occasions in New Orleans; it was not a habit she'd liked or adopted. But she was on the brink of revealing herself to someone relatively new in her life, a veritable stranger, and she needed some kind of fortification.

Tess offered her the box, and after lighting the cigarette, Bea stared at the smoldering orange tip, a tiny but implacable eye. Then she began to speak. If Tess was shocked or disgusted, she showed no sign of it. In fact, she said nothing but simply let Bea continue until she'd reached the end.

"So you do have children," she said. "Two daughters."

"Not really, not exactly—"

"Yes, really. Yes exactly. Two daughters."

"But one of them won't speak to me and the other has disappeared."

"That makes no difference," said Tess. "None at all." Then she gently took the cigarette, barely smoked, from Bea's hand, and tapped the end. Instantly, it collapsed into a tiny, velvety-gray mound of ash. "If they were ever yours, then they always are, and always will be. Always."

WINTER

CHAPTER TWENTY-SIX

ALICE

Brooklyn, 1924

In December, Alice watched how Catherine's in-laws began preparing for Christmas. If she'd thought their Thanksgiving celebration was lavish, she saw that it actually paled in comparison to this, their next big celebration. Catherine said Veronica Berrill approached the upcoming holiday as if it were a military campaign and Veronica was a general, orchestrating and plotting every move. First the house was dusted, mopped, scoured, and shined. Maids went up on stepladders, wiping down the chandeliers; all the silver was laid out in rows on the dining room table and furiously rubbed to a reflective gleam. Furniture was oiled, floors waxed, and everything that could succumb to bleach, ironing, and starch was bleached, pressed, and starched.

Then there were the interior and exterior decorations, which began early in December, the fragrant wreaths and swags and garlands, all interwoven with plaid ribbons and red berries. The tree wouldn't go up until a few days before the actual holiday, but the Moravian blown glass and Polish glazed ceramic ornaments were taken out of their excelsior-lined boxes in time for the tree-trimming party that Veronica hosted for the children. There was to be a gingerbread house dripping with sugar icing and studded with candies, and platters piled high with cookies of every sort. Christmas dinner would be a roast goose and a ham, as well as scalloped potatoes, creamed spinach, fresh rolls, and three kinds of pie—mince, apple, and chocolate cream.

Alice was grateful for all the distraction. Her mind pulsed with worry; her body was an outright traitor. Her breasts, her belly, and even her full face were a source of self-loathing; as her size increased, so did her disgust. Like someone unable to look away from a grisly crime scene, she tried to imagine what exactly had been done to her, and by whom. She'd been polluted by one or both of those boys, and didn't even know which of them was responsible for getting her in this condition.

The doctor to whom Catherine had insisted on taking her said she would be giving birth in a matter of weeks. Even though the weight of the baby was like a sack of rocks that she longed to set down, the thought of the actual birth was terrifying. Even more terrifying was what she was going to do with a baby—her baby. Would Catherine continue to let her live here? And if not, where would she go?

To calm herself, Alice continued to knit—socks made good presents, as well as mufflers. Then there was the afghan she was making for Catherine and her husband; she'd come up with a design of violet, saffron, and chartreuse squares because she thought the combination of colors would be something Catherine would appreciate. Crocheting was not something she'd ever done, but the nice girl in a notions store on the corner of Berkeley Place had given her a quick lesson and sold her a simple hook. She was able to pick it up easily after that, so she busied herself crocheting dresser scarves, doilies, and tea cozies.

But though her hands were sure, precise, and competent, her mind was not. She'd find a way to keep the baby; she'd give the baby up for adoption. She'd stay in Brooklyn; she'd go back to New Orleans. No—Belle Chasse. Or someplace else entirely. And then there was Bea—how could she right the wrong she'd done her? Was there a hope of forgiveness? Or was the woman she'd so looked up to lost to her forever? She had the feeling that her life, governed as it was by this large, cumbersome body, was galloping along without her control or direction. Sometimes she'd bolt out of sleep, clammy with sweat. On one such night, the knocking she heard in her head turned into a knocking at the door.

"Who's there?" she asked, still partially submerged in that murky dream state.

"It's me, Catherine. I heard you cry out. Are you all right?"

"Come in." Alice's breathing calmed. "Please."

Catherine entered the room, her dressing gown sash untied, her dark hair loose and untidy around her shoulders. "I thought maybe the baby was coming,"

"Not yet," said Alice. "I was just having a bad dream."

"Maybe you'd like some hot milk? It will help you sleep. You need your rest, you know."

"I'd love that," Alice said gratefully.

"Good. I'll bring it up. It will just be a few minutes."

"Oh no!" Alice didn't want to be alone in the room right then. "I'd rather have it downstairs."

So she put on her dressing down and accompanied Catherine to the kitchen. It was reassuring to watch her moving around the room, adjusting the tiny blue flame beneath the pot, pouring the heated milk into the cup, ladling in a spoonful of honey. "There," Catherine said. "This should help."

"I think of her all the time," Alice blurted out.

"Bea?" asked Catherine, and when Alice nodded, she said, "So do I."

"Really? I thought you were so angry that you never wanted to see her again."

"Never is a long time. And as for angry, I know I was. Very angry. But now, not as much."

"What changed?" The sweetened milk was flowing through her, calming her down.

"Having you here," Catherine said.

"I'm not sure I understand."

"Bea was alone once too. Pregnant. Frightened. I knew all that. She'd told me. But seeing you in the same situation somehow made it all much more real. Because if you hadn't been able to come here, what would you have done?"

"I think of that every day," Alice said. "And I'm so, so grateful." She downed the last of the milk. "Do you think we'll ever see her again?"

"I don't know," Catherine told her. "The last time we were together I was . . . harsh. Very harsh." She glanced outside, where the sky was lightening. "Let's go back up now. Do you think you can sleep?"

Alice fell into a deep, peaceful slumber, and when she opened her eyes again, a weak, wintery sun was trying to penetrate the gray morning. She swung her legs off the bed, and nearly fell to the floor. Something had shifted, like her center of gravity had suddenly dropped. When she stood, a gush of liquid poured out, soaking her nightdress, her legs, and the small rug beneath her feet. Was this what the doctor had told her would happen—the water? It must be. The water was breaking and the baby was on the way. God help her.

* * *

Hours later, Alice lay recovering from the birth in a bed at Methodist Hospital, where Catherine and Stephen had brought her. They were presumably somewhere in the building. She wanted to see them but was too exhausted to say so. The labor had been swift—Alice was aware of the nurses talking about how quickly things were progressing—and while it had been even more excruciating than she'd imagined, it was also over much sooner than she'd been led to expect. The pains that came at intervals soon blurred into an unending spasm, with no rest, no relief. She'd thrashed, moaned, cried, pushed, and pushed again, and then—

"Now that's the way to have a baby!" crowed the doctor, who pulled something wet and covered in slime from her body. "She didn't even need the ether!" The creature was whisked away and she was cleaned up and allowed to close her legs, finally, and then, her eyes.

When she opened them some time later she was alone. She looked around the room. A green wreath with a red bow hung on the wall and a paper chain of green-and-red-loops was draped over the doorway. Christmas—she'd forgotten. Just then a nurse appeared with the baby, tightly swaddled in a flannel blanket and head covered by a fitted cap. "Here's your boy!" she said brightly.

Reluctantly, Alice took the bundle in her arms. He was so, well, ugly. Were all newborns so ugly, or just this one? She stared at his mottled complexion, his lumpish nose, his eyes, with their heavy lids, that bulged, ever so slightly, like a frog's. Did he look like Artie? Or like Sheldon? In his tiny face, she saw their faces, jeering at her, taking off her clothes. Were these actual memories or just her imagination? It didn't matter. The baby revolted her.

"Do you have a name for him?" the nurse asked.

"A name?" asked Alice. She hadn't once thought about it.

"Well, yes. He needs a name."

"I haven't decided yet."

"You could always name him for his father. Men seem to like that."

Alice felt a prickle of fear. "His father? What do you know about his father?"

"The gentleman that brought you in—his wife gave me the name."

"She did? Why?"

"For the birth certificate."

The birth certificate . . . of course. "Where are they now?"

"That couple? Outside in the lounge. They've been waiting to see you."

"Can you send them in now? Please?"

"Of course. I'll go get them."

The nurse left the room. Alice looked down at the baby in her arms. He was dozing now, so she was spared those eyes of his, though even in repose, they still protruded. She had an urge to put him down, or better yet, get up and leave him behind. But she was still too wrung out from the birth to move.

"Alice! Congratulations!" Stephen's voice was so loud she wanted to put the pillow over her ears to muffle the sound. He carried a bouquet of white rosebuds wrapped in crisp white paper and tied with a blue ribbon. He was grinning broadly.

"And look, there's the baby." Catherine's voice was reverent. "He looks so solemn."

Solemn? Alice thought he looked like a gremlin. A troll. "The nurse said you told her his father's name," Alice said. "But how . . . ?"

"It was my idea. Stephen agreed though. He agreed right away." Catherine addressed her, but her gaze remained on the baby.

Stephen nodded. "We told them the baby's father was James Berrill."

"Who is James Berrill?" asked Alice.

"My cousin."

"How could you *do* that? What's he going to say when you tell him?" Alice saw them exchange glances.

"He's not going to say anything. He's dead—he was killed in the war, may God rest his soul."

"I still don't understand," Alice said.

"You see, we thought the father's name should be on the birth certificate, and so I thought of James. He was Stephen's first cousin and they'd always been close, like brothers really. James would have wanted to help if he could." Catherine was talking very fast.

"Help?" Alice was even more confused now.

"The baby needed a name. So James gave him one—think of it as a posthumous gift," said Stephen. "Unless of course you'd rather not—"

"No, it's fine. Fine. Thank you. Again. It seems I have so much to thank you for." The baby stirred in Alice's arms. "Let's call him James, then. James—for his 'father.'"

"That's a lovely gesture, Alice," Stephen said.

"Very thoughtful," added Catherine.

The baby was fussing now, his little face scrunched in—anger? hunger?—Alice was sure she didn't know, but his skin, previously just mottled, was now turning decidedly blotchy.

"Maybe he needs to be fed—" Catherine gestured to her own chest.

Alice felt a distinct sensation, a tingling, a tightening. She looked down to see two wet spots on the front of the hospital gown. They were spreading.

"No," she said, horrified at the thought of the baby suckling from her body. "No, no, no. Please, you take him." She thrust the baby toward Catherine, who looked surprised but immediately stretched out her arms.

"Hello, little James," she cooed. "Welcome to the world."

Alice was using the blanket to frantically blot the front of the gown. This liquid, this milk . . . it was disgusting. She just wanted it to dry up, go away—

". . . what about a middle name?" Catherine was saying. "Don't you think he should have a middle name?"

"You choose it, then! He's yours anyway!"

"What?" Catherine and Stephen said the word almost in unison.

"He's a Berrill, isn't he? He's practically one of you already. So take him, please just take him. Adopt him. Raise him. He's your present—Merry Christmas!" And she put her face in her hands, surrendering to the sweet, sweet relief of her tears.

SPRING

CHAPTER TWENTY-SEVEN

BEA

Manhattan, 1925

There was a day in April when Bea arrived at the hospital to find Raisa's crib empty. She immediately went in search of Tess, whom she still always called Nurse Morgan at the hospital. "I just found out about it myself," Tess said. "I was planning to tell you as soon as I saw you."

"Tell me what?" Bea felt the dread even before she heard the answer.

"There's a couple, the Coopers. They're considering adoption."

"Adopting Raisa?"

"Yes," Tess said. "You know that's what we hope for here, right? That these children will leave the hospital and have a chance at a new life, with a new family." She touched Bea's arm. "They're spending a little time with her now but she'll be back in her crib after that. You can see her later."

"Of course," said Bea. "Later." She went off to visit with other babies but when she returned to Raisa's crib, it was still empty. *Tomorrow,* she told herself. She would see Raisa tomorrow. They could
spend extra time together to make up for the visit they missed. But
the couple had reappeared the next day, and the day after that. By
week's end, they had made the decision and started filling out the
paperwork for the adoption.

Bea had a last morning visit with her. Unaware of the impending
change, Raisa greeted Bea in her usual gleeful fashion—the wildly
waving fists, the little gurgles of excitement. Bea put her in the push-
cart and they walked all the way to the East River. She let Raisa scat-
ter the breadcrumbs she'd brought to a flock of pigeons; the little girl
bounced up and down in the seat as they fluttered around her. Then
Bea took her from the cart and sat with her on a bench for a long
time. Why was she feeling so bereft? This was wonderful news for
Raisa. As she'd known from the start, the aim of the foundling home
was to place the babies with loving families. Bea wasn't prepared to
adopt a child, yet she didn't want to see Raisa leave, didn't want to be
parted from her.

The day the Coopers came for Raisa, Bea deliberately stayed away.
When she returned the following day, looking for solace in the smiles
of other children, the comfort was fleeting, and she went home early.
Back in her rooms, she pulled out a small bottle of vodka she'd stowed
away years ago. Over the course of the evening, she consumed almost
all of it, portioned out in small glasses. She fell asleep fully dressed,
and woke the next day thoroughly disgusted with herself. Stripping
off her clothes, she washed herself at the sink and put on fresh undergarments, stockings, skirt, and jacket. She then found her shoes and
hat and prepared to leave her rooms, but found she couldn't make
herself do it. The thought of stepping into the foundling hospital
knowing that Raisa wouldn't be there filled her with the most pro-

found despair. What was there for her anyway? Forging a bond to another baby who would also be spirited away by an adoptive family? It all seemed so pointless.

Finally, she got herself to leave but she didn't head for the foundling hospital. Instead, she walked and walked many blocks uptown until she reached Central Park. By this time, her feet were aching, and her mouth was dry. The day had turned unseasonably warm and muggy and even her new, streamlined clothing felt restrictive and uncomfortable. Sinking gratefully down on a bench, Bea watched the parade of people strolling by. Some were alone, but what she focused on were people together—couples, families, women with children, pairs and groups of women or men. She'd always prided herself on her ability to survive whatever life thrust at her, to rely on no one but herself. Now she felt like she'd been a fool, squandered her chances— for connection, for love—because she thought that would keep her safe. How wrong she'd been. How deluded. She was right back where she'd been decades ago, lying in that upstairs bedroom after she'd given Catherine away, stunned with loss, with grief. To have come so far in life only to find herself here again—it rankled.

Clouds gathered above and rain threatened. People began hurrying along, looking for shelter. Bea remained where she sat. The loss of her parents, her brothers, Clay Robichaud, and even her own infant daughter—these had been losses not of her making. But the later losses—Catherine, Alice—had been her fault entirely. She'd never made it clear to Alice that she'd loved her, valued her. When Alice had felt displaced by Catherine, had Bea reassured her, made her feel safe and protected and cherished? She had not. Alice had betrayed her—Bea didn't know the specifics but instinctively felt that the girl had been involved—but maybe Bea had driven her to it. She'd been so caught up with finding Catherine, getting to know her, trying, in her own way, to win her over and as a result, been guilty of neglect as far as Alice was concerned. Why hadn't she made sure that Alice had companions her own age, that she felt she had a hand in determining her own future? Instead, Alice had moved to New York with Bea, Bea who'd been thinking only of herself. And now she'd vanished to God only knew where. How was she managing? She was so young, so defenseless. She didn't have Bea's backbone, her impervious shell—she hadn't had the time to develop it.

And then what of her last exchange with Catherine? How proud she'd been, how haughty and cold. She had wanted to protect herself and succeeded only too well. Catherine thought her uncaring. Aloof. It was all an act, a facade, something learned so long ago that it had become part of her, and she couldn't let it go, even when she wanted—or needed—to. She should have apologized to Catherine, begged her forgiveness, if not for lying about her past, then for the hurt Catherine experienced when she learned of it. Why hadn't she ever told her daughters—the one she gave up, the one she'd found along the way—the depth of her feeling? She had never said *I love you* to either of them. Not once. Why not? They were her daughters, both of them. Tess knew that. And now Bea did too.

Above her there was a sharp crack of thunder and then the rain came pouring down. Bea remained rooted to the bench, letting the water first punish and then cleanse her. Her hat became a waterlogged mess, her dress stuck to her body, rain squelched in her shoes, yet there she sat. A policeman walking his beat came up to her, extending his umbrella so that it covered her as well. "Are you all right, ma'am?" he asked. "Do you need any help?"

She shook her head, and rain dripped from her cheeks, her chin. "I'm fine."

"Are you sure? Maybe you'd like to go inside and dry off?"

"Not just yet," said Bea. "But thank you for your concern." Looking into his face, Bea could see how young he was; he could have even been her son. She smiled and tried to make her situation—sitting here getting drenched, making no effort to cover or protect herself—seem perfectly normal, and the policeman finally moved along. Eventually, she walked back downtown slowly. Her shoes had become excruciating, so she took them off and walked in her stocking feet. The gutters ran full and horses splashed water when they shook their tails; the few people in the streets regarded Bea with open suspicion. They thought she was a madwoman. She kept walking.

When she reached her building, she saw that her stockings were in shreds, so she peeled them off and walked up the stairs barefoot, trailing water as she went. Inside, she took off the wet clothes, exchanging them for garments that were clean and dry. That was better. Then she poured the remainder of the vodka down the sink. She had something important to do and she didn't want to be distracted. After assembling what she needed—ink, stationery, the pen she had bought at Berrill's—Bea sat down at the apartment's largest table and began to write. She should have written this letter months ago—after that last, disastrous meeting with Catherine. Too late, of course. But she understood now why she hadn't wanted—or been able—to do it then, because writing it forced her to dredge up the worst and most painful part of her past.

Dearest Catherine,

I know how shocked and horrified you were to learn my true story, to have the glossed-over version I first shared with you exposed for what it was—a lie. And I know how disgusted and hurt you feel. Also betrayed. But I hope you can consider my position. I'd made such an effort to find you, and if I told you straightaway who I was and had been, you would have ended our relationship immediately. Can you see how difficult this was? That I couldn't risk losing you again? Yet it seems that is exactly what happened. I don't know if I can ever regain your trust, or if there will ever again be a place for me in your life. Still, I want to tell you what happened in my own words, and not let the salacious words of that newspaper article speak for me. To do that, I need to go back a bit, to the time before the events described—so coldly, with so little context or insight—in the hope that if I do, you may come to understand. Understand and even forgive.

The night of Clay's funeral, I stayed with a woman Bitsy knew, and in the morning, using the key I still had, I retrieved my bag from Clay's house. Then I made my way to the neighborhood where the houses of ill repute flourished. I avoided the more lavish establishments and tried my luck at the smaller, more derelict ones. The first three—or was it four?—turned me away at once, but Eloise, who presided over a house just off North Robertson Street, was willing to give me a chance, even though she stared quite openly at my waist; my condition had just started to show. She was a faded blonde in a tattered silk wrapper and liver-colored lip rouge; I could tell that her accent was British, but it lacked the smooth polish of Mr. Bixby's.

"Not with the fellows, you understand, though some of them might not mind," she said. "But I can use a girl to do the washing up. Girl I had just upped and left without giving me so much as a day's notice."

"I can do all that," I said. "I can do anything."

"What about when your ankles swell and you're big as a balloon in the front?" she asked.

"I can mend." This was a lie. "And I'll polish the silver. I can do it sitting down."

"Silver!" she brayed. "Where do you think you are, Buckingham Palace? I ain't got no silver here, missy, and not likely to have any either."

"Please let me stay," I begged. "I haven't anywhere else to go."

Eloise pursed her luridly stained lips and sighed. "All right," she said. "I'll give you a try. But if you're not useful, or I catch you stealing so much as a lump of sugar, it's back to the street, you understand?"

"Yes, I understand," I said. "You don't have to worry about me."

The atmosphere at Eloise's simmered with resentment and discontent. I grew accustomed to the sound of angry voices—the girls sniping and muttering when they woke around three in the afternoon and crowding into the kitchen for the bitter, chicory-laced coffee and stale bread Eloise called breakfast. As evening fell and the doorbell started ringing, I heard them arguing with her about what they were owed. They also argued with the patrons who began to fill the parlor or with each other; sometimes these arguments led to physical encounters—scratching, biting, or pulling out clumps of one another's hair.

The cursing and insults were my morning song and my lullaby; the rise and fall of the voices, the bursts of invective, the drunken punches thrown by the customers—I grew inured to all of it. Keeping myself apart, I scrubbed—dishes, pans, floors—until my fingers grew raw and chafed, emptied chamber pots, beat the dingy carpets out behind the house, grateful all the while for the distraction from my own thoughts.

I no longer roamed the city as I had when I had lived with the Phillipses. But I did come to know the immediate area. There were two more houses like Eloise's on the street; one a few doors down and the other at the corner. One of these was a house of colored girls only; whites and coloreds weren't allowed to work together. Also on the street was a bar with a back room where men gambled all night long—cards, dice, darts—and a pawnshop, its smeared and grimy window crammed with jewelry, firearms, and the occasional oddity, like a magnificent stuffed gray owl with golden glass eyes that seemed to reveal its soul. Once I ventured inside, lured by a necklace of tiny red-orange glass beads. The dense strands reminded me of the triple-tier coral necklace that had been one of my mother's most prized ornaments. She had promised it to me on my wedding day, but it was sold, along with most everything else we owned.

Still farther down was another bar, this one featured a band of scruffy musicians of dubious talent, and a place that sold po'boys, those sandwiches crammed with oysters or shrimp, which most of the girls loved. "No onions," Eloise barked whenever they would head down the block to buy one. "The gentlemen don't want to smell no onions on your breath." She may have had a point, but calling the patrons of her house "gentlemen" was a gross exaggeration.

I found most of the girls who worked for Eloise coarse and frightening. Several carried weapons, small knives, or in one case, a pistol. I saw a girl use the tip of her knife to split the bottom lip of a customer—blood splattered all over the floor.

But there was one, Consuela, who seemed less coarse, less brutal than the rest. When she saw that I couldn't tolerate the coffee that Eloise provided, she said, "Let me show you how to fix it." She then whisked some milk she had heated, poured it into a small bowl, and added a little coffee and a lot of sugar. I took a tentative sip. It was unfamiliar, but not unsatisfying. I smiled at her. "Much better."

"Café con leche," she said. "Or café au lait—that's what they say here."

We became allies first, looking out for each other when possible, and then friends. Eloise liked Consuela, and because of our alliance she came to like me as well. She said I had the manners of a real lady. And when I did become as "big as a balloon," she wouldn't let me scrub the floors or do any heavy lifting. "It'll hurt the baby," she said. One morning when I was in the kitchen making the coffee and porridge that she sometimes served her girls, Eloise approached me. "Do you have a plan?" she asked.

"A plan?"

"For what happens to the baby," she said. "You must have thought about it some."

It seemed to me I'd thought of nothing but for months. It was clear the Robichauds would be of no help to me; I wouldn't approach them again. "There are orphanages. I can bring the baby to one of them."

"Is that what you want?"

"Do I have a choice?"

"You could have the baby and raise it here. It's been done," said Eloise.

"Really?" I hadn't known, but the thought gave me no solace. Raise a child in a whorehouse? What kind of life was that for either of us?

"Yes, really. But there might be another way," she told me.

"And what would that be?"

Sylvia and Chantelle came into the kitchen. The light from the window was merciless, revealing their lined and spotted skin, and the gray roots sprouting where the brassy auburn or shoe polish black had grown out.

"I'll tell you later," said Eloise. When they had cleared out, she took me aside and told me about a man she'd known from way back who had made good, and even though he'd moved away, he still stayed in touch. "He's very successful now," she said. "He married a woman from a nice family. They're very happy, only she couldn't have children. Always wanted them though. And if yours was white, I know she'd take it."

"Do you really think so?"

"I know so." I was quiet so she went on. "Would you rather leave your baby in an orphanage with all those castoffs? Or give it to a well-to-do couple who'll dote on it from morning till night?" When I didn't reply, she said, "Besides, there's money in it—for both of us."

"Money?" I hadn't considered that.

"This couple, they'd pay you well for a baby. And then you could pay me a little something for the favor of bringing you together." I must have looked horrified because Eloise added, "We're all just selling our wares, dearie, old and young alike. So how's this any different? Someone's going to profit from your bad luck. Might as well be you."

I said nothing. There was much about Eloise's house that I found objectionable and offensive, and as I made my own way in the same underworld, I was conscious of wanting to distinguish myself from her. But *even so, I had to concede that there were times when she was absolutely right, and this, alas, was one of them.*

Eloise was with me when my water broke, soaking the worn and already stained carpet in her front room. She hustled me upstairs to bed, and then dispatched Consuela and some of the others to perform the necessary tasks—boiling water, gathering towels and blankets, sponging off my forehead—while I sweated and grunted with the effort of birth. As soon as one wave of pain passed, I was engulfed by another. It wasn't an especially long labor, but while I endured it, I felt it would never end.

"Here it comes!" cried Consuela as something slipped, warm and wet, from my body. For a few seconds, I luxuriated in the relief from the stabbing pain and didn't immediately connect the thin, mewling cry with anything that had to do with me. It's over, *I kept thinking.* Thank God it's over. *I think I even dozed for a little while, and when I opened my eyes again, Eloise handed me a small bundle wrapped in a piece of faded flannel that I recognized from one of my winter petticoats. "You should try to feed her now."*

I looked down at the baby. At you, Catherine. Your eyes were startlingly blue—just like your father's. Devushka, *I said softly. That had been my mother's word for me. When you were pressed close to my chest, you began snuffling, rooting even, like a piglet, for the breast I fumbled to offer. It took a couple of tries before you latched on but when you did, your gummy grip had surprising force and I winced.*

I tried to adjust to the unfamiliar and insistent tugging. There was nothing pleasurable about it—this was about survival and nothing else. When you had had your fill and drifted off to sleep, Consuela gave you to Eloise, who placed you in the dresser drawer she had emptied and prepared for this purpose. There was no point in buying a cradle—you wouldn't be staying with me for very long.

Consuela helped me wash and change while another girl cleaned up the bedding and floor. Then I lay down and slept for what felt like days.

It was only your urgent wailing that woke me, and this time, when you were placed at my breast, you knew exactly what to do. So did I. This went on for a few days. Eloise discouraged me from naming you, so I didn't.

You soon lost the yellowish cast to your skin and your face filled out nicely. You had a coating of fine brown hair on your head—not exactly blond, but much lighter than I would have expected given my own coloring. And every time your eyes locked on mine, I could have sworn the spirit of your dead father was staring back at me. I began to enjoy the nursing—the intensity of the suckling and the utter surrender, almost drugged, in its aftermath. But I knew all the while that this would need to come to an end, and by the close of the second week, Eloise had arranged for me to meet Sebastian. Meredith wasn't with him. He was very solicitous and never for a moment made me feel ashamed of the position I was in. And he was predictably smitten by the baby—by you.

"She'll want for nothing," Sebastian told me. "Her own room, the best wet nurse in the city, and a governess after that."

"Will she be educated?" I asked. You were snuggled in my arms, your blue eyes unblinking and solemn.

"Oh yes," he said. "Of course she will."

I nodded. How could I know whether he'd keep his word? We chatted for a little longer and I let him hold you. You didn't protest. And then I did what I had known I would do all along: I gave you to Sebastian Delgado.

He didn't take you right away but allowed me to have one last night with you, a night during which I stayed awake, watching you sleep. I was lacerated by my thoughts and I longed for something to numb my fevered brain; instead, I continued in this strange, suspended state until dawn, when I could finally get up and stumble to the kitchen for a cup of scalding coffee taken black, without my usual ameliorating portion of milk.

Sebastian arrived just as I was finishing the coffee. He gave me the money he had promised, and I gave him my daughter. I gave him you. He left and I never expected to see him—or you—again. All in all it had gone well. My shame was a hidden thing, behind me now. I could move on in my life as if it had never happened.

Yet after Sebastian took you away, I sank into the deepest despair that I'd ever experienced, and I was at a loss to explain why. Hadn't it all worked out, even better than I'd ever imagined possible? I knew that I couldn't have raised you alone, in a brothel no less. I had done what I'd had to do and I'd managed to spare you the grimness of a local orphanage. Instead, you would be raised by loving parents and remain forever ignorant of the circumstances of your birth. And yet, I mourned your loss more keenly than that of my father, my mother, my siblings, and even Clay. For days after Sebastian left, I could do nothing but lie in my attic room, sleeping or staring at the flaking paint on the ceiling above me. I was too numb and broken to cry, though sometimes tears seemed to rise in my eyes and leak down my face of their own volition. I was paralyzed by sadness, and confused by my reaction—I had not imagined I would be so stricken. Consuela came up as often as she could, but though I was grateful for her company, I felt too broken to talk.

Eloise was patient at first, but as the days turned to weeks, she grew less so. "You need to get up and get on with it, dearie," she told me. "You're doing yourself no good at all, moping around like this. Why, you've done something wonderful for that girl, yes, you have. Think of the life you've spared her, and the life she's going to have. The life you made sure she could have. And just think—you even got paid to do it. Paid quite handsomely, I would add." Of the fifteen hundred Sebastian had given me, I'd given Eloise five hundred for brokering the arrangement.

I was afraid she would turn me out, and in my state, the idea seemed terrifying. So I forced myself to get up, wash, dress, and fix my hair. I planned to remain employed in the kitchen or on the sidelines; I had proven myself to be capable and hardworking, and I knew Eloise would allow it. And I might have been satisfied with that, at least for a time.

But one evening, I began chatting with a young man who was waiting in a corner of Eloise's parlor for his turn with another of her girls. His expression was sensitive and his features, especially his large brown eyes, were fine, but the angry blemishes on his face diverted all attention from them. I could see he was made uncomfortable by his skin, which was badly pitted where it wasn't broken out, and he sat with a handkerchief pressed to his cheek. He told me that he worked in a bank but that he read poetry in the evenings and had even tried his hand at writing his own verse. I was touched by this, as well as by his excruciating self-consciousness. When he asked if he might go upstairs with me instead of that other girl, I agreed. I felt I was giving him a gift of my sympathetic regard; he in turn was so grateful for my treatment that he paid me twice the going rate.

That was how it began. Eloise was pleased, and was keen to steer me toward customers such as the shy, older man who, like Mr. Phillips, wanted only to watch me undress and loll about languidly as he touched himself, the man whose full height reached only my hip and who insisted our activities take place in the pitch-dark, and the portly man who stuttered so terribly that he wrote little notes rather than speak to me. All the strays, the misfits, the wounded, the damaged—they recognized a kindred spirit in me. We were gentle with each other, and I could tolerate them. By then I knew about the thin sheaths that could prevent both an unwanted child and the vile diseases of the trade, and I insisted that my customers use them.

I continued in this manner for the next couple of years; once a week, I would take my share of my earnings and bring it downtown, to the Whitney National Bank, where I had opened an account. As I added to the thousand dollars I had from Sebastian, I watched my savings grow steadily. I knew I could have sought another form of work: serving food or drink, cleaning. No one would hire me in a more respectable domestic position, not anymore. And even if they had, these jobs would have placed me once again at the mercy of my employers. I remembered those nights when Mr. Phillips would come to my room; I never wanted to be that beholden to anyone again. I was able to endure life as a prostitute because I saw the men who used my body as stepping-stones, part of a plan that had been burbling just below my consciousness until I finally recognized it for what it was. And when I did, it seemed like the most logical and sensible thing in the world—I would go into business for myself.

Once the idea was born, its possibilities unfolded and expanded, filling my mind entirely.

In an establishment of my own, the reins of control would be in my hands, and my hands only. Being a madam had its own kind of status, at least in the looking-glass world of the District. And in their own houses, madams made all the rules.

I tended my plan as a gardener tends her plot, making notes in a journal I kept hidden. I told no one about it, not even Consuela. But we remained close, and through her, I became less fearful of—and even friendly with—the other girls in the house. They eventually shared their stories over smudged glasses of rye or beer: sold into prostitution in Buenos Aires, raped by her foster brother, orphaned and left to wander the streets. The details varied but the underlying thread was the same: we were all women to whom harm had been done.

It wasn't long before I bought a small house of my own four blocks down from Basin. It was a run-down little place, but I did my best to improve its appearance with a fresh coat of paint, secondhand drapes bought from a junkman, and other furnishings I could scrounge or come by cheaply. I had secured the services of four girls and was able to open within six weeks of signing the deed at the bank; I'd been amazed to learn that in New Orleans, even unmarried women could own property. Consuela came with me and proved herself invaluable in so many ways. I needed her as much as she needed me. I am sorry I eventually lost touch with her—another regret among so many.

Several of my customers from Eloise's followed me and I was gradually able to shift them over to my girls, who were selected for their personalities as well as their looks. These customers told their friends, and their friends brought other friends and soon I had outgrown the house and amassed enough money to sell it and purchase another. This one was on Liberty Street, only two blocks from the opulence of Basin, but Basin Street was my goal. I had a vision for what kind of establishment I wanted to run and for the next ten years worked hard to make that dream come true. When I was finally able to buy a house on that most coveted of streets, I felt I had achieved something of value.

Again, I briefly considered opening a dress or perfume shop, but being a madam had suited me better. If I'd chosen something more respectable, my time as a prostitute would always be nipping at my heels, waiting to ensnare me. A former customer might recognize me and the word would spread. No, it was better that I stayed safely within the District, where I was known and respected. Instead of having to hide my past, it could walk in the open beside me.

If you can believe this, I had a reputation for being firm but fair. I would not employ girls younger than eighteen. I gave the women who worked for me more of their earnings than any of the other madams, as well as an allowance for clothing and cosmetics. I saw to their physical needs—feeding them decently, making sure they saw a doctor when they needed one, not forcing them to entertain too many customers in an evening. I did all this not only because I felt it was right, but also because I preferred to have the loyalty and gratitude of the women in my employ, not their resentment or hatred. My father had always treated his employees with that in mind, and they repaid him in kind. It was one of those employees who came to our house after the tannery had been burned down and tried to help us.

For many years, this life suited me well, or well enough. I had no desire to find another man, to fall in love again. No desire for a child. Even Alice didn't quite awaken those feelings, at least not then. I didn't feel like her mother. I didn't believe I had the right to. Now she's gone, who knows where, and I am tortured with guilt. I can only hope—I no longer pray—that wherever she is, it is somewhere safe and that she is happy.

I have made many mistakes, though none out of malice. The fates were not kind to me, but I did the best with what I had been given—and with what had been torn away. You were both. In finding you again, I had hoped I might if not mend, then at least soften, that savage tear in the fabric of my life. If it is ever in your heart to allow that, I will be here.

Always,

Bea

The rain had stopped and the sky cleared as Bea set out again, this time toward the subway that would take her to the house on St. Marks Avenue. Her daughter's house. The letter she'd written was with her, folded in thirds and slid inside an envelope with Catherine's name on it. But Bea wasn't going to wait for the mail. No, she would deliver it herself. She felt resolute as she emerged from the subway station, resolute as she walked along the streets of her erstwhile neighborhood, hesitating only when she reached the door. Ignoring the fear that had begun to fray her resolve, she rang the bell firmly.

The door was opened almost immediately by the maid Bea had seen the only other time she'd been here. The maid asked for her name, but Bea just handed her the envelope and said, "Please give this to Mrs. Berrill. I'll wait outside."

The maid looked puzzled but took it, and as she closed the door, Bea heard Catherine saying, "Nettie, was that—" only the rest of it was drowned out by what sounded like a baby. A baby! Whose was it? Bea waited in a quiet agony of suspense, trying to imagine Catherine's response to her words. She felt almost sick with apprehension and wanted to sit down on the stoop but instead remained standing, holding on to only her own crossed arms for support. The letter was long but not that long; surely Catherine had finished by now. Finished and decided that Bea's attempts to explain, to justify, were insufficient, that the transgression and the deception were too great. Bea should leave now, and not endure another minute of this, another second—

The door was yanked open, and there was Catherine, holding the letter in one hand. Her face glistened with tears. "Bea!" she cried before throwing her arms around her and hugging her tightly. "Oh, Bea!"

For a moment Bea remained still, frozen almost, until it sunk in— Catherine was not sending her away. Tentatively, she allowed herself to return the embrace.

"You must come in! Right now!"

Bea crossed the threshold of Catherine's house, a house filled with so much color, pattern, and texture as to be dizzying. She'd had a glimpse of the interior before, but only a brief one. Now she could look all she pleased. She sat on Catherine's sofa, gazing around, when a tall, bearded young man approached. "Bea?" He looked surprised but then extended his hand. "I'm Stephen Berrill, Catherine's husband. It's so good to meet you."

"Good to meet you too," said Bea. He didn't remember that he'd sold her a pen.

Stephen left the room and Catherine joined her on the sofa. She set the letter out on the low table in front of them, smoothing out the folds. "I'm sorry for the way I spoke to you that day. I've spent a long while regretting it. I could only see what you'd done from the outside. It took me a while to understand what it might have felt like for you, going through it. And this"—she touched one of the pages—"this told me everything I should I have been able to guess on my own, what I only began to understand when Alice showed up here—"

"Alice! Alice was here? Is she all right? When did you see her last?"

Before Catherine could answer, the maid appeared with a baby boy in her arms. Was this the baby she'd heard when she rang the bell? It must be.

"Oh, I didn't realize you had company, Mrs. Berrill. I thought you wanted me to bring him in but I can take him upstairs if you like," the maid said.

"No, Nettie, that's all right. Bring him here."

"This is the newest member of the family," said Catherine when the baby was settled on her lap, gumming his knuckles contentedly. "James Redden Berrill."

"Berrill?" Bea looked from Catherine to the baby, the baby to Catherine. "So he's—yours? So soon? I thought you said—"

"Oh, he's ours all right, though I didn't give birth to him."

"Ah," said Bea, "Then where . . . ?"

"Alice," Catherine said. Bea's astonishment must have been evident for she added, "That's right—you didn't know, did you? She never told you."

"Told me what?"

"That she was pregnant."

"Pregnant! What happened? Who was the father?"

"That's not for me to say," said Catherine. "But I can tell you that after she'd talked to that reporter, she was so ashamed of herself she couldn't face you, so she ran off and lived in Manhattan for a time. She'd gotten herself a job with a tailor in Greenwich Village. When she found out she was expecting a baby, she came back to Brooklyn looking for you, only you'd gone and she didn't know how to find you."

A grief, even a sickness, gripped Bea at the thought of Alice not being able to find her in her time of need. "So she came here? She came here and you—you took her in."

"We did. She had no one else to turn to. Like you, Bea. That's what happened to you."

It was exactly what had happened to her. The baby began fussing and Catherine called Stephen back in. "Can you ask Nettie to give him his bath now?"

"Of course." Stephen swooped James into his arms and whisked him up the stairs.

"So she's all right?" asked Bea. "You're still in touch with her?"

"Oh yes! She never left—she lives here now."

"Lives here? With you?"

Catherine nodded. "It seemed like it was for the best. She's a dear girl and we love having her."

"And the baby . . . little James?"

"We adopted him formally. It was Alice's idea. She didn't feel she could raise him on her own, and we'd become very involved during the pregnancy and the birth. It seemed like the natural thing to do."

"So you did come round to the idea of adoption," said Bea.

"Having Alice here, watching him grow inside her, being there when he was born. He was already a part of us. Part of me. I just didn't know it yet."

"And what about his father? Is Alice in contact with him?"

"I'm going to let her explain all that. She's out this evening but there'll be plenty of time."

"I'm just so relieved to know she's safe. I was so worried about her."

"And we were worried about you." Catherine reached over to take Bea's hand.

Bea sat quite still—had Catherine ever done this before? Initiated a touch? She didn't think so.

". . . we've already had our dinner but could I offer you something to eat or drink?"

"No, thank you."

"Then let's go up and visit Jamie in his room." She stood, her hand still clasping Bea's. "He's your grandson after all."

"Yes," said Bea. Her heart was so full it was spilling over. "Yes, he is."

CHAPTER TWENTY-EIGHT

CATHERINE, ALICE, BEA

Brooklyn and Manhattan, 1925

Catherine's days were now governed by baby James, the tiny tyrant, the precious prince. Oh, Bridget, Molly, and even Veronica and especially her own mother tried to get her to keep him on a schedule. Schedules, they chorused, were essential for a well-run home and a well-adjusted child. Catherine would nod her head and say *yes, yes, yes*, just waiting for them to stop so she could get back to doing things her own way. She didn't care about schedules or that the experts were so enamored of them and she left unopened the books on child-rearing that Bridget and Molly were constantly foisting upon her. As far as Catherine was concerned, she was the expert and she needed advice and guidance from no one. Her instinct told her to feed her baby when he was hungry and to pick him up when he cried. She didn't believe the first would upset his digestion or the second would spoil him. And he wasn't either of those things. He was mostly a happy, good-tempered baby, a little angel in her view. Of course he had his occasional temper fits, but he was a baby, for heaven's sake. That's what babies did. And Catherine was so happy to indulge his little whims, to let him snuggle between her and Stephen early in the morning or to have a taste of what he saw—and yearned for—on her plate. He ran her ragged sometimes, but it was a happy exhaustion, full and brimming with life, the life she'd always wanted and didn't think she'd ever have. But there was this meal for Bea she wanted to host—the meal she had been planning all those months ago until the hateful article appeared and both Bea and Alice had disappeared—and so she allowed Bridget to look after little Jamie, if only for a little while.

"I think a poached salmon would be nice," she told Nettie as they sat in the kitchen, putting together a shopping list.

"I can do a dill sauce with that, Mrs. Berrill. And asparagus Hollandaise."

"That sounds lovely. A salad too?"

Before Nettie could reply, Catherine heard the sound of the key in the front lock, followed by the sound of someone hurrying up the stairs. "Alice?" Catherine called out, and within seconds, Alice breezed into the room. "Hello, hello!" she said.

"Hello yourself." Catherine smiled. "Back so soon?" Alice had said she was off to the picture show with a group of Stephen's siblings and cousins.

"I haven't even gone yet! But I left without my coin purse and I won't get very far without that."

"Well, have a good time," said Catherine. "Will we see you for dinner?"

"Oh no, I've been asked to eat with the Berrills tonight. Is that all right?"

"Of course it is." Catherine watched her go. Alice was a different girl these days. Less shy, more open. She'd been taken up by the Berrill clan and found companions and friends among them. Even her attitude toward Jamie had changed; now that he was a quasi-brother, rather than a son, her revulsion had lifted. She'd bounce him on her knee or tickle him under his chin, though she drew the line at changing his diapers or bathing him. She'd get only so close, but that was all right with Catherine.

"We were talking about the salad," Nettie reminded her.

"Oh yes," Catherine said. "You plan to serve one?"

"Of course. And rice pilaf."

Catherine nodded. It was June, and the day might be hot, so the cold fish was a good choice. She'd decided on lunch rather than dinner because she wanted Jamie to be part of the festivities, but then she wanted him to be part of nearly everything. And she'd invited the Berrills too, at least the adults, no longer concerned about overwhelming Bea. No, this was who they were, and she wanted to bring Bea into their midst as soon as possible; there really wasn't any reason to wait.

"Now what about dessert?" Nettie asked.

"Well, we should have a fruit salad of some kind—peaches, plums, melon, that sort of thing. And then something else too . . ." She remembered the praline cake from the Union Street baker but decided against it. Making a reference to Bea's life in New Orleans seemed cruel; she would never bring it up again.

"I could do a lemon meringue pie," Nettie offered. "Or an angel food cake."

"The pie," Catherine said decisively. "Your pie crust is without parallel, Nettie."

"Thank you, Mrs. Berrill." Nettie was busy writing but Catherine could see she was pleased. "And a very nice menu, I might add."

"It is, isn't it? And I want to use my wedding china, the Haviland, and the flowers should be white, all white—"

"Not your usual colors?"

"I do love my bright colors," Catherine said. "But there's already so much color in the room. And we can do different kinds of white flowers—gardenias, roses, white lilac if the florist can get it." She could see it all in her mind—the colored vases, ruby, cobalt, emerald, amber—and the flowers rising above them, a pale garden, a dream of white. Her plan to enroll in decorating school was something she'd put aside just for the time being; she would do it later on. Right now, she had a baby who was quickly growing into a little boy, and soon would be a bigger one. She didn't want to miss a second of the journey.

"Very pretty," Nettie said. "You do set an elegant table, Mrs. Berrill."

"I hope so," Catherine said. "This is a special meal and I want everything to be just right." That desire extended to the behavior of the guests, most notably her mother. While Sebastian was open to seeing Bea again, Meredith was adamantly opposed. "What if she's recognized on the way here?" she asked.

"She'll take a taxi."

"Are you sure?"

"Yes, Mother. I'm sure."

"Well, someone might spot her standing on the stoop."

"I don't think so," Catherine said. "It's not like she wants to invite the attention. I'm sure she'll be—discreet."

"Too late for that," Meredith said quietly, but not so quietly that Catherine didn't hear.

"Mother, if you love me—"

"As if that were in question—"

"If you love me, you'll be gracious to Bea. She'll be a guest in our home. And while she doesn't share *our* history, *our* past, she's still a part of me. An important part." Catherine suddenly understood that Meredith's concern over how all this would look was really just a way to camouflage her own worry that she might be displaced in Catherine's affections. And though Catherine could find her mother exasperating in the extreme, she still did love her, and knew Meredith loved her. That mattered. She was a mother herself now and had to hope that Jamie would forgive whatever mistakes she was bound to make.

"You're asking me to do something . . . something I find deeply objectionable. Offensive even. I don't know this woman, but given her background I don't want to know her—"

"That's just it," said Catherine. "If you got to know her, you'd understand the choices she made. And the ones that were made for her."

"No," Meredith said. "I wouldn't."

Catherine looked at her mother. "Are you saying you won't be joining us?"

"That's what I'm saying. And I'm going to tell your father he shouldn't either."

"Don't you see how much this will hurt me?"

"I could ask you the same question, Catherine. It seems you haven't given my feelings much, or maybe any, thought at all."

"Of course I have," Catherine said.

"Then why? Why are you doing this to me?"

Catherine controlled the impatient sigh she badly wanted to release. "I'm not doing anything to you, Mother. I'm doing something for me."

"Your interest in her is . . . unseemly. It makes me feel insufficient."

"Unseemly? She did give birth to me. And I don't see how my wanting her in my life casts any aspersions on you."

"But it does!" Meredith was clearly upset. "If I'd been enough, you wouldn't need her."

Catherine said nothing. She was not going to make Meredith understand; she might as well resign herself to that. But as the days passed, resignation soured into resentment. Why was Meredith so inflexible? Yes, Bea had a scandalous past, but there were reasons she'd made the choices she had. Those reasons mattered. And what of forgiveness? Her mother called herself a Christian, went to church every week. But evidently she could not practice what she heard preached.

"It's like she's rejecting a part of me," Catherine said to Stephen when they were lying together, safe in the cocoon of their shared bed.

"She doesn't see it that way." He drew her closer. "She thinks your life began when your father brought you home and put you in her arms."

"She's wrong. And not just about that."

"What do you mean?"

"She's told me that she hopes Alice moves out, and that I never, ever tell Jamie about her."

"I don't see that happening."

"Neither do I." She was getting worked up; this conversation was not a good prelude to sleep. "Do you hear that?" There was a tentative cry from the nursery—*eh, eh, eh*—that caused Catherine to sit up. "The baby," she said. She kept the bedroom and nursery doors open at night —Alice had moved into one of the guest rooms—so she'd hear him.

"Do you want me to go?"

"No, I will." She headed upstairs; maybe she could rock him back to sleep. If not, she'd bring him downstairs and let him sleep with them. Those books that counseled against such a practice? Catherine ignored every single one of them.

* * *

Alice was nervous about facing Bea again after so many months, but she knew it would be better to see her alone at least once before the meal that Catherine was planning. She'd even tried to get out of that, saying she didn't really belong there, but Catherine was having none of it. "Of course you belong," she said. "You're the glue that holds us together. If it weren't for you, I don't know where we'd be." So Alice had reluctantly agreed, and in anticipation of the day had arranged to meet Bea on Ludlow Street, at a restaurant she'd discovered on one of her fabric-buying excursions. It was also not far from the Scorcios' tailoring shop; she had kept in touch with them and let them know when the baby was born. Mr. Scorcio had died in January, but Mrs. Scorcio was still alive.

Arriving a little early, Alice found just two men sitting at the counter and, at a table, a lone woman whose back faced her. Alice's gaze settled on the solitary woman. Bobbed hair, black crepe coat. As if she sensed she was being observed, the woman turned. Bea. That was Bea sitting there. Alice hurried over.

"I almost didn't recognize you!" she said.

"It's the hair," said Bea. "But sit down. Let me look at you. I was worried when you vanished. So worried."

"I do know and I'm sorry—sorry for everything . . ." Alice felt the tears coming. "I never should have have talked to him. Never. I don't know if you can ever forgive me, but I so hope you can."

"I already have," Bea said. "I think you hurt yourself as much as you hurt me."

The waiter appeared. "So what'll it be, ladies?"

"Borscht," they said, almost together.

The waiter rushed off and the two of them were left looking at each other. Alice couldn't see how to begin, but to her relief, Bea started talking.

"I didn't know how you felt," she said. "I didn't seem to know anything. Looking for Catherine made me a blinkered horse—I was so focused on that goal I saw only what was ahead of me. I understand how that hurt you."

That was unexpected—Bea apologizing to her? Before Alice could say anything, the waiter reappeared with two bowls of borscht, a basket of fresh, dark bread, and a dish of butter. "Enjoy!" he barked before disappearing again. They ate in silence for a moment and then Bea said, "Tell me about the baby. Please. Tell me everything."

So Alice told her the story—the party, the punch, the boys, the bedroom. To her surprise, it no longer ravaged her to recount it. That blurry day was slipping into the past, and almost seemed like it had happened to a different girl.

"Those boys—they committed a crime," said Bea. "A serious crime for which they should have been prosecuted. And punished."

"A crime?" She hadn't thought of it that way. "I assumed it was my fault."

"Women always do."

Then Alice told her about living with the Scorcios. "They would have let me stay," she said. "But it would have meant giving the baby away to the church, and as much as I didn't want him, I just couldn't do it. I kept thinking of you, Bea—how giving away your baby had shaped your life."

"It did," said Bea. "Only I didn't understand it at the time. There was no way I could have. I thought that once she was gone, it would be as if she'd never been, as if none of it had ever happened." She took a bite of the bread. "Instead, it colored everything."

"Giving Jamie to Catherine and Stephen—it's different. I won't ever have to wonder about what's happened to him, wonder if he's all right—I'll know. Now that I don't have to be responsible for him, I don't even mind him so much. And one day, when he's grown, Catherine's going to tell him about me."

"Really?"

"Yes. She says some secrets are like acid—they corrode your soul."

"She's right about that," Bea said.

"I was wrong about her. She's wonderful, Bea. She said I can stay with her as long as I like. I thought I could go back to work for Mrs. Scorcio, but she closed the shop and moved to the Bronx to be near her sister. I've stayed in touch with her and I want you to meet her too."

"I'd like that." Bea buttered a slice of bread and offered it to Alice. "I was going to ask if you wanted to live with me—we could find a new place together. But it seems you're better off where you are."

"Oh, Bea! I can't tell you what it means to have you say that. But you're right—I do want to stay where I am. It's not just Catherine and Stephen. It's his whole family, they've been so good to me. He has two younger brothers and a younger sister who invite me out with them. And they've introduced me to their friends. They tell everyone I'm an orphaned cousin, which is almost the truth."

"And how do you spend your days?" Bea asked.

"I have a job," Alice said proudly. "I'm doing alterations at Bonwit Teller and they're very happy with me. I might even get promoted."

"Promoted!" said Bea. "I'm so glad they recognize your gift."

Alice smiled and buttered another slice of bread. "And what about you? Where do you live now? What have you been doing?"

The waiter appeared, this time with a tray. On it were a platter of blintzes, two plates, and bowls of sour cream and applesauce. He practically slammed everything down on the table and rushed off.

"Did we order this?" Alice asked.

"No," said Bea. "But it looks delicious and I'm hungry. Aren't you?"

They began to eat. Alice was aware that Bea hadn't answered her; should she ask again? But there was something else that was distracting her, something else that she had to do. She reached down to her lap and pulled out the small pouch she had been carrying in a pocket. Inside were the sparkly necklace and earrings. Alice peeled back the layer of tissue to reveal them.

"That's my choker. My earrings. How did you get them? Did you—"

"Steal them? Yes, I did. And I don't even know why."

Bea lifted the earrings up and then set them down again. "You were looking for something. Something you couldn't find, no matter how hard you tried or how many things you took."

"What was that?"

"Love, of course." She pushed the earrings and choker in Alice's direction. "For you."

"For me? Don't you want them? I remember you wearing them in New Orleans. With your black dress—"

"I have plenty of baubles," Bea said. "I'd rather you have them. That's one of the things mothers do—they give jewelry to their daughters."

Alice took the pieces and held them tightly. "You never told me . . ."

"No," said Bea. "But I should have. And I'm sorry you had to go through so much grief, and go through it alone, before we both came to a place where I could tell you." She reached her hand across the table and placed it on Alice's cheek. "Because that's what you are—my daughter."

* * *

Bea entered Catherine's house bearing a large and somewhat unwieldy bag of gifts—a linen table runner embellished by strawberries done in needlepoint, a majolica pitcher whose brilliant glaze combined shades of green, teal, and pink, a delicate jade figurine of an owl. For Alice, she had a sterling silver thimble-and-scissors set tucked into a gold-embossed Italian leather case. They'd been chosen with deliberation and care; Bea thought Catherine's gifts would appear to her tastes and that Alice would find the set useful. Also in the bag were the toys she'd purchased at FAO Schwarz—a wooden train whose wheels spun round and round, a toy drum with a set of sticks, and a stuffed giraffe made by the German company Steiff. Jamie was too young for these things now but he'd come to enjoy them soon enough.

Bea was apprehensive about the visit. She already knew that Meredith Delman would not be present, and she didn't have to ask why. Also, this would be her first formal invitation; the only other time she'd entered the house she'd come unannounced. So the gifts were a form of protection, the offerings meant to secure future invitations. Catherine was delighted with everything and gave Jamie the giraffe on the spot. He began waving it around and then bit the creature right on the snout.

Bea followed Catherine to the dining room but stopped just before stepping inside, just to take in the effect. The focal point was a long table covered in a damask cloth and surrounded by a dozen or so chairs with needlepoint seats—her gift had indeed been apt. A rainbow of glass vases filled with white flowers acted as the centerpiece. Everyone was still standing and most of the faces were unfamiliar to her. But there was one she knew, a face she'd never thought she'd see again—Sebastian Delgado, Delman now. He looked older, of course. But his kind, forbearing expression? That had not changed in all these years.

Catherine touched her elbow and led Bea across the room, and Sebastian met them halfway. Before Bea could say a word, she felt herself embraced. "Bea," he said, clearly overcome. "Bea, is it really you?"

"It is." How extraordinary that they should meet again.

Catherine asked everyone to sit down and the meal was served. Bea had been placed next to Jack Berrill on one side and Stephen on the other. Alice was down at the other end, near one of Stephen's sisters, the one called Bridget—she remembered her from the shop. Stephen and his father did their best to put her at ease, but Bea sensed that the guests at this table were acutely aware of her, trying to reconcile the past they had heard about with the present they could see. Would she ever be fully accepted here? It certainly wouldn't be easy; it might well be impossible.

After the main course, Bea excused herself to freshen up, and Sebastian waylaid her before she returned to the table. "I still can't quite believe that you found her. Found us," he said. "I used to think of you back then. Almost every day."

"You did?" She was surprised, imagining that he would have wanted to banish her from his mind and memory, and start the story of Catherine's life on a fresh page.

"Yes. I used to thank you."

"What for?"

"For giving her up so we could have her. I always knew why you did it, I just couldn't imagine how. I still can't. But I've been grateful to you every day since. And I'll go on being grateful." He put his hands on her shoulders and leaned over to kiss her, once on each cheek. Then he turned and went back to the table.

Bea stood there for a moment. Voices and laughter floated in the from the other room, beckoning her, yet still Bea remained where she was. Finally, the girl who'd been hired to help Nettie with the serving sidled by her and began clearing the table so that dessert could be served.

Back in the dining room, smaller plates had been laid out and Stephen had taken out a bottle of champagne. Yes, it was unlawful, but his father had tucked a few bottles away and surely this was a moment to open one. The cork shot up and across the room, eliciting a delighted shriek from Jamie, who was now ensconced on his mother's lap. "Toast," Jack Berrill called to his son. "Toast, toast," the chant was taken up. The bottle was passed around the table and glasses were filled. Bea saw that Stephen was about to get up but she put a hand on his arm. "May I?" she said. She saw him glance over at Catherine, who nodded.

Bea stood and gazed at the people assembled around the table. She wanted to feel hopeful, to feel that there might, in time, be a way for her to truly belong. Everyone was quiet, even the baby, and they all waited for her to speak. "To family," she said as she raised her glass.

The morning after the party, the city was drenched by a chilly downpour. Even when it cleared, the sky remained cloudy, the days unseasonably cool and gray for June. Bea continued her work at the foundling hospital, though she found time to go to Prospect Heights too—she wanted to spend time with her daughters. Her daughters. How lovely those words sounded, what a satisfying ring they had.

Still, the thought of Meredith Delman was a small but persistent irritant, like a stone in her shoe. She said as much to Tess Morgan over a pot of Darjeeling one afternoon. "Does it really matter?" Tess asked. They were seated in a tearoom on Lexington Avenue, the steaming pot set between them, a scone on each of their plates. "You have Catherine, her husband, and her baby. You have Alice. And you even have Sebastian. If that woman can't find it in her heart to meet you, to get to know you, then the loss is hers."

Bea was quiet. She wanted to believe that, she tried to believe that. But she didn't, she couldn't. "It's like the circle is incomplete," she said finally.

"Does it matter to Catherine?"

"She says it doesn't," Bea said. "But I don't believe it. She looks so uncomfortable when there's any mention of her mother."

"So then write to her. Even better, go to Larchmont and see her."

"I can't do that."

"Why not? Bea, after what you've told me about your life, I can't believe there's anything you can't do. You're the bravest woman I've ever met."

The waiter appeared with the check and they said goodbye on Lexington Avenue, Tess heading in one direction while Bea headed slowly back to her rooms in the other. Tess thought she was brave. Brave enough to seek out Meredith Delman and risk being rebuffed? There was so much in her life now. She didn't need to know a woman who clearly didn't want to know her. But Meredith's absence became more and more like a presence, a presence that weighed on her. She couldn't ignore it forever.

By the end of the month, it had finally begun to feel like summer. The sky brightened, and the days were mild. It was on one of these fine days that Bea boarded the train at Grand Central Terminal. Looking out of the window, she watched the city's muted hues—gray, black, silver—give way to a half dozen different greens, from dark to light, and a riot of colorful flowers.

There were two taxicabs waiting at the Larchmont station and she got into one of them and gave the driver an address she'd memorized from a letter she'd spotted at Catherine's house. She hadn't wanted to tell Catherine what she was about to do. No, for now this was between her and Meredith. The ride took only a few minutes, and when she got out, she found herself in front of the house where her daughter had lived and grown into the woman she was now.

It was stone—like Bea's own childhood home—and well proportioned. An apple tree grew in the front yard, and there was a neat brick pathway leading to the front door. But Bea didn't approach the house. Now that she was here, her nerve was failing. Maybe it had been a bad idea after all—

She heard a sound, and saw a figure moving across the fence-enclosed garden at the side of the house. There was a woman, perhaps her age, perhaps a bit younger, in a wide straw hat that tied under her chin, and a basket over her arm. She was absorbed by her task—cutting roses—and didn't look up, so Bea was able to watch her unobserved. This was the woman who had been Catherine's mother—rocked her, fed her, bathed her, soothed her. She had been the one to worry when Catherine was sick, to feel pride in her accomplishments, to celebrate her milestones. She had done the job Bea could not; Bea was in her debt. She walked closer to the fence. "Mrs. Delman," she said.

Meredith raised her head and stepped closer. "Can I help you?"

"I'm Beatrice," she said. "Bea."

"Bea." Meredith stood quite still, though the basket that held the roses quivered a little. "Why are you here? I didn't invite you."

"I know. And I hope you'll forgive me for surprising you, but I didn't think you'd agree to our meeting if I proposed it."

"You'd be right about that."

"Could we talk? Just for a little while?"

"I'm sure I don't have anything to say to you."

"But I have things I want to say to you."

Meredith looked undecided for a moment, then she set down the basket. "If I let you talk, will you then promise to go away and never come back?"

Now it was Bea who hesitated. "I will," she said finally.

"All right," Meredith said. "I'm listening."

"I came because I wanted to thank you."

"Thank me?" Meredith was clearly not expecting this.

"Yes. For raising her, caring for her, loving her. I couldn't do those things back then—"

"Of course you couldn't! You were a woman without scruples, without any morals, without—"

"I was a woman without a family, without friends, without money or a home."

"You were a prostitute."

"Not when I gave birth to her."

"Of course you would say that."

"Mrs. Delman, you brought her up, and you did a magnificent job of it. Look at her. But I brought her into the world." Bea squinted; unlike Meredith's hat, the brim of her own was small and did nothing to keep the sun from her eyes. "She was conceived in love, and she grew inside me for nine months. I felt her move. I felt her turn. Kick. I endured the pain of giving birth to her, and of giving her up, which turned out to be the worst pain of all because there was no end to it. No end until I came to New York and found her again."

"But what about everything that came after? Catherine told me what happened. And then there was that perfectly horrid article."

"It was mortifying in the extreme. Yet Catherine has managed to forgive me—can't you?"

"Catherine's headstrong and stubborn. She's always been like that."

"Or you could say she's spirited and principled. She listens to herself, not the din and clamor of the world. You should be proud of her. Very proud."

Meredith said nothing but Bea felt something between them shift, just the slightest bit. So she went on. "It hurts her that you won't see me."

"She told you that?"

"She didn't have to. I can tell."

"She told me she feels close to you, that she can confide in you . . . She so rarely confides in me anymore."

"Sometimes the bond is so tight it can feel . . . restricting."

"But I'm her mother! And you're trying to take my place!"

"No, I'm not." So there it was. That was what was at the heart of this. Bea thought of Alice and Catherine and of Tess Morgan too. Maybe everyone clung to the precarious place she had carved out for herself, clung to it tightly, resisting—and resenting—anyone who could be seen as a threat. The human heart was resilient as rubber, durable as stone, and breakable as the most delicate, handblown glass. "Though I can see how you might think that."

Meredith stood there clutching her basket. So many roses, so many shades of pink, crimson, yellow, and white. She knew how to nurture, how to cultivate; her garden was lush and brimming. Then, to Bea's surprise, she leaned over and unlatched the gate. "You must be hot and thirsty after your trip," she said. "Won't you come inside?"

Although the day had become quite warm, Bea shivered a little as she followed her hostess. Two daughters. And now two mothers. Meredith turned and for a moment they regarded each other. Then they walked—together—toward the house.

Bea was pensive on the train ride back to Grand Central Station. Meredith Delman might never fully accept or welcome her into her family, but by the time Bea left, she had surrendered a little of her animosity. Even that felt to Bea like a victory. And when she told Catherine about it a few days later, Catherine clearly agreed.

"It was brave of you to do that," she said. They had gone into the park late in the afternoon and by now the sun was sinking gently toward the horizon, turning the sky a soft shade of pink.

335

"I don't know about that," Bea said. "I don't think of myself as brave." But Tess had used that word too.

"You're wrong," Catherine said firmly, and she linked her arm through Bea's. Bea did not instinctively pull away. She was growing used to this about Catherine, the ease with which she touched, hugged, embraced.

Just ahead of them walked Alice, who was pushing Jamie in his pram; Bea could hear his joyful babbling. She'd been so glad when Alice agreed to join them on this walk. Her aversion for Jamie was fading just as she herself was blossoming. The promised promotion at Bonwit's had become a reality, and she was now the assistant to the head of the alterations department. She'd also confided in Catherine that she was being courted by Henry, one of the numerous Berrill cousins. She would be eighteen soon, almost grown. Bea remembered how she had told Helen she'd allow Alice to start seeing men when she was eighteen. But Bea had somehow managed to spare Alice from such a fate—something else to give thanks for.

At the sound of her son, Catherine trotted ahead toward Alice and reached down to pluck Jamie from the pram. He immediately buried his face in her neck and began kicking his feet wildly; one of his little cotton booties flew off and Bea knelt to retrieve it.

The park had emptied out; it was the dinner hour and most people had gone home. The sun was no longer visible, and the pink of the sky had deepened to violet, but when Bea straightened up again, her eye was caught by a slight movement in the trees. She was instantly alerted. Was someone there? She kept her gaze on the trees. But the shape resolved itself not into a man or even a woman—it was a doe, large eyed, with even larger, quivering ears.

Bea stood still, not wanting to frighten the creature, who seemed to be regarding her so warily. And then she saw why—just behind her were a pair of fawns whose spotted coats and white bibs moved in and out of view. How unusual to see a single deer in Prospect Park; seeing three all at once was quite remarkable.

Stepping delicately through the twigs and grass, the doe was leading the way. Then she stopped, swiveled her long, elegant neck around and looked at the fawns. She was checking on them, making sure they were still with her; this small, intentional act filled Bea's eyes with sudden tears. Catherine and Alice were chattering up ahead and Bea longed to call out but if she did, she would risk scaring the deer away. So she remained where she stood, humbly watching, until the doe and her fawns had moved out of the range of her vision.

ACKNOWLEDGMENTS

For editorial suggestions, guidance, and all-around moral support, I'd like to thank Jennie Fields, Patricia Grossman, Michele Rubin, Sally Schloss, Adrienne Sharp, Alexandra Shelly, and Kenneth Silver.

For assistance with researching New Orleans, my thanks to Suzy Muery, Jari Honora, Rebecca Smith, and the staff of the Historic New Orleans Collection, as well as Carolanne Gardner for pointing the way.

The team at HarperCollins has been a joy to work with from start to finish. Emily Griffin is an incomparable editor—skillful, sensitive, and smart—and Heather Drucker is a superlative and tireless publicist. I am also so grateful to Micaela Carr and Katie O'Callaghan for everything they do. Olga Grlic created a beautiful—and bewitching—cover. Finally, this list would not be complete without a mention of my peerless agent, Susanna Einstein; I'm so lucky to be in your expert hands.

ABOUT THE AUTHOR

KITTY ZELDIS is the pseudonym for a novelist and nonfiction writer of books for adults and children. She lives with her family in Brooklyn, New York.